The

BEAUTY
DOCTOR

Second Edition, 2024, with Author's Preface

Elizabeth Hutchison Bernard

Black Rose Writing | Texas

First printing

This is a work of fiction. Names, characters, businesses, places,
events, and incidents are either the products of the author's imagination or used in a fictitious manner. Apart from well-known
historical figures, any resemblance to actual persons, living or
dead, or actual events is purely coincidental.

ISBN: 978-1-68513-350-4
Library of Congress Control Number: 20239430507
PUBLISHED BY BLACK ROSE WRITING
www.blackrosewriting.com

Printed in the United States of America
Suggested Retail Price (SRP) $23.95

The Beauty Doctor is printed in Garamond Premier Pro

*As a planet-friendly publisher, Black Rose Writing does its best to eliminate
unnecessary waste to reduce paper usage and energy costs, while never
compromising the reading experience. As a result, the final word count vs.
page count may not meet common expectations.

Author photo by Tina Celle

For my late father, Stanley P. Hutchison,
in whose footsteps I have followed more than I realized.

Preface to Second Edition

The story you are about to read is fiction, with plot and characters that spring from the author's imagination. But what inspired me to write this suspenseful mystery/thriller was something very real—the history of modern-day cosmetic surgery, which begins in the Victorian era. So, while the tale of *The Beauty Doctor* may shock you, it is not as improbable as you might think.

By 1907, when the novel takes place, women had just begun to break free from many Victorian-era constraints. The illustrator-created Gibson Girl (artist Charles Dana Gibson, 1867-1944), featured in many popular magazines, represented a new Euro-American ideal that equated beauty with strength and power. Beauty doctors, as they were called, capitalized on this evolving vision of women's potential. Between 1870 and 1909, the self-trained beauty doctor John H. Woodbury became wealthy by establishing a chain of beauty surgery *institutes* in six states as well as creating his own brand of soaps and cosmetics. The procedures that he and his staff of twenty-five doctors and surgeons performed included nose reshaping (rhinoplasty), eyelid trimming, facelifts, creating dimples, and filling wrinkles with paraffin wax. Other beauty doctors may have profited on a smaller scale; however, their aggressive newspaper advertising introduced the concept of beauty surgery to a wide audience.

But there were problems.

In the early 1900s, with the field of medicine struggling to regulate itself, opportunities for quackery abounded. This was certainly true in the nascent field of beauty surgery. Abuses in all areas of medicine eventually led to stricter guidelines for medical education and credentials. Because of the Flexner Report, published in 1910 under the sponsorship of the Carnegie Foundation, almost half of all medical schools in the United States were judged inadequate; eventually, these schools merged with others or were shut down completely. This caused at least one unfortunate side effect: Previously, women had made progress in obtaining medical school admission, but now fewer available slots for aspiring doctors meant that virtually all women were to be excluded. It would take some time to reestablish women among the ranks of medical students at American universities.

During the same period, the eugenics movement—which sought to create a "super race" through authoritarian control of human reproduction—was widely embraced by academic institutions and governments throughout the world. Many wealthy individuals like Carnegie and Rockefeller contributed sizeable sums of money for eugenics research. It was not until the 1930s that enthusiasm for the doctrine began its decline. By the end of World War II, eugenics was widely discredited. However, practices of forced limits on reproduction, as well as involuntary sterilizations and hysterectomies, continue in some countries to the present day.

Concurrent with the rise of eugenics was the public's fascination with people exhibiting rare congenital conditions, such as conjoined twins (then called *Siamese twins* because of the famous Siamese brothers Chang and Eng, 1811-1874). The cruel exploitation of such individuals is well documented. Only with greater medical knowledge concerning the causes of such afflictions did public attitudes begin to change.

These facts of America's Edwardian era converge in a fictional story full of unexpected twists and turns, as a young woman who dreams of becoming a doctor serving the poor of New York City discovers that appearances can be deceiving, and perhaps deadly. I hope you will be intrigued by both the history and mystery of this re-edited Second Edition of *The Beauty Doctor*.

Elizabeth Hutchison Bernard
January 4, 2024

Into whatsoever houses I enter, I will enter to help the sick, and I will abstain from all intentional wrong-doing and harm, especially from abusing the bodies of man or woman, bond or free.

–From the Hippocratic Oath, fifth century BC

The
BEAUTY
DOCTOR

CHAPTER 1

The maid assigned to the construction of Abigail's elaborate hairdo stood at attention, her smile reflected in the dressing-table mirror.

"Are you pleased with it, Miss Platford?"

Abigail sighed. Really, what difference did it make? What mattered was that everything had been done exactly as her future mother-in-law instructed. Her honey-colored hair was arranged over several layers of padding that rose nearly half a foot, and the formidable mass was ornamented with plumes and several strings of pearls from Mrs. Hennessy's own jewelry box.

"Very nice. Thank you."

"Will there be anything else then, ma'am?"

"No, that's all."

She was relieved when, finally, the door of the guest room closed, and she was alone.

It was April 19, 1907, precisely five months before her wedding date. That night, Mr. and Mrs. Hennessy were hosting a lavish banquet at Sherry's, one of the most expensive venues in Manhattan. The purpose was to announce their only son Arthur's engagement and, Abigail assumed, to ease her introduction into New York's high-society circles, if such a thing was possible. The invitations, handwritten in French, announced the theme of the night was a royal garden party. Mrs. Hennessy had invited three hundred guests and asked them to come dressed in eighteenth-century costumes—an ideal excuse for her to oversee Abigail's attire for the evening, likely fearing that otherwise her son's fiancée would fail to make the correct impression.

Abigail had to admit, the dress Mrs. Hennessy had selected for her was beautiful—deep blue to match her eyes, with a square neck, tight sleeves layered with ruffles, a flounced skirt, and a fitted bodice that emphasized her slim silhouette. And, as the final touch, an exquisite diamond choker, purportedly among the most precious of the venerable family's heirlooms. Abigail contemplated it now with mixed emotions. If security was what she desired, then she surely had found it in Arthur Hennessy. But as she lifted the borrowed necklace to her throat, it seemed only a symbol of her irrevocable captivity.

She thought back to the gloomy gray morning in mid-February when she had fled her mother's home. Finding Arthur at the bank, she had intended to ask him for a position. A teller, a secretary, anything that would enable her to move out and never again be subjected to the lewd advances of her new stepfather. She and Arthur had barely known each other. Still, he had taken pity on her, offering her temporary asylum in his parents' home.

How well she remembered the gallery of dour-faced family portraits under which she had unsuspectingly sat on that fateful night when Arthur proposed in a rush of words that seemed painfully well rehearsed. At the time, it seemed there was nothing she could say but *yes*. To a man for whom she felt not the slightest spark of passion. To a life she didn't want, one filled with the endless insincerities of polite social intercourse and the useless pastimes to which women of the Hennessys' class so ardently devoted themselves. And, of course, children. She had never desired them, but as certainly as all the rest she didn't want, they were ahead of her now. All because of one tragically foolish mistake that had stolen her father—and her future—forever.

There was a tap at the door. Before Abigail could reply, a gnarled stick of a woman, dressed in a lavish gold-and-burgundy brocade gown that trailed at least three feet along the floor, entered the room. Mrs. Hennessy was followed by Arthur's sister, Sarah, whose multi-layered costume of canary-yellow silk with orange chiffon only made her appear larger and more awkward than usual.

Abigail held her breath as Mrs. Hennessy slowly circled her, checking for any slight deviation from perfection. "You actually look quite lovely," she finally said, offering a subdued smile. "Doesn't she, Sarah?"

Sarah's tight-lipped expression made it clear she intended to be difficult. "That necklace belonged to Grandmother Hennessy. She wouldn't want it worn by a stranger."

Abigail reached to undo the clasp, more than willing to relinquish the family jewels. "Leave it, Abigail," Mrs. Hennessy commanded. She turned to Sarah. "It's only for one night, dear." Sarah gave a little sniff, turned on her heel, and stormed out, a suffocating cloud of French perfume lingering in her wake.

"I was thinking," Abigail began uncertainly, the choker now unbearably tight around her neck, "might this outfit look best without jewelry?"

"Don't be silly. The important thing is that tonight you appear like a lady."

Abigail ignored the inference that she could not appear so without the Hennessy diamonds at her throat. "Arthur should have been here by now."

"Oh, he telephoned from the bank. He's planning to meet us at Sherry's later."

She tried to hide her displeasure. How could he send her off to the party alone, knowing not a single soul among all the guests? "Couldn't we wait for him?"

"Come along now," Mrs. Hennessy said. "The limousine is in front."

They were about to head downstairs when the maid, the same one who had styled Abigail's hair, rushed into the room. Her eyes flitted uncertainly from the mistress of the house to Abigail and back. "Ma'am, did you mean to leave this behind?" she asked, passing something to Mrs. Hennessy who then turned to Abigail, her arm outstretched.

"For you."

It was a fan, mounted on a stick of ivory with inlaid mother-of-pearl. Carefully, because she could tell it was old and fragile, Abigail spread the silk folds. Exquisitely painted, the intricate design weaved a mythical tale of castles and sailing ships, mermaids strumming lutes, cupids peeking from behind clouds. She would have loved to linger, piecing together the various fragments of the artist's imagined story, losing herself in the magic, but there was no time now.

"Thank you," she said, uncertain if this was a gift or yet another item on loan. "It's beautiful."

Mrs. Hennessy's next comment was direct and deliberate, and Abigail had no trouble reading between the lines. "I always feel that a fan lends a woman an air of mystery, don't you?"

In other words, the less her future daughter-in-law might reveal about herself, the better.

· · · · ·

Abigail had never been to Sherry's, but even if she had, she would not have recognized it that night. An entire floor of the restaurant was decorated to create the ambiance of a royal French garden. Fresh sod had been laid over the marble tiles in a soft carpet of green. Arbors of cascading purple wisteria sheltered the banquet tables set with sparkling gold and crystal, each with a stunning centerpiece of pink roses paired with white lilies. Abigail hesitated in the doorway, intimidated by the overwhelming opulence, before Mrs. Hennessy turned to her with a stiff smile.

"You are not to call attention to yourself or discuss the engagement with anyone. Mr. Hennessy will make the announcement later in the evening, and I want it to be a surprise."

Abigail made no reply, her attention drawn to laughter in the hallway signaling the evening's first arrivals. As the guests came into view, she saw that all wore colorful period costumes as extravagant as Mrs. Hennessy's, likely modeled after famous portraits of Louis XV and his mistress Madame de Pompadour, or Louis XVI and Marie Antoinette. Certainly, none among the Hennessys' set would be caught dead in an outfit less than authentically regal.

"Go on and take your seat. You'll be at the head table." Mrs. Hennessy pointed toward the center of the room. Among all the round tables for ten was a long, narrow one with seating for twenty. "There's a place card with your name. Hurry now. Don't dawdle."

If Mrs. Hennessy wished not to call attention to her, this was not the way. Sitting alone at the head table would only make her more noticeable and encourage speculation as to who would merit such a prestigious spot and why she was unaccompanied. Nevertheless, she did as she had been asked, settling herself into the designated seat and trying to look as if she belonged there. She was glad when several others took their seats, followed by a few more, until the table was almost full. The chair to her left, however, remained empty, with a place card that said it was reserved for Mr.

George Kilroy, whoever he might be. The vacant seat on her right was Arthur's.

She had not yet seen Arthur in his costume but tried now to imagine him, with his long, serious face and sparse rust-colored moustache, dressed as a sword-wielding eighteenth-century Frenchman. The thought of it brought a brief touch of levity to her otherwise anxious, and increasingly annoyed, state of mind. However ridiculous he might look she would try to keep from laughing. Arthur was extraordinarily shy and, even if he might deserve a taste of humiliation such as she was being forced to endure, she didn't have the heart to embarrass him.

She need not have worried. The moment Arthur walked through the door it was apparent that he'd planned his late entry purely to maximize the attention he would receive. There was a swagger to his step, a flush to his cheeks, an exuberance that was palpably heady. In fact, Abigail had never seen him look so comfortable with himself as he did in that full-skirted and elaborately embroidered jacket, the long waistcoat underneath open at the neck to display a frilled shirtfront and lace cravat fastened with a black velvet bow. Even the powdered wig seemed to suit him well, tied at the back with another bow. He had apparently decided a sword was unnecessary. Instead, he carried in his hand, probably so as not to muss his hair, a three-cornered hat bound with gold galloon and sporting a trim of flat rosettes of ribbon.

Abigail watched as he went around to every table, taking his time, chatting amiably with the guests. He was animated, confident. Though she couldn't help a curious sort of admiration for his new attitude, her irritation far exceeded such kinder sentiments. Had he no appreciation of how uncomfortable she felt, surrounded by people she didn't know? People who obviously had very little interest in knowing her. And the way his mother had treated her! It was as if Mrs. Hennessy didn't trust her to open her mouth for fear of what might come out.

Suddenly, she felt the chair to her left move. Looking up, she encountered a gentleman who was noticeably out of place with his black evening suit and white bow tie. His neatly trimmed hair was dark and wavy, his moustache thick and waxed at the ends. He was older than she, likely in his forties, but he struck Abigail as one of those men who become even more handsome with a slight graying at the temples. The hesitancy in his manner led her to believe he realized he was at the wrong event.

"Pardon me," he said. "I believe this is my place."

"Mr. Kilroy?"

"No, Mr. Kilroy couldn't make it, I'm afraid," he said, proceeding to take the seat. "He's a little under the weather. But Mrs. Kilroy—" He nodded toward the head of the table. A stout woman, her costume adorned with stunning jewels obviously worth a fortune, stood talking with Mrs. Hennessy. She gestured toward the gentleman now seated next to Abigail. A slight frown creased the space between Mrs. Hennessy's painted brows.

"Mrs. Kilroy," he began again, "persuaded me to accompany her in place of her husband. And if you know Mrs. Kilroy, you'll understand I really had no choice," he said with a smile.

By now, Abigail had further assessed his appearance: the firmness of his jaw, the sharp angle of his cheek, the depth of his dark eyes. He was a distinguished-looking man, but the rakishness of his smile suggested an impetuous nature. She noticed, too, a peculiar scent about him, slightly acrid. It was so familiar.

An image popped into her mind. Row upon row of stoppered bottles and lidded apothecary jars, her face reflected for a moment in the glass of the medicine cabinet before she opened the door, reached inside ...

"It's rather embarrassing, however, to be the only one from the twentieth century in attendance."

She pulled herself back to the present. "Actually, it's a welcome relief to see a modern man. I was beginning to feel I'd been sent off in one of Mr. Wells's time machines."

"Ah, one of my favorite books!"

"Mine as well."

"An intriguing premise, traveling into the future to see what we humans have become."

"Yes, quite a fantastical story, but with a rather solemn truth at its core."

"Solemn truth?" He thought for a moment. "Yes, you're right. You're absolutely right." He gave her an approving nod, pausing only a beat before adding, "Tell me, what else do you like to read?"

He probably expected her to be a fan of Gothic novels, like most women of her age and education—proper young ladies who nonetheless harbor secret longings for surrender to reckless passion. In Abigail's case, such longings had always been overridden by what her mother liked to call a *morbid fascination* with the human body and the variety of afflictions that so mercilessly render it helpless.

"*Gray's Anatomy*," she said, realizing full well what an odd choice it must seem. Perhaps just as strange was her sudden and inexplicable urge to tell him how Father had always encouraged her to study science. How she'd grown up believing she would follow in his footsteps and become a doctor despite the many challenges women faced. To think that she had once imagined herself becoming a student at Johns Hopkins! Yet, since her father's sudden passing, that dream and so many others had died a slow, agonizing death.

"Excuse me—" The stranger was speaking again. "Since we appear to have no one offering to introduce us, allow me to do the honors myself. I'm Dr. Franklin Rome."

A doctor!

She inclined her head politely, a hot flush spreading over her face. He must think her incredibly pretentious to have mentioned *Gray's Anatomy*. He had no way of knowing the countless hours she had spent poring over that revered book. Eight hundred illustrations—all the skeletal parts laid bare of flesh, meticulously labeled as to the various bones, nerve openings, attachments of the tendons.

"I've only recently opened my practice here. Mrs. Kilroy is one of my first patients." He glanced at the elderly woman with what seemed a condescending smile. "I'm not sure what I can do for her, but I'll think of something. However—" He turned back to Abigail. "Far more important, you haven't yet told me who *you* are."

She thought of Mrs. Hennessy's warning. "Abigail Platford."

"A pleasure, Miss Platford. It is *Miss*, isn't it?"

Mrs. Kilroy had taken a seat directly opposite Dr. Rome and now called out across the table. "Dr. Rome, I see you have landed yourself a spot next to the loveliest girl in the room. I suppose I should be thankful you're the one sitting next to her, instead of my husband. I doubt poor George's heart could take it." She and everyone around her laughed.

"If my goal was to rub elbows with the loveliest of all the lovely creatures here tonight, then surely I would have maneuvered a seat next to you, Mrs. Kilroy." Dr. Rome turned to Abigail with a sly wink.

"Oh, Doctor! Are you sure your degree isn't in flattery?" Mrs. Kilroy snapped open her jeweled fan and fluttered it by her cheek. "I suppose I should explain how I came to be accompanied by this charming gentleman tonight. Lest you think," she said, turning right and then left to make sure everyone was listening, "that I've run off and left my poor ailing George for another man. Dr. Rome can attest to the fact I've done no such thing. You see, our own personal physician, Dr. Hannity, is on holiday overseas. Just when we need him, of course! But—and don't ask me how, because it's a very long story—I was fortunate to have recently made the acquaintance of Dr. Rome, who has been tending to George for several days now with uncommon devotion. Though my husband wasn't quite up to stepping out tonight, I wouldn't dream of disappointing our hosts. So, I convinced Dr. Rome to assume the role of my escort, an invitation he graciously accepted. And isn't it nice to have at least one gentleman around here without flowing curls or a velvet-bowed rat tail?"

"Most certainly," agreed a stylish woman sitting two seats to Mrs. Kilroy's right, who had been studying Dr. Rome with a keen eye.

"The pleasure is all mine," Dr. Rome replied. "Miss Platford and I were just discussing time machines. As a time traveler, I could hope for no better place to land than a royal banquet in eighteenth-century France. The perfect setting for one who enjoys excess in all things."

"Excess, Doctor?" said the same woman, who'd not taken her eyes off him. "But I thought those in your profession most often preach moderation."

He chuckled. "My calling may not be quite what you imagine. Anyway, how a doctor advises his patients and how he behaves himself are often two very different things. We are, after all, only human." Turning to Abigail, he leaned close to whisper, "I must admit you've intrigued me, Miss Platford. We'll have to discuss *Gray's Anatomy* in more detail later, all right?"

Arthur appeared the next moment, slipping into the chair to her right with a mumbled apology. She had never been happier to see him. His absence had left her vulnerable not only to the curiosity of others, but to her own curiosity about the handsome doctor on her left. Abigail hadn't spoken of her interest in medicine for so long, not even dared to think of it. What had made her bring up the subject—and to a total stranger?

Of course! It was that smell.

Antiseptic.

•   •   •   •   •

The meal proceeded uneventfully, if one could call a feast with eight separate courses uneventful. Abigail had never seen so much food, wave after wave of bowls and trays and platters piled high and steaming with the scents of tarragon, thyme, rosemary, and sage. There were four different soups, three kinds of salad, stuffed pheasant, roasted duck, veal, ham, and several whole fish, each entrée accompanied by its own exotic sauce. The procession of French champagnes of every variety and vintage was unending, the pop of a cork sounding every minute from somewhere in the room.

Surrounded by such abundance, Abigail merely picked at her food, apprehensive about what was to come. Soon there would be three hundred pairs of prying eyes trained on her. The flowery toast would be followed by discreet whispers and polite applause, Mrs. Hennessy's frozen smile fooling no one. Abigail *who*?

She was grateful to Mrs. Kilroy for dominating the conversation so completely that, throughout the meal, she scarcely had to speak. Careful to orient herself to the right, toward Arthur, she hoped to avoid further dialog with the doctor on her left—though she wasn't entirely sure why. It might have been that nervous flutter she'd felt when she first saw him; even now, the recollection was vaguely disturbing. More likely, though, it was the memories he had inadvertently evoked. Her Father quizzing her on anatomy and how hard she would try to impress him. The affection in his smile, his words of gentle encouragement. "Someday we'll practice medicine together," he'd say. "Someday we'll be partners."

Mr. Hennessy rose from his chair and tapped a knife against his glass, those seated around Abigail joining in. The clamor from the head table quieted everyone around the room. Abigail felt the urgent thumping of her heart as the host straightened his wig and began.

"I hope everyone is having a wonderful time. This entire evening was my lovely wife's idea. She never ceases to amaze me with her talent and imagination!" He paused for the mandatory applause while Mrs. Hennessy dipped her head in acknowledgment.

"Besides a desire to treat our many dear friends to a banquet to end all banquets, we have another reason for inviting you here tonight. A reason that we have kept a secret until now." Mr. Hennessy looked over at Arthur, beaming. "Our only son, Arthur, has long been our pride and joy. His accomplishments of the last several years, on behalf of our family's banking enterprises, show him to be a young man of exceptional abilities. I have always believed, as well, that he is a gentleman of refinement and taste, qualities confirmed by his selection of a most charming young lady to be his future wife."

An audible gasp arose throughout the room. "It gives me great pleasure," Mr. Hennessy continued, "to introduce her to you now." He turned again to Arthur. "Son, please assist Miss Platford to rise and let our guests get a good look at the two of you together, the future Mr. and Mrs. Arthur Hennessy!"

Arthur stood and offered Abigail his arm so she could display herself by his side while the elite of New York City applauded their impending union. Those at the head table were the first to stand. Soon all were on their feet, giving the couple an ovation more suitable, Abigail thought, for the stars of an opera or a nominee for political office. To her, the thunderous noise went on forever. But actually, it was less than a minute until the guests were back in their seats, choosing from among the decadent assortment of multilayered cakes, cream-filled pastries, and chocolates delivered to the tables on huge rolling carts.

It was then she noticed Arthur seemed to be in a heightened state of agitation. She could tell by the way he kept fingering the ruffles of his shirt, eyes down, mouth tight. He had lost the effortless grace she'd so admired earlier in the evening. Now he seemed more like a man awaiting execution.

"Arthur? Are you all right?"

He glanced uneasily toward the door leading to the hallway outside the banquet room. Abigail followed his eyes. There was a young man standing there, handsome in a delicate sort of way, with a look of distress that mirrored Arthur's distracted air.

"I'll be back." Arthur rose abruptly from his chair.

She watched him leave, feeling rudely abandoned. Had she done something wrong? Embarrassed him? She concluded he must be having second thoughts about his affections, or the wisdom of marrying someone of such little note. His proposal, after only a brief acquaintance, might seem imprudent to him now. Despite her own ambivalent feelings toward the marriage, it was intolerable to think Arthur might be similarly torn. He was to have been, if nothing else, her rock. But might he so easily crumble? Was he no stronger, no surer, than she?

"It seems that congratulations are in order." Dr. Rome leaned toward her, speaking in a confidential tone. "I didn't realize I was sitting next to the evening's guest of honor."

"I'm not really," Abigail said, aware that her heart was again pounding but for a different reason.

"And here I thought perhaps you aspired to practice the medical arts. Or was that only a passing fancy?"

"It was a long time ago."

"And no more?"

The effort to explain was too great. Besides, she felt ill. "I apologize, but I really must excuse myself."

Abigail jumped from her chair, ignoring the inquisitive glances from others seated at the head table. Keeping her head down, she maneuvered through the crowded banquet hall toward the exit and into the hallway. The stairs were straight ahead. Gripping the banister for support, she dragged herself to the top. Thankfully, the ladies' room was only a few steps away. She burst through the door, collapsing in disarray onto a tufted-velvet chair—praying no one would come along. Or, if they did, that she would have enough presence of mind to blame her condition on the champagne.

Not her sudden realization that, somehow, she must escape.

CHAPTER 2

There was only blackness before her eyes as the ominous ticking of the bedside clock marched toward dawn. She had been awake since her head touched the pillow, hours ago. Pulling the soft blanket tighter around her shoulders, she was again consumed with self-loathing. How undeserving she was of the luxuries that had been hers over the past two months. She had become the most odious form of parasite, feeding on the coerced sympathy of others. Mr. and Mrs. Hennessy had never truly welcomed her into their home; they had merely tolerated her presence.

But she had been safe.

And Arthur—how would he take the news? She remembered the look of shock on his face when she first told him of her stepfather's late-night intrusion into her bedroom. In her eagerness for solace, had she mistaken his sympathy for love? Had he accepted her gratitude in much the same way? She would be sorry to hurt him—though she wasn't sure he would be so very upset. She recalled the way he had appeared after his father's announcement of their engagement. The nervous fidgeting and the sudden pallor of his already pale complexion. Then the haste with which he'd excused himself. The young man who appeared to be waiting for him in the hallway ...

How easily she'd deceived herself into thinking it was possible to love almost anybody if only you put your mind to it. She and Arthur could never be right for each other; she should have known it all along. His generosity, coupled with her despair, had clouded her better senses.

But then her senses had been clouded, or at least dulled, for a very long time.

She thought of the doctor seated next to her at the banquet, Dr. Franklin Rome. He'd asked if she *aspired to the medical arts.* An odd way to put it! To her, medicine had always been more akin to a religious calling and a doctor not so different from a modern-day saint, rescuing countless poor souls from neglect, sickness, and death. Just as her father had done. Whatever dream she had of doing the same had ended that dreary afternoon when he fell to the floor of his office in an apparent seizure and she blindly rushed to administer treatment. There had been no time to think, just to act. Still, how could she have been so wrong?

She wasn't meant to be a doctor. It had taken her two years finally to accept it. But last night, the talk of *Gray's Anatomy* ... it had reawakened something. Not the old ambition; that was gone. Perhaps it was only a longing for her father, to watch him caring for his patients with that sureness of hand, calmness of spirit. How she loved helping him, and how special it made her feel to win his praise. She could almost hear him now, saying she had an aptitude for medicine. Someday she would make a fine doctor.

She sat up, thinking she'd heard a knock at the door. But it was only a branch from the enormous oak tree outside her window, scraping against the glass. She remained attentive for a while, hoping for some hidden message in the faint tap-tap-tap. Guidance from beyond, perhaps from Father, who had always directed her in everything. But there was no message, no guiding spirit, and there would be no simple escape from her predicament. Only a shockingly sudden one that surely would sully her reputation.

But then, what did she have to lose? She had no reputation, not among the Hennessys' set or any other. And though it might be cruel and ungrateful—in Mrs. Hennessy's eyes, proof of her deplorable lack of breeding—she was running away.

But first she had to find Dr. Rome.

· · · · ·

She felt awkward breakfasting with the Hennessys that morning, knowing what she planned to do, even if no one noticed her peculiar discomposure. Mrs. Hennessy, seated at the head, seldom spoke to her anyway, though she always had plenty to say to everyone else. Sarah was openly hateful, as usual, glaring at Abigail as if by doing so she might cause her to disappear in a puff of smoke. As for Mr. Hennessy, he was pleasant enough, but it seemed his mind was elsewhere. Nevertheless, through a bit of artful conniving, Abigail was able to find out where Mrs. Kilroy lived, and, on the pretext of having an early appointment, she hurriedly excused herself before anyone could question her.

On the chance Dr. Rome was still attending to Mr. Kilroy, she lay in wait. He was clearly surprised to find her loitering in front of the Kilroys' townhome. She explained that she was calling off her engagement and needed to find employment. He seemed interested. It wasn't until they were sitting across from each other at Café Le Jour on Forty-sixth Street that Abigail began to think she'd made yet another terrible mistake.

"You are a very beautiful young woman," he said, smiling at her over his coffee cup. "I suppose people tell you that all the time."

"Not so often, actually." That he had begun on such a personal note, and with the same overabundance of charm he'd displayed at the Hennessys' banquet, had an unsettling effect on her. As did his gaze, which was direct and insistent.

"I'm sure you're only being modest, but you need not be around me. I appreciate beauty for what it is and for the entitlements it brings to those lucky enough to have it."

"I've never been one to think much about entitlements. I was taught that if you desire something, you work for it. Which is why I wanted to speak with you—"

"There are lots of women who work very hard at being beautiful and still they can't hold a candle to you. I'd even go so far as to say that you, Miss Platford, are the embodiment of everything I hope to achieve for my patients. That's why you may actually be the perfect one to assist me with my new practice. You see, what I really need," he said, the excitement in his voice building, "is a *foil*. A stunningly beautiful foil."

"A foil?" She wasn't sure what the word meant, but didn't like the way it sounded.

"Yes. Someone to make the rounds with me at parties and events, anywhere we can meet women—the kind of women with both the desire and the means to avail themselves of my services."

This was not what she'd expected, nor was it a welcome development. Her purpose in approaching Dr. Rome was a far more serious one than his words implied. She had imagined herself working at his side, much as she had done with her father, helping to put patients at ease, assisting with their care. And though it was not her favorite duty, she would readily have consented to manage his schedule and fulfill the required paperwork if he were to ask her. But this business of attending parties and events—what did it have to do with doctoring?

"You speak of meeting women in need of your services, but surely you plan to take care of men as well. Mr. Kilroy is your patient, isn't he?"

"For the moment, yes—though that was only a favor. But let me explain." He took a hasty gulp of his coffee and set down the cup. "I'm about to embark on a new facet of my career, a new field. *Transformative surgery*. Have you heard of it?"

"I don't believe I have."

"Some call it beauty surgery."

She instantly recalled splashy advertisements she'd seen in the newspapers for practitioners who claimed to specialize in straightening noses, pinning back ears, and plumping up wrinkles with paraffin. At best, such solicitations had struck her as tasteless. At worst ... might Dr. Rome be nothing more than a charlatan?

"Oh—you're a *beauty doctor*." The inflection in her voice no doubt came across as somewhat disparaging. She dipped her head, hoping to obscure the visual evidence of her skepticism beneath the plethora of ostrich feathers on the brim of her blue velvet hat.

"Just imagine it for a moment, Miss Platford," he said, seeming not to have found anything disturbing in her reaction. "Your mere presence by my side would stimulate, in any average woman, an intense longing for beauty; then, arising quite naturally from that, a burning curiosity. With just a hint, she would be eager to learn what I offer in the way of beautifying procedures. That's how one goes about building a thriving beauty practice. Stimulate the need, offer the solution. Or, if you prefer, think of it this way: You would be helping to enlighten women about advances that can greatly enhance their lives. No different from selling a product. A product that people would certainly buy if they only knew its benefits."

So, he wanted her to help him *sell* the concept of beauty surgery to other women? That was not what a doctor does! To take part in such activities would compromise everything she believed in. "Your idea is to use me as a sort of walking advertisement?"

"I wouldn't put it like that."

"Forgive me for being blunt, but are you *really* a doctor?"

He shoved aside his coffee cup, almost knocking it over. "Would I call myself a doctor if I wasn't one?"

"I don't mean to offend you. It's just that I don't know any other doctors who are engaged in your kind of work."

"Because no medical school in this country has the foresight to embrace transformative surgery. That's why it was necessary for me to receive advanced training in Europe. I returned from Paris only recently."

"But you *did* train in medicine? Here in America?"

"Certainly, but the typical doctor's training only goes so far. The medical establishment is very set in its ways. It resists anything that might challenge the status quo. And that is exactly what transformative surgery does. The social implications are immense. It represents possibly the greatest force for the empowerment of women in all of human history."

"Empowerment of women?" Despite her disappointment, she had to smile. "I'm sorry, but I don't see what your transformative surgery could have to do with the movement for women's rights."

"Maybe you've never thought of it this way, but beauty is power," Dr. Rome said, with the calm certainty of a man who knows he speaks the truth. "And with enough power, Miss Platford, a woman can achieve anything."

She remembered what her father had always told her: As a woman, she would need to work doubly hard to convince others she had the skills to be a doctor. "I'm afraid I wouldn't feel comfortable encouraging vanity. It's not a trait I find admirable."

"Rubbish!" He leaned back in his chair with an exasperated sigh. But when he spoke again, his tone and manner were conciliatory. "Fine for a Sunday school lesson, but in the real world, appearances are everything. Beauty is a woman's greatest asset and the most reliable predictor of her future happiness. What you naturally possess, my dear, many others covet and believe impossible to attain. But what do you think they would give if they *could* achieve it? Not entirely, of course. But maybe half your beauty? A third? Maybe just enough to feel there was hope?"

"So, your patients will be paying you for *hope*? If that's all they stand to gain, I doubt they'd feel it was money well spent."

"Hope is only the beginning. Ultimately, what I offer is *happiness*. They say money can't buy it, but I'm here to prove them wrong." He paused, exuding a sense of drama. "Consider as well that *my* success will be *your* success. That *is* what you want, isn't it? To feel a sense of accomplishment?"

She considered telling him that her idea of accomplishment differed greatly from what he described. She could have reminded him, too, that curing the sick was the highest calling of a doctor, not pandering to the vanity of the wealthy. But she wasn't in a position to preach; the reality of her situation loomed over her like a dark cloud. If Dr. Rome was really a doctor, as he claimed, might she find his work interesting? Could it at least be a *start*—to tide her over until she could move on to something more worthwhile?

"And if you don't mind me saying so," he continued, "I'm not at all surprised that you've called it off with Arthur Hennessy. I could see right away, the two of you were not well matched. To be honest, Mr. Hennessy seems the sort to be uncomfortable in a conventional marriage. I have a pretty good eye for that kind of thing."

Abigail was startled by the shift of topic but couldn't stop herself from asking, "What *kind of thing* do you mean?"

"Let's just say it wouldn't be the first time a fellow has married in order to disguise his true proclivities. On the other hand, life as Mrs. Arthur Hennessy would have had its advantages. But now, here you are—in need of employment, you say. Tell me, is it really a need, or a desire?"

She didn't know how to answer him, having denied herself desires of any sort for so long. "I like working in a doctor's office. My father was a physician, until he passed away. I used to help him, and I—I had planned to go to medical school."

"Is that so?"

"Yes. I thought you might be willing teach me a few things— the way my father did. He was always very pleased with how fast I caught on. He said I had a natural talent for medicine. That someday I might—" She stopped, that same arresting image again before her eyes. Her father lying on the floor of his office ...

"Miss Platford?"

For a second, she couldn't breathe. "Forgive me, I was remembering something. About my father."

"No need to apologize." His tone was surprisingly gentle. "You know, sometimes it's better to look forward rather than back. As far as your immediate future, I would be more than happy to offer you a position."

"Kind of you, but I must decline. What you've described—a *foil*, as you called it—isn't at all what I'm looking for."

"I'm not saying that's all you'd be doing. I have a practice to run, and I could use the help of an efficient office assistant."

She paused, arguments on both sides playing out in her mind. It seemed there was something intrinsically shameful in the idea of working for a beauty doctor, even one as highly trained as Dr. Rome claimed to be. But what other options did she have? Where was she to go without a penny to her name? She could not continue her residence with the Hennessys, nor could she return home. She might look for a position with another doctor, but whether she would find one was uncertain. And though there were other types of labor at which she might excel, she could think of none that appealed to her.

"You can start right away. I'll give you an advance on your salary, if that would help. I can even suggest someplace for you to stay— that is, if you need help."

Was her desperation so obvious?

Giving up, she sighed. After all, it was only temporary. "Yes—to all of it. And thank you." She offered a wan smile, trying not to think of her father rolling over in his grave.

$$\cdot \quad \cdot \quad \cdot \quad \cdot \quad \cdot$$

When she arrived back at the Hennessys' home, she was elated to find that Mrs. Hennessy was not in. Dashing up to her room, she was finished packing in ten minutes. She'd come with almost nothing, and that was how she would leave. There were half a dozen exquisite new gowns hanging in the armoire that could have been hers for the taking. But they had been intended for Arthur's future wife. To realize that she no longer held that title was momentarily exhilarating, though what followed was a sense of how dreadfully she was behaving and what the Hennessys, especially Arthur, would think of her.

She found a pen and paper and hastily scribbled a note of thanks to the woman who would have been her mother-in-law, leaving it on the dressing table. She knew Mrs. Hennessy would be outraged but ultimately relieved by her departure. A second note to Arthur was more penitent. Asking for his forgiveness, she said that extended grief over her father's death had taken its toll on her emotions, and she believed him deserving of more than she could offer. Nothing was said about Dr. Rome, nothing about her plans except that she had secured a well-paying position. She asked that he not try to find her. *I will be all right*, she wrote, *and I am sure you will be better off without me.*

Downstairs, Abigail found a footman and asked him to fetch her suitcases and summon a cab. Dr. Rome had given her an address on a side street off Madison Avenue, close to the center of town. He had recently rented a two-story maisonnette, with the main level to serve as his office and the second as his living quarters. She was welcome to occupy a furnished basement room intended for the help; since his maid left every night after supper, the space was vacant. It would only be temporary, he assured, as she'd soon be able to afford something else—if things worked out.

She stared out the cab window as the horse plodded along Fifth Avenue, soon leaving behind the splendid mansions guarded by iron gates. The weather had changed; angry clouds were gathering, and the wind made shrill whistling noises through the cracks around the windows. Abigail pulled the lap rug tighter, thinking of the poor in New York City who tonight would have little or no shelter from the impending storm. She felt fortunate not to be among them. Instead, she was on her way to a new life, very different from what she would have had as a Hennessy and far better suited to her temperament. Now that she had made her escape, she couldn't believe she'd ever been willing to sacrifice her freedom for the promise of comfort and security. But then, people often do things that later seem out of character, only because they've forgotten what matters to them.

She must not make that mistake again.

The cab pulled up in front of a lovely brick-and-limestone building with tall windows and two small stone balconies on the second floor. The elegantly corniced doorway was at the top of a short flight of steps. The driver pulled a lever to release the cab doors and came around to withdraw the two suitcases stacked on the seat beside her, depositing them on the sidewalk. Abigail had already disembarked and was about to pay him, from the small amount of cash she had left, when Dr. Rome came up behind her.

"I'll take care of that." He took a few coins from the pocket of his trousers and dropped them into the man's outstretched palm. "Will fifty cents cover it?"

"Yes indeed, sir."

The driver nodded his thanks and left as Dr. Rome turned to Abigail with an expectant smile. "Are you ready?" He picked up her bags, one in each hand.

She nodded, feeling suddenly less sure of herself. The thought of living under the same roof as Dr. Rome, not exactly together but not so far apart either, was uncomfortable. She barely knew him. But the time for second thoughts was past. All she needed to do was keep her wits about her, and everything would be fine.

He motioned for her to follow. "The only access to the basement level is from outside," he said over his shoulder.

They took a short flight of steps down to a plain door painted black. To her relief, the basement was only partially below street level and had windows, though they were small and protected with iron bars. He unlocked the door, and they entered a damp-smelling room with brick walls. There were several colorful rugs on the cement floor, an obvious attempt at brightening up the place, and a few simple pieces of furniture—a narrow bed, a wooden night table, an overstuffed chair and matching ottoman in moth-eaten green velvet. Above a tiny stove and an enameled metal basin, with a ewer for washing dishes, were several open shelves where a few mismatched plates and cups were stacked. Abigail fleetingly thought of her former room at the Hennessys' Fifth Avenue mansion, with its polished floors and flowing drapes and intricately patterned Persian carpets in muted shades of blue, gold, and persimmon. How drastically her life had changed in a matter of hours!

"There's a small bathroom behind that door," Dr. Rome said, nodding to the left. He set down her bags. "I'm sorry, there's no electricity down here. But there are several oil lamps."

"All I need is enough light to read."

"We'll find someplace more appropriate, but for now—"

"It will do fine—for now," she said, hoping he would not sense her dismay. She didn't know what she'd expected, only that this was worse. She tried to console herself with the thought that a few homey touches might transform the dismal space into something more inviting. Lace curtains at the windows, a few pictures on the walls, maybe a patchwork quilt.

"Of course, I could put you up in my apartment for a while. I have an extra bedroom."

Instinctively, she took a step back. "Thank you, but I'll manage here."

She saw a slight smile flicker beneath his dark moustache. He had known she would refuse, which undoubtedly was why he'd offered. Such an arrangement would be unthinkable; quite different from Arthur's invitation to shelter her in his parents' home, though some might have raised an eyebrow even at that. It disturbed her that Dr. Rome would make the offer, however insincere.

"There are fresh linens on the bed. Soap and towels and that kind of thing in there." He gestured toward a rickety-looking chest of drawers shoved into a dark corner. "The lock on the door is sturdy. I tested it myself."

There was an awkward silence.

"If you need anything, you'll let me know," he said.

There seemed nothing else for him to do but leave. Abigail dreaded the moment he would shut the door behind him and she would be alone. Soon it would be evening. She glanced nervously through the bars of her tiny windows. The storm that had threatened all afternoon was beginning now, tiny droplets beading on the glass. She shivered to think of being down here, by herself, all night—the wind howling, rain pounding on the sidewalk. And inside, only the flickering of an oil lamp, a mouse scurrying silently along the wall ...

Dr. Rome was looking at her rather pityingly, as if he could read her mind. "Is your mother alive?"

"Yes."

"Where does she live?"

She couldn't tell him the truth. Not when she thought of what her mother had said on the day she left, how hatefully she had accused her. *You were always your father's, and he was yours. And now you want to take my new husband from me, too?* "She lives quite far from here. But I'll be fine. Honestly, I will."

"All right then, take tonight and Sunday to get settled. Monday morning we'll meet upstairs in the office at nine. I'll show you around the place, and then we have some work to do. There's an important event coming up, and I want you dressed up to the nines."

She pictured the outfits she'd brought with her, none of them chic. "I'm afraid my wardrobe is rather limited," she said, embarrassed to admit how destitute she was. The gown she'd worn to the banquet, though only a costume, had been extraordinary, and the diamond choker was worth a fortune; she assumed he realized both had been borrowed.

"Don't concern yourself about clothes," he said. "I have my own ideas about how I want you to look. I've planned for us to go shopping together on Monday."

"But—"

"I understand your circumstances, Miss Platford. Whatever you may need in order to perform your duties will be my responsibility to provide."

She couldn't help but feel the humiliation of her situation. But even if she must temporarily rely on Dr. Rome to provide her wardrobe, did that give him the right to dictate how she would look? She'd been through that once already, with Mrs. Hennessy.

"I'll pay you back as soon as I can."

Again, that amused twitch at the corners of his mouth. "I'm sure you will. But you needn't be in such a hurry. Give yourself a little time."

He turned to leave, tossing over his shoulder as he passed through the open doorway, "Good night, Miss Platford. Sleep well. Should you change your mind about the apartment, you know where to find me."

Abigail closed the door softly, as if afraid of the sound it would make. The finality of *everything* pressed in on her. Had it been a mistake to abandon Arthur? She had behaved so selfishly, and what had she accomplished besides stirring up scandal and placing herself at the mercy of yet another man? She supposed she was lucky to have a position as Dr. Rome's assistant; but in the long run, where would that take her? Might she have been better off as Mrs. Arthur Hennessy, wealthy and secure, devoting herself to an array of worthy causes? She would have done more for the good of others than she could ever hope to do now.

She removed her light cloak and tossed it onto the bed. Sitting on the edge of the hard mattress, gazing through the bars of her tiny windows, she craned her neck for a glimpse of the darkening sky. She hardly knew herself anymore. How she missed the girl who had so ardently believed in her mission to become a physician dedicated to the poor. That girl of long ago never would have resigned herself to grasping at straws, putting her fate in the hands of a virtual stranger—a beauty doctor, no less!

But it was no use thinking that way. Things could be worse, and her present situation was only temporary. For now, she must make the best of it.

And try not to worry about what might happen if she failed to live up to Dr. Rome's expectations.

CHAPTER 3

Abigail's debut as Dr. Rome's foil, only six nights later, took place at the famous Delmonico's. The annual spring banquet hosted by the Governors of the Cotillion of Eighty was a much-anticipated event among that social set, which, according to Dr. Rome, included names associated with some of the city's oldest money. The restaurant's immense reception hall had been transformed into a flowering garden with red wisteria, pink carnations, and yellow daisies, the flowers woven into trailing green vines of Southern smilax which trimmed multiple arbors positioned around the room. Somewhat ironically, it reminded Abigail of how Sherry's had looked on the night of her engagement party, when she'd stood with shaking knees next to Arthur and received the blessing of a similar cadre of New York's elite for their ill-fated union. She wondered if some of that group might be present tonight. Likely they had not yet gotten a whiff of the scandal but would no doubt find her presence on the arm of another man ample fodder for gossip—that is, assuming they even remembered her.

As soon as she and Dr. Rome entered from the foyer, two elderly patronesses rushed over to intercept them at the door.

"Ladies, how delightful to see you." Dr. Rome lifted a gloved hand from each, in succession, to his lips. "I'm Dr. Franklin Rome and"—he turned to Abigail with a broad smile— "this is the charming Miss Abigail Platford."

"A pleasure," the women said almost in unison, their eyes sweeping over Abigail as they not so subtly assessed her new satin gown with pearl-encrusted bodice and puffed sleeves. On Monday, she and Dr. Rome had spent several hours at Bergdorf Goodman; he'd paid extra for the dressmaker's promise that this dress, from among several they'd ordered, would be ready for tonight. Her final primping, which included a salon-styled pompadour hairdo, had required all afternoon at the beauty parlor. Still, she could tell that the ladies were wary. Might they be questioning the nature of her relationship with Dr. Rome?

"And the two of you are here as guests of ...?"

"Mr. and Mrs. Chapman," Dr. Rome said, his eyes scouring the room. "Yes, I think I see them right over there." He nodded toward the farthest corner, mumbled a quick thank you, and before the two patronesses could inquire further, he took Abigail by the arm and propelled her onto the crowded floor.

"Tell me about the Chapmans again?" She was nervous. Though Dr. Rome had been patient with her for the entire week, explaining in great detail about the office and how he wanted things done, she feared he might expect too much of her tonight.

"Roger Chapman is a big industrialist, mostly land and minerals. I've never met him, actually. But I *have* met his wife. They have a townhome only a few blocks from the office. I had the good fortune not too long ago to find and return her missing Pomeranian. Name is Buttons, I believe—the dog, that is. Mrs. Chapman was exceedingly grateful." He straightened his bow tie. "Now, do as I've told you. Make her curious, dying to know everything. I'll take it from there."

"But what if she doesn't approve of beauty surgery?"

"Don't worry about that. Some will think it's wonderful, others will be aghast. But in the end, they all want to hear about it in every fascinating detail."

They approached a couple, whom Abigail judged to be in their fifties, the man on the short side and portly, the woman tall and attractive but with the first telltale signs of advancing years—a slight slackness of the jawline, a deepness to the folds around her mouth. Dr. Rome had already begun teaching her how to assess a woman's appearance and what might benefit from correction, though there had been very little discussion of how he went about restoring the illusion of youth. It bothered her to think that, from now on, she must take a critical view of every woman she met, intent only on her physical flaws. Yet Dr. Rome appeared sincere in believing he offered a valuable service and one that many women wanted. In Abigail's mind, both assertions had yet to be proved.

"Mrs. Chapman!" Dr. Rome spoke her name as if she were a dear and long-lost friend. "How wonderful to see you!"

"Oh yes, Dr. Rome. I'm happy you could make it." Mrs. Chapman glanced at her husband, who was contemplating the selection of canapes on a silver tray held only inches from his nose by a white-coated butler. "Roger, this is Dr. Rome. I told you about him. The one who found our Buttons!"

Mr. Chapman interrupted his deliberations long enough to glance at the new arrivals. "Good evening. Roger Chapman here." He snatched a couple of appetizers from the tray before finally giving them his full attention. "Guess I owe you a debt of gratitude, Doctor. If anything had happened to Buttons, I'm afraid my wife would never have recovered from it. She's more attached to that dog than she is to me!"

Dr. Rome laughed heartily while Abigail offered an appropriately subdued smile.

"But tell us, who is this lovely young lady?" Mr. Chapman said, eyeing her as he stuffed foie gras on a cracker into his mouth.

"Please allow me to introduce Miss Abigail Platford, my—"

"Dr. Rome's assistant," she interjected firmly, before a less distinguished title might be assigned.

"Your assistant! What a responsible position for such a lovely young girl," exclaimed Mrs. Chapman. Though her response was gracious, she seemed circumspect; perhaps she was unaccustomed to socializing with working women.

"Yes, Miss Platford is very well organized. Setting up a new practice is a complicated matter. Countless things to attend to, most of which I must confess I have little patience for. With her help this week, I've settled into my new office and already am scheduling patients for transformative procedures."

"A good secretary is worth her weight in gold," said Mr. Chapman, signaling the butler to return with the tray of hors d'oeuvres.

"But, Dr. Rome, what was that you said? What sort of *procedures*?" Mrs. Chapman said.

Dr. Rome offered his most disarming smile. "Ah yes, I'd forgotten that the subject never came up when we met before. Understandably so, with our attention on that most exceptional dog of yours. A brilliant example of his breed!"

"Why, thank you. But what did you say about—"

"My field, Mrs. Chapman, is *transformative surgery*."

Abigail took her cue, just as they'd rehearsed. "Dr. Rome is too modest to boast of his reputation, but besides being fully trained as a general surgeon, he is among the world's most acclaimed beauty doctors. He's just returned from Europe, and the techniques he learned there are truly astonishing." She turned to Mrs. Chapman with a touch of playfulness. "Haven't you ever wondered why European women always appear so chic, so ageless?"

"Well, they do seem to have a certain *something*." Mrs. Chapman agreed.

"Before I arrived in New York, just a few short weeks ago," Dr. Rome interjected, "I was performing procedures alongside some of the leading beauty doctors in France. As in many scientific matters, Europe is far ahead of America."

"Well, if you ask me—" Though no one had inquired as to Mr. Chapman's opinion, everyone paused with an air of deference to hear his pronouncement. "I find it ludicrous that any genuine doctor would spend his time and the efforts of his training on such frivolity when far more important issues need to be addressed. What about tuberculosis, polio, influenza? And, certainly, no man in his right mind would ever allow his wife to indulge in that kind of tinkering with nature." He shot a meaningful glance at Mrs. Chapman. "That's why they have rouge pots and curling tongs, isn't it? I would think that's quite enough."

"Of course, such interventions are not for everyone, Mr. Chapman." Dr. Rome's response was perfectly composed, though Abigail noticed a slight rigidity to his jaw. "A woman such as Mrs. Chapman, for example, could scarcely improve on what nature has already endowed. But there are others whose lives might be transformed for the better if only they could look in the mirror without flinching. There is a wide range of conditions that can cause certain people to feel unsettled about their appearance. I've seen many instances in which such individuals withdraw completely from life, even shun those closest to them. Thank goodness, in their desperation, they have somewhere to turn—to a doctor, a professional who understands their pain and possesses the highly specialized surgical skill to alleviate it once and for all."

"Yes, thank goodness," Abigail chimed in, unexpectedly moved by Dr. Rome's seemingly heartfelt monologue. "Surely it's not for us to judge others' pain, wouldn't you agree?"

Mrs. Chapman waited a moment for her husband's reply, as if she dared not offer her own opinion first. But seeing that he was again distracted by the butler's tray, she spoke up herself. "Putting all that aside, what exactly *are* these techniques, Dr. Rome?"

His jaw relaxed. It was not Mr. Chapman he needed to convince. "They are quite varied, depending on the problem to be addressed. But, to give you an example, facial wrinkles and folds often can be treated with a simple paraffin injection, virtually painless, and the results are nothing short of spectacular."

"Is that so ..." Mrs. Chapman's expression was thoughtful, but before she could formulate her next question, they were being summoned to supper. "My goodness, I've scarcely had time to work up an appetite." She smiled at Abigail, examining her with a great deal more interest than before. "You must tell me the secret of such a lovely complexion. Or would that require giving away one of Dr. Rome's proprietary formulas?"

Abigail laughed lightly, glancing at Dr. Rome to see if he was about to answer. He offered her no such help. "I'd be happy to tell you anything you'd like to know, but I hope you will also share your beauty secrets with me."

Mrs. Chapman appeared flattered. Linking her arm through Abigail's, she said in a cozy tone, "Come along, dear. Let's get you and Dr. Rome settled at our table, and we can continue our discussion there." Then, propelling Abigail a few feet away from Mr. Chapman, she leaned in to whisper, "I suddenly feel as if the world has passed me by, and there is so much I must learn."

She had no further opportunity to question Abigail. When they arrived at the banquet table, her husband promptly seated himself to Abigail's left, with Dr. Rome occupying the chair on her right. But Mrs. Chapman apparently had taken a liking to Dr. Rome's youthful assistant, and at the end of the night she invited Abigail to tea on Monday afternoon with several other ladies who, she said, might enjoy hearing about Dr. Rome's work.

Though Abigail readily accepted the invitation, she did so with some trepidation. She was relieved that her first performance as Dr. Rome's foil had gone extraordinarily well. But on Monday, at Mrs. Chapman's party, she would be on her own.

·　　·　　·　　·　　·

"Good afternoon, ma'am. Won't you please come in?"

The butler dipped his head in deference as Abigail crossed the threshold of the Chapmans' elegantly appointed foyer.

"Thank you. Am I the first to arrive?"

"Oh no, ma'am. There are two others here already. Unless you'd like to visit the powder room, I can take you to them now."

"We can go directly."

"Of course, if you'll follow me, please."

Pausing at the foyer's gleaming rosewood console, she removed from her handbag one of her new calling cards that read "Miss Abigail Platford, Assistant to Franklin Rome, MD, Transformative Surgery." Below was the slogan "The Power of Beauty" and Dr. Rome's office address and five-digit telephone number. After depositing the card front and center on the console, she followed the butler down a wide hallway, past a spacious drawing room, a wood-paneled library, and a formal dining room where several maids bustled about the banquet table laying out fine china, crystal, and silver for the Chapmans' next exclusive soiree. Passing through a back parlor that smelled of fresh roses and cinnamon, they exited through French doors onto a tiny patch of lawn. Several wicker chairs and small tea tables had been set up in the shade of a willow oak. As Abigail approached the three ladies who stood chatting, Mrs. Chapman turned to greet her.

"Miss Platford, how good of you to come." Dismissing the butler, she took Abigail's arm and oriented her toward the others. "If I may interrupt for just a moment, I'd like to introduce Miss Abigail Platford, the young lady I've been telling you about."

There was a momentary hush as the two women surveyed Abigail's appearance. She took comfort in knowing that her afternoon frock from Bergdorf Goodman—lavender-dotted batiste with Swiss needlework and trimmed in baby Irish lace, with a matching hat and parasol—could hold its own against any of the other ladies' outfits.

"Mrs. Edwards"—Mrs. Chapman gestured toward an extremely thin woman with a lined and hollowed-out face— "and Mrs. Monroe, both of them dear friends."

Mrs. Monroe was an attractive woman with graying hair and lively blue eyes. "Loretta warned us that your youth and beauty would put the rest of us to shame, and I'm afraid she was correct." She flashed a mock-serious frown at Mrs. Chapman and then giggled. "Anyway, she told us to pay close attention to what you have to say about Dr. Rome and his so-called *transformative* surgery. Sounds frightening to me! But the implication was that we'd be smart to avail ourselves of it, whatever it might be."

"I would never make that kind of recommendation," Mrs. Chapman protested. "But all of us being modern women, we at least ought to know what's available to us. As I said to Miss Platford the other night, the world has changed, and there is no good reason to remain ignorant of the possibilities."

At that moment, three more women appeared on the lawn. Two of them were of the same general age as Mrs. Chapman and her other friends. Abigail judged the third to be no older than twenty.

Mrs. Chapman greeted the new arrivals and introduced Abigail to them as well. Rather quickly, however, she returned to the subject of beauty surgery. "Miss Platford, you were very mysterious at the Cotillion of Eighty banquet about Dr. Rome and his work. Of course, we've all heard about beauty surgery, but I doubt any of us have taken it too seriously. Nor has anyone we know."

"You haven't heard about Geraldine Langhardt?" said one of the new arrivals. "Last year she went to some beauty doctor out of town and apparently had the full treatment. All along, of course, she insisted she was doing it for her husband. Wanted to tame his wandering eye, she said. But when it was all done and paid for, she divorced him. And soon after, she ran off to Paris with some fellow fifteen years her junior!"

There were gasps and murmured exclamations.

"Whatever happened to accepting what God has seen fit to give you in the way of looks?" said Mrs. Edwards. "It's character that matters, is it not, ladies?"

"Have you ever heard a man say such a thing? No, my dear, it's what we women tell ourselves when we no longer can bear to look in the mirror!"

"But these beauty doctors—forgive me, Miss Platford, but their reputations leave much to be desired."

"Oh, but Dr. Rome seems quite distinguished," Mrs. Chapman said. "Not at all what one would imagine. He told me his degree is from Johns Hopkins!"

"That *is* impressive," Mrs. Monroe said. "Actually, I would find it fascinating to learn more about what he does."

There followed a general flutter of assent which Abigail found more terrifying than gratifying given that she had not expected to deliver a lecture but merely let slip a few hints in conversation. But it was obvious these women, or at least some of them, were determined to wring from her every drop of

information they could, not understanding that h
was extremely shallow.   fo

She was granted a few minutes' reprieve by the ap   ti
two manservants bearing refreshments, but once the
helped themselves to tea and blueberry scones, they se   n
in their chairs. Pacified by the warmth of the late-afterı   I
and the sweet scent of winter honeysuckle, they now lo
Abigail for enlightenment.

"So, tell us, Miss Platford, what is this transformative s
that Dr. Rome speaks about in such elusive terms?" said Mrs. (
man.

"Well ..." Abigail could feel droplets of perspiration gatheı
above her lip; she raised her napkin to brush them away. "Let ı
start by saying that Dr. Rome has the greatest respect for wome
and a most compassionate understanding of the difficulties w
may sometimes face in achieving and maintaining our natural
beauty. Because, as I'm sure everyone would agree, it is *natural*
beauty for which we all strive. The means, however, can be various."

"But what *are* the means?" prodded Mrs. Edwards.

"There are as many approaches as there are individuals. Which
is to say, Dr. Rome must first evaluate his patient and then design a
treatment specifically for her."

"Give us an example," chimed in one of the late arrivals. "What
sort of treatments are they?"

"Well, there are simple injections and there is actual surgery,
mostly minor procedures—all of it totally pain free, I should em-
phasize, thanks to the wonderful anesthetics available today. As
Mrs. Chapman mentioned, Dr. Rome is a graduate of Johns Hopkins and a fully trained surgeon, having studied both here in
America and abroad."

"But please, can you explain how the procedures are per-
med?" This time, it was the young woman, who spoke in a soft,
nid voice. "The various facial surgeries ..."

"And what about scars?" asked Mrs. Monroe. "Surely, there
ust be some telltale trace, something that would give it away—
mean, one would want to keep such a thing private. Can you im-
gine if something like that were to get around?"

"I can assure you, the goal of Dr. Rome's techniques is to
achieve results that appear totally natural," Abigail said again, at
this point feeling a bit like a trained parrot.

"You must be talking about cutting the skin, my dear. And a
cut always leaves some sign."

"That, Mrs. Monroe, is why the skill of the surgeon is para-
mount."

"You have, of course, seen Dr. Rome operate?" The way Mrs.
Edwards inquired left no doubt as to the answer she expected. Abigail could have saved face by just agreeing with her; yes, she'd seen
Dr. Rome's work, and it was extraordinary. But, having been careful, up to now, to speak only in vague generalities, she could not
bring herself to tell an unambiguous lie.

She was about to admit that she had only recently begun her employment with Dr. Rome and had yet to see him *in action*, so to
speak, when Mrs. Chapman jumped up from her chair, clapping
her hands in delight as a new guest entered the garden. Abigail
could not have been more thankful for the interruption—until
she turned to see the final latecomer. For a moment, she hoped
she was mistaken, that her memory of Mrs. Hennessy's sour,
pinched face already had been dulled to where she might easily
confuse her with someone else. But no, the slope of the woman's
long nose, the vulture-like sharpness of her gaze, the ropey cords
that stood out from her thin neck—there could be no doubt it
was Arthur's mother.

Abigail ducked her head, hoping her hostess would not notice. It was too late. Mrs. Chapman bent down with a look of concern, speaking in a whisper. "Is there something wrong, Miss Platford? Have we tired you with all our questions?"

The other women had risen to greet Mrs. Hennessy, and all were preoccupied for the moment. Abigail knew that if she was to avoid a scene, or at least an uncomfortable encounter, she would need to act right away.

"I—I'm so sorry, but I really must be going," she apologized, getting up from her chair. "Please offer my regrets to everyone."

"But, my dear, we were looking forward to hearing more about Dr. Rome's work."

"I'd be happy to return another time," she said weakly. "But I'm afraid I feel a bit faint."

"Oh, my! I'll walk with you back to the house. Perhaps you'd like to rest."

Mrs. Chapman stood up, looking genuinely worried as she linked her arm with Abigail's. They had just started off when Mrs. Edwards called out, "Miss Platford, where are you going? You mustn't leave without answering a few more of our questions about Dr. Rome!"

Out of the corner of her eye, Abigail saw Mrs. Hennessy's head turn sharply in her direction. "Abigail Platford!" she exclaimed in a piercing voice. "And what, may I ask, is *she* doing here?"

Mrs. Chapman froze, the rest of the ladies looking at one another and then at Abigail, their faces conveying a lurid curiosity.

"You know Miss Platford?" asked Mrs. Monroe with a raised brow, perhaps wondering if Mrs. Hennessy had already availed herself of Dr. Rome's services.

"Do I know her? I should say that I do, and most unfortunately so!"

Mrs. Chapman might easily assume the worst of someone she knew almost nothing about. Abigail sensed, however, that her hostess was less concerned with passing judgment than effectuating a rapid exit. "Miss Platford was about to leave. I was just seeing her off. If you'll excuse us—"

"I will *not*!" Mrs. Hennessy was beside herself now. "Do you ladies know anything about this young woman? Anything at all?"

"She's the assistant of Dr. Rome—the beauty doctor," someone said.

"Ha! Is that what she told you?" Mrs. Hennessy seemed about to burst out of her corset. "It doesn't surprise me. Not a bit. A girl like that will lie about anything." She puffed herself up like a rooster ready to crow. "Miss Platford is *not* Dr. Rome's assistant. She is his— his—" she spluttered for a few painful seconds. "His *trollop*!"

There was a horrible silence during which all Abigail could hear was the blood pounding in her ears. She waited for someone to rise to her defense. She had come here invested with a certain authority and, though she may have failed to deliver what was expected neither had she comported herself in a fashion supportive of Mrs. Hennessy's allegations. But when Mrs. Chapman spoke again, the chill of her tone was clearly directed toward the guest to whom she felt the least loyalty.

"It appears there's been a misunderstanding. Come along, Miss Platford. I'll see you out."

Abigail's mortification was second only to her fury toward Mrs. Hennessy, who had done nothing but belittle her from the very start of their association. Yes, she had allowed Abigail to take up residence in her home, an uninvited guest, but she had never thought her good enough for Arthur. And while, admittedly, the manner of Abigail's departure had confirmed Mrs. Hennessy's worst opinion of her, it didn't justify the humiliating accusation she had just made in front of everyone.

As for the rest of them—these women who most likely had never done a day's work in their entire lives—what gave them the right to assume so much about her, solely on the say-so of one of their own?

"If I might clarify the matter—" Everyone turned toward Abigail, astonished she would dare to say anything, having been so unequivocally dismissed. She swallowed, her throat tight. "Mrs. Hennessy is egregiously misinformed about my relationship with Dr. Rome. As he himself explained to Mrs. Chapman, I am his *assistant*—a responsible position for which I am to be paid a monthly salary." She glanced about, trying to gauge if her words were having any effect, but all she received were blank stares. "All of us here being *modern* women, no doubt we can agree there is no dishonor in such an arrangement," she continued, though struggling now. "In today's world, there is no way for a woman to get ahead and make something of herself other than honest employment. Unless she wishes to be nothing more than an extension of her husband."

She thought she detected a slight gasp from one or two of them, which gave her a momentary satisfaction. She tilted her hat back to its original jaunty angle. "It was a pleasure meeting you, ladies."

Abigail hurried from the garden, letting herself out the side gate. Ordinarily, she could have walked the few blocks home, but the moment she closed the gate behind her, she was overcome with a violent shaking in her knees. Luckily, a hansom had just deposited a passenger across the street. She signaled for the driver to wait until she felt steady enough to proceed. Once inside the cab, she gave him the address, leaned back, and tried to gather her senses.

She had made a mess of things, in all likelihood ruining Dr. Rome's reputation among Mrs. Chapman's influential set, and she was sorry for that. If she could have demonstrated expertise on the topic of beauty surgery, even slightly, Mrs. Hennessy's charges against her would have seemed preposterous. But as it was, she had little credibility on which to stand, nothing more than a calling card with her title and a catchy slogan meant to titillate the curiosity of unsuspecting women like Mrs. Chapman and her friends.

The whole situation was absurd. There was nothing in it for her—nothing but disgrace. Whether it was Dr. Rome's fault or her own, whatever might become of her, she could not continue like this. By the time the hansom pulled in front of the office, she had decided. If Dr. Rome wanted a foil he would have to find one somewhere else.

CHAPTER 4

D r. Rome's reception room was decorated much like an upper-class parlor. Heavy velvet drapes, brocade uphol-stery in deep shades of blue and burgundy, Tiffany lamps, and an array of interesting curios displayed in a glass cabinet, lit from within. On the walls were a series of gold-framed etchings, reproductions of Leonardo da Vinci studies of the female face. In this room, also, was Abigail's desk, mahogany with turned legs and a burgundy leather top embossed around the edges with a delicate gold leaf design. Sitting smartly at the corner was a Strowger dial telephone. In the nine days since she had begun her employment as Dr. Rome's assistant, it had yet to ring.

She was seated at her desk. This morning, she had dressed in one of her old frocks, not the prettily tucked white shirtwaist and dark pleated skirt that Dr. Rome had bought for her to wear in the office. Her hair was pulled into a simple bun instead of the more sophisticated pompadour and chignon that he preferred. Her only concession to his taste was her perfume, essence of gar-denia, which he had insisted was the perfect scent for her. Its exotic aroma, heightened by the nervous heat of her body, was intoxicating.

As she awaited the sound of Dr. Rome's footsteps on the wooden staircase down the hall, she wondered again how he would take the news that she was resigning. She had composed a letter, just to make it official, which she signed now with a decisive flourish. If she did not extricate herself from a situation that clearly required a compromise of her integrity, then in the future she would have no one to blame but herself.

"How did things go at Mrs. Chapman's tea party?"

Startled, she looked up. Dr. Rome was leaning in the doorway, dapper in a black morning coat paired with gray-and-black striped trousers. He flashed a smile brilliant as his starched white shirt. "Sorry if I caught you by surprise. You were deeply engrossed in your writing. May I ask what you're working on?"

"A letter."

"Ah, a letter," he responded dismissively. "Well, let me interrupt you long enough to—"

"A rather important letter."

"I doubt as important as the news I have for you," he said, with that cool self-confidence that she suddenly found terribly annoying.

"If you don't mind, I'll tell you my news first. I'm resigning my position as your *foil*."

His jovial mood instantly evaporated. "And what is this all about?"

"Dr. Rome, I find it difficult to understand how you could send me out to address a group of women without properly equipping me to answer the questions you knew they would ask." She was surprised by the vehemence in her voice. She'd meant to be firm, not abrasive. But did it matter now what he thought of her?

"Are you referring to Mrs. Chapman's tea party?"

"What else *could* I be referring to? Did it ever occur to you that you have yet to explain precisely how you intend to deliver on the promises you seem willing to make to anyone who will listen? You expect me to promote your expertise when I don't have the slightest proof of the abilities you claim."

"Now wait a minute—"

"Yet you've asked me to provide assurances, to instill faith and trust in your skill and experience. I'm sorry, but I can't. Ignorance can be no excuse for misleading others."

"Are you finished?"

"Yes, I suppose I am." She could have told him about her encounter with Mrs. Hennessy and how her virtue had been maligned. Though the incident was possibly the worst of all that had happened, she couldn't bring herself to admit to it, perhaps because she feared there might be a kernel of truth in what Mrs. Hennessy had said. Hadn't she accepted shelter and clothing from a man she hardly knew, a man who had been quite open about his intention to use her as nothing more than decoration? She supposed one could make the argument there was little substantive difference between a woman who would agree to such an arrangement and a so-called trollop. But there was no need to go into all that now.

"What I mean to say is that I can't be what you want me to be, Dr. Rome. I can't pretend to know things I don't, and I doubt anyone would believe me if I tried. There is something immoral about—"

"Hold on, hold on!" Dr. Rome raised his hand to silence her. "There's something I need to tell you." He pulled out his watch, glanced at it, and then returned it to the pocket of his waistcoat. "We have only five minutes to get ready."

"Ready? For what?"

He folded his arms over his chest. "If you assumed that your participation in Mrs. Chapman's tea party yesterday was to no avail, you are wrong. I had come downstairs early this morning, around nine, when the telephone rang. It was Mrs. Hadley. She explained how she and her daughter had met you through Mrs. Chapman and were curious to know if there was anything that could be done regarding the young Miss Hadley's rather prominent nose."

"They're coming here? Now?"

"Yes, in five minutes. Well, now it's four minutes." He smiled benevolently. "I'm very proud of you, Miss Platford. This is just how it's supposed to work."

Despite the vociferousness of her earlier protests, Abigail felt giddy. Her first effort had been a success! It almost seemed too easy. "But what should I do when they get here?"

"You'll greet them, thank them for coming. You'll complete the brief form that we designed the other day, if you recall. Name, address, and so on. You'll ask them to wait a moment, and then you'll come back to my office to inform me that the patient has arrived. You will then return to say *Dr. Rome is ready*, and you'll bring them to me, after which I will take over."

She glanced down at her outfit. It was drab and outdated. She should not have worn it; but at least the way she looked now, she wouldn't be mistaken for a trollop.

The bell rang, and Dr. Rome gave her an encouraging nod before retiring to the back.

"Good morning, ladies," she said cheerily, stepping aside for them to enter.

Miss Isabelle Hadley looked elegant in a pale blue walking dress of linen and lace, detailed with cluster tucks at the collar, shoulders, and sleeves. Quite the latest fashion and obviously expensive, which only made Abigail feel all the dowdier in her plain frock. The young woman greeted her with a self-effacing smile, no hint of disrespect. Abigail didn't know what took place after she left Mrs. Chapman's party, but apparently the Hadley mother and daughter had decided Mrs. Hennessy's accusations against her were not all that important.

"Good morning to you, Miss Platford." Miss Hadley's mother smiled at Abigail from beneath a wide hat on which several stuffed hummingbirds nested among an elaborate decoration of silk flowers, chiffon, and ribbon. "We're here to see Dr. Rome."

"Yes, of course. He told me you were coming."

After seeing to their comfort and politely gathering the necessary personal information, as she and Dr. Rome had discussed, Abigail escorted the women into his private office. When the three of them emerged half an hour later, Dr. Rome was smug as he led them over to her desk.

"Miss Platford," he said, "Miss Hadley would like to make an appointment for a procedure. Please find a time that would be convenient for her. I realize I'm scheduled already through this week—" He gave Abigail a look that meant she was not to contradict him. "But after that, I believe there should be several slots available. Please block out an entire morning, beginning at eight."

And with that, he turned to Isabelle Hadley and her mother, made a slight bow to each, and retreated into the hallway.

They agreed on a date in two weeks. Seeing the nervousness in Miss Hadley's face, the tightness of her mouth and the intensity of every blink, Abigail realized how much courage it had taken for her to come today. She admired her for it and wondered, were she in the other young woman's position, would she be as brave? She wondered, too, if there was anything specific in what she'd said yesterday that had encouraged such confidence. The thought troubled her. Though it was satisfying to imagine her powers of persuasion so finely tuned, she was uncomfortable with the responsibility such influence implied. Yet, as Dr. Rome had said, this was how it was supposed to work.

As they were leaving, Mrs. Hadley suddenly turned around. "Oh, I almost forgot." She opened her handbag and pulled out a checkbook. "May I borrow a pen?"

"Certainly."

Likely noticing Abigail's look of surprise, Miss Hadley said, "Dr. Rome requested a deposit. Is that not customary?"

"Oh yes. Very customary," Abigail replied, aware that the color had rushed to her cheeks. How could she have neglected to ask for a deposit, as she'd been instructed? But Dr. Rome had not told her how much it should be.

Before she could figure out what to say next, Mrs. Hadley had already handed over the check. "We'll see you in a couple of weeks," she said, and then mother and daughter quietly left.

Abigail glanced down at the paper in her hand. At first, she thought she'd misread the amount. One hundred dollars! Most people labored for months to earn that amount. And this was only a deposit? She realized with a jolt what had attracted Dr. Rome to his new field. Clearly there was an inordinate amount of money to be made from it—though she supposed it wasn't fair to assume profit as his primary motivation. For a surgeon, there must be a certain challenge in pursuing a field still in its infancy. Dr. Rome, if she read him correctly, seemed the type to thrive on adventure.

Maybe in her own way, she was as well.

.   .   .   .   .

That night, Abigail awoke to the screeching of a siren somewhere not far away. She sat up, felt around for the matches, and lit the lamp by her bed. It was eleven-thirty. She had been asleep for only an hour. Sighing, she extinguished the light and lay back down. Rolling onto her side, she pulled the comforter over her head.

Would she ever get used to living in this musty-smelling basement room with the bars on the windows? But maybe she wouldn't have to stay here too much longer. Dr. Rome said they would find another place for her—something *more appropriate*. Now that she had seen what his patients were willing to pay him, she should have no compunction about asking for a wage that could support her. Though she supposed it was a bit early to be haggling over money. He had, after all, supplied her with a place to live and several expensive outfits. And his elderly maid, Prudence, had even brought supper to her a few times.

She wondered what Dr. Rome did in the evenings after he left the office. Perhaps he had dinner out with friends. Or with a lady.

She contemplated, not for the first time, why a handsome professional man like Franklin Rome was unmarried. Recalling what he'd insinuated about Arthur, and how he claimed to have *a pretty good eye for that kind of thing*, she allowed herself a moment to consider whether Dr. Rome might himself have a hidden predilection. But no, that was impossible. She remembered the little flutter in her stomach that night at the banquet when he first smiled at her and then later, again, when he leaned close, saying she *intrigued* him. She couldn't deny he was immensely attractive.

Unsettled by the direction of her thoughts, she reminded herself that Dr. Rome was her employer and a person from whom she might learn a great deal. Yes, he was a beauty doctor. But his credentials were impressive. That very afternoon she had helped him hang half a dozen framed diplomas on the wall of his private office, tangible proof of his training and competence. Even her father hadn't so many certificates.

Yet as Mr. Chapman had rather indelicately questioned the other night, why would a doctor waste the efforts of all that training on something as inconsequential as beauty surgery?

Certainly, it might be the money. Her father would have been lucky to make a hundred dollars in six months' time. Most of his patients were poor; he not only treated them without thought of remuneration but often was forced to pay for the medicines they needed from his own pocket. Then she remembered how, at the Hennessys' banquet, Dr. Rome had referred to the work of a doctor as *the medical arts.* That was it, of course! He did, in fact, strike her as the artistic type; more than once, she had admired the gracefulness of his long fingers, imagining them holding a blade—cutting and shaping human flesh, much like a sculptor molds clay. If Dr. Rome was a physician with the soul of an artist, it was understandable why he might become a beauty doctor.

She thought again of Isabelle Hadley and how her first success as Dr. Rome's foil had given her an unexpected sense of pride. Already, she was embracing her new role with more enthusiasm than she'd anticipated. Why shouldn't she? It was surely better than the awful dispiritedness that had plagued her since her father's death.

Besides, she enjoyed the sense of collegiality she shared with Dr. Rome. Yes, she was only an office girl, but he occasionally spoke to her about medicine and surgery and how far it all had come in recent years. She remembered how effusive he had become last week when the autoclave was delivered to the office. He'd explained in great detail about the steam sterilizer. It was one of the most important inventions of the late nineteenth century, he'd said. Many problems could be avoided by sterilizing instruments before they were used in patients. When he'd unpacked it from the crate, he'd told her how—

She threw off the comforter, every nerve in her body alert. The delivery! How could she have forgotten to tell Dr. Rome about the man who had stopped by the office after he'd left for the day?

Hastily, she lit the lamp, jumped out of bed, and began dressing, all the while replaying the conversation in her mind from late that afternoon. It had been awkward and very strange. She was locking up around five o'clock when a squat, unkempt little man appeared on the doorstep. Right away, she noticed his nose, which was large and misshapen, with a red, bulbous tip. Assuming he was a prospective patient, she gave him a card and instructed him to call the office in the morning for an appointment.

With obvious impatience, he crumpled the card in his hand. "You can't get in touch with him?"

"Well, I might—"

"Yes or no."

She didn't answer, put off by his rudeness. Who was he to speak to her in such a manner?

"Just tell him Shark said to look for a delivery tonight, same time as before," he said without waiting. "Got it?"

"What kind of delivery?"

"He'll know. Tell him midnight, just like he wanted."

"Midnight? Why, that's ridiculous! Nobody makes deliveries at that hour."

"Look, lady, I ain't got time for parlor games. I make a lot o' deliveries. The day ain't long enough for all of 'em, so I work late. The doc says he don't mind. Just tell him, all right? And make sure you don't forget."

Pulling on her boots, she pictured again his dissipated look, the malicious twist to his lips, the wrinkled gray sack suit, and the shabby bowler perched precariously on his wide head. A shiver of revulsion ran through her. A rendezvous with such a fellow, alone and in the dark of night, was the last thing she wanted, but now there was no choice. She would conduct whatever brief transaction might be necessary and leave the delivery for Dr.

Rome to find in the morning. He would never have to know how irresponsible she'd been in failing to inform him.

She went to the door and stepped outside. The stars, covered by a haze of clouds, provided only scant light, but the glimmer of electric street lamps made up for any deficit. She climbed the half dozen stairs from her room and then the short flight to the office entrance, unlocked the door, and entered.

Inside was pitch-black. She felt her way to the desk and lit the lamp. Her eyes scanned the dim interior. The room in which she had grown accustomed to spending her days seemed somehow foreign at night, its sense of comfort reliant on sunlight streaming through the tall windows that now were shrouded in velvet drapery. She looked toward the dark hallway leading to the operating room and Dr. Rome's private office and felt a vague apprehension, as if something sinister lurked beyond her small circle of light.

Brushing off her fears as best she could, Abigail sat down behind her desk to await the man who called himself *Shark*. He had best not insult her again. She would report it to Dr. Rome, who surely would not stand for it. He'd find someone else to handle deliveries, someone who kept better hours.

With that mildly reassuring thought, Abigail leaned her head against the high back of the chair and closed her eyes. Before long, she was slouched down, asleep, until jolted awake by a single sharp knock. Immediately alert, she jumped up and hurried to open the door, eager to be done with the entire matter as quickly as possible.

Shark was dressed in the same shabby suit he had worn that afternoon, the same gray bowler balanced uncertainly on his head. Abigail could smell the liquor on his breath as he addressed her in a harsh whisper.

"Where's the doc?"

"He's running late. I'll take the delivery."

"You?" His eyes narrowed.

"I'm Dr. Rome's assistant. It's my job to take deliveries—all deliveries," she added for emphasis. How annoying this fellow was!

He looked her up and down. "Well, all right. But he needs to get started pretty soon. Before the chloroform wears off."

"Chloroform?"

Now he regarded her with renewed suspicion. "You sure the doc knows you're here?"

She recovered herself. "I told you so already, didn't I?"

Shark turned around and let out a low whistle. A horse-drawn hansom pulled up and came to a stop. The driver jumped down and positioned himself next to the passenger door. Shark's eyes scanned the street in both directions before he gave a quick nod to the driver, who opened the cab door, reached inside, and lifted out a long bundle covered with a sheet.

"Look out!" Shark pushed her out of the way as the other man, with his strange cargo, swept past. Shark followed him toward the back hallway, yelling, "Give us some light, for Christ's sake!"

Reaching the hallway, Abigail tugged on the pull switch and, having deduced the intended destination, went ahead to the operating room to do the same. The two men entered behind her, and Shark motioned for the driver to lay the bundle on the operating table. If there had been any question what it was, the scuffed brown shoes sticking out from under the sheet left no doubt. Shark looked at her expectantly.

"You got the cash?"

"Cash?" She hadn't thought about the possibility of having to pay for something. "I thought this was to be on account," she said lamely.

"On account! You think I'm a feckin' banker or somethin'?" Shark glanced at the bundle, which lay perfectly still on the table, as if he were considering whether to grab it and go. Abigail would have been happy if he did so, already convinced that whoever was under that sheet was dead. But she had come this far. She would do her job.

"You know Dr. Rome is good for it."

Shark thought for a moment. "Tell him to have it ready when I get back later."

"You're coming back?"

He leered at her again. "Just tell him to have it ready."

He nodded to his accomplice, and then, as speedily as they had appeared, they were gone. Abigail listened to make sure they closed the front door and then forced herself to take a few steps toward the table. Warily, she reached out and pulled back the top edge of the sheet. Before her was the placid face of a child, probably twelve or thirteen years old. Dragging the sheet down a little farther, she could see the rise and fall of his chest beneath his tattered shirt.

Thank God, he was alive!

Emboldened, she yanked off the entire cover and searched for any sign of blood or trauma. Nothing. He seemed to be peacefully sleeping. Then she remembered what Shark had said about chloroform. The child had been drugged! He could come out of it almost any time, and then what? What would she say to him? What would he do? Might he have been kidnapped, transported here against his will? But why?

There were so many questions running through her mind. It was inconceivable the boy would be brought here unless Dr. Rome had somehow arranged for it. Yet Abigail could not think of any reasonable explanation for why he would.

Perhaps Shark was trying to blackmail Dr. Rome, setting up what was supposed to be a routine delivery and then putting him in a compromised position from which he could extricate himself only with a cash payment. Yet a midnight drop-off couldn't be routine, and Shark made it sound as if he'd done this before.

There was only one thing she knew for certain: Dr. Rome would have to be summoned right away.

She went into the hall and began walking toward the back stairs that led to Dr. Rome's second-floor apartment. At the bottom, she hesitated—wondering how difficult it would be to wake him, thinking how embarrassing if he came to the door in his nightshirt. But there was no time for indecision. She hurried up the wooden steps, pausing again at the top, listening for any sound of activity inside. It was perfectly still.

She knocked once, gingerly. Then again, with a bit more force. She waited a while and then, with the heel of her palm, banged on the door as hard as she could.

"Hold on!" said a voice from inside.

The door opened a crack, and Dr. Rome peered out at her. "Miss Platford! Do you have any idea what time it is? What are you doing here?"

She tried her best to sound calm. "I'm sorry, Dr. Rome, but you've got to come down to the operating room. There's a boy there. He's—he's unconscious."

"What?" It was hard to tell whether he was shocked or angry. "I'll be there in a minute." The door closed.

Filled with a renewed dread of the disaster that surely loomed ahead, Abigail ran back down to the operating room to check on the boy. He hadn't moved. She gazed down at him, a sweet-looking lad wearing the typical uniform of a street urchin, torn overalls and a shirt of coarse cotton, dirty and badly frayed at the collar and cuffs. A checkered wool cap was the only item of apparel that appeared new, likely snatched from some hapless vendor or the head of a more fortunate child. The boy's face had that unmistakable look of the Irish, upturned nose and freckles across the cheeks. His hair was reddish brown, stringy, and too long; his ears protruded from beneath it.

Abigail had seen plenty of youngsters like him when she used to volunteer at the parish soup kitchen, poor immigrant children forced to fend for themselves. Weary and hungry and already hardened by life's heartlessness. She had once dreamed of helping them as a doctor. They were the very ones to whom her father had devoted the entirety of his practice, those who were habitually ignored and pushed aside and trodden over as if they didn't matter.

The clatter of boots on the back stairs prepared her for Dr. Rome's rushed entry into the operating room. Breathing heavily, he stood beside her and looked down on their young visitor. He felt the boy's pulse, lifted one of his eyelids.

"Is he all right?" Abigail asked hesitantly.

"Yes, yes, he's fine." When Dr. Rome turned to her, his dark brows were drawn together in a scowl. "And what are *you* doing here?"

"I came to accept a delivery. I'm sorry—I—" She regarded the boy uneasily. "I never expected it would be something like this."

"I imagine you didn't. In the future, I would prefer that you inform me when any deliveries are expected. That *is* your job, you know."

"But, Dr. Rome—" Perhaps she had no right to question him, but some kind of explanation was needed. Whatever was going on, she had inadvertently become part of it. "I'm sure you can't be in the habit of receiving comatose children in the middle of the night. And who is this fellow Shark?"

"There are some things you don't know and, frankly, would be better off not knowing." He eyed the boy on the table. "I need to get started on this young man."

ELIZABETH HUTCHISON BERNARD | 59

"Get started! What do you mean?"

"Let me make this brief," he said sternly. "A beauty doctor is like an explorer without a compass, without a reliable map. As I've told you before, there are very few who will admit to doing the sort of work I do. My medical colleagues don't talk about it; they like to pretend it's beneath them. So, how do you think I must learn my craft?"

"But you studied beauty surgery in Europe. You performed it with the masters."

"True, but techniques become outdated quickly. Others come along to replace them. Sometimes I have no choice but to find out for myself what works best in my hands. You wouldn't have me experiment on one of my patients, would you? On someone of means, someone whose result will be admired or, God forbid, disparaged by those in the higher echelons of society? Because, remember, my success depends on a sterling reputation among that very class of people."

She was beginning to understand what he was saying, though his explanation did not lessen the shock. "This boy—you're going to operate on him?"

"Look at his ears!" He waved his hand around the boy's head. "Now, would *you* want to go through life with ears that stuck out like *that*?"

"But has he agreed to this? Why didn't he just come into the office by himself? Why was he delivered by that man, that *Shark*—and unconscious?"

Dr. Rome placed his hands firmly on her shoulders and leaned in close. His breath was hot and slightly stale with the remnants of smoke and liquor. "Others would pay a fortune for the operation I'm going to give him for nothing. It's not as if he'll be harmed by it. His life will be much better, I promise you."

He stepped away from her. "The field of medicine has always been like this. For every new treatment, every important breakthrough, some patient, somewhere, has to be the first."

"But I thought surgeons practiced on dead people. Or pigs."

"One can do that, of course, and I've done it many times. But nothing compares with living tissue, especially for a beauty doctor."

Looking again at the boy, knowing the innocent cruelty of children, she could imagine the teasing and bullying he'd endured because of those ears. Even so, someone must be accountable for whatever might happen.

"What about afterward? How will he be taken care of?"

The boy stirred on the table.

"Get me the chloroform."

By the tone of his voice, she understood it was not a request, but a command. Yet she hesitated. If the boy had indeed been kidnapped, did she wish to be an accomplice to a crime?

"Get it now!" he thundered.

Shaken, Abigail hurried to the medicine cabinet, found the bottle of chloroform and the mask, and brought them back. Dr. Rome placed a few drops of the liquid onto the cloth and held it over the boy's nose and mouth.

"This is the end of our conversation," he said, without looking up. "And since you're here, you might as well assist me with the surgery."

"Assist you?" She was incredulous. What could he be thinking to ask such a thing of her?

"Yes, isn't that what you've wanted all along? To be with me in the operating room?"

She was only half-listening. What if the boy *had* been kidnapped? Shouldn't she go to the police? She had nothing to fear. She'd done nothing wrong—not so far. But now Dr. Rome wanted her to help him operate. Someone could easily find out. She might even go to prison.

She looked at the boy and felt a surge of sympathy. And yet, what Dr. Rome had said was true. He would look much better if his ears weren't so prominent; yet it was doubtful he could ever afford an operation to fix them. And the other part—about *her*. That was true as well. She was curious about Miss Hadley's surgery but hadn't had the courage to ask Dr. Rome if she could watch. Assisting him with it? The responsibility was too great. What if she made a mistake?

"I know the circumstances of all this seem strange to you," Dr. Rome said, still pressing on the mask, "but I assure you, it's not an unusual occurrence. No harm will come to the boy. He'll be better off. One day, he'll be grateful—when he finds a young lady he wants to marry, and he need not fear rejection because of his unsightly ears."

Again, she scarcely heard him, but this time because she was back in her father's office, kneeling on the cold tile floor, holding him in her arms, weeping. The rhythm of blood pounded in her ears.

"Miss Platford? You'll need to give me an answer. Either you'll assist or I want you to leave. Go back downstairs to your room. We'll discuss things in the morning. Maybe you're not a good fit for this practice after all, but I'll do my best to help you find something else. Perhaps a sales position somewhere. You seem to have an aptitude for that."

Her head jerked back as if she'd been struck across the cheek. "I have an aptitude for medicine, Dr. Rome. And I didn't spend all that time poring over *Gray's Anatomy* for nothing."

"Very well, then." He removed the mask from the boy's face. "There's a butcher's apron in the closet over there. Let's get started."

CHAPTER 5

More than a week had passed, and still she found it impossible to sleep, impossible to put out of her mind the helpless young boy who had lain unconscious on Dr. Rome's operating table. Impossible to forget what had happened to him and how she had been a participant—if not a willing one, a compliant one.

But no, she *was* willing. She wanted to assist Dr. Rome. When faced with the alternative—to give up the rare opportunity onto which she had blindly stumbled—she'd made her choice.

A choice that, since then, she had examined and reexamined until she was worn out and nearly ill.

Dr. Rome had said what took place was not uncommon; surgeons often found cases from among the poor. But the child had been frightened and uncooperative; he needed slightly stronger measures.

And now Dr. Rome wanted her to assist with Miss Hadley's surgery. He'd found it convenient to have her with him in the operating room, fetching whatever he needed, handing him each instrument on demand, wiping away the blood after every cut. She should have been ecstatic, and would have been but for her niggling doubts. Was what had taken place with the boy justifiable, as Dr. Rome claimed, or had he crossed a boundary that no doctor ever should?

She wondered, too, if he sensed her unease; if he did, he surely must resent it. Who was she, knowing next to nothing, to judge his actions as a surgeon? And how timid she must seem to him. The first genuine opportunity to work side by side with him, much as she had with her father, and she was ready to retreat into her shell like a little box turtle.

Yet, no matter how hard she tried, she couldn't stop worrying about the boy. She had to know. She had to have proof that Dr. Rome, and she along with him, had not violated the doctor's sacred oath to do no harm.

It was Friday morning, the tenth of May. Dr. Rome was at his desk, casually thumbing through the morning paper, when she finally found the courage to approach him with a plan.

"Excuse me for interrupting."

He looked up with an expression of mild annoyance.

"Yes?"

"I need to speak with you."

"Go on."

"I have a request. I want to see the boy—the one we operated on."

He shoved the paper aside. "What in God's name are you talking about?"

"I need to see him."

He looked at her with an expression of disbelief. "I wouldn't have the slightest idea how to find him. Not now. Besides, what reason would you have for wanting to see him?"

Again, she pictured the boy's innocent face, freckles scattered like stardust across his nose and cheeks. It was an image that would haunt her forever unless she could find out what had become of him. "That fellow Shark must know where he is. Can't you tell him to take me there?" She lowered her eyes, aware of how very strident she must sound. "I don't mean to be a burden to you—really, I don't. But my worry over the boy gives me no peace."

Dr. Rome retrieved his newspaper and began folding it slowly, deliberately. "Are we going to have trouble between us? I hope not, because I have no intention of spending another second of my time trying to appease the person whose job it is to appease *me*."

"I'm only asking to see that the boy is all right."

He didn't answer right away and, though his displeasure was obvious, she was encouraged that he seemed to be considering her request. "And there will be no more of this nonsense talk?"

She nodded, realizing with a desperate longing just how much she wished to put her doubts behind her. If the boy was fine, if no harm had been done, if Dr. Rome was telling the truth about everything ...

"All right. No promises, but I'll see if I can arrange it." He raised a finger and shook it at her. "But you're not to speak with him. Do you understand? Not a word."

· · · · ·

The next afternoon, Abigail mounted the step of a horse-drawn hansom in which Shark already sat, smoking a fat cigar that filled the closed compartment with a stinking cloud of smoke.

"Good afternoon," she said pleasantly, determined not to give him the satisfaction of even a single complaint.

"Ma'am." He tipped his gray bowler, as she settled herself into the seat, as far from him as she could.

"And where are we going?"

"Not any kind of neighborhood you'd know about. Down past Canal Street."

There was no reason to explain she was not a stranger to such places. Her father had allowed her to accompany him on many an occasion to the Lower East Side tenements, where he went to treat victims of dire diseases like influenza, typhoid, tuberculosis—always at the behest of distraught relatives suspicious of the official public-health doctors. They'd heard Dr. Platford had no political agenda, nor did he distinguish between those who could pay for his services and those who could not. Remembering her father's heroism, she felt a swift stab of remorse. Her current mission was not one of mercy, but guilt.

Shark blew a smoke ring and watched it drift upward, dissipating at the cab's low ceiling. "Course, I can't guarantee we'll find the boy. Didn't count on nobody havin' a soft spot for him." He yelled up through the hatch, "Let's get goin'." The cab lurched forward, and they headed toward the chaotic traffic of Madison Avenue.

"Where do you expect we'll find him?"

"Most likely hangin' around the alley next to Shorty's Tavern. Got kind of a business goin' there."

"What sort of business?"

"The sort that ladies like you wouldn't want to talk about. They call it the oldest profession in the world, if you catch my drift."

What he said brought a knot to Abigail's stomach. Child prostitution was a scourge on the city that no one seemed willing or able to eradicate. Especially when the victims were immigrants, who much of American society persisted in viewing as a notch or two below human.

She sank into silence as Shark puffed away on his steadily dwindling cigar, wondering suddenly if Dr. Rome's motivation in having her assist with the boy's surgery was to make certain she kept quiet about it. If she was involved, she would have good reason not to talk.

She pushed the thought aside, reminding herself again of all that Dr. Rome had done for her. Wasn't he the one to recognize how capable she was, to elevate her from a mere office girl to a surgical assistant? He had seen her potential. He believed in her—perhaps more than she believed in herself.

They arrived at the eastern stretch of Canal Street, an area that, prior to the turn of the century, was a favorite of journalistic muckrakers aiming to expose the city's rampant violence and squalid living conditions. As a young girl, Abigail had read their shocking articles, so graphic as to be almost unbelievable. Even a few years ago, prior to the enactment of sanitation reforms, one could not walk these streets without wading through a thick layer of human waste. Rotting carcasses of rodents, dogs, and horses routinely littered the pavement; trash was piled everywhere in small mountains of smoldering stench that had become permanent features of the landscape. Even now, Five Points, as it was called, was not a place to find oneself alone and defenseless, not by night or day.

Shark was barking orders at the driver through the rear hatch. "Wait a minute!" He stuck his head out the window, craning his neck to the right, excited as a dog on a scent. "Go back 'bout half a block."

The driver turned his horse around in the middle of the road, almost colliding with a cart full of watermelons, and they headed back. Abigail felt a rush of anticipation but also a touch of apprehension. What if the boy had not fared as well as Dr. Rome expected?

"That's him all right! See?" Shark pointed just ahead. "Right there, next to that shack with the green awning."

She recognized the boy immediately. He was leaning against a huge trash barrel, aimlessly tossing a ball in the air, dressed much the same as on that starless night when Shark's accomplice carried him into Dr. Rome's operating room wrapped in a sheet. She remembered how Dr. Rome had pinned a note to his shirt, saying not to remove the bandages for a week. It had been eleven days now. From this distance, he appeared fine. He had slicked back his hair, exposing his ears. Abigail felt a tiny burst of hope. Might he be proud of them?

"Tell the driver to pull over," she said.

Shark flashed a look of warning. "Those ain't my orders from the doc."

She extracted a few coins from her handbag. Defiantly, she tossed them on the seat between them. Shark wasted no time in snatching up the money, instructing the driver as Abigail had told him.

The cab came to a halt. She eyed the boy, not sure what she intended to do next. She had agreed not to approach him directly and, until this moment, had not planned to do otherwise. But she was no longer satisfied with merely seeing him from afar. She wanted to get a better look. To hear him say that all was well and his ordeal had not been too horribly painful or frightening. That he'd been well taken care of afterward, not just dumped in an alley somewhere. And—though it might be asking too much, too soon— she wanted to know if he was indeed happier than before. Wouldn't that prove beyond any doubt that everything Dr. Rome had promised was true? Perhaps he really *had* made this boy's life better; if that were so, wasn't it possible that even the poor lad himself might agree the end had justified the means?

The driver released the door, and Abigail jumped from the cab, knowing full well she was being more than a touch reckless. In neighborhoods like this, outsiders were often looked on with suspicion, if not outright malice. She was aware of the reasons, among them that despicable entertainment of the wealthy, called *slumming*—strolling through the poorest areas of the city to gawk at the desperate conditions in which the other half lived. Such was not her intent, of course, and neither did she appear especially affluent. She was dressed in a simple black skirt and white shirtwaist; her ostrich-feather hat, though she was inordinately fond of it, was far from new, and the dark shade of blue didn't really match the rest of her outfit.

She started walking, keeping her eyes on the sidewalk as she passed by a crowd of men drinking and laughing. She could hear snippets of their conversation, none of it suitable for a lady's ears, but was determined to let nothing rattle her or cause the sureness of her step to falter. One of them called out to her—something about her hair that she couldn't quite make out, but certainly not a compliment in the usual sense. She ignored it and kept walking with her head down, fearing even an innocent glance, a smile, the swish of a skirt or less, was apt to be misinterpreted.

The boy stood in front of a butcher's stall, where a few emaciated chickens, a rabbit, and a small goat dangled from fierce metal hooks. As Abigail approached, he raised his head and stopped tossing the ball, peering at her intently.

"Hello," she said, smiling uncertainly as she stopped in front of him. He kept staring, with a mildly insolent look, and did not reply. "You don't know me," she began again, "but I've been watching you and—"

He took a step back, as if he might bolt at any second.

"And I've noticed you look different." She touched her own ear and smiled again, hoping he'd understand.

His eyes narrowed.

"I hope you're well and everything is all right. I—I have a little something for you." Reaching into her handbag, she took out some change and held out her hand, offering it to him.

"What's that for?" he said. She was surprised by his voice; it was deeper, more mature than she'd expected.

"Nothing in particular. I just thought maybe you could use some help."

He glanced around. Then, with a quick motion, he scooped the coins from Abigail's gloved hand and shoved them into the pocket of his trousers.

"Good," she said, still smiling. "So ... you're all right?"

"You best get out of there!" Shark was yelling at her, and, from the tone of his voice, there must be trouble. She looked behind her and saw that several of the men she'd passed before had ceased their revelry and turned their attention to her.

Just then, her purse was ripped from her hand. Startled, she turned back to the boy, instinctively grabbing at his arm to stop him, but he was too fast. He easily evaded her and took off sprinting down the street. It was no use calling after him. In a matter of seconds, he had ducked down the nearest alleyway and was gone.

Shark shouted again. "Listen up! I ain't riskin' my hide to save yours! Get over here now!"

Abigail looked over her shoulder. Two rough-looking characters were headed in her direction, one of them wielding a large stick. Why would they be coming after her? She'd done nothing wrong. She'd only been talking to the boy. Why should anyone care?

Her mind flashed back to the only time she'd ever been threatened by a man—the night her stepfather came to her bedroom, drunk and intent on violating her. She remembered his smell, the sweet and salt of liquor and sweat, and the feel of his hands grabbing at her breasts through her nightgown. She remembered his animal grunt and her own scream and the flailing of arms and legs before she threw him off and he fled amid curses condemning her to hell.

But if violation was what these men had in mind, what hope would she have of repelling them? It was crazy to think her good intentions would save her. They cared nothing for who she was or her motive for trespassing into their territory. To them, she was fair game.

She glanced about, looking for a weapon she might use to defend herself. There was nothing. Her eyes darted to the cab and then back to her would-be assailants as she tried to measure how much time was left before it would be too late. But what did measurements matter? It was obvious she hadn't a moment to lose.

"Hey, blondie! I ain't seen nothin' fine as you around here for a long time!"

She took off toward the hansom, not quite running but walking fast, making a wide circle to avoid the two thugs who now veered to the left in a direct line to the cab. They appeared to have calculated the distance better than she, with no need to break a sweat. They might merely have been out for a stroll except for the lust in their eyes and how the one with the stick kept slapping it into the palm of his hand.

Abigail's heart was pounding as she approached the hansom, near enough now that she could smell the smoke from Shark's cigar through the open door. She saw him motioning for her to hurry, the driver tense and ready, the horse shuddering in anticipation of the whip. She was almost there, almost safe. There was no way they could catch up to her now, and it seemed they weren't trying very hard. It was more of a game than anything else—she hoped.

But the thin film of muck coating the bricks—perhaps a bit of washed-down horse manure, or maybe only a light coating of mud from a recent rain—had laid a trap for the smooth leather soles of her boots. Down she went, her ostrich-feather hat landing next to her, upside down in the slime. Her skirt, stockings, gloves, even her face, were splattered with brown sludge.

The laughter behind her was alarmingly close.

The next thing she knew, Shark was at her side, swearing under his breath. Roughly, he grabbed her arm and yanked her to her feet. "Hurry up, get in the feckin' cab!"

He dragged Abigail the last few feet to the hansom, where she somehow managed to mount the step and climb inside. Shark jumped in beside her, slamming the door shut just as the man with the stick swung it halfheartedly at the side of the cab. The driver cracked his whip; the horse whinnied in protest but obligingly broke into a trot.

Headed north, toward relative civilization, they rode most of the way in silence. How embarrassing to have needed Shark, of all people, to rescue her. And what if he was angry enough to tell Dr. Rome what she'd done? She dared not imagine the consequences if he did. Most likely, she would lose her position. On top of that, she'd been robbed. One would think the little ragamuffin might have shown greater consideration to a stranger who so obviously wished only to help him! But perhaps having a little less sympathy, she might find it easier now to accept things as they were. Not that the child's actions justified hers, but at least she was reminded that sometimes each of us does what he must in order to survive.

With a sigh, she leaned back in the seat. It was over now. The boy had come to no harm, and neither had she. Isabelle Hadley's surgery was in three days. If Dr. Rome still wanted her, she would assist him and be grateful for it.

When the driver finally pulled up in front of the office, Abigail turned to Shark with a sheepish look. "Thank you for helping me back there. I appreciate you put yourself in danger to save me."

He appeared almost bashful. "I wasn't really in all that much danger. Them fellows, they look worse 'n they are."

"I'm afraid I lost my purse. But I can pay the driver tomorrow. And I'll have something more for you," she said, thinking she would ask Dr. Rome for an advance—that is, if she had the nerve to face him.

"Aw, forget it." Shark retrieved the coins that Abigail had bribed him with earlier. "This'll cover the fare, I reckon." Despite her distaste for the man, she couldn't help but find the gesture touching. Perhaps she might have judged him too harshly.

The driver already had opened the door to the cab and was waiting for her to step down. Waving away the hand he offered so as not to befoul him with her soiled glove, she exited the cab and rushed down the short flight of steps to her door, praying Dr. Rome had not seen them arrive from his window.

It was only when she stood in front of her door, thinking her ordeal was almost over, that she realized what was missing. The key to her room. It was in her purse.

She turned and flew up the stairs, frantically waving her arms to attract the attention of Shark or the driver, or both. "Stop! Please!"

Shark opened the door of the cab. "What's the matter?"

"How are you at picking locks?"

He seemed flattered by the invitation. "Pretty feckin' good, ma'am, if I do say so myself!"

CHAPTER 6

A t eight o'clock sharp on Tuesday morning, Isabelle Hadley walked through the front door of the office. She looked exceptionally pale. Her mother held her by the elbow as if otherwise she might collapse.

"Good morning, ladies." Abigail approached them with her most reassuring smile, though she doubted it would help.

"Hello, Miss Platford." Mrs. Hadley seemed nearly as apprehensive as her daughter. "Is the doctor ready for us?"

"Actually, Mrs. Hadley, Dr. Rome suggests that you leave your daughter now and return home. You may telephone the office around noon, and I'll let you know when Miss Hadley can be discharged. I promise, we will take good care of her."

Mrs. Hadley seemed reluctant to let go of her daughter's arm. "Would you rather that I stay?" she asked, searching the girl's anxious face.

Miss Hadley glanced at Abigail, probably hoping she would say it was all right, but a slight shake of Abigail's head told her Dr. Rome's orders stood. "No, Mother. It's all right. Go home, as Miss Platford said."

Mrs. Hadley took a deep breath, gave her daughter a peck on the cheek, and proceeded to the door. She paused with her hand on the knob, turning around for one last look at her darling Isabelle. "You're sure you want to do this?"

Miss Hadley nodded, her lip quivering.

"Then I'll be back in a few hours. Be brave."

Abigail, grappling with her own uncertainty, turned to the patient. "If you wouldn't mind following me, please ..."

Miss Hadley trailed her down the long hallway and into a small room with a sofa and two chairs, a dressing table and mirror, and an armoire. She was instructed to remove all her clothing, except for her knickers, and hang everything in the armoire. Abigail handed her what she authoritatively called the *surgical gown*, explaining it should be tied loosely at the neck and left open in the back. "I know you'll be glad when this is over," she said, unable to restrain herself from expressing the empathy she so strongly felt for this young woman, who was not all that different from herself.

"But Miss Platford—" Miss Hadley's eyes were wide and searching. "Is there really no reason to worry? I mean, could anything go wrong?"

At that moment, there was nothing Abigail wanted more than to put Miss Hadley's mind at ease. But how could she possibly tell her something that she, herself, didn't know for certain?

"Have faith in Dr. Rome" was all she could think of to say, until she remembered the question that had stymied her at Mrs. Chapman's tea party, happy she could now answer it. "I've seen him operate. He has excellent hands."

• • • • •

Abigail entered the operating room, having changed into her oldest and plainest dress, covered with the same butcher's apron she had worn once before. She went over to the long metal sink against the wall and scrubbed her hands and arms with soap, then donned a pair of rubber gloves.

Harsh lights above the narrow operating table shone down on the patient, who lay flat with a white sheet covering her from the chest down. Dr. Rome, his clothes protected by an apron similar to Abigail's, stood by Miss Hadley's side. Abigail took her place across from him.

"What we are going to do today for Miss Hadley is to remove that bump on her nasal bridge so that she will have a straight, pretty nose like she's always wanted." Though his confident tone was meant to put his patient at ease, Miss Hadley looked up at him with fear in her eyes.

"Now, you remember," he said, "a little while ago, I gave you that injection so you won't feel what we're going to be doing next." He touched her nose with his finger. "Already numb, isn't it?"

She nodded.

Several gauze strips and a bowl filled with a soapy solution sat atop a small wooden stand next to the operating table. Abigail watched as Dr. Rome thoroughly cleansed the front portion of Miss Hadley's nasal cavity.

"Miss Platford, please remove the instruments from the autoclave."

She hastened to do as he asked, retrieving the instrument tray and setting it onto a second wooden stand positioned on her side of the table.

"All right, we're ready to begin. Hand me the blade, please." Abigail's heart was pounding as she picked up the small blade and passed it to him, then observed him poke the sharp instrument deep inside Miss Hadley's nose. The patient cried out, and Abigail gasped in alarm. Dr. Rome shot her a stern look before filling a syringe and administering another dose of anesthetic, a solution of

boiled water and cocaine that Abigail had earlier helped him prepare.

A second probe with the blade elicited no complaint and, after making an incision, he passed the instrument back to Abigail.
"Chisel," he said.

She handed him the chisel, which he inserted into the same
nostril. "I'm positioning the chisel just at the portion of the nasal
hump we want to reduce," he said, this part of his commentary apparently for Abigail's benefit. "Hammer."

She passed him the small hammer and watched as he used
it to lightly tap the chisel. "I'll be able to feel the bone give way."
After several taps, each of which sent a tiny shiver through her, Dr.
Rome seemed satisfied. "Forceps."

Abigail took the chisel and hammer from him, then gave him
the forceps, which he used to remove the piece of bone he'd broken off. He laid the fragment on the sheet that covered Miss
Hadley's chest. At first, she was surprised such a small morsel could
make any difference at all. Yet, when she looked at Miss Hadley's
profile, she saw the change. It was shocking to realize the power of
that tiny bit of bone, how it could distract from the sparkle in Miss
Hadley's eyes and the sweetness of her smile. When viewed from
such a perspective, the act of removing it seemed perfectly sensible.
Was it fair to say what had brought Isabelle Hadley to Dr. Rome
was nothing more than *vanity*? Or might it be, in fact, a rational desire to make the most of the other fine attributes with which she
had been blessed?

A sudden alarm went off inside her head. How swiftly and
easily her sentiments were falling into line with those of Dr.
Rome! Was such a drastic change in her thinking a matter of evolution or expediency? Had the thrill of the operating room
already begun to erode values she'd held for her entire life—a belief that beauty comes from within and that a doctor's calling is
to cure the sick?

"Miss Platford, pay attention! Wipe up that blood."

She brushed her misgivings aside as she grabbed a clean cloth and dabbed beneath Miss Hadley's nose. Out of the corner of her eye, she watched Dr. Rome's face, trying to gauge whether this amount of bleeding was excessive. He appeared not to be concerned, calmly moving her hands aside and applying pressure to the nose for several minutes.

She had thought they were finished, but he surprised her by asking for what he called the *rasp*. When she hesitated, he pointed to it a metal file. "I'm going to make the bone nice and smooth." Inserting the rasp in the same way he had done with the chisel, he moved it back and forth over the area where he had chipped off the fragment. Then he handed it back to her and ran his finger along the bridge, checking for any irregularities he could detect through the skin. A second time he asked for the rasp, smoothing a little more. Finally, after studying the nose from every angle, he proclaimed the surgery a success.

They moved Miss Hadley into the recovery room to rest; she promptly fell asleep, seeming none the worse for her ordeal. Abigail thought everything had gone splendidly, especially her own performance. She had made no glaring errors. Her hands had been steady, her responses quick. The anxiety she had felt earlier quickly subsided; she was too engrossed in Dr. Rome's every maneuver to question the correctness of violating healthy tissue, chipping away at bone, allowing life-sustaining blood to trickle out like water from an open faucet. If anything, she wished the surgery had not been over so soon. She could easily have gone on, with never a thought of wanting to be anywhere but there—standing across from Dr. Rome, making a mental note of each step in the procedure, each nuance of Isabelle Hadley's transformation.

Determined, going forward, to make herself indispensable.

CHAPTER 7

New York City was fast entering the season when ladies of means depart in droves for Newport and other beach-side getaways where the monotony of idleness is assuaged by cool breezes and the soothing rhythm of waves lapping at the shore. In the month that followed Isabelle Hadley's surgery, there were few social events to attend, which might have called into question the value of Abigail's services as Dr. Rome's foil. Realizing this, she took it upon herself to make the rounds of local beauty parlors, chatting up the owners and any patrons within earshot and leaving behind her business cards touting "The Power of Beauty." This strategy resulted in enough consultations and surgeries to keep Dr. Rome reasonably happy. Advertisements in the *New York World* and other city papers also drew potential patients, many of whom were unprepared for the exorbitant fees at which Dr. Rome's more affluent clientele barely batted an eyelash. But for some, so great was the desire for beauty, by whatever sacrifice they found the means to pay.

From the middle of May to the middle of June, Abigail assisted with nineteen procedures on noses, ears, lips, jowls, and eye bags, as well as countless injections of paraffin into facial wrinkles and folds. She watched Dr. Rome prepare the mixture of paraffin and goose grease, listened as he debated with himself each time whether to modify the formula, perhaps try mixing it with white oak bark instead. Though he cared nothing for her opinion, it made her feel important that he would share his thoughts with her, like her father used to do.

For the first time in so long, Abigail was happy. If her life might lack some of the simple pleasures that others took for granted, the comforts of a home and loved ones, she scarcely noticed. Her thoughts were constantly on surgery. She even dreamed about it. When she wasn't dreaming of Dr. Rome himself. Dangerous dreams that she regretted when she awoke, even as she tried to remember every shocking detail.

At every opportunity, she endeavored to expand her knowledge of medicine. Her collection of used textbooks burgeoned to more than a dozen, and she spent many an evening in her basement room poring over them with the zeal of someone who, with no real plan, still believed she might someday use the information they contained.

As for how Dr. Rome occupied himself on the many nights when there were no parties or banquets to attend, Abigail didn't know. Then one day toward the end of June, he surprised her with an invitation for dinner at the Park Avenue Hotel's exclusive restaurant, one of the city's very best. He called the evening a *celebration*.

They arrived at the restaurant around eight, the head waiter greeting them as if they were his most important guests of the night. Abigail wore her one and only Parisian gown, silk in a light coral shade, trimmed in gray chiffon and lace. Its off-the-shoulder neckline exposed the graceful curve of her collarbone and the creamy smoothness of her skin. She knew Dr. Rome had a keen eye for such things. He had been the one to favor this dress when they shopped together at Bergdorf Goodman on the first morning of her employment, when she had feared he would try to make her into something she could never be. The frock had set him back a pretty penny, but it made an impression. As did Dr. Rome in his well-tailored black tuxedo, top hat, and white gloves—an outfit no different from that of any other man in the restaurant, but on him it looked splendid.

They were seated at a table for two, not tucked away in a corner but out in the open, where they were bound to be noticed. Dr. Rome wasted no time in ordering an expensive bottle of champagne. The sommelier poured each of them a glass and put the rest on ice. Abigail sat stiffly in her chair, unsure how to behave in so intimate a situation. Though they had often gone out together in public, she had never spent an evening alone with Dr. Rome.

"To success!" he said, raising his glass. She did the same, their crystal flutes colliding with a delicate clink. Smiling, she sipped her Dom Perignon, trying to convince herself there was no reason to be nervous. Over the past two months, she had spent five days a week in the office with Dr. Rome, often just the two of them. He was not so frightening. Not really ...

The champagne soon exerted its effect. Lulled by golden candlelight and the hypnotic murmur of voices woven like silk into soft strains of music from a balcony above, her tension eased. Dr. Rome reached into an inner pocket of his jacket and withdrew a slender silver case. Even something as simple as the way he opened it and extracted a cigarette captivated her. The waiter rushed over to offer a light and then discreetly stepped away, out of earshot. Bringing the cigarette to his lips, Dr. Rome inhaled deeply, his gaze fixed on Abigail's face.

"A penny for your thoughts."

The openness of his query caught her by surprise. If she truly trusted him, and if she wasn't so tipsy, there were many things

she might have said. She could have described to him the joyous relief of once again having a reason to get up in the morning, to
imagine there was hope for the future. She could have thanked
him for the opportunity to observe him, to learn from him. Already he'd allowed her to do much more than she would have
dared to ask. But she was reluctant to expose her feelings; best not
to get too personal.

"I was thinking how very much I'm looking forward to
Thursday's operation on Miss Vanderbout. You mentioned you
might try a slight variation of your usual technique for the ears. I
was wondering what you have in mind doing differently?"

He puffed on his cigarette, still watching her intently. "If it's all
right, Miss Platford, I'd rather not talk about work. There's time
enough for that in the office." He flicked an errant ash from his
lapel. "I don't mind telling you what *I* was thinking, if you like."

"Yes, of course. Please do." She was happy to let him steer the
conversation. Apparently, she had done a poor job of it so far.

He savored his smoke a moment longer. "I was trying to picture what you do at night, when you are alone downstairs in your
room."

Abigail paused, her cheeks warming. "I doubt you would find
it interesting."

"I would find it fascinating."

She reached for her champagne and raised it to her lips,
stalling for time. Did she dare tell him how last night she'd been
reading one of her old journals, from a time when she still thought
of a doctor's work as a heroic struggle between the joy of health
and the calamity of sickness and death? A time when she'd been
disheartened by the difficulty of saving for her medical education,
with so many of her father's patients too poor to pay him anything at all for his services. When two hundred dollars a year for
tuition seemed like a fortune, and she would never have dreamed

how easily one might earn that, and more, performing a single beauty surgery.

But she doubted Dr. Rome would understand. Worse, he might think she was questioning the value of his work, comparing him to her father. A comparison that always threatened to stir up her own ambivalent feelings about the path she had lately chosen.

"Mostly I read. And I study my medical textbooks—hoping they're not too out-of-date."

"Ah, studying." He nodded slowly. "So, you're telling me there isn't another side to Abigail Platford? Maybe an imaginative side? A romantic side?"

She shifted uneasily in her chair. "I like to think I am rather imaginative. And what woman doesn't have a romantic side? But I guess I've always had a more scientific bent than most."

"You never fantasize about having a lover?"

Embarrassed, she looked away. He had no business asking such questions; she found it unsettling that he would presume to be so familiar with her.

"Arthur Hennessy couldn't have been your only beau," he remarked casually. "Not an enticing girl like you."

"I don't have a beau, and neither am I in the habit of entertaining such fantasies as you suggest. And if you don't mind, couldn't we speak of something else?"

"Come now, I assumed you were a modern woman," he said, ignoring her indignation. "You certainly seem like one in many respects."

"And so I am, but I'm sure you would agree a woman can be modern in her thinking without sacrificing her morals. And besides, a woman's needs are of a different sort than what a man imagines."

"I doubt that very much. The days of labeling a woman's natural desires as *hysteria* are fortunately over. There is no reason that a woman, especially one in the prime of youth, shouldn't experience as much pleasure from intimacy as a man. If she has a lover who knows a little something about such things." He paused. "A young woman often finds the greatest satisfaction with an older man."

He retrieved the iced champagne from the bucket, waving away the waiter who came rushing over to assist, and filled Abigail's glass to the brim while she waited, barely breathing, to hear what he would say next. "I find it refreshing that a modern woman, such as you profess to be, has the freedom to do whatever she chooses, as long as she remains discreet. Wouldn't you agree?"

She lifted the crystal flute to her lips, saying nothing.

"I'm sorry, Miss Platford—do I frighten you?" Dr. Rome snuffed out the burning tip of his cigarette, the smoke rising in a spiral between them. "It's just that I thought I might be candid with you. Especially since I believe we are very much alike."

His odd declaration jolted her yet again. Her father had often said the same—that the two of them were alike. But to hear it from Dr. Rome! She didn't understand how he could have come to such a conclusion.

"There's an ancient saying," he said, inclining toward her. "*Water flows to what is wet*. It means that those who are alike always come together, eventually." He smiled. "But maybe you doubt our affinity?"

Though he'd said he didn't wish to discuss work, now it seemed the only safe subject. "All I know is that I admire you greatly. I wish I had your skill in the operating room—though, of course, that could never be."

"You're too impatient for things that take time. So am I. But I've learned to wait. Provided it's not *too* long." He leaned in close enough that she could breathe in his scent—smoke, sandalwood, and that acrid hint of antiseptic that had evoked so many memories on the night they met. "Would you like to know a little something about me? What made me who I am?"

She nodded, curious and slightly afraid.

"I have an older brother. People always said he was the smart one, I was the handsome one. I suppose they thought I should be content with that. True, my success with the ladies was not an insignificant accomplishment. I'd be lying if I said such pursuits didn't keep me happily occupied for a good part of my youth and beyond. One might say I have a weakness for beauty, and beautiful women seem to have a weakness for me. But there came a time when I decided that was no longer enough."

As he spoke, the candlelight played on his face, softening the lines and creases, burnishing his dark hair with a touch of gold. She could imagine him as a younger man, just as he had described himself: a bit of a rake, charming and reckless.

"What was it that made you want to pursue medicine?"

He settled back in his chair. "I was tired of everybody writing me off. My brother studied hard and became a doctor. It was no surprise to anyone. They didn't expect so much from me."

"Surely you didn't become a doctor just to prove you could?"

"No, to prove I could do it better than anybody else. To beat them at their own game."

"Game? Isn't that a rather odd way to speak about your profession?"

"Maybe so. I suppose it's just the gambler in me talking. I'm proud that I've always been willing to take a risk. When I finally found my way and decided I wanted to be a doctor, I was no longer a young man. But that didn't matter. I pursued my goal like a hunter stalks his prey, and once I had it in my sights I went in for the kill."

"So ..." Abigail was still thinking about what he'd said earlier: that they were alike. Was it possible they were? "I shouldn't think it's too late for me?"

A look came over him that was at once amused and puzzled. "Too late for what?"

This could be the moment to speak plainly about her earlier ambitions. To admit to him what had happened to her father, how it had been her fault despite what everyone said later. To explain why she had given up her dream of becoming a doctor. The guilt, the fear of making another mistake. The loneliness. Her lack of funds. But now, if there were someone willing to help her, to believe in her ...

"Miss Platford?" He cocked his head, waiting for an answer.

"I think I told you before, I had planned to go to medical school."

"Ah yes, I remember." He crossed his arms over his chest. "Tell you what! Just to show how much I think of you, Miss Platford, I'm going to arrange a little surprise. Maybe this week sometime, I can't say when, but we'll have a special lesson. Should be very exciting for you."

"What sort of lesson?"

"You'll just have to wait and see. But I promise—you will be enthralled." He rubbed his palms together, his dark eyes dancing. "But now, let me tell you the reason for our little celebration. I got a telephone call last night from a friend—well, he's only an acquaintance really—but that part doesn't matter. The important thing is that I have received a very special invitation to the home of Mr. and Mrs. Joseph Radcliff, who are hosting Countess Alexandra Gagarin of Russia at their country estate in Scarsdale. It seems the countess has a mole that she might like to have removed and wants to consult with a beauty doctor."

"A mole?" Removing a mole hardly seemed worthy of celebration with an expensive bottle of Dom Perignon.

"You sound disappointed. Don't be. A tiny mole today, something much bigger tomorrow! Who knows where it might lead? The point is, having a countess as a patient is nothing to sniff at. If I can make her happy, she's likely to send others of her ilk my way. That's how one builds an *exclusive* beauty practice, which is the only kind worth having. Do you see what I'm getting at?"

"Yes, of course. Countess Alexandra will tell her friends, and they'll tell others." She wanted to be enthusiastic. But the fact was, he'd treated other wealthy patients and, so far, they'd not seen fit to send their friends. Perhaps because none wished to admit having consulted with a beauty doctor.

"That's not all." Dr. Rome smiled as if the best was yet to be revealed. "You'll be coming with me."

She hesitated. "Coming with you, where?"

"To Scarsdale. I'm borrowing a motorcar. We'll leave a week from Friday."

He couldn't be suggesting that she accompany him to the Radcliffs' estate. "But it's *you* the countess wants to see."

"Yes, but Mr. Radcliff encouraged me to bring a guest, and I thought it only appropriate that it should be my esteemed assistant."

His words were so complimentary, his manner so matter-of-fact. There seemed no question in his mind that she would come. Or perhaps that she had no other choice.

"But what will I wear?" she asked, without thinking how foolish she would sound. Dr. Rome had just invited her to spend a weekend with him! "What I mean is, I wouldn't want to embarrass you."

"Miss Platford, are you uncomfortable about the idea of traveling with me? I will, of course, make it clear to everyone that our relationship is purely a professional one."

"It's not that I care what anyone else thinks, but—"

"Oh, you care very much. Especially what *I* think. Even though I've said that I find the old rules stifling and would regard you with no less esteem if you rejected them in total. Chances are, I would admire you even more."

It was then the waiter reappeared, offering menus and a recitation of the specialties of the night. Abigail paid little attention. She was far too preoccupied with thinking about what Dr. Rome had said earlier—that a young woman often finds the greatest satisfaction with an older man.

• • • • •

It was close to midnight. Open in her lap was a worn volume written in 1816 by the famous European surgeon Joseph Constantine Carpue, which she had purchased that afternoon from Grumper's Rare Book Store. Entitled *An Account of Two Successful Operations for Restoring a Lost Nose*, it recounted not only Carpue's early surgical experience but also two of the older methods of nasal reconstruction, the so-called Indian method and the Italian method, dating back to 600 BC and the late sixteenth century, respectively. She hoped to impress Dr. Rome with the depth of her knowledge on such an esoteric subject. Though perhaps far afield from beauty surgery, surely there were parallels to be drawn.

She paused her reading, glancing nervously about the basement room. On the table next to her, a flickering oil lamp cast shadows that played on the bare brick walls. The constantly changing shapes were like demons in some wild dance—

taunting, threatening. Perhaps laughing at her, too. She had not yet learned to feel comfortable half-below ground, without electricity, surrounded by a hollow stillness. Especially late at night, when the sounds of traffic diminished and only a pale light from the street lamps found its way between the window bars.

Closing the cover of her book, she leaned her head against the back of the overstuffed velvet chair and shut her eyes. Soon she was again reliving her evening with Dr. Rome, two nights ago at the Park Avenue Hotel. Once again wondering what it all meant. The things he'd said, the provocative remarks he'd made ... there must have been a purpose behind them.

A week from tomorrow they were to travel to Scarsdale together and stay the weekend at a country estate among people as wealthy, or maybe wealthier, than the Hennessys. Among guests that included a countess. It had been generous of Dr. Rome to suggest she come with him. Unless it wasn't generosity, but something else.

She had never had a lover. She'd always believed, as girls are taught early on, that she must *save* herself for marriage. But at twenty-two, she was no longer a girl and lately seemed to care less for propriety than she used to. Yes, she had balked at Mrs. Hennessy's public insinuations about her relationship with Dr. Rome; but as he'd said, what a modern woman does in private is her own business.

Still, a woman's virtue is a commodity that mustn't be squandered. She didn't know what to make of Dr. Rome, though, for his part, he'd acted as if they knew each other well. Admittedly, his familiarity had been thrilling. A bit indecent. Perhaps he had just been having a little fun at her expense, and she shouldn't take it too seriously.

But neither should she deceive herself. Playing at romance with Franklin Rome would be utterly foolhardy. It might easily end as most affairs do. A complete disaster. She would find herself without a position, without a future—at least, not like the future she was starting to imagine. Sometimes when she was with him in the office, it felt almost like the old days with Father. The way he would explain things to her, smile when she asked a question he regarded as astute. She was learning from Dr. Rome. True, he was a *beauty* doctor; but he was a *doctor*. A surgeon. And everything she'd seen so far made her believe he was a skilled one.

Her thoughts were interrupted by a sharp knock at the door. Strange. The only person who had ever called on her was Dr. Rome's maid, Prudence, with a warm plate of supper. But not at this hour. She rose from her chair but remained where she was, unwilling to approach the door without first knowing who stood on the other side.

"Who's there?"

"Dr. Rome says to come to the office. Now."

She recognized the voice. Shark!

The first thing that came to her mind was that finally he had told Dr. Rome about what happened with the boy on Canal Street—that she'd spoken to the lad and he'd stolen her purse. It didn't help that she had lied to Dr. Rome about how she'd lost the key to her room. But she had needed a new one. And it was so long ago now, she had stopped worrying.

She took only a minute to ready herself, smoothing her hair and throwing a light shawl over her shoulders. She stepped outside, trying to think of something she might say to make Dr. Rome forgive her. Climbing the half-dozen steps to the sidewalk, she noticed a horse-drawn hansom at the curb, parked in the dim area between the electric street lamps. Shark stood on the sidewalk, waiting. Suddenly, the door to the office opened, revealing Dr. Rome haloed in the light from inside, dressed in his butcher's apron. Abigail mounted the second short flight, leading to the entry, filled with a different sort of dread, worse than the fear of Dr. Rome's wrath. No need to look over her shoulder; she already knew what Shark and his accomplice were up to.

"Step aside," said Dr. Rome as the two men swept by her with their long, sheet-wrapped bundle. Once they had passed, he turned to follow them, calling back to her, "Come along."

She closed the door and grimly made her way to the operating room. The overhead lights were blazing, the bundle already in place on the narrow table but still covered with a sheet. Dr. Rome was handing some cash to Shark, who shot Abigail a sly glance.

"What time you want me back, boss?" he said to Dr. Rome.

"There's no rush on this one. I'm keeping the office closed tomorrow. You can come for her tomorrow night around nine."

"You got it." Shark gave his partner a rude shove, and the two men exited the operating room. Abigail heard the front door open and then slam shut.

"Run out and lock up, would you?" Dr. Rome said, approaching the operating table. "And hurry back."

Abigail didn't move. Perhaps Shark had said nothing about the boy or the key; she was glad of that. But the thought of assisting Dr. Rome with another operation like the last, another patient subjected to surgery without his knowledge or consent ... She had justified it the first time, even convinced herself it was all for the best. She wasn't sure she could do so again.

Dr. Rome looked at her in surprise. "Did you hear me?"

"Yes, but I'm not staying."

"I've arranged this whole evening for you, so let's have none of your silliness."

"Silliness?" He knew how uncomfortable she had felt before. How many sleepless nights she had suffered. Why had he forced her into another situation so untenable? He had conducted his experiments without her in the past; why did he need her now?

Dispensing with any semblance of ceremony, Dr. Rome ripped away the sheet covering the body. There was no way for Abigail to avoid looking at her, a slender young woman likely only a little older than she was, naked and clearly dead. There was a fresh cut on her abdomen, from the navel down. Abigail knew enough to recognize an incision for a Cesarean section.

"What happened?" she asked, her voice a whisper.

"Complications of pregnancy. They don't all make it, you know."

"And the baby?"

"I wouldn't have any idea."

She raised the back of her hand to her forehead and closed her eyes. She was loath to admit it, but she felt faint. "Why is she here?"

"Because you once complained that you hadn't spent hours on end studying *Gray's Anatomy* for nothing. But the fact is, you can't learn anatomy from a book. Tonight you will have a proper lesson."

He really *had* done this for her! But did that change how she felt?

"Dr. Rome—I don't know what to say. I appreciate it greatly, but—"

"You're not pleased?"

"I need to know ... where did she come from?" Abigail recalled what she'd read once about anatomists in earlier times who would buy corpses from professional body snatchers. There were even those who engaged in *anatomy murder* to get the fresh cadavers medical students used for their dissections.

Of course, Shark had not murdered anyone ...

"Good God, what's wrong with you? Where's your curiosity? Your guts? She was on her way to the potter's field on Hart Island. Far better she should contribute to science."

Abigail dared to gaze down on the young woman's face. Her eyelids were closed in repose; her long, dark hair cascaded softly over her shoulders. She was only slightly blue, her body not yet stiff. The odor emanating from her was not unpleasant, almost like a sweetly pungent flower. She could not have been dead for long.

Dr. Rome rubbed his palms together, in that voracious manner of his. "Now, let's consider this woman's lips, which are rather thin," he said, seeming to have moved on from his momentary irritation. "In a few minutes, I'll show you how to make them voluptuous. We'll also raise the angle of the mouth, just to give her a pleasant expression. I'll let you inject some paraffin all by yourself. You'd like that, wouldn't you? As for the nose, you've seen how I remove a hump. This time, we're going to elevate the tip— even though she has a perfect nose as it is." He ran a finger down the bridge. "A shame, really. She wasn't at all bad looking." He brushed his hand along her neck. "There's something else I want to try—a way to lift the neck through incisions inside the mouth. I've read about it. Novel, but apparently there are some problems. We'll see. You need to understand that operating on a corpse isn't quite the same as working with living tissue, but often we need to make do."

She was trying to listen, to focus on what he was saying, but all she could think of was the poor woman laid out on the table. Did she have a family somewhere? Was there a man who loved her? And her baby—what had happened to it? She wondered if the young mother had even known whether her child lived or died.

"Miss Platford!" Dr. Rome had paused his lecture long enough to notice she was not paying attention. "I hope you realize that our time is limited. A fresh cadaver, especially one as nice as this, is a precious thing."

Abigail pulled her eyes away from the woman's ripped abdomen. "It's sad. She's so young."

He sighed, coming over to her and laying his hands on her shoulders. "You've never seen death before?"

An image of her father's face, devoid of life, flashed before her eyes. She mustn't think about it now, not when Dr. Rome expected her to act like any ambitious student should: eager to take the knife, to make the first cut.

He gave her an encouraging pat on the arm and took a step back. "I suggest you ready yourself, and we'll get started."

She glanced again at the body. The *woman*. What they were about to do felt somehow irreverent. Perhaps it was only the way she had been brought here, by Shark and his partner, wrapped in a dirty white sheet. Or maybe it was seeing her laid out on the same table where Isabelle Hadley's surgery had taken place. Miss Hadley—so lovely, so full of hope, her whole life ahead of her.

"Miss Platford, I'm going to ask you once more, and that will be the last time."

With difficulty, Abigail reined herself in. How could she refuse such an opportunity? If she did, Dr. Rome would never again take her seriously.

She donned her apron and readied the instruments, all the while struggling with her emotions. But once they got started, hesitation gave way to wonder. It was no less than the discovery of a whole new world—as Dr. Rome had said, a world impossible to know or imagine from the pages of a book.

He proved to be a wonderful teacher, giving her ample opportunity to make the mistakes he knew she inevitably would; eager to show the depth of his knowledge, to dazzle with the quick precision of his hands. She had recognized his talent before, watching him day after day in the operating room, but this was different. He was allowing her inside his mind, telling her the reason behind every movement of the knife. By the time she took the blade into her own hands—so she could not only see the cut, but feel it—she had all but forgotten it was only beauty surgery.

"When you analyze a face for beauty," Dr. Rome explained, "you need to understand that the great philosophers and artists have already agreed on certain criteria, a certain ideal form and proportion. But the truly great beauty doctor does not stop there. He brings his own unique vision to bear on every case so the result is far more than a mere replication of some theoretical standard of perfection. What I envision and ultimately achieve is the ideal for *my* patient, a person unlike any other. One does not use a cookie cutter on the human face. One molds it by hand, with the greatest attention to nuance. And *that*, my dear, is the difference between a crass technician and an inspired artist."

"But how do you know if what you think is beautiful will also please your patient?"

"I know because already I have made her believe in me more than she believes in herself."

Abigail did not doubt his assertion; he had succeeded in convincing her of the same.

It was past midnight when they undertook the gross dissection, peeling away the facial skin to expose the crisscrossed muscle layers underneath. Dr. Rome showed her the nerves that run along the sides of the face, like the branches of a tree, pointing out the ones that control movement and expression and those responsible for sensation. She observed the facial artery just lateral to the corner of the mouth and one of the salivary glands nearby—structures, he warned, that no knife must ever transgress.

"These nerves and muscles," he said, pointing to those he had identified as responsible for expression, "are the ones that cause deformities of the face, meaning those wrinkles and creases that too soon turn a woman into her grandmother. If one is very careful, they can be dissected subcutaneously—that is, beneath the skin—and no one will ever see the slightest sign of it, except that the expressions of the face will be pleasantly subdued."

Another hour went by as he entertained her with stories from his days in Paris about the women who came into the clinic seeking treatment. "*Ah yes*, I remember one of them saying, *I used to be so beautiful and now—well, I'm not sure why I'm not anymore. Perhaps you can tell me. I have the same nose, same eyes, same lips. But when I look at them all together, nothing is the same.*" He chuckled. "It was an apt observation. Fading beauty can be subtle. One day a woman is lovely and desirable, the next day she isn't anymore. It takes the eye of a beauty doctor to figure out what's out of place and, with enough skill, put everything back where it belongs."

Though Abigail smiled politely, some of what he said troubled her and in a way she had not expected. Like the women of whom he spoke so dismissively, one day she, too, would no longer possess the bloom of youth sufficient to draw his approving eye. She was aware, of course, that to think in such a personal way about matters that were purely clinical was not to think like a doctor. But though she'd never intended to feel this way, suddenly she cared whether Dr. Rome found her attractive. Perhaps she had cared all along.

At half-past two, Dr. Rome announced he was ready to quit, promising they could have another round or two tomorrow. Abigail stood silently while he spread a formalin-soaked cloth over the body before covering it with a rubber sheet like a cold black shroud. Though it felt as if she was being laid to rest, tomorrow would bring fresh insults to her weary flesh—all for Abigail's sake.

She had tried to show the young woman proper respect. Perhaps, under the circumstances, it was impossible. But of one thing, Abigail was certain.

She would never forget her.

CHAPTER 8

D r. Rome switched into neutral, throttled down, and put on the park brake. He removed his goggles and leather gloves and, with an abundance of energy, leaped from the driver's seat of the open-top Ford.

"What a place this is!" he said, shrugging off his black motoring coat and flinging it onto the seat.

Abigail looked with awe upon the Radcliffs' stately home, three stories high, with long wings spreading to the left and right. The red-brick Georgian-style structure had a front veranda embellished with four massive white pillars and surrounded by tiered beds of blossoming flowers and fruit trees.

Dr. Rome came around to the passenger side, opened the door, and helped her out.

"Thank you." Carefully, she removed her black cape and the veiled hat adorned with silk peonies tied onto her head throughout the windy ride. In its place, she pinned an elaborate millinery creation matching her afternoon frock; the ensemble was sure to make a favorable impression.

They made their way up the flagstone walkway to where their host stood waiting on the veranda. At first glance, Mr. Radcliff was not at all what she'd expected. Rather than tweed and

knickerbockers, or perhaps a summer suit and tie, he wore something resembling the uniform of Theodore Roosevelt's Rough
Riders—khaki pants and a belted jacket, tall boots, and a wide-
brimmed canvas hat. He was a big man, not in height but girth,
with a round face and spidery veins like a red rash across his
cheeks.

"Welcome, welcome! Nice to meet you, Doctor." Mr. Radcliff took a step forward to shake Dr. Rome's hand before turning
to Abigail. "And this must be the lovely Miss Platford," he said,
his expansive grin revealing tobacco-stained teeth that were large
and square. "I can see already that this is going to be an extraordinary weekend."

"Good afternoon, Mr. Radcliff. It's a pleasure to make your acquaintance."

"Very gracious of you and Mrs. Radcliff to issue the invitation
through my friend, Mr. Harber," said Dr. Rome. "He had nothing
but wonderful things to say about you and your various enterprises, Mr. Radcliff."

"First off, you'll address me as Joe. Around here, we're what they
like to call *avant-garde*. First names only, preferably two syllables or
fewer. So much more efficient." He let out a booming laugh.

"By all means," Dr. Rome said. "Then it's Franklin." He turned
to Abigail with a smile. "And Abigail."

"Very good. As for our mutual friend, Mr. Harber, he's done
a fair job with some investments of mine. I've got no serious complaints yet. Nice enough fellow. I see he even loaned you his
motorcar," Mr. Radcliff said, casting an admiring glance at the
red Ford with its brass side lamps, red wheel spokes, and black
leather seats. "I'm an automobile enthusiast myself. Got three of
them in the garage in back that I'll show you later, Frank. You, too,
Abby—that is, if you're interested. But then I'm sure you'd rather

be sipping Veuve Clicquot with the ladies than sticking your nose under the hood of a car."

She smiled. Though his joviality struck her as a bit forced, Mr. Radcliff, or *Joe*, could not have given them a more welcoming reception. Still, she wasn't at all certain she could accustom herself to such overfamiliarity, especially with people of distinction like the Radcliffs and their guests.

"I'm afraid I know nothing about motorcars, except this one gave me quite a drafty ride."

"Well, it beats the train any day. But listen, everyone is waiting out at the gazebo. Unless you two would like to be shown to your rooms now ..."

"No, that won't be necessary." Dr. Rome replied, before Abigail could say she'd love a few minutes to freshen up.

"All right then, come this way." Joe Radcliff beckoned them to follow with a sweep of his arm. "The servants will take your bags upstairs in the meantime."

He led them around to the back of the house and then down a long path through a field of yellow and blue wildflowers, all the while engaged in an animated monologue about how tiresome it was to be the sole man in a household full of women. They soon arrived at a maze-like configuration of high hedges. In the center, flowerbeds bursting with masses of red roses were arranged in a circle around a large white gazebo with arched openings and a gently sloping green roof. Abigail heard the murmur of voices followed by a peal of high-pitched laughter.

Joe stepped aside to let her pass through the arches. Two women sat together on a white wicker settee, a third in one of several matching chairs arranged around a low round table. As Abigail approached, they stopped talking, their eyes fixed on her as if she were some rare species of bird that had alighted on a nearby branch.

"Miss Platford!" A short, chubby woman rose from her chair, grasping Abigail's white-gloved hands with her bare and lightly freckled ones. "Welcome. And Dr. Rome," she said, turning to him with a smile. "We're so glad you both could make it."

"We've already agreed, dear, to use our given names. Frank and Abby, this is my wife, Lillian," Joe said, nodding toward the woman who stood before them. Outfitted in an embroidered linen shirtwaist and pleated walking skirt, her graying hair pulled into a frizzy knot, she did not fit Abigail's image of the mistress of such a palatial estate. Perhaps the only clue to her status was the gigantic diamond she wore on her left hand. Abigail had never seen a stone so large.

"And comfortably arranged on the sofa, in her usual outlandish style," Joe went on, "is Countess Alexandra Fedosia Gagarin. Quite a mouthful, isn't it? You can forget what I said about two syllables. Countess Alexandra takes great pleasure in ignoring all the rules of the house. She believes a title gives one that prerogative."

Even if the countess had not acknowledged Joe's remarks with a droll smile, Abigail needed no one to tell her which of the two remaining women she was. She could have picked her out among a hundred, so distinctive was her bearing. Her hair was fashionably brunette, almost black, and she wore it piled on top of her head in a mass of ringlets, some of which had either broken loose or had been styled that way to make her appear reckless. Her features were delicately beautiful, her porcelain skin so white it could have been enamel. Abigail barely noticed the tiny black mole near her upper lip. If anything, it made her even more exotic.

Perhaps the strangest thing about her was her costume, an embroidered Japanese kimono, beige with tiny pink and yellow flowers and flowing sleeves, bound tightly around the waist with a yellow sash. Her feet were bare, the toenails stained with red oil and buffed to a shine.

Alexandra offered an imperious smile. "You may call me *Countess*."

"It's a pleasure," Abigail said, feeling uncomfortably overdressed and prudish. "I go by Abigail," she added, hoping Joe would take note; she despised the nickname *Abby*.

"And this," the countess said, reaching over to touch the hand of the woman sitting next to her, "is my dear Ronnie." Without further explanation, she raised her dark eyes, lined with lamp-black, to Dr. Rome. "How lovely to meet you, Doctor."

"All right, everyone, enough of pleasantries," Joe said. "Have a seat, and let's pop open another bottle of bubbly. It's not too early for you, is it, Abby?"

He gestured toward a wicker chair across from the countess where he wanted Abigail to sit. Dr. Rome took the seat beside her. Lillian tooted on a little whistle that she wore around her neck, and a servant appeared, carrying a silver tray with a fresh bottle of champagne and a set of chilled crystal flutes.

"I was just remarking to Ronnie how spoiled rotten I've become since having the good fortune to be a guest of her magnanimous brother and his wife," the countess said, smiling at Lillian. Though she spoke with an accent, her English was impeccable. "You will be amazed," she continued, directing the rest of her remarks to Abigail. "Nothing you can think of hasn't occurred to them already. I guarantee Joe has planned all sorts of clever surprises. He always does."

"Wonderful ones, I'm sure."

"But tell us—" Now it was Ronnie who spoke, which gave Abigail an excuse to look at her more closely. She bore a strong resemblance to her brother, intense gray-blue eyes and large, protruding teeth. Her hair was done in a short, blunt cut, quite unbecoming for a woman. She wore a shapeless tan skirt and a white cotton blouse, and the soles of her boots were caked with mud as if she'd been tramping across the fields. "What's the most shocking thing you've ever seen in Dr. Rome's operating room? I'm sure he wouldn't tell us. Probably none of it is shocking to *him*. But we've never met a beauty doctor before, and we're curious."

"What exactly do you mean by *shocking*?" Abigail glanced nervously at Dr. Rome.

"I believe what Ronnie means," interjected the countess, "is that there's a certain ..." She paused, searching for the right word. "A certain *ghastliness* about the idea of cutting people up, moving things around, and then sewing them back together. I'm intrigued by it. We all are. But one has to wonder, how far can it go?"

"I'm afraid that's something you'd have to ask Dr. Rome," Abigail said, automatically shifting into her customary role. "He is the world's foremost expert in transformative surgery. If Dr. Rome can't do it, then I assure you no one can."

"*Transformative* surgery?" echoed the countess, crinkling her brow.

"Beauty surgery, that is."

"Yes, do tell us, Doctor," piped up Lillian. "Will we soon be able to change anything we want about the way we look? For example, might you make me tall and slender?"

"I believe your husband prefers you just as you are, and I concur with his taste," Dr. Rome answered diplomatically. "But as for the limitations of transformative surgery, we don't yet know what they are. I feel confident in saying we're just at the beginning. What we ultimately achieve may be limited only by the imagination."

"The famous Dr. Frankenstein started out wishing to create something of beauty," said the countess, pulling out a cigarette from beneath the sash of her kimono. Ronnie was quick to offer her a light. "But, of course, the result was not as he imagined."

"Ah, the perils of invention!" said Joe.

"But surely, Doctor," the countess insisted, "you must have had a disaster or two in your career. No one could expect otherwise. I've heard some awful stories. I remember one in particular, about a young woman, a dancer. Apparently, all she wanted was a prettier pair of legs. Of course, it wasn't you, Frank, but one of those other beauty doctors—he did something to her. I don't remember what, or I never knew. But it didn't work. It was such a complete failure that they ended up having to cut off her legs entirely. Can you believe it? A dancer without legs!" She burst into laughter. "It isn't funny, I know, but it *is* ironic."

"The keys to avoiding such unfortunate occurrences are skill and restraint," Dr. Rome said, seemingly unfazed by the countess's story, or her behavior. "Never push beyond what is prudent. One can always do a little more, but undoing a mistake already made is often impossible."

"And have you ever?" Ronnie asked.

"I'm sorry? Have I ever *what*?"

"Have you ever stretched the limits, pushed beyond what's prudent? Have you undertaken something that you wished, in retrospect, you hadn't? Or maybe taken it further than you should have. Further than a reasonable man might."

Dr. Rome smiled. "I can promise you I've not done anything *un*reasonable. As for having regrets, I'm afraid I don't indulge in that kind of negative thinking, which always does more harm than good. It leads to timidity, and in my profession, one must always remain fearless."

"That's what I like to hear!" Joe exclaimed. "Fearless! Today's imperiled world calls for nothing less."

"And what about you?" The countess turned again toward Abigail. "Are you fearless as well?"

Abigail could feel her heat rising. "The requirements of my position are very different."

"But I'm sure you must be quite a Florence Nightingale. Otherwise, you'd not be working for a man with such exacting standards as your Dr. Rome."

"If Abby is really that tough," Joe interjected, "you'd never know it from looking at her. Why, that face is right off the cover of a magazine. Like one of those Gibson girls."

Abigail shifted in her chair. "Thank you, but you ought to see me dressed for surgery. I assure you, I look quite unglamorous."

"Well, it's a good thing. Otherwise, I don't know how Frank could keep his mind on his blade."

"Joe, you're embarrassing Abigail," Lillian chided. "You forget she's a professional woman."

"All right, I stand corrected—or should I say reprimanded?" Joe quipped. He raised his champagne flute with a flourish. "Here's to new friends and fresh adventures!"

Abigail toasted with the others, already wishing the weekend was over.

"Frank—" Joe took a gulp of bubbly. "Before dinner, I'd like us to sit down and chat for a while. All kidding aside, I'm very interested in your work. I want you to tell me all about it. And then I'll fill you in on my little idea. I'd be curious to know what you think."

Dr. Rome nodded. "I've been looking forward to it."

●   ●   ●   ●   ●

Everyone gathered in the dining room for dinner at eight o'clock. The long table was elegantly appointed, fine white porcelain and cut crystal glassware shimmering beneath tall silver candelabras. Red roses and honeysuckle from the garden were artfully arranged in ample bouquets at each end of the table, filling the room with a seductive sweetness. In the kindness of candlelight, Abigail could almost imagine the room's garish wallpaper and overly ornate furnishings as quaintly eccentric.

Earlier, she had received a perfunctory tour of the first floor of the grand house. The architecture was magnificent. The various rooms in the wings off either side of the expansive foyer were of stately proportions, with high ceilings, tall sash windows, and pillared fireplaces. They were spaces designed for furniture of distinction, fine Chippendales and Hepplewhites, Persian carpets, upholstery and drapes of rich textures and hues. But the items with which the Radcliffs filled them could have been plucked from a seamy French brothel. Louis XIV furnishings, gilded and velvet-covered in brash shades of red. Patterned draperies and walls papered in dizzying designs. Worst of all were the paintings, especially in the drawing room which contained a series of amateurishly executed female nudes in provocative poses. She wondered why the Radcliffs, who obviously could afford better, would decorate their home with such offensive rubbish.

From her seat at the dining table next to Dr. Rome, she observed her hosts with a critical eye. Joe was strapped into an evening suit that was embarrassingly tight around the waist, while Lillian had chosen a puffy-sleeved dress of white lace more suitable as a tablecloth. She wore several substantial pieces of jewelry—a huge peacock brooch with every color gem imaginable, pearl drop earrings, and an amethyst-and-onyx choker—the sum of which utterly confounded the eye.

And then there was the countess, decked out in a flowing green taffeta gown, the fitted bodice notable for its nearly complete exposure of her ample bosom. A massive diamond-and-emerald necklace hung like a chandelier around her neck. She wore her hair loose, the dark mass puffed out around her face and dropping past her shoulders in a frenzy of curls. The woman was striking, dramatically so. Abigail cast a glance at Dr. Rome. From the way he was staring at the countess, surely something other than her mole had captured his attention.

For a moment, Abigail regretted her selection of the coral-colored Parisian gown that she and Dr. Rome had picked out together, the same one she'd worn for their celebratory dinner at the Park Avenue Hotel. The dress was beautiful and fit her to perfection, but it paled in comparison with the countess's flamboyant outfit. How disappointing to feel so outdone, even in her finest frock!

Suddenly she felt a weight on her thigh, underneath the table. With a start, she realized it was Dr. Rome's hand. He leaned over to whisper in her ear, "Is your room upstairs satisfactory?"

"Yes, it's lovely," she said, her heart racing.

"Mine is just across the hall," he said, giving her thigh a slight squeeze before moving away to say something to Joe, leaving her dizzy from his touch and the warmth of his breath in her ear.

It was then that Ronnie entered the dining room. At first, Abigail didn't recognize her, dressed as she was in a suit similar to what Joe was wearing. She glanced at Dr. Rome to gauge his reaction, but if he was in the least surprised or disturbed, he didn't show it. Everyone else, too, acted as if it were nothing out of the ordinary. Looking about the table, Abigail felt like a player in some odd drama with a cast of characters who seemed not to belong on the same stage.

A butler began making the rounds, filling their glasses from a bottle of what was announced to be fine old Bordeaux. Joe, rising from his chair at the head of the table, cleared his throat.

"Welcome, welcome! We have an exciting evening ahead of us, sure to be a memorable one. But how could it be anything else with such an outstanding group as we have gathered here tonight?" He clasped his hands, gazing down at his guests with a beatific smile. "I thought we could begin by entertaining ourselves with a little game intended to challenge the intellect and stimulate the imagination. Does anyone object?"

"Are we allowed to keep our clothes on?" the countess quipped.

Joe smiled. "You may, of course, Countess. Though I'll be disappointed."

Abigail stole a glance at Dr. Rome, who maintained an air of amusement.

"All right then, let us begin." Joe sat down and placed a small notebook and a pen on the table in front of him. "The theme of our dinner tonight is, appropriately, *beauty*. I would therefore like to start with everyone offering his or her definition of beauty, with one stipulation: Each of us must define it differently. Which means the one who goes first will have the easiest time of it, and the last may find it difficult." He turned to Abigail. "It's a definition that has eluded influential thinkers throughout history, but I have every confidence that among us tonight is the one who can finally put to rest all speculation as to the true meaning of beauty. Who shall it be? I don't know—but, Abby, why don't you go first?"

All eyes turned toward her as she frantically tried to recall her fireside readings in philosophy, hoping to come up with an applicable quote from one of those *influential thinkers* to whom Joe had alluded. It shouldn't be so difficult, yet at that moment she could think of only a single word in response.

"Nature."

Joe raised a skeptical brow. "But some things that occur in nature are aberrations, wouldn't you agree? Why else should we refer to that which is unexpectedly awful as a *freak of nature*?"

Aberrations? Strange that he would think of nature in such a way, when most would picture the majesty of mountain peaks or the dazzling hues of a spectacular sunset. "I would argue that nature in all its forms, even the strange and unexpected, is beautiful."

"Not an opinion I would expect from someone employed by the world's foremost beauty surgeon," Joe countered. "After all, what *is* a beauty doctor if not someone whose purpose is to alter nature? Right, Frank?"

Realizing the truth of Joe's statement, Abigail could only hope Dr. Rome might amend her too-hasty declaration to suit the purpose of their visit.

"Let's just say that, as a beauty doctor, my goal is to elevate nature to its own most perfect standards."

"How truly poetic," Countess Alexandra gushed, smiling over her wineglass at him. "I can't wait to hear *your* definition of beauty, Frank. Whatever it is, I shall try my best to exemplify it."

Joe had been scribbling in his notebook, but now he stopped. "We'll come back to Frank later. Ronnie, you're next."

Ronnie, sitting to Joe's immediate right, straightened her bow tie. "All right. I like what the English writer John Ruskin said: *The most beautiful things in the world are the most useless.*"

"So, you see no value in beauty?" Joe asked, seeming to regard her remark with great seriousness.

"I didn't say that. Something can have value without being useful. You know, art for art's sake. That's the point, I guess."

"Fair enough." Joe turned to the next in succession around the long table. "Countess?"

"Very simple. Beauty is power."

Abigail caught her breath. How shrewd! She'd known precisely what to say to win Dr. Rome's approval. But how?

"And I must disagree with Ronnie," the countess resumed. "Beauty is indeed very useful. It can be used for good or evil. But it can always be used for something."

"Beauty is innocence." It was Lillian who chimed in. "That's why we lose so much of it with age and experience."

Joe swirled his wine before finishing it in a single swallow and turning his attention to Dr. Rome. "Frank, if anyone can give us a precise definition of beauty, it should be you. Tell us, why do we see some people as beautiful, others as merely plain, and still others as unattractive or even hideous? Is there a single formula for beauty that we all recognize, whether or not we realize it?"

Dr. Rome sat back in his chair, a finger tracing the rim of his wineglass. "I can't speak as a philosopher, only as a surgeon. But what I define as beauty is a certain balance and harmony among the features. If we're talking about a beautiful face, that balance is different for each individual. In answer to your question, Joe, I don't believe in an absolute standard of beauty, though some have proposed it. To my way of thinking, there is no precise measurement, no one formula that can apply to everyone. If there were, then anyone skilled with a knife could be a superb beauty doctor. But beauty is elusive, even deceitful. It requires an artist's eye to envision it, an artisan's hand to mold it. That is what I find so gratifying about my profession. The sculptor of human flesh can take his place among the ranks of Michelangelo and Leonardo da Vinci. Perhaps it may seem an overstatement, but to a beauty doctor, the product of his labor, though mortal, is no less a work of art."

"How inspiring," Lillian said. "I had never thought of beauty surgery that way, but it makes great sense."

The countess lifted her brows as she raised the wine to her lips. "I agree. Dr. Rome is most definitely the winner of Joe's little game. But then, we haven't heard from our host. Joe, we're all dying to know *your* definition of beauty."

"Very well, Countess." Joe closed his notebook and slipped it back into his pocket. "I see beauty as the engine of evolution."

"And we are supposed to understand what *that* means?"

"Those who are beautiful are desirable; therefore they have the advantage in attracting a mate and reproducing."

"Well, if that's true, then why are there still so many ugly people in the world? Shouldn't *beauty* plus *beauty* equal *beauty*?"

"A very astute question indeed, Countess." Joe paused, looking through the dining room's open doors toward the hallway. "Well, well—I think the rest of our guests have arrived."

Abigail had not been aware more guests were expected but, mildly curious, turned to see the newcomers. In the shadowy doorway appeared a form that, at first, made no sense to her. Was the flickering candlelight playing tricks? Had she suddenly developed double vision? She blinked several times to clear her sight.

But no, this was not a trick of light or eyesight.

The figure that emerged from the semi-darkness was a pair of Siamese twins of the rarest variety—a single body with two heads, one slightly tilted to the left, the other at a somewhat greater angle to the right. They were adolescent girls, perhaps thirteen or fourteen years old. Their faces were virtually identical and quite pretty—dark eyes, well-angled cheeks, and small chins, the most distinguishing feature of each being a prominent and high-bridged nose. Their shoulders and chest were wide, but the rest of their torso, obscured by the soft folds of a loose-fitting garment of white silk with blue embroidery, appeared to taper somewhat normally. They had two arms, and a single pair of buttoned boots peeked from beneath the hem of their dress.

As they paused in the doorway, taking in their surroundings and the company, it was clear they were accustomed to polite society. They stood for a moment, nodding and smiling. One spoke quietly to the other and then to a man in evening attire who had just come up behind them.

"Come in, come in!" Joe called out. "Valencia, Melilla—I have a special place for you girls right over there." He pointed to the far end of the long table, well away from the other guests. "And you, Baron, I've seated you next to the lovely Miss Abigail Platford, for which I'm sure you will thank me later."

The twins, walking with a limp but exhibiting excellent co-ordination of their shared body, circled the table to their assigned chair, while the man who accompanied them was shown by the butler to the seat on Abigail's left.

"Friends, this is Baron Ludwik Rutkowski. He and his charges arrived late last night." Joe gave the baron a big-toothed grin. "I trust you've recuperated from your travels?"

"Very much so, thank you," the baron said, taking his seat. "Miss Platford," he acknowledged, his lively blue eyes moving past Abigail to Dr. Rome, who leaned forward to get a better look at him. "And Dr. Rome, I presume."

"It's a pleasure, Baron Rutkowski."

"Come now, we're all on a first-name basis around here," Joe interjected. "As I always say, titles are for those who feel the need to make themselves appear important."

While the others exchanged brief pleasantries, Abigail conducted a clandestine assessment of the gentleman on her left. He had a clean-shaven face with strong, smooth features that would catch any woman's eye. His wavy blond hair was brushed back from a high forehead in a style longer than the current fashion. Abigail thought he must be in his early thirties; yet, in some ways, he had the manner of an older man. A stiffness and formality which might have been simply a sign of discomfiture with his present surroundings. She was curious to know his connection with the

Radcliffs and what reason he had for being their guest. And his relationship with the Siamese twins.

"But excuse me," Ludwik said, "I've neglected to introduce my girls, the two lovely Miss Rosas. On the left is Valencia, and Melilla on the right. The twins are delighted to join everyone tonight, aren't you, girls?"

Both nodded, smiling but saying nothing.

Joe was staring at the girls with shameless fascination. "They speak very little English," he said to no one in particular.

Ludwik was quick to correct him. "Actually, their English is not at all bad," He leaned back so the butler could fill his goblet. "By the way, I took the liberty today of borrowing a few books from your library. Reading is the best way for them to develop their vocabulary. English and Spanish have many similarities."

"They're Spanish?" the countess asked, glancing disdainfully at the girls. "Parents were gypsies, I suppose."

An awkward hush fell over the table. Without answering, Ludwik turned to Dr. Rome. "Joe tells me you're in the beauty business."

Dr. Rome sprang to attention. "Yes, though it's actually quite more than that. My field is *transformative surgery*."

"Sounds formidable."

"I'd be happy to explain, if you're interested—that is, if the others don't mind. I wouldn't want to bore them."

"I, for one, should never tire of hearing you talk about your work, Doctor," Countess Alexandra said with a charming lilt to her voice.

At that point, several servants entered the dining room and began serving the first course, a cream soup with lobster and shrimp. Abigail couldn't help her own somewhat puerile curiosity about the twins. Would they share a single bowl or would each have her own? Would they eat simultaneously? But manners kept her from observing them too closely.

"Before you arrived, we were having a discussion about the definition of beauty," Joe said, ignoring Dr. Rome's offer to expound on his profession. "Abby's opinion was that beauty and nature are synonymous. Yet, as we can see, nature left to itself often makes terrible mistakes."

There could be no doubt in anyone's mind what, or whom, Joe was referring to.

"Nature plays with us as she chooses, sir." Ludwik's voice was tinged with anger. "It behooves us to show others the compassion we would wish for ourselves. Especially when one considers that he who is strong today may find himself helpless tomorrow."

"Ludwik makes an excellent point," agreed Dr. Rome. "However, more than compassion is required if we are to provide hope to those afflicted with sometimes shocking but potentially explainable medical conditions."

Joe stopped eating, his spoon suspended in midair. "You're not implying that something could be done to help these poor girls, are you?"

The countess threw back her head with a laugh. "Ha! I suspected you might be some kind of mad scientist, Frank. What are you going to do? Cut off one of their heads and sew it onto a spare body?"

The soupspoon fell from Abigail's hand, clattering against the rim of the bowl before falling into her lap. "Excuse me," she mumbled, lowering her eyes.

"Bring Miss Platford another spoon," Joe barked at the servants.

Lillian smiled at the twins. "Tell Dr. Rome what you told me this morning, Valencia."

Valencia bit her lower lip, glancing nervously at Ludwik. "Our noses?" she said in a tiny voice.

Joe's head popped up from his soup bowl. "What about their noses?"

Lillian nodded again at Valencia, encouraging her to speak, but to no avail. The girl refused to say another word. "Then I'll tell him myself. Valencia and Melilla ran across one of your advertisements in the newspaper, Frank, and now they've got it in their heads to have you fix their noses. You know, take off the big bump in the middle."

Out of the corner of her eye, Abigail saw Ludwik reach for a glass of water, his expression taut.

"I'll be damned!" Joe wiped a trace of cream from his mouth with a napkin. "That would be something, wouldn't it?"

"Is there any reason it couldn't be done?" It was Ronnie who addressed Dr. Rome. "I mean, I'm just wondering."

"I honestly don't know. I'd have to examine the girls, understand their anatomy. Evaluate their overall health. There are lots of things to consider—that is, if one were to consider it at all."

Ludwik cleared his throat. "Let's not talk about such nonsense."

"But why?" Joe was enjoying himself tremendously. "These girls want to be beautiful. What's wrong with that?" He glanced from Dr. Rome to Ludwik and back to Dr. Rome.

"Ludwik is right," Dr. Rome said, to Abigail's great relief.

Joe looked disappointed. "I guess I'm overruled. But it doesn't seem like so very much to ask, just to straighten out a bump or two. Why not make a couple of beauties out of these girls? Why, I would think any beauty doctor worth his salt would consider it a challenge, if not a duty."

Abigail should have spoken up. Whatever merit there was in Dr. Rome's work, the ignorance of Joe's comments only belittled it.

But to say so would not serve the purpose for which she had promised to devote herself this weekend. Though now she regretted coming here at all.

．　．　．　．　．

"I was hoping you might have been a bit more charming tonight."

Dr. Rome stood with Abigail before the door to her bedroom. She had been quiet all evening, passing up many opportunities to bolster his reputation in the eyes of the Radcliffs and their guests. But she had been too upset by the behavior of people from whom she would have expected better.

He touched her arm. "Abigail, Abigail ... what am I going to do with you?"

His use of her given name startled her, even though she'd been called Abigail, or Abby, all night long by everyone else. Except the baron.

"I'll do better tomorrow," she said contritely, turning toward the door.

"May I come in?"

Her hand paused on the knob. To invite him into her bedroom, especially as a guest in someone's home, was far from proper. What would the Radcliffs think? But then, how were they to know? Besides, Dr. Rome might have something important to discuss with her.

"As you wish—for a minute."

Abigail entered the room, Dr. Rome behind her. Softly, he shut the door. As she hurried to light the bedside lamp, she heard the snap of the lock.

"You must be in seventh heaven out here in the countryside, surrounded by all this beauty," he remarked, almost too casually. "I didn't know you were such a nature lover."

She froze. Was his comment a jab at her earlier attempts at profundity? Had he asked to come in only to scold her?

Abigail removed her gloves and tossed them on the bed. "I'm sorry, but Mr. Radcliff put me on the spot. I'm sure he wanted to embarrass me. And since we're talking about him, my impression of Joe Radcliff is not terribly favorable."

"I'm not asking you to approve of him, or any of them. Just remember, they could be important to me. Besides, others are entitled to their opinions. Not everyone is as enlightened as you are, my dear."

So, this *was* all he wanted. To lecture her. She spun around. "So, you still think removing the countess's mole would be such a boon to your practice?" she asked, with a hint of petulance.

"I'm not sure I should encourage her to get rid of it. One might regard it as more of a beauty mark, don't you think? And it rather becomes her."

Overcome by a burst of exasperation that felt suspiciously like jealousy, she swept past him toward the window. The drapes were open, the sky a vast black ocean littered with pinpoints of light. She thought again of Joe in his role as the evening's master of ceremonies. Her answer in his little game of definitions had been correct; what greater beauty than this could there ever be? Nature surpasses all else.

In the glass, she caught a faint reflection of movement. The next second, Dr. Rome was close behind her.

"Alexandra is quite a beautiful woman," he said softly, "but certainly no more beautiful than you."

He placed his hands at her waist. She stiffened. "I'm afraid that—that Countess Alexandra and I could not be more different." How frightened she sounded!

"That's very true. And isn't it wonderful that we live in a world of opposites? One has so many choices."

His hands slowly followed the curve of her hips. "Alexandra's costume this evening did nothing to flatter her. She should know better. A beautiful woman never allows the sparkle of her jewels to outshine her own brilliance."

She felt his lips soft against her ear, his moustache like the tease of a feather. "You, however, looked ravishing." He ran his tongue down her neck, sending a ripple of sensation through her. "I love this gown on you. But I must admit that all night long, I've been trying to imagine you without it."

With deft fingers, he undid the topmost button of her dress, hesitating only a moment before moving to the next and the next—all the way down her back. She did nothing to stop him as he slid the coral-colored silk off her shoulders; it pooled around her waist, leaving her exposed in her corset and shift. Shaking, but not from the night chill.

"Don't tell me you haven't thought about this." Turning her around, he slowly ran his finger along the length of her collarbone, his gaze lingering on her bosom. "Don't tell me you haven't wanted it."

Somehow, she found her voice. "Dr. Rome—"

"*Franklin*," he said, removing the laced butterfly ornament from her hair. "Say it. I want to hear how it sounds on those gorgeous lips of yours." She closed her eyes, terrified to look at him. "Say it now."

"Franklin," she whispered.

"That didn't hurt, did it? And the rest won't either. I promise you."

She knew then, beyond any doubt, what he meant to do. No longer could she pretend to be surprised. Hadn't he hinted at it that night in the Park Avenue Hotel? Hadn't she been waiting all this time to see when and how it would happen? But she could not give in, even if she wanted to. There was far too much at stake.

She opened her eyes. "I'm sorry. I can't."

"You can't? Or you won't?" He took her hand and lifted it to his lips. "There's a difference, you know."

She remembered how he had spoken so openly of his many affairs with women. How he'd admitted to a weakness for beauty. He would tire of her quickly, perhaps come to loathe the sight of her.

"My dear Abigail, I know what you're thinking, but you mustn't be afraid. Fear is the enemy of passion. The enemy of everything you want but think you can't have." He looked at her hungrily. "Do you have any idea how beautiful you are?"

He began again to kiss her neck, and again she didn't stop him. Shutting her eyes, she was back at the Park Avenue Hotel. His head bent toward her; his dark hair touched with gold. *A young woman often finds the greatest satisfaction with an older man ...* Was it her imagination, or had he said it again, just now?

"She does?" she murmured as his lips caressed the soft swell of her breast.

CHAPTER 9

I f I might ask," the countess said, in that droll manner of hers, "what reason on earth did Joe have for inviting that Ludwik fellow and his little monster to Scarsdale?"

"You'd have to ask Joe," Lillian replied, spreading a thick layer of strawberry jam on her corn muffin.

"Where is he this morning? Tinkering with one of his silly machines?"

"No, he and Frank left early. Something about a meeting with the Scarsdale Town Club. He said not to expect them back until this afternoon."

It had been hard enough waking up alone, wondering why Franklin had left her, what he'd been thinking when he did. But the news that she wouldn't see him until this afternoon sent Abigail into a tailspin. Didn't he know how anxious she was, how much she needed his reassurance that what had happened was all right? That she had nothing to regret?

Her thoughts drifted back to last night. How intently he'd watched her, how persistent his efforts to please. She would not have guessed him to be capable of such tenderness. He knew he was her first—or if there had been any question in his mind in the beginning, there could be none now. He had taken the bloody towel with him; the maid would likely think he'd cut himself shaving. She was glad to be rid of it. But there was still that uneasiness, the questions. The need to know: What were they to each other now?

"It's disturbing to think of those girls sleeping under the same roof as the rest of us." The countess was back to ranting over the Siamese twins. "In my estimation, they're not quite human. I'm going to talk to Joe—"

"They're as human as you or I." Everyone at the table turned to look at Abigail.

"She's right," said Ronnie. "They're people, just like the rest of us. Just put together differently." Her face assumed a thoughtful expression. "I sometimes wonder if all of us aren't freaks, each in our own way."

"Or maybe all of us are beautiful in our own way." Abigail spooned more sugar into her tea, remembering how she'd promised to keep her opinions to herself.

Ronnie grabbed another muffin from the platter. "I believe you really mean that."

"Yes, I do."

"But what if we don't see ourselves as beautiful?" Ronnie smiled ruefully. "I suppose you'll say we should telephone Dr. Rome, and he'll take care of it?"

"It's not quite that simple, but often there's something he can do."

"But he can't change everything about a person, can he?"

"I'm not sure what you mean." Abigail was uncomfortable with the direction of Ronnie's questions. Too often, people had bizarre misconceptions about Franklin's work.

"What's the old saying—you can't make a silk purse out of a sow's ear?"

"No, I suppose not. But no one should think about herself that way. Or himself," she added, remembering the several men Franklin had treated in the time she had been with him.

"What about paraffin? They use it for all kinds of things, don't they?"

"Mostly for wrinkles, sometimes to build up a nose when the bridge is depressed—a *saddle nose*, they call it."

"And Frank does that?"

"Paraffin injections are one of his specialties."

"What about testicles?"

"I'm sorry, *what*?" Abigail thought she must have misheard.

"Testicles. I read somewhere they can be fashioned from paraffin wax. You know, if someone had lost them, maybe in an accident or something."

Alexandra broke in. "Oh, Ronnie, why don't you just come right out and say what's on your mind? You see, Abigail," she said snidely, "Ronnie has this notion that she's some sort of unique being, defying all the usual categories. She thinks, in her case, God made some sort of mistake. And she keeps trying to figure out how to correct it, but I'm afraid to no avail. Really, I find it hilarious."

"That's enough, Alexandra," Ronnie snapped, her face scarlet.

Abigail's shock at Alexandra's cruelty was exceeded only by her sympathy for Ronnie. How she would have liked to tell the countess what she really thought of her—or, better yet, break the news that Franklin, with whom Alexandra had flirted so shamelessly, had chosen *her*.

"Oh, very well! My point about the twins was that I don't understand why Joe would find it necessary to invite them to dine with us. Honestly, Lillian, I don't know how you live with that man."

"At least it's not dull. I guess I'm able to put up with his eccentricities because I understand him so well."

"What is there to understand?"

"Well ..." She sighed. "I shouldn't talk about him, not like this. But I have to say, Joe has a tremendous drive to achieve something grand. One might even call it an obsession. Maybe it's only to make himself feel important. We all need that sometimes, don't we?"

"Sounds like a typical man to me. Don't they always think they're something special? And yet Joe professes such humility. Everybody by their Christian names, he says. No respect for titles, as if they mean nothing at all when, in fact, they mean a great deal."

"Let's just say my husband is a mass of contradictions. Always trying to reconcile opposites. For example, he has it in his head that the world would be better off if humans could be as predictable as machines. Silly, isn't it? I told him—"

"Tell him to stop wasting his time. Human beings will never be predictable. And wanting to save the world gets no one anywhere, except into trouble. Isn't that right, Abigail?"

Abigail looked up in surprise. Why would the countess single her out for such a question? "I can't agree with Joe's notions about humans and machines, but I find the impulse to change things for the better quite admirable. Without it, there would be no such thing as progress."

"One person's idea of progress is another's treason," Alexandra shot back with a vehemence that came out of the blue.

"Alexandra is remembering her father," Lillian said with a sympathetic shake of her head. "A tragic story."

"My dear Abigail," the countess said in a tone that sounded more like anger than sorrow, "my father was part of an elite group called the People's Will, which directed the assassination of Czar Alexander the second. Their goal was to incite revolution among the Russian peasant class, but, unfortunately for them, the peasants did not share their zeal. My father and the others in his circle were arrested and killed. Which is why I say that it's best to leave things as they are. One person, or even a group of fanatics, cannot hope to change the world. In matters of social class, we are what we are. As my late husband, the Count, used to say, *Without the rich, the poor would have nothing to complain about.*"

Abigail was disturbed by Alexandra's story, especially her cavalier attitude. Perhaps it was only a cover for her pain.

"But come now, one can easily become melancholy from such deep thoughts so early in the morning," Lillian said, glancing at Ronnie with a worried look. "It's a lovely day, and I thought it would be fun for the four of us to take a little walk. Unless you ladies are too concerned for your complexions."

"I would enjoy a walk," Abigail answered, happy to move on to a lighter subject. She recalled the stunning impression the orchards and gardens had made on her when she and Franklin first arrived. It would be delightful to take a leisurely stroll among them.

"I'll come along," Ronnie said, pushing her chair back from the table.

"And you, Alexandra? Would you be in favor of some fresh air?"

The countess blotted her lips with a napkin. "I'm afraid not. Why don't the three of you go? I have other things to do."

"You're sure you don't mind if we leave you here alone?"

"Not at all. I can entertain myself."

Whatever Alexandra's reason for not joining them, Abigail was glad of it. Though she and the countess might have something in common—both had lost their fathers under trying circumstances—she still could not stand her.

. . . . .

After changing into her walking suit and a pair of sturdy boots, Abigail joined Lillian and Ronnie in front of the house, and they started off down the gravel driveway. From the east, a light breeze carried the fragrance of roses and butterfly bushes. Ahead, the Radcliffs' private road followed the soft roll of grassy fields on either side of it. To the west, there was only the deeper green of summer woods, ash and maple and oak stretching their branches to the sky in an intricate mosaic.

Abigail tried to picture how it would be to live in a place like this, so different from the gray city streets where she'd spent her entire life. It would be a wonderful setting in which to raise children—that is, if she were so inclined. But she was not, and couldn't imagine a single circumstance under which she might ever settle in such a remote spot. For her, the world revolved around Manhattan. And, perhaps, Franklin Rome.

"We've a decision to make," Lillian announced. She had stopped at the edge of the woods, just to the right of where the driveway ended and the private road leading to the public thoroughfare began. Ahead, a dirt path wound under a thick canopy of trees, a lovely dapple of sunlight lighting the way into what appeared a haven of tranquility.

"If we take a shortcut through these woods, it's about a mile to the asylum."

"Asylum!" Abigail thought Lillian must be joking.

"Are you up for the walk?"

"Of course, but—"

"Then let's go."

The path was just wide enough to walk two abreast; after a minute or two, Ronnie fell back. Abigail slowed her pace accordingly until Lillian assured her that Ronnie often liked to wander off alone, and they should leave her be; she would catch up. As they continued walking, silence settled over the two of them, broken only by the crunch of a twig beneath their boots or the scurrying of a squirrel among the leaves. Abigail's thoughts turned back to Franklin. In the light of day, the memory of last night's intimacy felt awkward, and she wondered again whether she had made a mistake. Would it have been better to leave things between them as they were before?

She remembered the night he surprised her with a private anatomy lesson, taking her step by step through the intricate dissection. He had explained his philosophy of beauty, recounted his favorite stories from Paris, as if he were speaking with a friend, a colleague. Or at least someone more important than his office girl.

Now that he was her lover, how would things change?

"Would you like to hear about the asylum?"

Abigail came back to herself with a start. "Asylum? Oh ... yes, of course."

Lillian pulled a white handkerchief from beneath the cuff of her shirtwaist and blotted her forehead. "It all began seventeen years ago, in 1890. Dr. Hans Schwann came here from Germany and spent two years planning and building what was to be an institution for the insane and mentally deficient. Then, just before the facility opened, the poor fellow died. The building sat there for another six years, until Joe came along and bought up forty acres to build our house, including the five that were part of Dr. Schwann's estate. I think everyone assumed Joe would knock the place down, but he's always wondered if there wasn't something he could do with it."

"No one was interested in taking it over for its original purpose?"

"Funny you should say that. There was a psychiatrist who made an offer at the same time Joe did. I remember bumping into him one afternoon when we came out to take another look at the place. He and Joe got into a terrible argument. Joe has quite a temper. But turns out he needn't have spouted off like that. As luck would have it—actually, not luck but misfortune—the other fellow had some kind of accident soon after, and he dropped out of the bidding. Joe was the only one left. Our neighbors in Scarsdale were relieved. The town wasn't happy at the idea of a mental institution in our midst. A lot of strange folks wandering about, and one never knows how good the security is at such places. I'm afraid they think Joe and me strange enough."

"I'm certain they don't," Abigail objected, though probably Lillian was right.

"I'm not ashamed to admit it, though Joe wishes I wouldn't, but neither of us comes from money. As for education, I don't have an awful lot of it, and neither does Joe, though he reads everything he can get his hands on. He's not literary, mind you, but very practical. If you look in our library, you'll see what I mean. It's full of how-to books, a bit of history, and not much else. He's always been good with machines, good at figuring things out for himself, or at least knowing where to look for answers. I suppose that's what has made him so successful."

"May I ask, what is his field?"

"I thought you knew. Joe is an inventor."

An inventor! At least that helped explain his eccentricity; creative people often could be unorthodox.

"What kinds of things does he invent?"

"Oh, I don't know. Just *things*—mostly for industrial purposes. Rather boring, I'm afraid. I think that's why he's so keen on branching out. You can only do so much with machines before you tire of them. Human beings are vastly more engaging—and complex. He's recently become obsessed with the field of medicine, how it might actually alter the course of human destiny."

"Well, yes, if someday we could find cures—"

"That's not what I mean. Of course, curing disease is important. But Joe is more interested in changing human beings themselves. He's just not sure yet how to go about it, but he's definitely fascinated by Frank's work."

"Many people are intrigued by Dr. Rome's work, but very few really understand it. If they did, it might lose much of its glamour. In fact, Joe would likely find a visit to Franklin's operating room rather boring." Something about what Lillian had said made her nervous. She was glad they were leaving tomorrow. There was no reason to have come at all—not if Franklin planned to dissuade the countess from removing her mole.

She was about to ask Lillian whether she knew if Alexandra was still considering the procedure when the trail ended, and they stepped from the shelter of the woods into intense heat and blinding sunlight. Stretched out before them was an open field of tall, reedy grass. At the far end, partially hidden by a tangle of trees and overgrown shrubbery, an immense structure was silhouetted against the cloudless blue sky. The three-story Gothic-style building was constructed of blood-red brick, with tall, arched windows and a circular tower capped by a domed peak.

"There's something spooky about it, don't you think?" Ronnie said, having caught up with them. She raised an arm, using her shirtsleeve to wipe her sweaty forehead.

"Ronnie knows the story. The reason the workers won't come out here. When Dr. Schwann passed away suddenly, there was a rumor that he'd hung himself from the tower. Completely false, but you know how those kinds of tall tales get passed along. Maybe that's one reason Joe could buy the property for a bargain price." Lillian gave Ronnie a questioning look. "Would you mind if we take Abigail for a closer look?"

"Fine with me." Ronnie started off, tramping through the high grass with her heavy boots, like the leader of a jungle safari. Lillian fell in behind her, and Abigail brought up the rear, taking advantage of the flattened path forged by the others.

The closer they drew to the asylum, the more foreboding it appeared. Abigail had once read the journalist Nellie Bly's 1887 exposé on the Blackwell's Island Insane Asylum. The horrors had made a lasting impression. She recalled how dozens of women inmates were forced to bathe in the same filthy tub of water, one towel to share among them. They were fed rotten food, forced to endure the freezing cold, condemned to torturous punishments. If they were sane—and some clearly were—it didn't matter. The authorities decided their mental status. These women, abandoned by family and society, were utterly powerless. She shivered to think of their fate and the suffering of so many others like them. Thankfully, in the last twenty years, people had become a great deal more enlightened about mental illnesses.

As for the legacy of the imposing structure before her, apparently there wasn't one. Lillian said that Dr. Schwann died just after the construction of his hospital was completed. This asylum had never housed a single patient. There was no history of abuse here. It was and always had been only an empty shell.

Hot and weary, they finally reached a driveway that wound in a circle in front of the building. Weeds had overtaken it, and everything else as well. A rusty wheelbarrow, rake, and hoe were tossed off to the side as if someone had thought to make a start at cleaning the place up. But nothing had been done here for a very long time. Lillian said the workers were afraid. Staring up at the massive edifice, Abigail could understand why they felt intimidated by its looming presence. It seemed like a relic from another age, a monstrosity. All the windows were boarded up. The massive double doors at the entrance were secured with a heavy chain. And the tower ... her eyes were drawn to the peaked dome, the black spiral. Yes, one might easily conjure up the image of Dr. Schwann's lifeless body swinging back and forth in the breeze.

Abigail was just about to make a comment about the power of imagination when she heard an automobile. A black Stoddard-Dayton touring car came lurching around the curve of a dirt road off to the right, barreling toward them at top speed. Joe was at the wheel. Franklin was with him.

Her pulse quickened. She'd been waiting all morning for the reunion that now was just a few moments away. How would it feel when their eyes met? What secret message would she read in his smile? Reassurance? The promise of pleasures to come? Perhaps something more?

Joe pulled up in a flurry of dust and shut down the engine. As he and Franklin disembarked, they exchanged a few words, and Joe let out a hearty laugh. Abigail's attention was all on Franklin, handsome in his stylish suit, the jacket left open to reveal a smart burgundy-and-gray striped waistcoat. She waited, breathless, for his approach. What would he say to her? Would they touch—a brush of the hand that no one else would notice?

"Ladies, if I may have everyone's attention," Joe shouted, hurrying toward the three women as if they'd been expecting him and he was late. The exertion made his face even redder than usual. When he reached them, he paused only long enough to plant a swift kiss on Lillian's cheek before clapping his hands like an excited child.

"Listen up, everybody! I have big news! Are you ready for this?"

"Go on, Joe," Lillian prodded. "Don't keep us in suspense."

"All right, all right! I'm delighted to announce that Dr. Franklin Rome and I have just consummated the deal of the century." He turned to Franklin, who was just a few steps behind him. "I trust I'm not overstating it, am I, Frank?"

"Not in the least."

Coming up beside Joe, smiling broadly, Franklin acknowledged Abigail with an indifferent nod. His gaze was fixed on the building rising to the sky behind her, casting its giant shadow over them all.

Joe raised his eyes to the peak of the circular tower, placing a hand over his heart with a look of reverence. "Dr. Schwann, I know things didn't turn out as you planned, but all is not lost. Meet Dr. Franklin Rome, my new partner and the proprietor of your little hospital, henceforth to be called the Rome Institute of Transformative Surgery!"

CHAPTER 10

"Hope everybody's hungry for lunch!" Lillian took her seat at a round table on the porch overlooking the estate's rear property. "I thought it would be pleasant to eat out here," she said brightly. "Abigail, why don't you sit next to Frank. Alexandra, Ronnie—over here. Joe, you mustn't start eating yet!"

Her head pounding, Abigail took the assigned chair, careful to avoid brushing against Franklin who was already seated. After returning from the asylum, each had gone to their separate rooms to dress for lunch. They had not spoken. They had not touched. She might as well have been invisible.

He must have known this was coming, even before they left for Scarsdale on Friday. He'd hinted at something important. More important than Alexandra's mole. And Lillian had seemed aware of it, too. In fact, Abigail might be the only one for whom the Rome Institute of Transformative Surgery was a complete surprise. But why hadn't he told her?

Was it because he no longer would have any use for her?

"What do you think about this Typhoid Mary?" Joe said, his mouth full of salad greens. "The one they say made all those people sick? I say they should put her away. Can't have her running all over the place, infecting everybody. It's in the public welfare to lock her up. Don't you agree, Frank?"

"Apparently she shows no symptoms herself, but at least some period of isolation would seem mandatory," Franklin responded, assuming his most judicious air.

"I've always said you can't be too careful with the help," declared the countess, "especially if they're Irish."

Abigail had just picked up her fork but now set it down abruptly, her frustration finding a suitable enough target in Alexandra. "Typhoid fever is neither a matter of class nor nationality."

"Oh my, seems we have a reformer among us." Alexandra, her lips curled in a half smile, reached for her wineglass. "Unless what I said offended you personally, Abigail, in which case I apologize. I didn't realize Platford was an Irish name."

"I'm sure Abigail was only trying to clarify the situation," Franklin interjected, shooting her a sharp sideways glance. "However, there's no denying that the woman's occupation as a cook in various households might offer ample opportunity to spread the disease."

"Precisely my point!"

"If we're looking for something to worry about, they say this latest recession is more likely than typhoid fever to do us in," Lillian said, circumventing any further disagreement among her guests.

"Don't be ridiculous!" Joe broke open a hot roll and slathered it with butter. "Stock market fluctuations are inevitable. You either have the stomach for it or you don't. And if you don't, you shouldn't be in it. Besides, I doubt the recession is going to last too long. And even if it does, I'm not worried."

"That's good to hear," Franklin said, giving Joe a meaningful smile—a smile between partners, Abigail thought bitterly.

"Fact is, it's going to take a boatload of cash to finance this new institute, but I'm looking forward to getting started. I've already got an architect in mind for the renovation. And it's not too early to think about personnel, Frank. This won't be some hole-in-the-wall place like you're in now. It's got to be run like a hospital, with only the best and the brightest. How many nurses do you figure you'll need?"

"Well ..." Franklin appeared surprised by the question. "I haven't really thought about it yet—maybe two or three."

"Come on, you've got to think bigger than that, my friend! I'm expecting you'll need at least a dozen. You'll want to bring another doctor on board—not as a partner, of course. We'll limit that to the two of us. But you'll need an extra pair of hands, won't you? Someone to assist you, maybe take some cases of his own when you get too busy? We'll take a percentage of everything he brings in. Don't worry, I won't be greedy." He laughed. "Like I told you, my interest is purely scientific. You're going to teach me everything you know, Frank, and I'll figure out how I want to use it. Which reminds me, I want you to conduct a thorough examination of those girls, the twins. This afternoon. Where are they, anyway?"

His comment shook Abigail from the morose contemplation of all she'd just heard.

"Went somewhere with Ludwik this morning," Ronnie offered.

"But they're back now," said Lillian. "They weren't interested in lunch. I believe they're out in the gazebo, reading."

"Splendid!" Joe beamed at Franklin. "You can head over there when we're done eating."

"Why should Frank want to examine them?" The countess crinkled her nose in disgust. "It's horrible to imagine living like that, isn't it?"

"They actually do very well," Joe said. "I admit to being quite taken with them. I'd like to study them, test their physical capabilities, their intelligence. How they handle duress."

"I suspect you were one of those awful little boys who like to capture centipedes and then pull their legs off, one by one," the countess said, laughing.

"But, Frank," Joe began again, "I really think we're onto something here. Wouldn't this be just the thing to catapult you onto the front pages? 'Beauty Doc Operates on Freak Show Star Attraction.' I love it!"

"I don't know, Joe—"

"Well, you'll examine them." Joe motioned to the servants to remove his salad plate. "I'll be eager to hear what you think after that."

"Ordinarily, removal of a nasal hump is safe and predictable. But for them—" Franklin shook his head. "In all likelihood, one would not consider them suitable candidates for any type of surgery. Certainly not for an operation that, in their case, is unnecessary."

"Is beauty surgery ever *necessary*? Of course not! But I'm sure you're not in the habit of turning patients away. I'd be willing to bet you have no qualms about operating on virtually anyone who walks through your office door with cash in hand. Am I right?"

Franklin cleared his throat. "Well, I wouldn't say *that*. But it's true that what one person considers unnecessary can be of the most vital importance to another. That's what makes beauty surgery so different from other branches of medicine. The impetus can be as much psychological as physical."

"A very important point! It will be helpful to our little enterprise if more people understand that *need* takes many forms. Which is why performing beauty surgery on the Siamese twins is the greatest publicity stunt ever conceived." Joe leaned back in his chair with a self-satisfied grin. "If we're going to be partners, Frank, you're going to have to trust me on certain things. I'm a businessman. An entrepreneur. I know what sells." He pulled a cigarette from his pocket and lit up. "Listen, nobody goes overnight from being an obscure doc in a tiny Manhattan office to being the world's most acclaimed beauty doctor—not without doing something pretty jaw-dropping. An opportunity like this, operating on the rarest Siamese twins on the planet, doesn't come along every day. We'd be fools not to take it."

And Joe was no fool, Abigail thought bitterly. There seemed, in fact, only one idiot among the group seated at the Radcliffs' table. How could she have been so trusting?

"Joe is right," said Alexandra. "After all, not feeling beautiful is its own sort of tragedy, isn't it?"

"Maybe so," Lillian said, absently smoothing her unruly hair. "It's true that sometimes, without meaning to, I'll see my reflection in a mirror or a window, and suddenly realize the old witch with all the wrinkles is me. But would I ever go under the knife?" She shrugged. "Don't be offended, Frank, but I'm not sure I would trust anyone that much, not even you. And I don't know, when all is said and done, if I'd be happy with a face different from the one I'm used to."

"The art of the beauty doctor is not to give his patient a *different* face, only a *better* one," Franklin replied smoothly.

"Nicely put, Frank!" Joe pulled out his ever-present notebook and made a quick scribble. "Let's remember that one. 'Not a different face, just a better one.' Great slogan!"

•　　•　　•　　•　　•

"Franklin, wait."

With lunch finally over, and everyone going their own way, Abigail had silently trailed him into the hallway. He turned around as if surprised to see her.

"I thought you'd be headed upstairs for a nap."

His words seemed a wicked reminder of why neither of them had slept much last night—and how little it meant to him now.

"I need to talk with you."

"We can chat on the way out to the gazebo, if you like."

"I'm not going with you to the gazebo. And I don't want to *chat*. I want to *talk*."

She half expected him to say he hadn't time. "All right, but you'll have to walk with me."

They circled around the house in silence. Abigail didn't have a hat, and it was too late to go back for one. The sun beat down on her face, and the dry, dusty air made it hard to breathe. Somewhere close by, she heard the harsh cry of a sentinel crow.

"What's on your mind?"

Her anger seemed to have lost its edge. All she wanted now was to pour out her heart to Franklin, to make him understand what last night had meant to her, how lost and alone she felt today.

"Why didn't you tell me about your plans?" She stared at the ground, barely able to place one foot before the other, as they turned down the trail leading to the gazebo. "Why did I have to hear it first from Joe Radcliff?"

"I didn't realize I had to consult with you about such matters."

"You' don't *have to*. But I thought—" She could feel the tears coming. Ferociously, she swiped the back of her hand over her eyes. "You might at least have given me some warning before you pulled the rug out from under me."

"I haven't pulled out any rug, and I won't have you talking that way. What's the matter with you? Why are you so quick to assume the worst?"

Was he right? Was that what she was doing?

"It just seems as if everything has changed overnight. It wasn't what I expected. None of it was."

He stopped, grabbing her by the shoulders and turning her so he was looking straight into her eyes. "I want you to listen carefully. I've stumbled on an opportunity far beyond anything I imagined possible. And if you are really as smart as you pretend to be, you'll recognize it and embrace it."

"What am I supposed to embrace? I know nothing about your deal with Joe. Or what it means for—" She stopped, unsure whether to say *for me* or *for us*. Perhaps there was no *us* and never had been.

"Now isn't the time for that conversation."

"Why not?"

"Because the details have yet to be worked out."

"The details of *what*?"

"You know very well I'm speaking of the Rome Institute."

"And I am speaking of more than that. I thought last night was the start of something. Not the end."

"Abigail." His tone was gentler. He took her hand and lifted it to his lips. "I'm sorry not to have told you about the Institute. It was a very sudden thing. I honestly wasn't sure until this morning whether Joe was serious. And when he's serious, he moves fast. I've learned that much about him already. There was absolutely no chance, not a single moment, for me to talk with you alone."

She brushed a renegade tear from her cheek, determined not to fall apart in front of him. "We wouldn't be talking even now if I hadn't insisted on it."

"Just be quiet for a moment and listen to what I have to say. Can you do that?"

She prepared herself for another of his lectures about how she should or shouldn't feel.

"Now, close your eyes."

"What for?"

"I want you to use that very fertile imagination of yours to form a mental image of everything I'm about to say. Just try, will you?"

"I suppose," she said, rolling her eyes before she closed them.

"Now...visualize the Rome Institute. Imagine it, Abigail! Patients coming from across the country, around the world, women of virtually every description but with one thing in common: a thirst for beauty. And paying handsomely, I might add, to be artfully molded in the hands of the world-famous Dr. Franklin Rome."

Abigail opened her mouth to say something, but he pressed a long finger to her lips.

"Quiet. Just think of it. Those women staying at the Institute not just overnight but for days or even weeks at a time. Enjoying customized beauty treatments, lounging in lavish suites with all the panache of a luxury hotel, pampered by a professional nursing staff, their meals prepared by a superb private chef. You see? The Rome Institute won't be a beauty *hospital*; it will be a beauty *destination*!"

She opened her eyes. "But the people who come to you for surgery want it to be quick and painless. I don't see what can be accomplished by pretending it's a vacation. No one will want to stay a second longer than they must."

"You're wrong. Even some of the city hospitals are now offering luxury accommodations for those who can afford them—fancy rooms and gourmet meals. And that's for people who are sick. A beauty institute with patients who are there by choice, not necessity, should be expected to do even better. And Scarsdale is the perfect location. Close enough to the city for convenience, far enough so no one has to know. A woman can disappear for days or weeks or however long it might take for her transformation. And when she returns home, everyone will look at her and scratch their heads, wondering what she's done to look so refreshed, so beautiful and youthful. Was it only a vacation, they'll ask? And she'll insist, of course, that it was." He chuckled. "Joe's concept is brilliant."

She had no intention of saying so, but it wasn't Joe's *concept* that bothered her. It was the other things he'd said only an hour ago at lunch. At the Rome Institute, Franklin would have plenty of trained doctors and nurses to assist him. What use would he have for her? Perhaps the only thing he'd ever wanted from her was what she'd foolishly surrendered to him last night.

Franklin pulled out his pocket watch. "It's getting late, and I need to examine the twins. Come on along."

"I'm sure you don't need me."

He heaved an exasperated sigh. "Look, I've already said I'm sorry. But Joe's concept is the future. I never dreamed it would happen so fast, but once again, fortune has smiled on me. I would be remiss not to smile back."

"Well, congratulations then. I wish for your good luck to continue."

"Don't sound so glum. This is an unbelievable opportunity for you."

She sniffed. "For *me*? I don't see how."

"You will if you'll just open your mind to the possibilities."

Open her mind? It was easy enough for him to say. He had everything to gain.

Unable to meet his eyes, she let her gaze wander down the path leading to the gazebo. A long, empty trail; one would never guess what waited at the end, the beautiful white gazebo with its fragrant rose gardens. One would never know until almost there, when the first line of hedges came into view and the gazebo's sloping green roof appeared against the bright blue sky.

Could Franklin be right about opening her mind? It was doubtful he realized how much she had done so already, the effort of will it had taken to alter her long-held beliefs about what a doctor is and does. And now the Institute—a hospital masquerading as a vacation resort.

There was nothing to do but wait and see. Did Franklin truly care for her? Or would she soon be on her own and again without hope?

·　·　·　·　·

"Good afternoon!"

Ludwik looked up from his book, strikingly handsome in a light tan suit and blue silk tie that played brilliantly off his eyes. "Miss Platford. Dr. Rome. What brings the two of you out to the gazebo on this lovely afternoon?"

He stood, tipping his straw boater toward Abigail before he and Franklin shook hands.

"I was intrigued last night to learn that your girls would like to have me fix their noses." Franklin smiled at the twins, both of whom had stopped reading and were watching the three of them intently. "I wondered if I might have a look at them to determine whether the idea is workable."

Ludwik glanced at the twins with a stern expression that suggested they'd already discussed the matter. "Very kind of you, but I'm afraid you are wasting your time, Doctor."

"Maybe so. But I thought, with your permission, I might give them just a quick examination."

"Really, you needn't bother."

"It's no bother."

Ludwik drew himself up so he appeared almost as tall as Franklin. "Maybe you didn't hear me, Doctor. I said you are wasting your time."

"But Mr. Radcliff thinks—"

"Mr. Radcliff has nothing to do with this. The twins are guests here, nothing more. This idea they have about their noses is just a passing fancy. A reaction to the insensitive comments of others. They'll get over it." His face softened a bit. "It's not that I don't respect your work, Doctor," he said in a more conciliatory tone. "But save it for those who can benefit from it. Not my girls."

"Let's discuss all this later between the two of us. You understand, I've promised Joe that I'll at least examine the girls. No harm in that, is there?" Franklin lowered his voice to a confidential whisper. "Chances are they're not candidates for an operation. I can tell them so today, right now. The verdict of the good doctor will put an end to it!"

Ludwik looked again at the girls, who hastily buried their heads in their books.

"Well, you might have a point," he said, seeming to ease up somewhat. "They've been nagging me to no end. Sometimes it's like having two wives, if you can imagine the bloody pain of that!"

"Of course." Franklin barely cracked a smile, clearly impatient to get down to business. "I wonder if you can tell me whether the girls have separate hearts and lungs."

"I've been told they do."

"And they are in good physical health—both of them?"

"As you might expect, they have a few problems."

"Such as?"

"Each twin controls her half of their body, so one must always coordinate her movements with the other. They've mastered the technique well, but you may have noticed they walk with a limp—because Melilla's leg is shorter than Valencia's."

"That should have no impact on whether surgery can be performed on their noses," Franklin said brusquely. "They have no trouble with their breathing?"

Ludwik again seemed annoyed. "All these questions—it doesn't sound to me as if you've ruled out the possibility of operating on them, Doctor."

"Mr. Radcliff is only thinking of the girls. He wants them to be happy."

"I assure you, they're quite happy as they are."

"I know that's what you believe, but—perhaps you don't understand."

"I understand completely."

Franklin lowered his voice. "What I mean is, Mr. Radcliff realizes what a rare and valuable specimen the girls are. Apparently, there's nothing else like them alive in the world today. He's willing to compensate you accordingly."

Abigail looked at him, aghast. He surely meant something different from the way it sounded. Ludwik was fuming.

"I will do my best to forget that Mr. Radcliff, and you, as his messenger, ever dared suggest such a thing to me. My girls are not specimens, and they are not for sale at any price."

"I didn't mean to insult you, Baron, but Joe led me to believe that *you* paid a rather substantial sum for them yourself. So, naturally, we thought—"

"I've made a commitment to these girls, and I plan to honor it. I'm afraid I don't share your willingness to breach any oath as long as there's enough money on the table."

"That kind of remark is entirely uncalled for, sir," Franklin said imperiously. "There's no shame in desiring to be beautiful. I have devoted myself to assisting those who have such a desire, and I will not apologize for it."

"You are free to devote yourself to whatever you choose, but your help is not needed here. Now, if you'll be so kind as to excuse us, the twins and I are heading back to the house."

Ludwik turned to the girls, who already were rising from the wicker sofa. "Let's allow the doctor and his assistant to enjoy the gazebo," he said, motioning for the twins to hurry along. As they limped past, Melilla turned her head and slipped Abigail a furtive smile.

*   *   *   *   *

It was eight o'clock that evening when Abigail entered the dining room. She had hoped Ludwik might be there and she could have a word with him before Franklin arrived. She wanted to apologize and let him know she had nothing to do with what happened earlier. She agreed with him about the twins.

But only Lillian and Ronnie were seated at the table, and there were just four places set for dinner.

"Sad to say, we've lost all our gentlemen," Lillian said apologetically. "Joe and Franklin are tied up in some sort of meeting, and I'm afraid Ludwik won't be joining us either."

So, she was to dine with the ladies while Franklin and Joe discussed their plans for the Institute.

"I'm sure Alexandra will be down any minute," Lillian said.

"No, she won't." Ronnie picked up her linen napkin. "She's not feeling well. Best if she stays up in her room."

"What a pity," Abigail murmured, though she was relieved to be spared the countess's company. Especially with so much of importance on her mind. Literally overnight, her world had been turned upside down. Everything she cared about was in jeopardy. Worst of all, her fate largely depended on Joe Radcliff.

Lillian pushed back her chair, preparing to rise. "I'll have a tray sent up to her."

Ronnie held up her hand. "Please don't. Honestly, she wants nothing. Leave her alone. She'll feel better in the morning."

Lillian hesitated, her eyes searching Ronnie's face. "One of *those* evenings?"

Ronnie nodded.

"I hope it's nothing serious," Abigail said, just to be polite.

"It never is," Ronnie replied.

A casual dinner of roasted chicken and braised vegetables from the Radcliff's garden proceeded pleasantly enough. The conversation, though far short of scintillating, at least kept Abigail from examining and reexamining everything that had happened over the last twenty-four hours. Still, it was difficult to keep her eyes from glazing over as Lillian went into excruciating detail regarding the trials of managing her household staff, while Ronnie recounted her various adventures abroad, which consisted mostly of eating, drinking, and cavorting with a great number of extraordinarily wealthy people.

What a strange bird Ronnie was! Abigail thought it astonishing that she and Alexandra would be friends, let alone...well, the basis of their relationship remained a mystery. If, by adopting men's clothing and short-cropped hair, Ronnie had become a so-called *New Woman*, the countess did not strike Abigail as that sort. Not the way she constantly flirted with Franklin—unless that was only subterfuge. As Abigail had learned over the past few months, appearances can be deceiving.

Such thoughts kept her occupied for the duration of dinner. After they had finished their dessert of rhubarb pie and a selection of cheeses, Ronnie left to check on Alexandra. Lillian asked if there was anything special Abigail would like to do.

"I'd love to read for a while—if you don't mind showing me to the library," she added, hoping Lillian would understand she wished to be alone.

Even a library full of books to explore could not distract Abigail from her troubles. Once Lillian had said good night, her thoughts turned again to Franklin. She wondered if he would come to her bedroom tonight. And if he did, how should she respond? This morning, the answer would have been simple. But his behavior toward her since then suggested their romantic liaison meant one thing to her and something entirely different to him. Perhaps he had thought of last night as his best chance to seduce her, before she found out the office in Manhattan was, for him, just a brief stop along the way. The Rome Institute was his future. He and Joe were partners.

She pictured herself on the path to the gazebo, remembering how, for a second, she had embraced the unknown. But it seemed impossible now to recapture that moment or have any faith in the kindness of fate.

Weary of thinking, she lifted her gaze to the volumes lining the shelves of the Radcliffs' library. For people without a literary bent, as Lillian had admitted, they had a lot of books. Somewhere among them must be a great classic or at least an interesting work of fiction.

She approached the nearest shelf and skimmed the titles. They seemed in no particular order. One on fishing was next to a manual on mechanical engineering, and beside that was a thick volume on the history of Western Europe. One title captured her interest: *In Pursuit of Human Perfection* by Theodore Gallagher, published in 1905. Sliding it off the shelf, she tucked the book under her arm and went to sit by the empty fireplace.

Flipping through the pages, what first caught her attention were the frequent instances of underlining in black ink. Someone had read this book and thought it important enough to make notations. She stopped to read a few pages in one of the early chapters, in which the author had made a list of what he labeled the most *desirable* facial characteristics. Falling unthinkingly into her old habits, she wondered if this could have any relevance to beauty surgery—and if Franklin might be interested.

She went back to the foreword at the book's beginning. By the time she had finished reading it, she understood that

Gallagher's interest and intent had nothing to do with either beauty or surgery. His goal was the creation of a super race. Gallagher wished to design human beings like Ford designed cars. The more she read, the more she found his ideas not only flawed but deeply disturbing. What he suggested was a view of humans that favored certain groups and gave those in authority the right to purge society of all others. It was not a standard of beauty he sought to impose as much as standards of *normalcy* and *acceptability*—rigid standards that would automatically exclude vast segments of the population. His proposals, he said, were aimed at rooting out hereditary defects and "perfecting the species." He placed these principles within the context of what he called *eugenics*.

She was engrossed in a particularly troubling chapter, advocating the most shocking methods to speed this process of *favorable evolution*, when the door to the library swung open.

"Miss Platford!" Ludwik was dressed as she had seen him that afternoon, minus his straw boater. "I don't mean to intrude, but I saw a light and thought I might find Mr. Radcliff."

"I believe Joe and Dr. Rome are over at the old asylum, mapping out plans for its renovation. But then, I don't suppose you've heard about Joe's idea for a hospital."

"Yes, I caught wind of it." He glanced around the room as if making certain they were alone. "By the way, I hope you'll forgive my behavior this afternoon. But I'm sure you understand my concern about Valencia and Melilla."

"No need to apologize. I understand perfectly. Surgery is a serious matter. Besides, the girls are lovely as they are," she said, hoping he would understand how sorry she was for all the insensitive comments the twins had been forced to endure since their arrival in Scarsdale.

"I'm glad you see it that way. I wasn't sure. I wondered if your views might be the same as Dr. Rome's."

"This afternoon, I believe he was speaking for Joe more than for himself."

"Really? I didn't get that impression. His desire to operate on the twins was obvious to me."

"Oh no, I'm sure not." There followed an awkward silence. "Won't you come in and sit down?" she asked, gesturing toward the vacant chair opposite her. Though she'd sought solitude in the library, the chance to learn more about him was not unwelcome.

He entered, closing the door behind him. As Abigail watched him approach, she recalled what Franklin once said about the entitlements of beauty; it was much the same, she supposed, for a handsome baron. Ludwik must be used to women competing for his attention. She was intrigued that he had chosen the rather staid role of guardian for a pair of Siamese-twin girls.

"I must confess, I find the whole concept of beauty surgery a bit off-putting," he said, settling himself into the other fireside chair. "Clearly, you don't."

She didn't know how to answer him. When she had accepted the position with Franklin, it was only a matter of expediency. Now, her feelings were more complicated.

"I've always had an affinity for medicine—the old-fashioned kind. But then I met Dr. Rome. He's taught me a great deal."

"This *transformative* surgery, as the doctor likes to call it— you believe it has value?"

She hesitated, again battling herself. "I have seen instances where patients seemed happier as a result," she said, realizing suddenly how much she wanted to believe it was so. How else could she justify the path she'd chosen, even temporarily.

"I'm in no position to argue with you, Miss Platford. All I know is that it's not for my girls. They're just children. What do they really know of such things and the consequences, good or bad?"

"I agree. But do you mind if I ask, what brings you and the girls here? Have you been friends with the Radcliffs for long?"

"I wouldn't call us friends. I'm an investor in Mr. Radcliff's project—or at least I was."

She was incredulous. "The Institute?"

"No, no. The other project—Mr. Radcliff's museum."

He ran a hand through his hair in a manner that conveyed an undercurrent of frustration. "I should start at the beginning. A few months ago, I met Mr. Radcliff in London through a mutual acquaintance, an old friend of my father's. A newspaperman named Samuel Storey."

"Storey? What a perfect name for someone in the newspaper trade!"

He nodded. "I've often thought the same. A fine fellow, he is, too. I'm not sure how Mr. Radcliff was acquainted with him, but we both were in attendance at a small dinner party at Mr. Storey's home when Mr. Radcliff mentioned he'd always had a fascination with, as he called them, *freaks*. Though I was put off by his use of an appellation I find abhorrent, once we got to talking, he seemed uncommonly appreciative of these rare human beings. Their resilience and determination to thrive. He said he was putting together a collection of historical displays intended to counter the prejudices that still exist against them. I thought the concept was interesting and so I wrote him a check."

"I didn't realize Joe was in need of other people's money," Abigail remarked drily, remembering how their host had boasted of the *boatload* of cash he'd be spending on the new institute.

"It was a nominal sum. I meant it only as a show of support, to encourage the endeavor if it might truly do some good."

She still wondered about his motive for assuming guardianship of the twins. Might he have profited from them personally? There were enough unscrupulous sorts who made a living by displaying their unfortunate charges for the public's amusement.

"This summer, my girls and I had planned a trip to New York. When we arrived from London a few days ago, I telephoned to see if we might stop by and see what progress had been made with the museum. Mr. Radcliff did not bother telling me that nothing has been done at all. It doesn't take much to see his enthusiasm now lies elsewhere."

"You believe he's abandoned the idea of a museum altogether?"

"There's been a change in his attitude—a change I don't like. He now refers to his project as a museum of *human oddities*. And his behavior toward my girls has been nothing short of deplorable."

"I agree." She was glad to know someone else shared her ambivalence toward Joe.

"I'm disappointed, but he's certainly free to do whatever he wishes. As things stand now, the twins and I have no reason to stay."

"You're leaving?"

"Yes, tomorrow morning."

She hesitated, unsure if she was being too inquisitive. But she felt a rapport had developed between them that might allow her curiosity. "If you don't mind my asking, how did you come to be the twins' guardian?"

"It was a matter of mutual necessity, Miss Platford."

"Mutual?"

"Yes, they needed me and, though it may surprise you, I needed them just as much. You might say that I had a debt to pay." He folded his hands, resting them in his lap. "I won't trouble you with *that* story. It's not a pretty one."

"But I'm interested," Abigail insisted.

"I wouldn't wish for you to think poorly of me," he said, staring into the cold fireplace.

"I'm sure there would be no reason for me to judge, in that way or any other."

"You are very kind. I could see that about you from the moment we met. I'm sorry if I didn't act like it this afternoon, in the heat of the moment."

"Please, don't worry about that."

"Well...when you've heard my tale, I think you'll understand why I am fiercely protective of the twins."

His look was so earnest, she felt ashamed of her earlier doubts about him.

"When I was twelve, my stepmother gave birth to a baby girl with severe defects. Rather than suffer the disgrace, she arranged quietly to have the child destroyed. Thinking myself the hero, I snatched the baby and took her away. There was a chap who claimed he and his wife would give her a fine home but insisted I pay him a large sum of cash to cover the care she would need. An amount of money not easy for a twelve-year-old to get his hands on, other than by a bit of shrewd deception. I thought I had done well for my little sister, until quite a few years later when I learned the truth of what happened to her."

Abigail's heart stalled. His words seemed to presage something nightmarish. After all, maybe she didn't want to know.

"It turns out the man ran a carnival," Ludwik said. "One of those despicable sideshows where they exhibit people with defects like circus animals. My sister had become one of his star attractions. You may have heard the argument that people like her should count themselves lucky to have work, and carnival life isn't really so bad? Don't believe it. The man was a monster. I saw the proof of it myself." He swallowed hard. "I tried to rescue her. Unfortunately, all I got for my efforts were a few broken ribs.

Seems that carnival folks stick together, and it was me against ten or twelve of them. By the time I was ready to try again, the show had moved on. When I finally tracked it down, months later, my sister was no longer with them. I was told she had died of a severe illness. It took me a while, but eventually I had the proof. It was cholera. I was too late to save her, but at least I knew she wasn't still suffering. That, I'm afraid, is my only consolation."

"So. you saved Valencia and Melilla instead." Abigail was on the verge of tears. "The twins became your little sisters."

"I suppose you could say that." He regarded her with a worried frown. "I'm sorry. I didn't mean to upset you. You must have more pleasant things to think about on a lovely night like this."

"Not really. And I'm glad you told me. I only hope you won't continue to torture yourself with thoughts of your sister. You were only a child yourself, and you tried your best to help her."

"All that is true, but the heart tends not to look at things so rationally."

"Yes—I know," she said, realizing that both of them carried the same burden: a failed attempt to save someone they loved.

Just then, the stillness of the library was shaken by a loud clatter from the hallway, followed by a shriek. The door to the library burst open. Wobbling in the threshold, the countess was a sight to behold—half-naked, wearing only a shift and a loosely fastened white corset. Long garters held up her black silk stockings, her feet clad in shiny patent leather boots with big gold buckles. A pair of opera-length evening gloves added to the absurdity of the ensemble,

"Well, well. What have we here?" She steadied herself with the door frame, a crooked smile on her lips, her voice oozing like syrup. "When the cat's away, the mice ..." She fixed her bleary-eyed gaze on Abigail. "I wonder what Frank would say if he knew his little virgin was carrying on with another man. But then, I guess you're not so lily pure. Not after last night." She threw back her head with a derisive snort.

Ludwik's face had turned bright red, though he could not have been as mortified as Abigail. She had known Alexandra's room was next to hers, but never stopped to think her neighbor might be listening through the wall.

"Ronnie said you weren't feeling well," Abigail said, trying to maintain her composure. "Maybe you need me to help you back upstairs."

"*Maybe* I don't want to go upstairs. *Maybe* I want to stay right here, with the two of you—and read a book!" A glistening string of spittle dribbled down her chin.

Ludwik took a step toward her. "Countess Alexandra, I'd be more than happy to escort you to your room."

"No, I'll wait for Frank. He'll be coming after me any second now." She turned her head to toss Abigail a wicked smile.

Astonishingly, the next moment, Franklin appeared from the hallway, jacketless, his tie loose around his neck. Abigail had not realized he and Joe were back. But there he stood, just behind the countess, who was propped against the threshold as if she might collapse without it. She rolled her head around and looked up at him.

"Frank, I knew you'd come." She tried to stand straight, but began to tip over. He reached out to steady her. Abigail watched as she swooned in his arms, babbling some incoherent nonsense about stars and tea leaves and satin sheets. She'd never witnessed such a disgusting display of debauchery!

"Let's get you upstairs, Alexandra," Franklin said, acknowledging neither Abigail nor Ludwik.

"Do you need a hand, Doctor?" Ludwik offered, jumping up from his chair.

"I can manage."

"Of course you can, darling," the countess said in a slurred drawl. "Let us leave these bibliophiles to their sophomoric inquiries. I prefer to explore the deeper meaning of life—upstairs."

She looped her arm through Franklin's, took a few tentative steps and, finding her legs solid enough, allowed him to lead her away. After they had disappeared and the sound of her drunken laughter faded, Ludwik turned to Abigail.

"Bloody disgraceful, wasn't it? She probably had no idea what she was saying. All such rubbish."

She was grateful for his diplomacy but hastened to change the subject. "Her head will be pounding in the morning."

"Yes, no doubt." He inhaled deeply, pressing his palms together. "Well, now that all the excitement is over, I'll wish you a good night. Unless—" He eyed her with a look of concern. "You'll be all right?"

"I'm fine."

He smiled. Mercifully, she thought, for no one could imagine her to be *fine* after such a humiliating encounter.

"I wish you the best, Miss Platford. Though we've only just met, I won't soon forget you."

Before she could decide whether it was proper to return the compliment, Ludwik was gone.

CHAPTER 11

A bigail awoke before five, the lamp at her bedside still lit. Franklin had not come to her last night.

She was ashamed to have left the door unlocked for him. After what she'd seen in the library? He'd offered no explanation, ignoring her completely, as if she wasn't there watching every moment of the disgusting little drama as it played itself out.

Yet she'd waited for him, wanting him to come. Needing to know if he still desired her. She longed to hear him say that he did and there was no reason to worry; he cared for her and would not let her down. The Rome Institute meant nothing to him without her.

But that was ridiculous. She'd been crazy to think she was important to him. In his mind, she was just a homeless waif he'd taken pity on—before robbing her of her innocence and her pride. Forever, she'd have to live with her disgrace. To be desired by him once, but not again, was worse than if he'd never wanted her at all.

Half the night, she had lain awake trying to imagine a way she could carry on. Pretend their affair had meant as little to her as it did to him. Act as if, all along, she had expected nothing to come of it. But how could she go back to being just his assistant, standing across the operating table, passing instruments with gloved hands while she so desperately longed for the warmth of his touch? It would be intolerable. As was the alternative: a future without Franklin Rome as her mentor. Or her lover. At that moment, she wasn't sure which was more vital to her happiness, but having arrived at such an impasse was perhaps the most frightening thing of all. Had she lost all reason?

With a heavy heart, she pushed back the covers and got out of bed. In the bathroom, she sponged herself down, brushed her teeth, and rinsed her mouth with Odol before dressing for a walk—a simple skirt, white blouse, and boots. Arranging her hair in a loose chignon, she was ready.

Opening the bedroom door, Abigail made sure no one was around and then tiptoed along the hallway and down the stairs. The first floor was also deserted. allowing her to escape without need of explanation.

The sun was still low in the sky. Even the birds had not yet left their nests. The only sounds were the faint rustling of leaves blowing in the breeze and the occasional chirp of a cricket in search of a mate. Though she had counted on nature to lift her spirits, her thoughts kept turning back to Franklin.

An honest accounting of their professional relationship could lead to only one conclusion: She was of limited value to him. Franklin had taught her enough to make her useful, but she was not indispensable. And with Joe willing to pay for whatever he needed in the way of assistance—doctors and nurses far more qualified than she—why would Franklin want to keep her on?

Yet an honorable man does not presume to take a thing as precious as a woman's virtue without paying the proper respect. Neither does he create expectations with no intention of fulfilling them. Nor leave in tatters a heart that has opened itself so trustingly, believing there was nothing to fear.

"Good morning!"

She spun around, her hand flying to her chest. Behind her on the path, Ludwick was only a few yards back. He carried a black leather bag over one shoulder and a camera in his hand. His face glowed with a light film of perspiration.

Abigail nervously poked a loose strand of hair back into her chignon, hoping she didn't look too unkempt. "I didn't expect to see anyone out here this early."

"Nor did I." He held up his camera, a black box with an accordion-like extension, at the end of which was a round lens. "I wanted to get a few more shots of the landscape before the girls and I leave. I like the way things look in the early morning light."

"I didn't know you're a photographer."

"Just a hobby. They're doing so much with cameras these days. I've recently started experimenting with color, so I can occasionally pretend to be something more than an amateur. But I am most fond of my little folding camera. Easy to carry around and enough of a challenge." Squinting into the rising sun, he lowered the brim of his straw boater. "What brings you out so early?"

"A last look at the rose gardens around the gazebo. Everything is so beautiful here. I don't want to forget."

He gave her a curious look. "You sound as if you don't expect to be back. But aren't you going to work at Mr. Radcliff's new institute with your Dr. Rome?"

Abigail bristled. "He's not *my* Dr. Rome. And I don't know if I'll be continuing on at the Institute."

"I thought you enjoyed your work."

"I do, but it would be impractical for me to stay on. I'm too accustomed to city life." She touched his leather bag, desperate to change the subject. "What's in there? Your film?"

"Yes, and a few of my albums."

"Albums?"

"I like to make up books with some of my better photographs. The ones I brought with me are all landscapes. Nothing too exciting."

"Could I see them?"

He seemed pleased by her request. "Why, of course—if you really want to." He glanced around and, seeing no place where they might sit, suggested they walk the rest of the way to the gazebo.

Along the trail, the conversation remained light. Ludwik stopped twice to take photographs. Abigail was surprised at what drew his attention; rather ordinary things, it seemed to her.

"How do you decide what will make an interesting picture?" she asked, as they walked the last stretch to the gazebo.

"Just the feeling I get from it. What I've learned about photography is that it's not as much about capturing an image as an emotion. The wonderful thing about an inspired photograph is its ability to touch each viewer in a unique way. Without that personal connection, a picture is just a moment in time, with no significance. Like the tree in the forest that crashes to the ground with no one around to hear it. Does it make a sound?"

"I think it does. Why must human beings always be at the center of everything? Nature's beauty exists with or without us."

"But without us to appreciate it, nature might be rather lonely."

She smiled. "I would be lonely without nature, that's for certain."

"I thought you said you're a city girl."

"I'm not sure what I am anymore."

Arriving at the gazebo, they settled themselves on the white wicker sofa. Ludwik removed four leather-bound albums from his bag, stacking them on the floor. Over the next hour, they flipped through them all, pausing often to talk about the pictures Abigail especially liked. Ludwik had an unusual way with landscapes that made them appear eerie and dreamlike, as if they were floating in mist. He said it was all in the lighting and insisted he was only occasionally so lucky; most of his photographs had to be discarded because they were too dark, over-exposed, or out of focus. But Abigail thought the ones he had kept showed genuine talent.

"Truth is, photography was not my first love. I always wanted to be a sculptor. Turns out I wasn't bad—but not very good either. I suppose, if I'd been serious, I should have studied at the university." He closed the cover of the last album. "So, now you've seen my hobby. But tell me, Miss Platford, what do *you* do for fun?"

"Fun?" She was reminded of her long-ago conversation with Franklin when he asked her about the *other side* of Abigail Platford. She hadn't much of an answer then, and she still didn't. "I'm all about work, I guess," she said, wondering if that was true anymore, now that she had allowed other desires to interfere.

"Then what are you going to do if you're no longer assisting Dr. Rome?"

"I don't know."

"I take it you don't really want to leave him?"

Tears sprung to her eyes. Blinking fast to hold them back, she turned away.

Ludwik pulled a handkerchief from his pocket and offered it to her, but she waved it away. "Maybe it's not as bad as you think," he said. "But if there's anything I can do to help ..."

She was startled by the touch of his hand on her wrist. "I don't need help, thank you." She jumped up from the sofa, confused and flustered. "Will we see you later this morning, at breakfast?"

Ludwik started gathering up his albums, shoving them into his black bag. "No, I'm afraid not," he replied, without looking up. "I'm going to stay out a while longer. The Radcliffs have some outstanding horses down at the barn. I thought it might be interesting to photograph them."

He didn't offer to walk her back to the house, and she was glad. She didn't trust herself. What silly thing might she end up saying or doing? Twice already she had been too eager to throw herself on the mercy of a man she scarcely knew; she mustn't make the same mistake again.

"Good luck. I hope the pictures turn out well." She stepped from the gazebo onto the grass. "Oh, I forgot to ask," she said, pivoting to look at him, feeling safer at a distance, "did you ever find Joe last night?"

"Yes, I did. He wasn't happy about me leaving with the twins today. Seems awfully taken with the idea of them having surgery at this new institute of his and Dr. Rome's. I'd say it's become a bit of an obsession and an absurd one at that. But he'll get over it."

"Yes, I'm sure. Well..." She felt awkward and ashamed of her earlier skittishness. His gesture had been one of kindness, nothing else. "I guess this is goodbye."

Ludwik raised his eyes, clear and blue as the morning sky. A sensitive soul. How could she ever have questioned it?

"Goodbye, Miss Platford. I trust you'll find your way."

Before she might change her mind, she turned and started up the path, her wrist still tingling.

•　　•　　•　　•　　•

She had expected that Alexandra would take a breakfast tray in her room, too indisposed to get out of bed. But when Abigail arrived at the back porch around ten, having redone her morning toilette and changed into a suitable day dress, she was dismayed to find the countess seated at the round table.

Alexandra looked stunning in one of her elaborate kimonos, a slight puffiness around her eyes the only sign of last night's intemperance. Franklin sat across from her, quietly sipping his coffee. He appeared tired; Abigail tried not to imagine what had kept him from sleep.

"Good morning, Abigail," Lillian chirped.

"You're looking bright-eyed and bushy-tailed," Joe boomed from his usual place at the table.

Franklin looked at her, his eyes conspicuously bloodshot. She headed for a seat as far from him as possible. Unfortunately, the only other setting was next to Alexandra. As soon as she sat down, a servant came with a platter of French toast and another of scrambled eggs, both of which she declined.

"I had a few more thoughts early this morning, Frank," Joe announced. "Made a couple of revised sketches I want to show you before you head back to New York."

Abigail allowed the butler to pour her tea. Adding sugar, much more than needed, she sullenly watched the granules dissolve.

"Don't you ever sleep, Joe?" Alexandra asked glibly.

"As little as possible. Seems I've always got too much to do. For me, the shortest distance between two points is seldom a straight line. Lillian says I change my mind more often than my socks, but it's not without good reason. Just when I decide to do things one way, I start to think another might be better. And sometimes, things that seemed to fit together just don't, and I have to modify one or the other—or even start over completely. But that's what an inventor is all about, no matter what you're trying to invent. Trial and error." He scratched at his thinning hair. "To tell the truth, I never know myself if what I've thought up will really work. Not until it does, and then I'm as surprised as anyone."

Abigail thought of asking Joe if his museum of human oddities was one of those things about which he'd changed his mind, and whether the Rome Institute might be next. But what would be the point? She was starting not to care—or maybe not as much.

"Has anyone seen Ludwik and the girls this morning?" Lillian asked. "I assumed they'd be joining us."

Joe's expression turned sour. "Ludwik and I had it out last night. I doubt he'll show up for breakfast."

"What do you mean—*had it out*?"

"Doesn't matter now. Forget it."

"If it's about those girls having surgery—"

"If you ask me," the countess interrupted, "I think the twins would be lucky to have Frank operate on them. There could be no one better."

But Lillian appeared upset. "Maybe I shouldn't have told everybody the girls wanted surgery on their noses. I never thought it would cause such a fuss."

"It's not your fault, Lillian," Abigail exclaimed with an unexpected burst of indignation. "The problem is, Joe doesn't understand the risks of surgery."

"Abigail, I believe I'm the doctor here."

"Of course, Dr. Rome, but even you insinuated there were too many unknowns." She heard the countess stifle a giggle. It infuriated her, as did Franklin's patronizing attitude. "I was merely pointing out that—"

"You've made your point."

"You know, Abby," Joe said through a mouthful of blueberry muffin, "that's why women shouldn't be allowed to practice medicine. It's a risky business, there's no doubt. But nothing ventured, nothing gained. A man takes it all in stride. But women—now, don't get me wrong; there's a lot to love about them! But when it comes to real guts, they just don't have 'em."

Abigail waited for Franklin to say something that would put Joe in his place. He didn't.

She rose from her chair. "If you'll excuse me, I need to go upstairs and pack."

Sweeping past Franklin and into the hall, she hurried upstairs to her bedroom and locked the door. Crossing the room, she threw open the armoire and began to rip her dresses and gowns off their hangers, flinging the once treasured creations onto the bed in a careless heap. Why had she ever allowed Franklin to buy them for her? He believed he owned her now, that he could take or leave her as he chose. And Joe Radcliff—he had certainly shown his true colors, and it wasn't the first time. Even if Franklin begged her, she would never consent to work for someone with attitudes like his toward women. He disgusted her! As for Franklin, he had only been pretending to respect her. Just long enough to carry out his seduction.

She started toward the bathroom to gather her toiletries, but stopped short. Frantic shouting could be heard coming from the backyard. She went to the window, parted the drapes, and peered out. A horse-drawn cart careened across the wide expanse of lawn. The driver, a gardener or field hand, yelled something she couldn't make out, As he sped by, she glimpsed a long bundle laid out in the cart. It took only a second to figure out it was a man— and then to recognize the straw boater someone had placed over his face.

Her heart pounding, Abigail threw open the bedroom door and ran downstairs, reaching the foyer just as three of the Radcliffs' workers burst through the front entrance carrying Ludwik. He appeared unconscious. The men had no stretcher; one of them held Ludwik's legs and another his shoulders while the third attempted to provide support for his head.

Franklin and Joe were already there, Joe barking orders like a military commander. He opened the dining room's double doors. "Put him in there. Lay him out on the table."

A couple of housemaids, busy with their mops and dust cloths, looked up in alarm before scurrying out of the way. The workers moved Ludwik inside and laid him atop the polished walnut slab.

Franklin immediately positioned himself at Ludwik's head, examining a bloody gash at his temple that extended about four inches into the hairline. He turned to the maids, huddled together along the wall. "Bring me some clean towels. And a basin of hot water, soap, and some long strips of cloth, something I can use to wrap his head."

"You're sure he's breathing?" Abigail said, peering over Franklin's shoulder.

"I've not pronounced him dead, have I?"

Her eyes traveled the length of Ludwik's body, searching for other signs of trauma. He was missing one of his boots, and his pant leg on that side was ripped. She moved away from Franklin. Rolling down Ludwik's long sock, she saw his ankle was beginning to swell.

"Dr. Rome, look at this."

He glanced at the ankle, but then turned his attention back to the temple wound. "Let me deal with his head first, then I'll worry about the rest."

"Is it serious, Frank?" Joe came closer, craning his neck for a better view.

"Any wound to the head can be serious, but we'll have to wait and see how fast he comes out of it."

The servants swiftly brought everything he had asked for. Using a towel, Franklin applied firm pressure to stop the bleeding, as Abigail had seen him do so many times in the operating room. "Abigail, run upstairs and get my medical bag."

Joe turned from the table to confront the three men who had carried Ludwik from the wagon. "What happened out there?"

She lingered a moment, wanting to hear what they would say. But the men just looked at each other.

"Well?"

"We was workin' in the barn. That's where we found him layin' on the ground. Looked like maybe he tripped on somethin' and hit his head on a rock. He was out cold."

Joe shook his head, clucking his tongue. "Nobody's fault, I guess. Just lucky you fellows happened along to find him."

She glanced at Ludwik, thinking how only a few hours before she had sat with him in the gazebo, admiring his photography. She recalled how kind he was, asking if there was anything he could do to help her. His touch on her wrist—how it had unnerved her! If only she had gone with him to the barn…

"I'll be able to sew up that gash without too much problem, but he may have sustained a concussion," Franklin was saying to Joe. "In a few minutes, I'll look at his ankle. Could be broken."

"Broken! But he was going to leave today."

"He won't be going anywhere right away, that much is certain." Franklin looked over at Abigail. "Didn't I ask you to bring my bag?"

"I'm getting it now."

"That's some rotten luck," Joe mumbled as she passed by. "Some rotten luck!"

.   .   .   .   .

Their departure was delayed until the afternoon, but by three o'clock Abigail and Franklin were standing next to the red Ford waiting for the servants to bring their luggage. The only words they had exchanged all day were whatever was necessary in tending to Ludwik's head wound and setting his broken ankle. But now, seeing there were two suitcases sitting in the driveway, neither of them familiar, Abigail thought she had best say something; obviously, there was a mistake. The servants had brought the wrong luggage.

"A little of the country life to take back with you." Joe's heavy hand on her shoulder, from behind, startled her. Reluctantly, she turned to face him. In his other hand, he clutched a fresh bouquet of red roses which he presented to her with an exaggerated flourish. "The twins should be here any minute. They're in the house saying goodbye to Lillian and Ronnie."

"Saying goodbye? But they can't be leaving today! Ludwik shouldn't be out of bed."

A conspiratorial look passed between Joe and Franklin. "Guess you haven't told her."

"Not yet." Franklin forced a smile. "We're taking the twins into the city. They'll be staying at my apartment."

"Just temporarily, of course," Joe said. "Best if they don't see Ludwik right now. Not the way he looks. No sense in upsetting them. But you're sure everything is all right with him, Frank?"

"As long as he stays quiet and in bed with his head elevated. I gave instructions to your maid, Nessa. She seems able enough. I expect he'll have quite a headache in the morning."

"We'll see that he's well taken care of. In the meantime, I appreciate you and Abby watching out for the twins."

"We're happy to do it," Franklin said. Abigail held her tongue, but only because the twins were loping down the walkway toward them, giggling and chattering like they hadn't a care in the world. It was wrong not to let them see Ludwik. He was their guardian.

Valencia spoke first. "We ready go with you to New York!"

Melilla gave Abigail a shy smile. "Pretty," she said, reaching up to touch the tip of Abigail's nose.

Lillian and Ronnie had joined everyone in the driveway, the countess apparently deciding to ignore their departure. Joe beamed at the twins, patting each on the head, as he would his favorite hunting dogs. "Now you two behave yourselves and do whatever Dr. Rome and Miss Platford tell you. I'm sure you'll have no trouble with them," he whispered to Abigail. "They're used to traveling."

By now, all the luggage had arrived. She watched as a servant strapped her bags, along with the others, to the back of the motorcar. Again, Franklin had sprung a surprise on her, something he and Joe had concocted on their own. But why should she care? The girls were his guests, not hers. Still, she couldn't help but be concerned. The twins seemed perfectly happy leaving without Ludwik, which made her wonder what Joe had told them—or hadn't.

Franklin assisted the girls into the fold-down seat in the back of the motorcar while Abigail, wearing her motoring cape and veiled hat, settled herself in front. She was determined to put on a pleasant face, mostly for Lillian, who had tried her best to be a proper hostess. Ronnie, too, had been cordial enough, in her peculiar way. Abigail wouldn't wish to offend either of them.

And so, with a toot of the horn and hands waving like a family off on vacation, the four of them departed for New York City.

* * * * *

"Excuse me, Doctor, but how many will there be for dinner tonight?"

Prudence stood in the small foyer of Franklin's apartment, her plump cheeks pink from exertion. The group's arrival from Scarsdale half an hour earlier had caused quite a commotion. She'd not been prepared for houseguests, especially ones as unusual as Valencia and Melilla. But once over her initial shock, she was remarkably gracious and eager to make the girls feel at home, fluttering about like a mother hen, asking them what kind of food they liked and how they would be most comfortable in their room. The twins, responding to her kindness, already seemed at ease.

Abigail had remained silent all the way home, as had Franklin. Though she'd relented enough to come upstairs and help the girls get settled, now that Prudence had taken over she considered her work done and was eager to leave.

Franklin turned to her. "You'll join us for dinner, won't you?"

"I think not."

"Hmm." His brow furrowed slightly. "Then I guess it will be only the twins and me," he told Prudence, dismissing her with a distracted nod, his eyes on Abigail. "You have plans for this evening?"

"Not really. I'm just tired."

"I assumed you would want to help the girls get adjusted to their new situation. You disappoint me."

"Valencia and Melilla are not my responsibility. Besides, they already seem quite comfortable with Prudence."

Again he frowned. "You don't seem yourself, Abigail. You didn't say a word the entire trip back from Scarsdale. And you look rather peaked. Are you not well...or is something bothering you?"

Could he really be so obtuse? Or was he baiting her, playing some sort of cruel game? "Actually, yes—I'm worried about Ludwik." She took pleasure in his look of surprise.

"He'll be fine."

She had not intended to say more, but now she couldn't stop herself. "It seems awfully strange that an accident like that should befall Ludwik just after he and Joe had a big argument. And the workers who found him at the barn—they seemed nervous, as if they were afraid to speak. Didn't you notice?"

"You have quite an imagination."

"It wasn't my imagination."

His eyes narrowed. "You're suggesting that Joe had something to do with Ludwik's accident?"

"You act as if you think it's impossible. But what do you really know about Joe Radcliff?"

He snorted contemptuously. "I dare say, a great deal more than you do."

"Have you heard the story about how he was able to purchase the asylum?"

"How he was *able*? I don't know what you're talking about, unless you mean that the fellow who built it died. That's no secret."

"But there was someone else who wanted it. Before some sort of accident befell him, and Joe ended up the only one to bid on the property."

"So what? Things like that happen all the time, accident or no accident. People change their minds, or it turns out they don't have the money. There's no reason to suspect anything, unless you're of a mind to pull conspiracy theories out of thin air."

She flashed back to the morning. Ludwik on the dining table, bleeding and helpless, and Joe hovering about, trying to look sorry. Why did she have the feeling he wasn't?

"Forget about Ludwik. Let's talk for a minute about the Rome Institute." Franklin brushed her cheek with the back of his hand. How dare he! "I know you're apprehensive, and I don't blame you."

Abigail felt a lump swell in her throat. What was he going to tell her? That it was over between them—all of it? Hadn't she figured as much that night in the library when he appeared out of nowhere to escort Alexandra upstairs to her bedroom?

"Let's sit in the parlor?" he said. "It's uncomfortable standing here like this, isn't it?"

"You can dismiss me just as easily standing as sitting."

"Dismiss you? Is that what you think I'm going to do?"

"Hasn't Joe commanded it?"

He drew himself up. "Joe does not command *me* to do anything."

She stared at the floor, silent.

"I have convinced Joe that we can make a handsome profit by developing beauty products bearing my name—soaps, tonics, and such. Whatever a woman needs for a more radiant complexion. Looks like we're going to have a special section of the Rome Institute devoted to dermatology. I was thinking of putting you in charge of it. After all, what woman wouldn't want skin as fresh and lovely as yours?"

She raised her eyes. From the triumphant smile on his face, it seemed he expected her to be elated.

"Selling creams and lotions is not my idea of medicine, nor do I have any interest in dermatology. You trained me to be your surgical assistant. But I guess that doesn't matter anymore. There are no promises to be kept, except the ones between you and Joe."

"Exactly what promises are you referring to?"

"I'm not privy to what has gone on between the two of you, remember?"

"You seem to have assumed some kind of plot against you."

"I heard what Joe said—a dozen doctors and nurses to assist you. Where does that leave me?" She was losing control—but why not speak her mind? She was tired of hiding her true feelings. "If you hadn't raised my expectations, it might be easier now. But—" She choked back a sob. "I didn't expect the rest of it, no matter what you may think, nor did I ask for it. I wish I'd refused."

"If you're referring to our night together—"

"You actually remember it?"

"You know I do. And I don't believe you wish you'd refused. As I recall, you seemed to enjoy yourself well enough. Look, there's no reason we can't continue to enjoy each other, but there can't be any pressure about it. You understand that, don't you?"

"What you mean is that I shouldn't allow myself to have the normal feelings any woman would, under the circumstances," she said defiantly, though she felt anything but that.

"Listen to me, Abigail. I don't want to hurt you, but neither can I allow you to assume too much. Maybe I was wrong, but I thought you were mature enough to handle a discreet relationship, one in which personal and professional interests are combined."

She bristled. "Hawking skin tonic is *not* my professional interest."

"I never meant to suggest that sort of thing would be the extent of your role at the Institute. But I thought you'd jump at the opportunity to be in charge of something."

"Joe doesn't believe women should be in charge of anything more complicated than assigning seats at the dinner table."

"Joe will come around. Don't worry."

"Honestly, I'm not interested in Joe *coming around*, as you put it.. Though it may not appear so, I still dream of doing something worthwhile with my life. What you were teaching me—I thought someday I might put it to better use than taking bumps off noses or making dimples in the cheeks of rich debutantes."

Franklin shook his head with a look of disdain. "I'm surprised at you, Abigail. What young woman in your position would take such a foolish attitude?"

"I suppose only one as foolish as I am." She turned to go, but he grabbed her arm, swinging her around to face him.

"Wait. There's something else. It's going to be at least a few months, I'd say longer, until the Institute is ready for business. And I don't want you living down in that basement room anymore."

Tears welled up in her eyes. She had assumed he'd ask her to leave, but not immediately. Couldn't he at least give her a little time to prepare?

"Fine, I'll start packing tomorrow."

"You misunderstand. I'm saying that I've decided you need a flat of your own. A pretty little one-bedroom on the second or third floor of a respectable building. Close by—maybe two or three blocks from here. What would you think about that?"

Her breath had stopped after his first sentence. "You're right. I don't understand."

"It's time you moved up in the world. Come now, don't you think you deserve better than to go on living in the servant's quarters?"

So much had happened, so much she hadn't expected, but this was beyond it all. "There's no way I can afford what you've described."

"Oh, but you can. I'm raising your monthly wage, by a substantial amount."

A minute ago, he had told her not to assume too much. And now this? It was bad enough she had surrendered her chastity to a man who, the very next night, was chasing after another woman. Now she should allow him to install her in a fancy apartment, with all that such an arrangement implied? Was she to have not a shred of dignity left? "I'm sorry, Dr. Rome. But no."

"We're back to *Dr. Rome*, are we?" He chuckled. "Well, you think it over. Sleep on it, as they say. If you change your mind, we can start looking tomorrow."

"Please—you must excuse me for tonight." She was weary. Too weary to know her own feelings, let alone speculate on his.

All she wanted now was to retire to her solitary basement room, climb into bed, and pull the covers over her head. To sleep ... and forget what she knew she could not.

CHAPTER 12

Abigail smoothed the last wrinkle from her satin sheets and stepped back to admire how they looked on the gauze-canopied featherbed. The only other furniture in her new apartment were a couple of electric lamps and a few shabby but essential items retrieved from the basement room. The over-stuffed velvet chair, battered chest of drawers, and rickety nightstand. Three days had passed since she moved into new quarters. Since then, Franklin had spent every night there.

Accepting his offer was easier than she at first thought. Her reasoning had taken a practical turn. Whatever might happen in the future, why shouldn't she have a decent place to live right now? She hadn't lost her position yet, and, as a doctor's assistant, she was entitled to a living wage. With the amount of money Franklin's patients paid for his services, he could well afford to increase her salary. Why he had suddenly offered to do so was another matter. Might he be sincere in his assurances of a role for her at the new institute—even if it was a role she didn't want? Or was it that he felt guilty for his behavior at the Radcliffs' home and wanted to make it up to her?

Or maybe the reason for the new apartment had nothing to do with her. With the twins occupying his usual residence, he preferred having someplace else to go.

Despite all these uncertainties as well as her suspicions about Alexandra, she had welcomed him into her bed. The memory of their first night together was too powerful to forget. She wanted him again.

Even if she might come to regret it.

. . . . .

On Thursday morning, Abigail arrived at the office to find Franklin with the twins, who were sitting atop the operating table, fully clothed. Franklin smiled as he turned to greet her.

"You're just in time," he said. "I have my two favorite patients here, and we're ready to listen to their hearts and lungs."

"Hello, Miss Abby," Melilla said cheerily, while Valencia offered a tentative smile.

Franklin held the stethoscope to their chest, listening intently. Next, he had them open their mouths, stick out their tongues, breathe deeply, and cough. Using a metal speculum, he looked inside their noses, palpated the nasal bones, and studied the front and profile views. It all seemed very thorough, very serious—even if he was only going through the motions so he could tell Joe that surgery was out of the question.

"Very good," he said when he was finished. "I wish all my patients were so cooperative."

The girls looked at him expectantly.

"You give us pretty noses?" Melilla asked.

"You'd like that, wouldn't you? And what about you, Valencia?"

Abigail felt like giving him a hard kick in the shin. Why torture them like this? He should come right out and tell them: No surgery. Finish it, once and for all.

Valencia chewed anxiously on her lower lip. "Will it hurt?"

"No, don't worry. Besides, you two are tough. I can see that." Franklin gave them a playful wink. "We'll talk more about this later, all right?" He turned to Prudence, who had been hovering in the background. It was clear from the uneasy look on her face she was growing fond of the girls and cared about their welfare. "Take them upstairs, please. We are done for today."

The twins jumped down from the exam table and, chattering excitedly to each other, hurried ahead of Prudence to the back stairs leading up to Franklin's apartment. Abigail listened for the uneven patter of their boots on the steps and then the closing of the door.

"That certainly accomplished nothing except to raise their hopes."

"On the contrary, I found out what I needed to know. And weren't they the model patients? It's refreshing not to be barraged with questions about every insignificant little detail. All these two wanted to know was if I'd make them pretty, and would it hurt."

Abigail was too disturbed to let it go. "But why would you mislead them? You could have explained the reason it's too dangerous. I'm sure they would understand."

Franklin was already putting away his exam equipment into the medicine cabinet, his back toward her. "I'm actually thinking there's no good reason why they can't have an operation—or two. They seem much fitter than I had imagined. Their breathing is good, Valencia's better than Melilla's. Both of their hearts appear to be strong. I'd have to plan things out carefully. The anesthesia could be tricky."

"But you know you can't operate on them! Ludwik will never allow it."

Franklin slammed the cabinet door shut. Dozens of bottles behind the glass doors rocked on their shelves. "Since you're so concerned about Ludwik," he said tersely, turning to face her, "you'll be pleased to know that I'm making a trip to Scarsdale this very afternoon to have a chat with him. Joe has assured me there's a way to work this out, but he needs my help. I hope by the time I get back you will have changed your attitude and resolved not to question me at every turn. I *am* the doctor here, and you would do well not to forget it."

So, Ludwik had been right. Franklin *did* want to operate on the twins, but it was all for the sake of pleasing Joe. True, the idea seemed to have originated with the girls themselves, or with their discovery of Franklin's advertisement in the newspaper, but they couldn't possibly understand the risks. Or Joe's intention to make public what should be a private affair. Using the twins for publicity was cheap and degrading, just another way of putting them on display.

"Yes, *you* are the doctor, which is why Joe should have nothing to say about it. He is putting you up to this, and it isn't fair. Not to the twins...or to you."

"No one is putting me up to anything. I don't know where you've gotten this idea that I answer to Joe Radcliff. It's plainly not true. He has his job to do, and I have mine. His is to get the Institute built and manage the business end of things. Mine is to manage patients, and that is what I intend to do—in whatever way I judge appropriate."

"I see," she said contritely, though she did not believe for a second that Franklin wasn't being pressured to operate on the twins. Joe was averse to ever taking *no* for an answer. But there was no point in arguing. Franklin would find out soon enough that Ludwik was not about to be persuaded. And perhaps it wouldn't be long before he tired of Joe's bullying. Thinking about it, she took heart.

The Institute was far from being a fait accompli.

. . . . .

Franklin did not leave for Scarsdale until two. At the last minute, he instructed her to clear his schedule for the next morning; the implication was clear. He would not be returning that night.

As soon as the snappy red Ford disappeared around the corner, Abigail closed the office for the day, partly out of spite for being left behind. But she also had a charitable motive. Her exchange with Franklin that morning had renewed Abigail's indignation at the injustice of Melilla and Valencia's situation. Despite the girls' enthusiasm for visiting New York, Franklin had ordered Prudence to confine them to the apartment, not allowing them even a short walk outdoors. She could somewhat understand; the twins were bound to attract attention anywhere they might go, and there were always unscrupulous characters seeking an opportunity for mischief. But now that she had seen Franklin's willingness to operate on the girls, she wondered if the greater concern wasn't keeping them under wraps until the launch of publicity for the Rome Institute.

But the girls were never going to become the Institute's star patients, regardless of what Joe wanted. If sending them off to New York was intended as a stalling tactic to wear down Ludwik's resistance, it wouldn't work. Soon he and the twins would be reunited, and the three of them would be on their way. No harm would come to them.

After a quick trip to the local five-and-dime, she climbed the stairs to Franklin's apartment and knocked on the door.

"Miss Platford!"

Prudence's look of surprise made it seem Abigail was the last person she had expected, perhaps assuming Dr. Rome's assistant would have accompanied him to Scarsdale.

"I hope I'm not interrupting, but I'd like to spend some time with the twins."

"Oh, wonderful! Please, come in."

Abigail entered the foyer, with its outdated wallpaper of peacocks amid blooming flowers, and listened for signs of life. How quiet the place was! Surely the girls weren't sleeping at such an hour.

"Where are they?"

"In the parlor, reading." Prudence nodded toward the closed double-doors to the left.

"I've been shopping," Abigail said, grinning as she lifted the big cloth bag in her hand. "I hope they like board games. Hand of Fate is a very popular one, and Game of the District Messenger Boy teaches children the value of work."

"They'll be grateful for the amusement, certainly. Shall I announce you?"

"Please, don't bother."

"All right, I'll be in the kitchen if you need me." Prudence turned and headed down the hall.

Abigail approached the door to the parlor, then opened it quietly. The twins didn't look up, so engrossed were they in their books. She watched them, fascinated as always by their appearance, which seemed to her at once strange and yet, by now, perfectly natural. They wore a blue cotton frock, finely sewn with a white ribbon-and-lace trim. Their hair was styled identically, plaited into long, thick braids tied with matching bows. Lying on a large pillow, their legs stretched out in back, each had an open book in front of her on the floor.

"Hello, girls," Abigail said softly, afraid of startling them.

They looked up in unison, smiles breaking over their sweet young faces.

"Miss Abby!" Valencia squealed.

Abigail crossed the room to where the twins lay, dropping to the floor beside them and curling her legs underneath her skirt. "I thought maybe you could use some company."

Melilla sighed, rolling her eyes. "Boring! We want to see New York."

"We go to Central Park?" suggested Valencia. "Oh yes, please! Central Park best place!"

The two of them regarded her eagerly, as if she might be the one to override Franklin's pronouncement that they were to stay in the apartment. How she wished she could!

"I'm sorry, girls, not today." Eager to change the subject, she pointed to the book Valencia had been reading. "*Fortunata y Jacinta*," Abigail read from the page header, stumbling over the pronunciation. "What's it about?"

Valencia giggled. "Two señoras with husbands—*and* boyfriends."

"Oh, my!" Judging from Valencia's reading material, it seemed the twins might be worldly beyond her expectation. "And your book, Melilla?"

"*Marianela*," she said, holding up the cover so Abigail could see. "About ugly girl. Her boyfriend blind, but when doctor make him see, he fall in love with pretty girl. He make Marianela cry."

Melilla suddenly looked so dejected that Abigail wished she hadn't asked—or she had another book to offer her, something to make her laugh. "Then the boyfriend wasn't worthy of her after all, was he?" she said, though she doubted either of them understood what she meant.

"When Dr. Rome make my nose pretty, all the boys want *me*!" Melilla said, her dark eyes flashing.

"No, *me*!" Valencia made a face at her sister before reaching up to grab Melilla's nose. With a wicked laugh, she gave it a sharp twist. "Then we marry and make babies, like Eng and Chang."

She was referring, of course, to the famous Siamese twin brothers who, it was told, had fathered over twenty children. Abigail had read about them and marveled at how they had managed it. But they were men, each with a relatively whole and separate body connected by a thick band just above their waists. As for Valencia and Melilla, what effect might childbearing have on their health? Or was it even physically possible for them? Yet it was understandable they would dream of motherhood, like any other adolescent girls.

"Will it hurt?" Valencia asked. "The nose ..."

Abigail hesitated, caught off guard by the sudden change of subject. It would be easy to frighten them both so badly they'd be unlikely ever to mention surgery again. But would that be fair? Didn't they, like anyone, deserve the truth? "People rarely feel anything during the operation. Afterward, though, your nose might be swollen and stuffy, maybe tender."

"See, I tell you!" Melilla gloated, sticking out her tongue at her sister. "We be pretty when Ludwik come for us."

"Well, let's see what Ludwik has to say about it. I'm sure when Dr. Rome returns from Scarsdale, he'll be able to tell us how the baron is doing."

"His father sick."

Abigail's puzzlement must have been obvious. "You not know?" Melilla said. "His father maybe die. That why Ludwik go back to Poland."

Abigail needed only a moment to figure everything out. Of course! No wonder they had not seemed the slightest bit worried about their guardian. "Who told you this?"

"Mr. Radcliff."

"And when did he say Ludwik would return?"

"Mr. Radcliff not know. But he promise we have fun in New York," Valencia said with a pout. "Not like this."

Why would Joe lead the girls to believe that Ludwik had gone to Poland? Did he wish to spare them worry, as he'd claimed? Though she doubted compassion had motivated Joe's latest deception, for now she would leave things as they were.

Abigail clapped her hands. "I'll tell you what! We're going to have some fun right now. Are you ready?"

The afternoon sped by in a flurry of activity. After they had exhausted their supply of parlor games, for which both girls displayed a strongly competitive spirit, Valencia suggested baking. They spent two hours making a chocolate cake; considering all were amateurs in the kitchen, it turned out well. Abigail admitted to the girls, with a touch of pride, that she had done her best over the years to avoid anything suggestive of domesticity.

"You no want to get married?" Valencia's eyes were wide with wonder.

"I don't think so," she said, thinking of her time with the Hennessys and how narrowly she'd escaped a life that would have stifled her every natural impulse.

"But if handsome man ask you?" This time it was Melilla's question, and Abigail sensed there might be more behind it than idle curiosity.

"Love isn't just about the person being handsome or pretty. More important is what's inside."

"You mean, if he nice?"

"Nice, of course. And trustworthy. That's the most critical thing of all. Being able to trust someone."

"Like Ludwik," Melilla said, sighing and going back to swirling little chocolate roses in a circle on top of their cake. Abigail suspected Melilla might have a crush on her guardian, neither unusual nor difficult to understand.

"Oh dear, did something explode in here?" Prudence had come into the kitchen to check on them. The twinkle in her eye made it clear she was not in the least upset to find the place a mess—flour everywhere, bowls and spoons and baking pans scattered over the countertop.

"I take full responsibility," Abigail said, laughing. "But oh, it's wonderful to feel like a child again!"

"I know what you mean," Prudence said, giving Melilla an affectionate pat.

After retiring again to the parlor, the girls barraged Abigail with questions, wanting to know if she had any brothers or sisters, and what her mother and father were like. When she was around their age, Abigail told them, her father had introduced her to the illustrated *Gray's Anatomy*, which sparked her interest in medicine. "I still have that same copy downstairs in my writing desk," she said. "I will never part with it."

At their insistence, she went down to retrieve the treasured volume. Together, they thumbed through the pages of illustrations and diagrams, Abigail teaching them how to pronounce some of the scientific names.

After a while, Valencia looked up, scratching her head. "Something missing,"

"Missing? What do you mean?"

"Us."

"You and Melilla?" Abigail smiled. "I guess you're right."

"I have idea! You draw us."

"Oh—I'm not much of an artist."

"You draw us," Melilla echoed.

Abigail didn't wish to disappoint them. "All right, I'll try. But don't expect too much."

The girls jumped up, striking a silly, convoluted pose that Abigail sketched to the best of her ability. The rendering didn't do them justice, but they seemed happy. So was Abigail. After her emotional struggles of late, the sweetness of this afternoon's childish play had brought her back to herself. Maybe not all the way, but enough to know, whatever might be next, she would not let the twins down.

At six o'clock, Abigail said her goodbyes. Closing the apartment door behind her, she took the staircase down to the office. In the reception room, she placed her *Gray's Anatomy* into the desk drawer and was about to turn out the light when there was a knock at the front door. She went to open it, prepared to explain that the office was closed.

"Help us, ma'am!"

Two children stood huddled together on the doorstep. Abigail recognized the boy, with his freckled face and scraggly reddish-brown hair slicked back behind his ears. With him was a little girl, no older than six or seven. The front of her raggedy blouse was stained red. The boy pressed what looked like a wadded-up shirt against her face.

"My little sister—she got bit by a dog."

"Come in, hurry!" Abigail shepherded them through the door and fell on one knee in front of the little girl. "Let me see." She pulled the blood-soaked cloth away and caught her breath. A large chunk of the child's cheek and lip had been ripped away but was still attached, hanging like a mangled scrap of meat.

"When did this happen?"

"'Bout half hour ago," the boy said. "A man brought us here. He drove fast."

She swept the little girl into her arms and ran toward the hall. Once inside the operating room, she had the boy pull the light-cord above the operating table as she laid his sister on the white sheet.

"Good lord!" she breathed, looking down at her. The harsh light only made the gaping wound appear ghastlier. But trying to get her to a hospital now had its own risks. According to the boy, at least half an hour had passed; it was difficult to judge how much blood she had lost.

Abigail hurried over to the medicine cabinet and pulled some clean towels from a drawer. Returning to the child's side, she pressed one of them against her face and watched it turn scarlet.

"She's not gonna die, is she?" the boy asked, his voice shaky.

"No, she's not."

Abigail stared down at the injured girl. She was shivering, and her eyes were glazed over. The little whining noise she made sounded like a frightened puppy.

"Aren't you going to do something?"

"Yes, of course." She tried to order her thoughts. The necessary sequence was obvious: Stop the bleeding, clean the wound, sew it up. She mustn't act precipitously. The first part might be easy, but after that ...

"Keep pressing hard on this towel." She took the boy's hand and placed it where hers had been. Then she sprang into action, rolling up her sleeves on the way to the metal sink, where she vigorously scrubbed her hands and arms with soap and water. Next, she sterilized a small basin of water in the autoclave and went to the medicine cabinet for a bottle of iodine.

Returning to the table, she took over from the boy. A few more minutes of pressure halted the bleeding. Once it had stopped, she washed out the wound with water and iodine. Thankfully, the bite had missed the artery; still, the repair job would be considerable. She had learned from watching Franklin how to close a wound with finesse, running the stitches in such a way as to minimize the eventual appearance of the scar. But even with her best efforts, the little girl would be badly disfigured. She could only hope there would be no infection to complicate matters further. A sudden thought gave her pause. What if the dog was rabid?

She looked over at the boy. He was leaning against the sink, his arms crossed over his chest, head down.

"Was it a stray dog?"

He looked up with a start. "You won't tell nobody, right?"

"Who would I tell?"

"The police maybe."

"Why would the police be interested?"

"They wouldn't," he blurted. "But the dog—they might try to take him away. He didn't mean to do it. He's a good dog. Really, he is."

Abigail heard the anguish in his voice, and her heart went out to him. She had always wanted a dog; her mother had forbidden it. "He's your dog?" she asked gently.

"Yes, ma'am. I found him in the alley. Somebody'd beat him up pretty bad, left him for dead. I took care of him 'til he got better. My sister—she likes him. Sometimes he licks her face. This time, though ... it was just an accident."

"Things like that happen sometimes," she said, trying to reassure him. "You're certain the dog isn't sick? Was he acting strangely before?"

"No, ma'am. Not strange at all. Somebody came up behind him and made a loud noise, that's all. It scared him."

"All right then." She could only hope he was telling the truth. "Why don't you go lie down on the bed in there," she said, nodding toward the adjacent recovery room. He shuffled off, and within a minute or two she heard him snoring.

So far, her patient had stayed still and mostly quiet. Abigail wasn't even sure the child heard her soft reassurances. But despite the little girl's compliance up to now, Abigail would need her unconscious to complete the job; otherwise, the pain of the needle would be intolerable. This was the decision she had dreaded, though she'd already settled her mind on using chloroform. She had observed Franklin administer it several times. But there were dangers. Determining the proper dosage was critical. Too little would not have the desired effect on the central nervous system. Too much could paralyze the lungs, leading to death. In determining the dosage, she must consider that her patient weighed less than fifty pounds.

Her patient. Her responsibility. Was she truly ready? Was she right to take this innocent life into her own hands—acting as a doctor without being one?

Plagued by uncertainty, she went to fetch the chloroform and mask, a nose-shaped metal cage with a hinged rim to hold a cloth in place. Stopping the bleeding, cleaning the wound—those things were relatively simple. But anesthesia could be deadly. What if she made a mistake?

She went back to the table and stared down at the child. Such a beautiful little angel entrusted now to her, alone. Suddenly, she was in her father's office, on that dreadful afternoon when she was called on to make a judgment that would change everything, forever. Her father fell to the floor, hyperventilating, his arms flailing, his body contorted. For a moment, she watched in horror, unable to comprehend what was happening. He had no history of epilepsy. But she must do something! She went to the cabinet, saw the grim reflection of her face in the glass. Opened the door, searched for the bottle of potassium bromide, reached for it ...

Abigail squeezed her eyes shut, so tightly it hurt. Would she never forgive herself? Would she never believe what the others had said—that even a doctor would likely have made the same decision and treated him for epilepsy? There was no way to have known it was his heart.

She opened her eyes and, hands shaking, dripped a small amount of the sweet-smelling liquid onto the cloth. "I'm going to put you to sleep for a little while," she said in a soft voice. "And when you wake up, you'll be much better." She held the mask to the little girl's nose and mouth. If done properly, the effect should be gradual, possibly taking several minutes, during which she must remain vigilant, focused on the child's breathing, alert to any irregularity, any sign of weakening.

The seconds ticked by ... one minute, then two, three. The child's breath stayed steady. Finally, when she thought it must be long enough, she removed the mask.

For the next two hours, Abigail worked on sewing up the wounds. It was nearly ten when she finished. Having placed over eighty stitches, she was tired but satisfied. She had done a competent job.

"Where am I?" To see the little girl's eyes flutter open, to hear her voice, was the most wonderful feeling Abigail had ever known.

"Don't talk just now. You're fine, and your brother is asleep in the next room."

The child's eyelids drifted down, but she opened them again, raising her hand to touch her face. Abigail stopped her. "Leave your face alone for a while, all right? It's nice and clean now."

"My brother—"

"I'll take you to him." Abigail had decided to keep both children for the night. In the recovery room, there were two beds and plenty of blankets, and she could remain close by, sleeping on the couch in the reception area. Thank goodness Franklin was away. Everything had gone well without him, but she would never have the chance to boast of it.

Because she had figured out how the boy found her. The purse: There had been several of her business cards inside.

"Let's see if we can sit you up," she said. "You let me do it. I don't want you straining." She slipped her arm beneath the girl's back and helped her into a sitting position. "I'm going to lift you now and take you into the next room where your brother is. You just relax, and don't wiggle around. I won't drop you; I promise."

Abigail carried the child into the recovery room and carefully laid her down on the bed, elevating her head with a couple of pillows and pulling a warm blanket up to her chin.

"How's that?"

The child didn't answer. She was already asleep. Abigail looked down at her, tears welling up in her eyes. She was such a sweet-looking little girl, pale-complected with light freckles across her nose and cheeks. Shark had hinted at what her brother did to earn money. For all Abigail knew, this little one might also make her living on the street. A sickening thought, but not impossible to imagine.

The boy was now awake and sitting up in his bed. "You fixed her?"

"Yes, she's all fixed. But it's very important that she stays quiet and rests. Will you help me make sure that she does?"

He nodded soberly.

"That doesn't mean I want you to stay up all night, though." She came over to him and plumped his pillow. "Go on, lie back down. You can go to sleep. You'll hear her if she wakes up."

He seemed hesitant, but lay down.. Abigail felt a sudden urge to tuck him in, as she had his sister, but he might consider himself too grown up for that. She watched as he finished settling in.

"What do your friends call you?"

"Paddy."

"And your sister? What's her name?"

"Shaena." He gave her a sly smile. "I already know who you are. Miss Abigail Platford."

She was startled before remembering again. The business cards. Which meant Paddy knew Franklin's name as well. But did he realize their connection to what had happened to him? She hoped not.

"You get some sleep." She patted his arm beneath the blanket. "And if Shaena wakes up, you come and get me right away. I'll be down the hall, in the room where you first came in tonight."

"Yes, ma'am."

Abigail glanced once more at her patient, who was sleeping soundly, her mouth open. Then she switched off the light.

"Miss Platford?"

She turned around. "Yes, Paddy?"

"Are you mad about the purse?"

She hesitated. "Why do you ask?"

"I was just afraid you might be mad. I wouldn't have fleeced you, 'cept—well, that's what I do. I mean, it's what everybody does."

A lump rose in her throat. "That doesn't make it right. But no—I'm not mad."

"Good."

She turned again to leave. "Miss Platford?"

Abigail sighed, pivoting around once more. "What is it, Paddy?"

"Are you a doctor?"

She was about to say no, but then thought better of it. "Not exactly."

"But you seem like a doctor."

Her heart made a tiny skip, and she smiled.

CHAPTER 13

E arly the next morning, Abigail took Shaena to her apartment, bathed her, and tucked her into the luxurious featherbed. It was obvious from the child's awed response she had never seen or felt anything like it. Abigail hated leaving her alone while she went to work, but there was no choice. If she were to bring the little girl with her, what would she say to Franklin when he returned in the afternoon? She dared not tell him she'd ignored his orders to say nothing to Paddy, nor could she admit the boy had stolen her purse, knew their names and where the office was, and may have figured out the rest as well.

The best she could do was to ask her neighbor, Mrs. Krueger, an elderly lady who lived alone, if she would mind watching her young "niece." She explained the child had suffered an accident; when Mrs. Krueger saw her, she was moved to tears. The dear woman told Abigail not to fret. She'd keep an eye on the little one, she said, and see that she had a healthy lunch as well. As for Paddy, Abigail had already sent him on his way with instructions to come back to the apartment for his sister at six o'clock that evening. By then, Shaena should be stable enough to go home—that is, if she had a home. Abigail planned to find out what she could about the children's circumstances, though she feared what Paddy would say.

She was at her desk in the office at half past four when Franklin walked through the door. The openness of his smile suggested he was in a considerably better mood than when they had last parted. With everything that had happened, she'd forgotten her anxiety over whether he might be spending the night with Alexandra. Seeing him now, however, it all came back.

"Any calls while I was gone?"

She pretended to be absorbed in her paperwork. "Yes, but only one. I'll tell you about it after you're settled."

"Why don't you come with me now?"

Reluctantly, she set aside her pen. "Fine. I'll be there in a minute."

Her eyes followed him down the hall toward his private office. The jauntiness of his step could have nothing to do with his meeting to persuade Ludwik about the twins' surgery, an encounter that undoubtedly had ended in failure. Franklin's change of mood meant only one thing. She tried to dismiss the tortuous image from her mind—Alexandra's seductive smile, her porcelain skin, the exotic beauty mark above her lip, those voluptuous breasts spilling from the tight bodice of her green taffeta gown. But there was no escape.

Abigail entered Franklin's office just as he was withdrawing a bundle of oversized documents from his briefcase. He set them down on the desktop and feverishly began spreading them out across the entire surface.

"Can you believe that Joe and his architect have already developed preliminary drawings for the surgery center?" He unfolded a huge blueprint, laying it over the others. "There's a lot they got wrong, but it's a start. Very encouraging, I must say. Seems he's really serious about my institute."

Standing next to Franklin, Abigail stared down at a maze of lines and scribbled notations.

"Right here is the operating theater," he said, pointing to one of many rectangular boxes. "Designed so that thirty spectators at a time can watch surgeries being performed. Several tiers of seating, all providing a superb view. And above the table, a wide mirror; even the most subtle maneuver can be seen from almost anywhere in the room. Houdini himself won't be able to top such a display of quick-handedness as that of Dr. Franklin Rome," he bragged, chuckling to himself.

"I guess I've never thought of surgery as a magic show." Abigail had abandoned her speculations about the countess to focus on a new threat. Plans for the Institute were taking shape too rapidly. She'd counted on having more time to assess her future, both personal and professional.

"There are many things you've never thought of, Abigail. Fortunately for both of us, I have. The Rome Institute is to be built on my reputation, and mine alone, so it only makes sense to display my skills to their best advantage. A fine old tradition, that kind of teaching. I should think you would appreciate it, having aspired once to be a student of medicine." He looked up from the drawings with an amused smile. "Surely by now you realize that medical school would be a complete waste of your time. You would find it excruciatingly boring. Day after day, endless lectures delivered by a bunch of old men hopelessly set in their ways, with no vision of the future. Why would you need *them* when you've got *me*?"

As he spoke, her mind wandered back to the night before. She saw herself meticulously cleansing Shaena's face, then placing the mask with chloroform over the little girl's nose and mouth. How nervous she'd been, afraid of giving her too much; but the dose had been correct. Her fingers were steady as she sewed up the wound, making sure the edges met perfectly. Franklin could not have done it any better.

"Abigail?" He paused. "I asked you a question. How do you like my idea?"

She hadn't heard a word, but suddenly remembered what had been foremost in her mind when he left for Scarsdale yesterday. "Did you see Ludwik? How is his recovery going?"

Franklin's lips tightened. "It's going as well as could be expected. However, though you didn't bother to ask, I have excellent news. Ludwik and Joe have worked out a deal."

"A deal?" She was immediately wary.

"First, I must tell you that Ludwik is a fraud." He paused, letting his words sink in. "You remember how he pretended to be so outraged that Joe would offer him money for the twins? It was all an act. He had every intention of striking a deal with Joe right from the beginning. That's why he brought the girls to Scarsdale."

No, there had to be some mistake. "But he loves the twins. And they love him."

"I don't know about all that, but it seems the baron has fallen on hard times. Then, lo-and-behold, along comes Joe Radcliff with money to burn and a fetish for freaks—a fortuitous situation for both." Turning back to the blueprint, he picked up a pen and made a hasty notation in the margin, casually adding, "Whether the girls have surgery is now entirely up to us."

"Us?"

"Yes, Joe and me."

"Oh, of course." The entire situation was reprehensible. The twins had been with Ludwik for eight years. They were a family.

"The fact of the matter is that Ludwik no longer wishes to be the girls' guardian, and Joe has agreed to assume that responsibility. Apparently, Lillian has always been unhappy that she and Joe couldn't have children. And she's very fond of the girls."

Abigail only partially processed this latest tidbit. How could she have so completely misjudged Ludwik's character? She would have sworn nothing could ever separate him from those girls. "Are you sure about all this?"

Finished with his notes, Franklin straightened up and lazily stretched his back. "The details are not my business, nor are they yours. I want you to stay out of the matter, do you understand? No meddling." He sat down at his desk. "Now, you said there were calls to the office?"

After what she'd just heard, it was difficult to turn her attention to office affairs. But this call was important. "Mrs. Moser. You injected her with paraffin, remember? She was very upset on the telephone, and I couldn't make sense of anything she said, except that something appears to have gone wrong."

His brows drew together sharply. "Telephone her and tell her to come in without delay. This afternoon." He opened a drawer and removed a small notebook, which he tossed on the desktop.

"But it's almost five."

"I can't have a patient like Mrs. Moser complaining about me all over town. All I need is for Joe to get wind of it! I've told you what I want done; just do it." He slammed the drawer shut. "Telephone her and get her in here—pronto."

She dared not object further. But Paddy would be in front of her apartment at six to pick up Shaena. If she wasn't there, might he come to the office looking for her? She could only hope Mrs. Moser might suggest coming the next morning instead.

But that was not the case, and it was already six by the time Mrs. Moser walked through the door, dressed in an expensive turquoise-and-black plaid dress with a fitted jacket that made her appear quite chic despite her matronly figure. She wore a lovely matching hat, turquoise with tan ostrich feathers and a black bow, its black chiffon veil drawn over her face.

"Where is he?" Mrs. Moser demanded, preempting Abigail's standard greeting. "I want to see that man right now."

"If you'd like to take a seat, Mrs. Moser, I'll let Dr. Rome know you're here."

"I will not take a seat, young lady. How dare he keep me waiting even one second, after what he's done to me! How he's ruined me …"

It was hard to imagine that something as benign as a paraffin injection could cause anyone's ruination. She wondered if Mrs. Moser was merely disappointed that her wrinkles had only softened and not actually disappeared.

Abigail hesitated, wondering if she should attempt to find out more. It would be helpful to Franklin if he could be forewarned. "May I tell Dr. Rome what specifically is bothering you?"

With a dramatic sweep of her hand, Mrs. Moser lifted the veil. Abigail caught her breath, unprepared for the appalling sight before her. The woman's cheeks and lower face, all around the areas where she had been injected, were riddled with large, angry-looking lumps, some of them oozing thick, yellow pus.

"Look at this!" Mrs. Moser waved her gloved hand around her face as though she was swatting flies. "I can't be seen in public. Thank heaven my husband is away on business. It's a nightmare! And your Dr. Rome said everything would be fine. Does this look *fine* to you?"

Abigail wanted to reassure her but the only words that came to her seemed woefully inadequate. "Naturally you're anxious. But I'm sure Dr. Rome can help you. Please, try not to worry."

"Don't worry? How would you like to wake up one morning and see this?" Mrs. Moser snapped, her eyes filling with tears as she again gestured toward her disfigured face.

"The doctor will know what to do. Please, come this way." Abigail led the patient into the exam room. She had planned to intercept Franklin before he went in, but then the telephone rang, and by the time she was finished with the caller, he already had entered and closed the door behind him. Lingering in the hallway, she could hear the hysterical pitch of Mrs. Moser's voice followed by the Franklin's deep, steady baritone. She had always admired his way with patients; he was equally adept at exciting their imaginations or diffusing their anxieties. But in a case like this, how much could words help? Mrs. Moser was right: Abigail couldn't imagine what it would be like to be in her position. Even worse, she felt partly to blame for the woman's misery. Hadn't she been the one to hand Franklin the loaded syringe with which he'd created this disaster?

She could hear Mrs. Moser sobbing and the quiet murmur of whatever Franklin was saying to comfort her. Abigail went back to her desk in the front room and sat down. Her stomach was churning. She had known beauty surgery carried risks, but until now they seemed only theoretical. Franklin had never dwelt on complications.

But his training must have prepared him to handle the unexpected. He would know what to do.

After another fifteen minutes, he and Mrs. Moser exited the exam room. Her entire head was wrapped up like a mummy, her face covered with a white bandage so that none of the lesions were visible. He guided her by the arm toward Abigail's desk.

"Miss Platford, please schedule Mrs. Moser for the operating room tomorrow. Just a quick procedure. Give us an hour, starting at ten."

"Are you sure it's going to work?" Mrs. Moser whined. "Because if it doesn't—"

"You'll be beautiful. In the meantime, don't remove those bandages. I want you at home, not going out and about. You said your husband is away for another few days?"

"Yes, until next Wednesday. I can't let him see me like this."

"He won't." Franklin reached for her hand and gave it a squeeze. "This is our little secret, right?"

She sighed, dabbing at her eyes with a handkerchief. "It will have to be. I wouldn't want a soul to know how stupid I was to have done such a thing." Then, with a sudden burst of mettle, she raised her finger and shook it in front of Franklin's face. "I'm warning you, Dr. Rome, I know a lot of people in this city—important people. I can destroy your reputation in a minute if I choose to. And believe me, if you don't fix this mess you've created, and fast, I'll make sure no woman of means ever steps across the threshold of this office again."

"Mrs. Moser, trust me."

Her eyes stared out through the round openings in her bandages. It was obvious, despite her bluster, how helpless she felt. "Very well, Doctor. I'll see you at ten o'clock."

Abigail watched, her breath suspended, as Mrs. Moser exited the office. Through the front window, she saw her climb into the hansom that had been waiting for her. In another minute, she was gone.

"My goodness, Franklin! What happened? What caused such a thing?" She hoped he would say it was something Mrs. Moser had done herself, through negligence or ignorance, and not his fault at all. A woman like that might easily think herself above following a doctor's orders.

Franklin didn't answer; he just shook his head. His silence was unsettling.

"She'll be all right, won't she?"

"Yes, yes," he replied distractedly.

"But there were so many of those awful-looking lesions. She won't be permanently scarred?"

He snapped. "This is not the time for an interrogation, Abigail. Don't make this any harder for me. You think I enjoy seeing one of my patients look like *that*?"

"But you *will* be able to help her?"

He slammed his fist on the top of her desk. "Now I must answer to *you*?"

She was startled by the extreme of his anger. But maybe he was right; her job was to assist, not antagonize him. "Tell me what I can do to help."

"Make sure no other patients are scheduled for tomorrow, not until Mrs. Moser is well on her way."

"Tomorrow is Saturday. No one is scheduled to come in."

"Good. Now leave me alone."

He stormed off, and a moment later she heard the door to his private office slam shut. She could imagine what he was doing on the other side—pouring a brandy, pacing in front of the window. Perhaps cursing her under his breath. When would she learn to keep her mouth shut? He'd told Mrs. Moser he could fix it. He'd promised everything would be all right.

She consulted the clock on her desk. It was half-past six and unlikely that Franklin would need her further. It seemed certain, in fact, that he would prefer her out of his sight.

Abigail hurriedly gathered her hat and parasol and made her escape. She only hoped Paddy would still be waiting.

·   ·   ·   ·   ·

"You ain't told nobody what happened, right? About the dog?"

Paddy and Abigail stood outside the door to her bedroom, about to look in on Shaena. She had assumed the boy would be concerned for his sister's condition, but obviously the matter of the dog weighed at least as heavily on his mind.

"I've told no one, and I don't intend to. In fact, I need you to help me keep it a secret. You can do that by promising you won't ever come to my office again, all right? If you need me, you'll come here. Around this time. No earlier, no later."

"I'm not stupid, you know."

"I didn't mean to suggest that you are. It's just that—"

"I know why you don't want me at your office." She could guess from the steely look in his eyes what was behind his attitude; he understood more than she had hoped. "It's okay. I'm not sorry what he did to me."

Abigail wanted to throw her arms around him and plant a big kiss on his grimy cheek, so elated was she by that simple declaration which seemed almost a vindication. Whether what they had done to him was right or wrong, he was glad for it. Wasn't that all that really mattered now?

Abigail took his hand. "Let's go check on Shaena."

She opened the door. The window shades were closed, but the lamp on the night table was lit. "Shh," she whispered.

They stopped at the end of the bed, peering over the footboard.

"Jaysus! She's a wreck!" he exclaimed loudly, turning to her and pointing an accusatory finger. "You said you fixed her!"

Abigail was startled not only by his tone, but somewhat his threatening gesture. She glanced at Shaena, who kept on sleeping with the same tiny smile on her lips. "It takes a long time for scars to heal, Paddy."

His eyes narrowed suspiciously. "How long?"

"Months. Maybe years." She wished there were a way to make the prognosis sound better, but there wasn't. "Your sister is going to need your support. She's going to need you to tell her she's beautiful and you love her—because not everyone is going to be so kind." She hesitated, afraid to ask but needing to know. "Are your parents prepared for this?"

Paddy looked down at the floor, tracing an imaginary circle with the toe of his shabby boot. "I ain't told nobody nothing."

"But they must have asked where she was last night—where you both were. They must have been worried."

"Nope," he said. "Da's wrote off the map mosta the time, and Mum—she would be worried, 'cept she's dead."

Though it was not what Abigail had wished to hear, she wasn't surprised.

"But is there someone we can trust to take care of Shaena? She needs to be very gentle with her face, you know."

"My auntie. She watches after her now. She's real nice."

Abigail felt slightly more hopeful. "You must tell your auntie to make sure Shaena keeps her face clean, but no harsh scrubbing. A week from today, I want you to bring her back here so I can take out the stitches. Six o'clock just like tonight. I'll try to be more prompt next time. Can you remember to do that?"

He nodded, still staring at his sister with a look bordering on revulsion. Shaena stirred, and then her eyes fluttered open. "Paddy!" She smiled and raised herself up. "Where'd you come from?"

"Where do you think?" he replied grudgingly.

"Can Paddy stay here tonight with me?" she asked, looking up at Abigail with pleading eyes.

"No, sweetheart. Paddy's come to take you back with him." Shaena's face fell.

"But I like it here. I like this bed." She lay back down, pulling the covers up around her chin. "It's soft."

Abigail would have given in and told Paddy to leave his sister for another night. But with Franklin around, that wasn't an option.

"Let's get you up and dressed," Abigail said.

"But I don't want to go." Shaena clung tighter to the comforter. "I want to live here, with you. Please?"

The lump in Abigail's throat made it difficult to answer. "How about this: Paddy will bring you back here in a week, and then I can take the two of you to the soda shop? Would you like that?"

The little girl's lips settled into a pout.

"Come on, Shaena," Paddy said gruffly. "I got stuff to do."

With a mournful look, Shaena tossed off the covers and wriggled to the edge of the bed. Abigail retrieved her clothes, which had been washed, and helped her to dress. When they were finished, she lifted the child down and gave her a kiss on the forehead.

"Now you be a good girl and take care of yourself. Don't touch your face except to wash it. And don't rub it."

Shaena nodded glumly. "What's a soda shop?"

Abigail felt another stab of pity. Such indulgences were not part of life's fabric for children like these. "A place where they serve ice cream. You'll love it," she said, kneeling down to wrap Shaena in her arms one last time. Feeling the child relax in her embrace, she was at once astonished and frightened by the affection she felt for the little girl. Was it because Shaena was her first patient, the only patient that had ever been her own? She gave the child a gentle squeeze and released her.

The three of them walked together to the front door, where Paddy stopped to pull something from the pocket of his trousers. "Here, maybe you want this," he said, extending his hand.

Abigail saw the glint of silver. Smiling, she took the key, though she was long past needing it. "And I have something for you." She extracted a thin wad of bills from under the edge of her sleeve. "You take this to your auntie. Tell her it's to help out with you and your sister." The way Paddy snatched it from her hand,

Abigail had to wonder if she was a fool to trust him. "You'll give it all to your auntie, won't you? I want you to promise me."

"Yeah, yeah, I promise," he said, shoving the money into his pocket.

"Paddy, look at me when you say that."

Sheepishly, he raised his eyes. Was that a glimmer of conscience she saw in them?

"Yes, ma'am. I'll give it to her. I promise."

CHAPTER 14

I couldn't sleep a wink last night, not with this horrible bandage on my face." Mrs. Moser handed Abigail her parasol, gloves, and yet another magnificent hat, this one fashioned of blue felt, draped with black chiffon, and decorated with huge red silk rosettes and bird-of-paradise plumes. The sort of hat that announces clearly its wearer is a person of importance.

"Your hat—I've never seen anything so lovely and colorful," Abigail said, trying to lighten the mood. After the way she'd upset Franklin yesterday, she was determined to be a steadying force today.

"Should be, for what it cost me. They think they can charge you three times as much just because it's from Paris. I had a hard time fitting it on my head the way I'm all bandaged up." Mrs. Moser nervously twisted the lace handkerchief in her hand. "I've never been so humiliated in my life, hiding away like a recluse, like some awful freak. I sent my entire staff on holiday, even my driver, just so no one would know. This morning, again, I had to come here in a common cab. But this time, the fellow who dropped me off refused to wait, even after I offered him extra for the fare. I suppose I shouldn't blame him. Probably was frightened, thinking I was some ancient mummy, risen from the dead."

"I'm so sorry. I know all this is a terrible inconvenience for you. And coming in on a Saturday, too."

"Inconvenience! That's what you call it, when he's ruined my face? Absolutely ruined it!" Her voice had risen to a hysterical pitch. "I'd sooner be dead than go through life like this. I'd sooner be dead!"

"Please, Mrs. Moser. You mustn't say such things. You heard what Dr. Rome said. He promised everything will be all right."

Mrs. Moser looked at her with pleading eyes. "So, he's fixed problems like this before? The patients recovered? They looked fine? Beautiful?"

Just then, Franklin entered the room bursting with energy, the exuberant spring in his step undoubtedly manufactured for Mrs. Moser's benefit. "Well, well," he said brightly, "are we ready to get started?"

"As ready as I'll ever be," Mrs. Moser replied glumly. "What exactly are you going to do to me, Doctor?"

"One thing I'm *not* going to do is trouble you with the details, my dear. You just leave it to me. There's nothing to fear. I'm going to numb you up so you won't feel a thing, and soon it will all be over."

"I want to know what I'm going to look like after you've done whatever it is you're doing."

"Mrs. Moser—" He licked his lips, a bit of nervousness showing through his bravado. "Sometimes, through no fault of anyone, a patient has an adverse reaction to paraffin. When that happens, the only thing to do is extract the offending substance."

"And afterward?"

"You can expect to be black-and-blue for a while."

"Black-and-blue! For how long? I have an important gala to attend in only a week, after my husband returns from London."

"You may have to miss the gala," Franklin said, his tone somewhat stern. He seemed to have determined that a change in strategy was in order; the gentle approach was not helping. "I will do the best I can to return your face to its original appearance, but it will take some time."

"But I don't *have* time! You promised me—"

"I could not have foreseen this type of reaction. It's very rare and totally unpredictable. I'm afraid you're just going to have to accept—"

"I accept nothing! You never told me there was any possibility of a reaction. You never said there was any risk at all. Yet you knew it could happen any time, to anyone. Why didn't you say so? I certainly had the right to know." She turned to Abigail, her eyes wild with conjecture. "I'd call that malpractice, Miss Platford. Wouldn't you? A doctor failing to inform his patient of the danger of an operation? And then there's the matter of incompetence." She turned back to Dr. Rome. "Perhaps you're not aware, but my husband owns a good chunk of Manhattan. And my father—he may be almost ninety, but he's still a powerful man; there's not a judge in this city he doesn't know."

The color had drained from Franklin's face. There was nothing he could do that would satisfy her. Abigail saw that now. She dreaded the prospect of watching him fail—for Mrs. Moser's sake and for his as well. Franklin's reputation was everything to him.

"We can continue this discussion some other time, madam," he said firmly, moving toward the hallway. "Miss Platford will escort you to the dressing room."

Abigail took a moment to place Mrs. Moser's personal belongings in the small closet by the front door. When she came out, she turned to the patient with a tense smile. "Let me help you get ready," she said, linking arms with Mrs. Moser's arm, afraid at any moment she might again become combative. "Once this is over, you'll be on your way to recovery."

∙   ∙   ∙   ∙   ∙

After two hours of poking all over Mrs. Moser's face with a tiny, sharp pick until every fragment of paraffin had been removed, Franklin finally stepped away from the operating table. Abigail had never seen him so sapped of energy.

"That's it. We're done," he said, though without a trace of jubilation. Looking at Mrs. Moser's face, Abigail could see why. It was a mess of tiny incisions, none of them any longer than a sixteenth of an inch, but each one a future scar.

"Let her rest for a few minutes before I bandage her up," Franklin said.

"I have to wear that awful bandage again?" Mrs. Moser cried.

"Just for tonight." His throat sounded husky, as though he was so tired he had to struggle with every word.

"Let me have a mirror. Let me see before you cover it up."

He glanced over his shoulder at Abigail with a slight shake of his head that only she could see. "It's best if you don't bother yourself about it right now, Mrs. Moser," he said.

Angrily, she threw back the sheet as if she meant to leap off the table and go after the mirror herself. "What is this, some kind of conspiracy? I have every right to see my face. Now bring me a mirror!"

Abigail waited to see what Franklin would have her do. He sighed. "As you wish."

She retrieved a hand mirror from the medicine cabinet drawer and gave it to Mrs. Moser, who held it up before her ravaged face. There was a long silence while she studied her image. Possibly it would be all right. Somehow, Mrs. Moser might see past the raw wounds inflicted by the blade and the pick and imagine herself healed.

"God in heaven," she breathed, the mirror falling from her hand. It clattered to the floor, shattering on the tiles. The next sound Abigail heard was Mrs. Moser sobbing uncontrollably. She rushed to her side.

"Please, Mrs. Moser, you need to stay calm." Looking over at Franklin, she saw he had opened the medicine cabinet and was rummaging among the different colored bottles. He pulled out one of them, unscrewed the top, and loaded a fresh syringe.

"What's that?" Abigail asked quietly, massaging Mrs. Moser's shoulders, hoping to pacify her.

"Just a sedative," Franklin answered grimly. He went over to Mrs. Moser, who was crying so hysterically that she seemed not to notice either of them, and quickly administered the injection. "You stay with her. I'll be right back."

Tossing the syringe into the sink, he hurried from the room. Abigail heard him sprinting up the back stairs. How could he leave her alone at a time like this, with a woman who, at any moment, was apt to become completely unhinged? But to her relief, Mrs. Moser's eyes already were drifting closed, her breathing shallow but steady. Abigail remained at attention, thankful her charge had quieted down, but unsure how long she might stay that way. Though she tried not to think about it, she couldn't help wondering whether Mrs. Moser would eventually make good on her threat to destroy Franklin. Would there be any among his happier patients who might rally to his defense? Or would they be too embarrassed to admit they had been to a beauty doctor themselves?

Her speculations were interrupted by the ringing of the telephone. Ordinarily, she would have left whatever she was doing to answer it. Franklin was adamant about never missing a call; a prospective patient might be lost for good, he always said. She looked down at Mrs. Moser, who by now appeared comatose. Deciding there was no harm in leaving her briefly, Abigail dashed into the reception room and grabbed the telephone from the corner of her desk.

"Dr. Franklin Rome's office." The line crackled with some sort of interference. "Dr. Rome's office," she repeated.

"Miss Platford?" The voice on the other end was distorted, but she could hear well enough to make out her name. "Thank God it's you! This is Ludwik Rutkowski. Listen carefully, I beg you. It's very important. I need your help to—"

The line went dead.

"Ludwik?" Frantically, she jiggled the cradle. "Ludwik?"

It was no use. She jammed the earpiece down. Forgetting Mrs. Moser, forgetting everything, she circled to the back of her desk, yanked open the top drawer, and retrieved the office appointment book. Furiously, she flipped backward through the pages until she reached the one on which she had written the Radcliffs' information. Within a few moments, she was reciting their five-digit telephone number to the switchboard operator. A few rings, and the butler, whose name she couldn't remember, answered.

"Radcliffs' residence."

"Hello, this is Abigail Platford. I just received a telephone call from Baron Rutkowski, but we were disconnected. Could you please find him for me and put him on?"

"Certainly, Miss Platford. Excuse me for one moment."

She drummed her fingers on the desktop, anxious for Ludwik's voice on the line. It might have been her imagination, or the poor connection, but he had sounded awful. She must find out why he'd called.

"Abby!"

Her stomach plummeted. "Good morning, Joe."

"Morning? It's quarter past noon!"

"Oh, of course. Good afternoon, then."

"I hear you're looking for Ludwik."

"Yes. He—" There was no way she could admit that Ludwik had just tried to reach her, that he had seemed desperate. She grabbed at the first excuse to pop into her mind. "He had promised to tell me the name of the camera he uses. I'm quite interested in photography, you know. But with everything that happened, there was no opportunity. I was hoping, before he leaves, I could get that information from him."

"Unfortunately, you're too late. He left early this morning for London. Last I saw him, he was all set to board the ship."

She hesitated, unsure whether she dared challenge him. "He's walking now?"

"With crutches. Hope it doesn't get too choppy for him out there on the Atlantic. Hate to see him slide right off the deck!" She could picture so well that grinning mouth, the large square teeth. "Frank made it home all right?"

"Yes, certainly." She suddenly remembered Mrs. Moser. She had to get back to her. "You're sure about Ludwik? Might he have changed his mind about leaving?"

"No, he was ready to be on his way." There followed a brief interlude of silence, punctuated only by the intermittent buzz of static on the line. "Well, good talking to you, Abby. Give my best to Frank—oh, and remind him we've got an important meeting on Tuesday."

"A meeting? May I tell him what it's about?"

"Just assure him it promises to be a most enlightening evening."

CHAPTER 15

W hat are you thinking about?" Franklin asked, speeding past a slower-moving motorcar, the driver sporting a duster and hat that matched the cerulean blue of her automobile. "You've been very quiet."

Behind her motoring veil, Abigail frowned. "I was wondering why the Radcliffs didn't ask us to bring the twins. I would think they'd be eager to see them now that the plans for their future are settled."

"I'm sure they have their reasons."

She looked away, her frustration mounting. Any other day, she would have enjoyed observing the scenery along the highway. Despite the scourge of industrialization, the Hudson River was a mighty force of nature. If one looked past the docks, railroads, and other apparatus of burgeoning commerce that lined the shores, and focused on the lush greenery beyond, it was almost possible to imagine what it was like in the days when Henry Hudson made his famous journey into unknown territory. But this afternoon, with her thoughts troubled and far away, the ever-changing scenery was little more than a blur.

She had been surprised when, at the last moment, Franklin insisted she accompany him to Scarsdale, which meant leaving the office unattended on a Tuesday afternoon. Just another example of how unpredictable he'd become, often like a man obsessed. Most evenings he spent in his private office poring over blueprints and diagrams and journal articles detailing the latest advances in hospital design. Invariably, he would show up at Abigail's apartment around midnight. They'd make love until he collapsed in exhaustion, falling asleep instantly while she lay awake, wondering how much longer either of them could go on like this.

The idea that Franklin's mentorship might somehow substitute for a real medical education had been wishful thinking. Never mind that throughout much of the nineteenth century apprenticeship had been the primary means of medical training, especially for a surgeon. It was not the type of education she'd always envisioned, nor would beauty surgery have been her chosen course of study. But then, her relationship with Franklin had other rewards; his tutelage in the art of lovemaking sometimes felt as important as what she learned from him in the operating room.

Still, she was weary of how he played with her emotions. He could be warm, even tender, but so easily turn cold and secretive. And she had started, again, to question his judgment. What upset her most was his collusion with Joe regarding the twins. In her mind, the scheme to operate on them for the sake of publicity was not only irresponsible, but a violation of the oath he'd taken as a doctor. She didn't understand how he could justify going ahead with it. That would never have been possible, of course, if Ludwik hadn't relinquished his guardianship to the Radcliffs.

That odd telephone call from Ludwik still haunted her. Had she imagined the desperation in his voice? *Thank God it's you,* he'd said. He needed her help for something. But what? And where had he been calling from? He couldn't have been on his way back to London, as Joe had told her. Unless at the time of his call he'd not yet boarded the ship, or the departure was delayed, or maybe he'd changed his mind about leaving. None of it made sense.

She turned her face toward Franklin, shouting into the wind, "But why should the twins remain in New York, holed up in your apartment with nothing to do? It's not fair."

"Best to keep them secluded for now. It will be even more stunning when they're finally introduced at the Institute's grand opening. No one will ever have seen anything like them."

The twins certainly would be protected from prying eyes if they were back at the Radcliffs' estate, and they would have acres of countryside to play in. But why bother pointing out the obvious? Nothing would change his mind, or Joe's, and voicing her opinion might only provoke an argument. Franklin was already edgy. She assumed it was mostly because of Mrs. Moser. The pain of seeing a patient in such emotional anguish had affected her, too. Yet, as far as she knew, Franklin was doing nothing to make the situation any better. Three days had passed since he sent Mrs. Moser home in a horse-drawn hansom. By now, he should have checked on her at least once. Abigail had volunteered to telephone, but he'd forbidden it, insisting it would only make matters worse by encouraging more complaints. He wanted to wait until the healing was farther along, and then he would examine her in the office. Though Abigail's instincts told her he was wrong to delay, she was in no position to protest. She just wished there was something she could do to help. Perhaps if the crisis with Mrs. Moser were finally resolved, Franklin would be more himself.

She stole a glance at him in the driver's seat, wearing a smart black cap and driving goggles, his long leather-gloved fingers wrapped around the wheel. No matter how he'd disappointed her, the intensity of her attraction to him seemed always to return.

Sometimes she could hardly believe that this elegant, distinguished man—a Johns Hopkins-trained surgeon—was her lover. Recalling the night when they first met, she'd been drawn to him even then. Perhaps, without her realizing it, the encounter had given her courage to break her engagement to Arthur Hennessy. And now, though Franklin seemed distant, and they often disagreed, she looked for ways to excuse his behavior. Why? Perhaps because she was afraid of going back to the way things were? To having nothing? And no one?

There was, of course, another possibility—the most disturbing of all. Despite everything, and all his faults, might she actually be in love with Franklin Rome?

"What's the purpose of this meeting that Joe has called?" she asked, suddenly desperate to know.

"I'm not sure. He was rather mysterious about it."

"But he's aware I'm coming?"

"Yes, I insisted on it. I want him to get used to the idea of you being involved in the Institute."

His remark confirmed that Joe did not welcome her presence, during this visit or any other. "I hope he's not still thinking of putting me in charge of selling magic potions," she said, though clearly Joe was not thinking about her at all.

"You've heard of John Woodbury, haven't you? He made a fortune as a dermatologist—at least, that's what he called himself. A few years back, he sold his soap and cosmetics line to the Jergens company for two hundred thousand dollars! Of course, he eventually lost it all, but that was sheer stupidity. The point is, you should not underestimate the importance of dermatology. I want the Rome Institute to be a leader in the field."

"I'd rather be a surgeon," she said, not caring if she sounded ridiculous. Or if he assumed she was talking about beauty surgery.

"Be realistic. You may imagine people's attitudes have changed, but they haven't. Most patients don't *want a fe*male doctor, and I guarantee no patient would want to go under the knife at the hands of a woman surgeon. The public isn't ready for it—especially the sort of clientele we see. They want only the best."

Abigail bridled at his arrogance. Yes, her own prospects were limited—he was right about that. But there was no need for him to cast dispersions on all women aspiring to become doctors or surgeons.

"You'll like dermatology. After I teach you about it."

"And what do *you* know about the subject?"

"All that is necessary to know. Creams, lotions, tonics. Whatever makes a woman imagine herself more beautiful than before."

Just as she'd assumed. They planned to turn her into some sort of glorified beautician. What would be in those tonics and lotions that they wanted her to sell? Would products bearing Franklin's name be any better or different from what one could pick up at the local drugstore?

Abigail stared off into the distance. What was the point of trying to fool anyone, least of all herself? She would never be a doctor. Stitching up a little girl's face didn't make her a surgeon, no matter how she might pretend that it did. Maybe Franklin was right. She should be grateful for the opportunity he was offering her.

Like it or not, what else did she have?

·   ·   ·   ·   ·

They arrived just in time to dress for dinner. There was no effusive greeting from Joe, no chilled champagne waiting in the gazebo. Only the butler met them at the door. They were promptly shown to their respective rooms, the same ones to which they had been assigned before.

Setting her handbag on the night table, Abigail went to the window and looked out. Several horses grazed in the grassy fields and, beyond, the sloping green roof of the gazebo could be seen peeking through the trees. She located the path she'd taken that morning when Ludwik caught up with her, and they had talked of nature and beauty and inspiration. With a heavy heart, she recalled watching him take photographs, his determination to find just the right light, the right angle.

Regardless of what Franklin said, she couldn't believe Ludwik would abandon the twins. Something about his story didn't ring true.

She turned to the pretty young maid who was helping her unpack. "Is the countess still here?"

"Oh yes, ma'am. In the room next to yours."

"And Baron Rutkowski?" she asked, thinking the maid might have useful information.

"Oh no, ma'am. He's not around anymore. But there's two other guests. New ones, just arrived today before you got here."

"More royalty, I presume," Abigail said drily. Funny how Joe liked to surround himself with titled guests.

"I believe they're doctors, ma'am."

Abigail wondered if they might be beauty doctors and if Joe was about to spring yet another surprise.

· · · · · ·

Abigail did not learn the identities of the new guests until everyone was gathered in the dining room.

"Welcome!" Joe stood at the head of the table, smiling down at his guests. He had put on a pound or two since Abigail last saw him; she marveled he could still fit into his evening suit. "Dr. Genworth, Dr. Sorrell—I hope your trip from Indiana was not too tiring," he said, apparently making an exception to his rule of first-names only.

Dr. Francis Genworth and Dr. Martin Sorrell were distinguished-looking gentlemen, moderately overfed, sporting neatly trimmed gray beards and round wire spectacles. In fact, they looked remarkably alike, as though both had been cast from the same mold.

"Fortunately, we rested for a while yesterday when we arrived in New York City," said Dr. Genworth. "However, our meeting with Andrew Carnegie ran until late last night. Of course, I'm not complaining! We're finding a great deal of support for our efforts here in New York. And it's certainly a pleasure to visit your home in Scarsdale, Mr. Radcliff. What beautiful setting!"

"A pleasure to have you." Joe tasted a sample from the first bottle of wine, approved it, and directed the butler to make his rounds. "The good doctors are engaged in some very important research. Possibly the most important in human history."

"Mr. Radcliff is referring to our research related to the field of eugenics."

They were eugenicists? Abigail remembered distinctly the book in Joe's library, *In Pursuit of Human Perfection.* Mr. Gallagher's book, what she'd read of it, had left a decidedly unpleasant taste in her mouth.

"Hear! Hear!" Joe bellowed. "Please, tell the others about it. A bit of intellectual discourse over dinner aids the digestion, you know."

"Yes, *please* tell us," Alexandra drawled in that absurd manner of hers. "I've grown tired of Mr. Radcliff's obsession with machines and monsters. I assume you gentlemen are involved in something infinitely more civilized?"

"Oh yes." Dr. Genworth glanced around the table. "If you're sure you'd like to hear more ..."

"Go ahead," Joe said. "We have a very curious group here."

"All right, then." Dr. Genworth cleared his throat. "The concept of bettering the human species through the strict control of reproduction dates back to Plato. More recently, some of the best thinkers have determined the most effective long-term strategy to eliminate inferior human beings from our ranks is to isolate those with hereditary defects and render them incapable of reproducing. Along with that goes a policy of encouraging reproduction among the fittest of our species."

"Makes sense," Joe interjected. "As an inventor, I'm always looking to create gadgets that run better, faster, more efficiently. Why shouldn't we expect the same from humans?"

"Absolutely, Mr. Radcliff. Our research, and that of many other scientists, is aimed at further identifying the hereditary factors that lead to superiority. Ultimately, we hope to refine the general makeup of vast populations, such that human evolution may take a giant leap forward. Imagine someday having eliminated the weak, the sick, and those who exhibit an inferior nature by their chronic state of poverty—all of which causes a significant drain on society's resources."

Dr. Sorrell jumped in to complete his colleague's explanation. "Such widespread effects will take the cooperation of many governments and may take generations to achieve, but the work must begin now. Earlier this year in our home state of Indiana, we convinced the legislature to pass a law, the first of its kind, permitting the involuntary sterilization of criminals, rapists, and mentally deficient persons within our public institutions."

"Physical defects, as well as traits of the feeble- and criminally minded, are vestiges of a darker age of our animal ancestry," Dr. Genworth said. "Personally, I would like to see their elimination sped up considerably, but that would require measures that some might find objectionable. But, as people appreciate the necessity, I imagine we will be granted the authority to do what must be done."

Abigail was reeling from the full realization of what they proposed, stated in even more shocking terms than Gallagher had described in his book. "If I may ask," she said, indignation causing her to throw aside her customary caution, "what gives you the right to decide who is superior to whom? Wouldn't such determinations, if they had any place at all, be within the purview of some higher intelligence than ours?"

Drs. Genworth and Sorrell exchanged a smile. "Be assured that these are not moral judgments as much as societal ones," said Dr. Genworth. "We live in an environment that demands a human species able to withstand countless assaults on its physical and mental stamina. In order to create a more perfect world in which to live, we must first weed out the imperfections in ourselves."

"You'll have to forgive our lovely Miss Platford," Joe said condescendingly. "I think sometimes accepting these realities is more difficult for women than for men."

"I don't find it difficult at all," the countess said with an imperious air. "The world would be much better off if we were to rid it of human parasites."

"Society cannot neglect the weak and the helpless—or simply destroy them," Abigail countered. How could she sit quietly by while others showed such disrespect for their fellow man? It was astonishing to hear such talk coming from doctors.

Franklin had been unusually quiet, but now he entered the fray. "Many would say it's a modern way of thinking to regard the future as something within our power to control."

"A good way to put it," Dr. Sorrell replied. "There is no reason that human reproduction should continue willy-nilly, with those most unfit often producing the greatest number of off-spring. Such a situation can only spell misfortune for humanity."

"I promise you, Miss Platford, we have no desire to usurp the role of God." Dr. Genworth's muted smile insinuated that he'd corrected such absurd misconceptions a thousand times before. "However, if you believe God endowed man with the ability to think and, by thinking, to improve his lot, then you must agree it is our duty to revere those qualities in mankind that have proven themselves most godly. It is our duty to create a more perfect human race."

Lillian was tapped a knife on the rim of her crystal goblet, which produced several sharp *pings*. "Forgive me, but I'm afraid this conversation is way over my head."

"I'm so sorry, Mrs. Radcliff," Dr. Genworth apologized. "We rarely start out like this in mixed company, unless we're asked. Certainly, let us go on to other subjects."

"I just have one more question—if you don't mind." Ronnie hadn't said a word until now. Abigail noticed with interest that tonight she wore a gown. Could it be that Joe, in light of the new houseguests, had asked her to forego her usual trousers and dinner jacket? "This eugenics of yours ... how do you know it will work? What if it somehow backfires, and we end up worse off than before?"

Dr. Genworth again traded amused glances with his colleague. "That's the purpose of our research. To determine what works."

"Undoubtedly you're familiar with the book *The Time Machine*." The edge to Abigail's tone was confrontational. And confident. "I'm curious to know which creatures of the future you think better off in the end—the pretty Eloi who'd been bred into uselessness or the bestial but more adaptive Morlocks?"

"Neither fate would be one I'd choose for humanity, Miss Platford. But I'm sure you already know that H. G. Wells is on record supporting the concepts of eugenics. Or if you weren't aware, perhaps that fact might better inform your reading of his work."

Abigail reached for her water. Having thought her literary allusion so clever, it was embarrassing to be outdone by Dr. Genworth, who now turned to Franklin. "Mr. Radcliff tells us you're a surgeon. *Beauty* surgery, is it?"

"That's right, though I prefer the term *transformative* surgery, which better represents the aim of my work. Interestingly, my goal is in some ways the same as yours—to improve on nature," Franklin said, offering a collegial nod.

"But if I might say so, doesn't this beauty surgery of yours actually run counter to what we are trying to accomplish?"

Franklin's smug look vanished, though he managed not to appear flustered. "There is no contradiction in our aims. As you said, the achievement of your goals will take generations. In the meantime, my work provides people with an immediate path to self-improvement. As I always say, let those who seek perfection in the here and now find it through transformative surgery!" He glanced at Joe, perhaps hoping for his support.

"Eloquently stated, Dr. Rome. But such perfection as you may achieve with your knife is not true perfection. It can be only superficial, failing to address the underlying cause of inferiority while lulling people into a false sense of well-being. Masking their true defects, which then are passed on to the next generation." By now, all pretense of tolerance had vanished as Dr. Genworth mounted ever more vociferous objections. "Is it not possible, Dr. Rome, to alter traits indicative of inferiority, thus allowing an individual to masquerade as something he is not? Can you not see how this beauty surgery of yours can be a very dangerous thing?"

Franklin paused for a sip of wine, a transparent stalling tactic. Undoubtedly, he'd not expected to spend the evening defending beauty surgery and found this turn of events troubling, especially when he needed Joe's unquestioning enthusiasm for their new business venture. "You misjudge my work, Dr. Genworth. Anything that allows healthy individuals who are productive members of society to further enhance their opportunities for marriage and reproduction should be applauded."

"But Doctor, I remember distinctly the writings of one of your predecessors, John B. Roberts. He was quite proud of the fact that undesirable characteristics of the nose can be entirely corrected with surgery—the Roman nose, the Jewish nose, and so on. And, of course, we're all painfully aware of the saddle nose indicative of syphilis. And isn't it true that the large features so clearly identifying persons of base sensuality, laziness, and low intelligence can be made small, to suggest virtue and delicacy where none exists? I'm sorry, sir, but these are not solutions to the problems of humanity. These are mere tricks to fool the eye, while the deeper defects continue. Breeding is the answer, Dr. Rome. Not beauty surgery."

"My goodness, I'm sure we won't solve the problems of the world around this dinner table," Lillian said, motioning to the servants for more wine. "Can we possibly discuss something a little less contentious?"

"Nothing is more stimulating than a healthy debate," Joe protested. "What's wrong with offering our guests both food for the belly and food for thought? After all, didn't Socrates say that the unexamined life is not worth living?"

Lillian gave her husband a mildly scolding frown. "I know nothing about this Socrates fellow, but sometimes one is better off not thinking so much."

"Ha, but that's the only way to arrive at the truth."

"The truth is always a matter of opinion," the countess said, idly stroking the stem of her wineglass. "I prefer to keep life simple and pleasurable. Delicious food, well-aged wine, sound sleep, and—" Her coquettish smile was aimed at Franklin. "I think it best not to say what else."

Chuckling, Franklin leaned back in his chair. He must be thankful for the interruption of what had turned into an uncomfortable debate.

"Let's just say that curling up with a good book is what the countess had in mind," Joe quipped, which occasioned laughter from almost everyone.

.   .   .   .   .   .

After dinner, Joe herded the men into the drawing room for a nightcap and cigar. Abigail, having excused herself from the table, was eager to retire to her room. But first, she wanted to stop by the library and retrieve the book by Thomas Gallagher, *In Pursuit of Human Perfection*. If the subject of eugenics should come up again, she would be better prepared to challenge its tenets.

She hurried down the hall, passing by the open door to the drawing room. The four men, standing before what Abigail considered the worst of the nude portraits, were engaged in animated conversation. She continued past the billiards room, its well-appointed bar stretching along an entire wall, and then the music room with its sprawling concert grand, crouched like a silent black beast. She wondered if it was ever played. Or was its purpose only to make an impression?

Joe's office came just before the library; its door was partly open. She paused, taking a furtive peek inside. An object on Joe's desk captured her attention. A camera—similar, if not identical, to the one Ludwik had carried that morning when they encountered each other on the path to the gazebo.

"Lost, are you?"

Abigail spun around. "I—I was just admiring your office. For-give me for intruding. But then, a bit of nosiness is a woman's prerogative, is it not?" she said with a coy smile, playing to Joe's misog-yny.

"Oh, I don't know about that." His gaze rolled over her in a way that made her cringe. "You're welcome to step inside with me, if you like."

"I can see it well enough from here." Her gaze returned, fleet-ingly, to the camera. Was it the same one? "You know," she said, forcing herself to look at Joe, "a man's office says a lot about him."

"Oh? You really think so?"

"Yes, I believe it does."

"And what does mine say about me?"

She thought for a moment, knowing she was treading on dan-gerous ground. "Well ... if this were my office, I expect I would have the desk positioned so I could look out the window, onto that glo-rious landscape. But I see you prefer to be facing the door."

"Ah, so you think I have no appreciation of beauty. Or I don't like anyone sneaking up on me."

"One could draw either inference."

"It's not so unusual to position a desk to make the best use of light. It's all about the light, you know. But then, I remem-ber you said you're a photographer. So, you understand what I mean."

Her mouth went dry. "Indeed."

"I do a bit of photography myself. Since you missed your chance to examine Ludwik's equipment, maybe you'd be inter-ested in seeing mine."

She looked away, suddenly nauseous. "Perhaps in the morn-ing. I'm rather tired tonight."

"But you came down this way for something." He raised his untamed brows, waiting. She suspected he was setting a trap, though she had done a good job of ensnaring herself. She should have known better than to spar with Joe.

"I was just going to borrow a book from the library to take up-stairs. But, on second thought, I'd be asleep before I could make it through the first chapter."

"Well then, I won't invite you to join us in the drawing room."

"I wouldn't dream of interrupting," she said, certain he had never intended such an invitation. "By the way, your newest guests are such fascinating men, obviously brilliant. I hope my questions at dinner didn't offend them."

"No, they weren't offended in the least. They're accustomed to it. As an inventor, so am I. One always has to answer to the skeptics—and those who lack imagination."

Ignoring the insult, and her earlier misgivings, she forged reck-lessly ahead. "I take it you're in sympathy with what the doctors wish to accomplish?"

"And you're not?"

"I guess I haven't the inclination to give it much thought. These days, my mind is entirely on Franklin's plans for the Rome Insti-tute."

"Is that so? Hmm." He nodded slowly. "Most women your age spend their time thinking about marriage and children."

"Perhaps, but not every woman has those aspirations, admirable as they are."

"Still, for a young woman such as yourself, marriage is inevi-table. You shouldn't delay it too long. Encourages rumors, you know. Speculation about this and that—never very flattering. Pretty soon, no decent fellow will want to chance it. Men are funny that way. They put great stock in being the first to raise the flag on conquered ground."

Though his comment was disgustingly malaprops, Abigail cared more about its not-so-subtle suggestion. Was he hinting that he knew the nature of her relationship with Franklin? Could it be that everyone did?

"My fascination has always been with medicine. And, perhaps unfortunately, I have no particular affinity for children."

"Odd, isn't it, that you've developed such a burning interest in the Siamese twins?"

She steadied herself. The twins were a subject about which she might easily become emotional, especially after what she had heard at dinner. "It surprised me to learn that you wish to adopt them."

"*My* fascination has always been with the macabre," he said, crossing his arms over his chest as though baiting her to challenge him.

Abigail shuddered. This was how he thought of his new charges? "Well, it's been an enlightening evening, just as you promised. Good night, Joe."

She turned and began walking down the hall toward the foyer, aware that he was monitoring her every step.

After a few seconds, he called out, "Good night, Abby. Sleep well … and sweet dreams."

CHAPTER 16

U pstairs in her room, Abigail stood in front of the open
window. A breeze brushed over her face, light as butterfly wings, bringing with it a hint of sweet lavender. In the
distance, an owl broke the stillness with its wavering cry.

The sickening tightness in her stomach wouldn't let go as the
events of the evening replayed in her mind. The doctors from Indiana were a frightening duo, so sure of their moral authority
that they would stop at nothing to enforce it. While their hardened hearts might be moved by the lush scenery of Scarsdale's
countryside, how blind they were to the innocent beauty of their
fellow man. What gave them the right to question nature's wisdom? To turn people against each other, denigrating the
infinitely unique qualities that make each of us special. Valuable.

And Joe. He thought himself such a master of efficiency, readily dispensing with anyone who might get in his way. Their
encounter in the hall had been chilling. He'd practically admitted it was Ludwik's camera on his desk. And the rest of his
comments—about marriage and children, rumors and raising
the flag on conquered ground. What little respect he had for
women, he showed even less for her.

Macabre! Choosing such a word to describe the twins, for whose care he and Lillian supposedly had assumed responsibility, was worse than deplorable. But why should she be surprised? Joe had applauded the misanthropic preaching of his new friends, Dr. Genworth and Dr. Sorrell. Men who hadn't the slightest appreciation for the special beauty of Melilla and Valencia. Their extraordinary intelligence and courage, their hopes and dreams not so different from those of other girls—none of that mattered. They were *defectives* for which society had no use.

Overcome with weariness, she shut the window and closed the drapes. She had not felt so alone since the day she fled her mother's house, not knowing where she would go or how she would survive. If only she could turn to Franklin; but tonight, he had disappointed her again. Why hadn't he spoken out against Dr. Genworth's hate-filled monologue? And the way he'd played along with Alexandra's silly flirtations! Was he so in need of admiration that he would willingly compromise his dignity? In front of everyone?

Yet even with Franklin having failed her in every way, she still desired him. There could be only one reason. Their lovemaking had become an intoxication, like a drug she couldn't do without. She wanted it, needed it ... even knowing its potential to destroy her.

·   ·   ·   ·   ·

She was still awake at half-past two when he finally appeared. Making no apology for the hour, he shed his clothes and crawled into bed, casually draping his leg over her with an air of entitlement.

228 | THE BEAUTY DOCTOR

"Tomorrow you'll go over to the Institute with us," he announced, kissing her cheek. "Joe wants to show Genworth and Sorrell what he's done with the north wing."

She raised herself up on one elbow. "Are you saying the renovation for the Institute has begun already?"

"Not for the Institute."

She cocked her head. "I don't understand."

"You've seen how the building spreads out from the center, north and south? Joe has started work on the first floor of the north wing. That's where he's putting his museum."

Could he be talking about Joe's so-called museum of *human oddities*, the project that Ludwik believed had been abandoned? "I thought the entire building was to be your hospital."

"I know, but this museum is one of Joe's obsessions. And don't forget, he owns the building; if he wants to use part of it to house his collection, I can't stop him. Look, it doesn't matter. There's plenty of room for the Institute—all three floors of the south wing and the upper two of the north."

"But Franklin—" Maybe he didn't truly realize what sort of museum it would be. "Have you seen any of the exhibits? Do you understand what Joe wants to do?"

"I've seen nothing yet, but yes—I know what it's about, more or less."

"And what will your patients think?"

"Joe isn't opening it to the public. It's more for his personal entertainment. I imagine he'll offer a tour every once in a while, just to impress his guests or the few people who might have a scientific interest. Like Genworth and Sorrell."

She was far from convinced, but this seemed like a good time to find out what he really thought of the doctors from Indiana and what they'd said about his work.

"Dr. Genworth seems not in the least impressed with beauty surgery. I imagine Dr. Sorrell feels the same."

He sniffed contemptuously. "Those two have no understanding of what I do. No concept of what creates beauty. I've made a study of it, as you know, and I can tell you without a doubt that the mixture of different types creates the most compelling beauty in a woman. That's why the Gibson Girl is so admired. She's a composite. The artist himself said she's the product of America's *melting pot*. She's unique. That's what I keep emphasizing to everyone—there is no single standard of beauty. And yet these myopic scientists—Genworth and Sorrell—they would have us all go back to the *Mayflower*. Their vision is for every woman to look like her grandmother. I don't know too many modern women who would be happy with that!"

Good. Franklin was as disgusted by the eugenicists as she was ... though perhaps for slightly different reasons.

"But I've had enough talk for one night, haven't you?" With a grunt, he hoisted himself on top of her. "Relax," he whispered, kissing her neck and then her breasts, teasing her nipples with a light flick of his tongue.

"Franklin—"

He raised his head, clearly piqued at the interruption. "What?"

"Do you find Alexandra attractive?"

"And where, may I ask, is this coming from?"

"I don't know. A few things she's said ... and Joe's snide comments." She was embarrassed, and almost sorry she'd brought up the subject. She could have chosen another time. But better now than never. "Are you and Alexandra lovers? Have you ever been?"

Franklin rolled off her, onto his back, and stared up at the ceiling. He was silent for what seemed forever. When finally he spoke, his tone was flat. "Alexandra is a striking woman and obviously taken with herself. I've known many like her. They easily become tiresome. But whether she and I are lovers, or have been—" He turned to look at her. "What if we were? Would it matter to you?"

"Yes, I suppose it would."

"And why is that?"

"Because—" She stopped. What did he expect her to say? That she wanted him all to herself? Was that so terrible?

"What never ceases to amaze me," he said, "is how women always want to equate love and possession."

Confusion gave way to indignation. "And men don't? It seems to me marriage is all about a man possessing a woman, and not so much the other way around."

"Which is why I thought that you, as a modern woman, might be beyond all that. Apparently, I was wrong."

She'd had enough of being told she wasn't *modern* enough. "I want to know. Have you been with Alexandra?"

"No, of course not."

Her heart was beating fast. Too fast. "But what about that night in the library? You came looking for her. You took her upstairs, and you never returned."

"Yes, that's true. Looks incriminating—I'll give you that. But does it prove I took Alexandra to bed? What if I told you Ronnie asked me to find her and bring her back upstairs?"

"That's the truth?"

Franklin sat up, his face red with anger. "What is this, Abigail? You want a sworn statement signed in blood? Look, I'm not used to being cross-examined by a woman—any woman. I never promised fidelity. But when I tell you I haven't been with Countess Alexandra, I expect you to believe me." He stopped, scrutinizing her with a look more suspicious than curious. "Just as I would believe you if you told me there was nothing between you and the baron."

What a clever way to stop her cold. But was it only cleverness? It must be. He couldn't possibly know how once, for the briefest moment, she had entertained a silly romantic fantasy about Ludwik. On that morning when they sat together in the gazebo, poring over his photographic albums. When he touched her hand ...

Suddenly, Franklin was on top of her. With a quick motion, he lifted her arms above her head, pinning her wrists as though he was daring her to resist. Perhaps she might have, just to prove she could, if she had not been swept away by a force stronger than pride. Stronger even than her instinct to survive.

They made love so long and arduously that time was forgotten. Afterward, Franklin sat up and swung his legs over the side of the bed. The bedside lamp was still lit. Abigail watched as her lover stood and walked over to the chair where he'd draped his clothes. Franklin's physique was like that of a younger man. The graceful curve of his back and waist, his broad shoulders and muscular calves. It excited her to think how well she knew his body—even down to the little strawberry-shaped birthmark on his left buttock.

A minor imperfection. But proof, after all, that he was only human.

．　．　．　．　．

In the morning, Abigail just vaguely remembered Franklin leaving. The last thing she recalled was his parting kiss—and that he had whispered something in her ear sounding like *I love you*. But she'd been half-asleep, and now she wasn't sure.

She was downstairs by ten, ready to accompany the men to the Institute. But Joe, Franklin, and the doctors from Indiana had already left. The gentlemen had an early train to catch, Lillian said.

That explanation didn't lessen Abigail's disappointment, or her annoyance; she felt as if her invitation to join the tour had been summarily revoked. When Lillian suggested that Eric, the stable master, drive her over in the horse cart, she eagerly accepted the offer.

It was unbearably hot in the open cart, and the wheels stirred up so much dust that she had to hold a handkerchief over her nose and mouth the entire way. She was moist with perspiration when they finally pulled up in front of the building that someday would house the Rome Institute—and, she thought with a shudder, Joe's museum of human oddities. The incongruity of both under the same roof apparently bothered nobody but her.

After Eric had departed, Abigail stood alone in the overgrown driveway, gazing up at the redbrick façade and trying to imagine it somehow transformed into the luxury beauty hospital that Franklin had described. The structure looked the same as the first time she had seen it, except the windows were no longer boarded up. She noticed that they all had iron bars, a stark reminder of the direful purpose for which this facility had originally been designed.

The Ford was parked off to the side, but not Joe's Stoddard-Dayton. She must be too late for the official tour. Most likely, Joe had already left with the Indiana doctors for the train station. But Franklin was still here.

The soles of her boots crunched on the gravel as she approached the building and then passed through the wide arch onto the portico. The entry doors had been left open. She hesitated with a mixture of anticipation and antipathy. The anticipation was for what this place could mean to her future; the antipathy was the same.

Dermatology was not a field she had ever thought much of, but Franklin was convinced of its merits. Formal training was unnecessary, he'd said. Her position at the Rome Institute would automatically impart credibility; patients would assume she was knowledgeable. She would extol the benefits of his proprietary products, and that would be that.

But *that* was not good enough. If dermatology was to be her path, she would approach it responsibly. Scientifically. A thorough understanding of the skin and its disorders was a necessary prerequisite to developing products for its beautification. She would need to study, then experiment and test. One could easily whip up a lotion that felt smooth and smelled pretty, then slap on a label with a doctor's name to give it "legitimacy." But what if the concoction did nothing? If Franklin was to tie his reputation to a line of products, they must successfully solve a woman's most vexing skin problems: blemishes, redness, dryness, dullness.

All this was running through her mind as she took her first tentative step into the foyer. The entry chamber was long and narrow, with high coffered ceilings and walnut paneling polished to a deep luster. Its floor was designed with large squares of gleaming white Carrara marble laid in a diagonal pattern, with a black marble border. The only light, other than what filtered through the open doorway, came from a huge iron lantern that hung in the center. Beneath it, on a tall marble pedestal, was a life-size bronze bust of Plato. Coming closer, she read the inscription: *The good is the beautiful.*

Despite herself, Abigail felt a tiny spark of excitement. There was something thrilling about the opulent entry—something that imparted seriousness and dignity to whatever might take place within these walls.

To her right, a pair of ornately carved doors closed off the south wing. Franklin had said the Rome Institute would eventually occupy that space, while Joe's museum was located opposite, in the north wing.

She turned north. Walking over to the tall doors, she gripped the brass handles and gave them a sharp twist. A firm push and, with a low groan, the doors opened. The room before her was dark. She groped her way along the wall until she located the porcelain base of a mounted switch and turned the key.

The illuminated scene was, at first glance, what one might expect of a museum in progress. Wooden crates were scattered about the floor, some opened and empty, others still sealed. Straw was everywhere, the air infused with its raw, slightly rancid smell. But amid the chaos were the assembled beginnings of Joe's grand plan. The shelves of four enormous display cases, positioned at equal intervals along the wall opposite where she stood, were populated by glass containers of various sizes. From a distance, what they held was unclear. But as she approached and discerned their contents, her initial curiosity quickly turned to anguish.

The first specimens to draw her attention were the babies, fully developed or nearly so, suspended and preserved in fluid. There was a human cyclops, with a single, centrally located eye. Twins joined at the stomach, their faces pressed together, arms twisted like pretzels beneath their chins. Babies with unsightly tumors growing from their foreheads and mouths. In one container, a child's head had the top of the skull removed, exposing the brain. In two other receptacles, the heads of a man and a woman were displayed in the same manner.

Sickened, Abigail turned away, only to be confronted by several characters straight from a carnival sideshow—a bearded lady with long black hair flowing over her voluptuous breasts, a wolf-man, and a tiny woman with slanted eyes and a beak-nose. All three appeared as though they might spring to life any second.

Abigail approached the trio cautiously, her hand trembling as she reached out to touch the bird-woman's peculiar face. The skin was cold and smooth. Wax.

Abigail's gaze roamed to a shadowy corner where several skeletons stood together in repose. A giant, a dwarf, and, between them, a child's skeleton with two skulls—Siamese twins similar in form and stature to Valencia and Melilla.

Two large poster-board displays were leaned against the wall nearest to her. She bent down to view them at eye level. The first poster was a series of illustrations comparing the embryonic development of humans and pigs. At the bottom was the attribution "Courtesy of the American Breeders' Association, founded in 1903." The other board featured photographs taken at carnival sideshows, unfortunate human beings half-naked and caged like animals, or mockingly portrayed in dignified poses, dressed like kings and queens.

Ludwik said that Joe once claimed his museum would celebrate the strength and courage of the human spirit. Abigail saw nothing of the sort here. No celebration of anything, only grim reminders of human frailty—and callousness.

She rose to her feet, returning to the first cabinet where babies floated in formalin, like aimless ships in a bottle. If these sad, rejected ones could speak, what would they say? She turned to view again the skeleton of the Siamese twins whose anatomy so closely resembled what she knew of Melilla and Valencia. They were obviously young. Had they died of natural causes? Had they ever been loved, or, like Ludwik's young sister, were they cast out and subjected to unthinkable cruelties? And the others—what were their stories? Did anyone know or care?

She closed her eyes, fighting an overwhelming impulse to flee. She could return to the Radcliffs' house, pack her suitcases, and catch the first train to Manhattan. She didn't belong here. But what about Franklin?

She tip-toed back to the entrance, found the light switch, turned the key. The room plunged into darkness. Gently, as if afraid of disturbing someone's sleep, she closed the double doors behind her.

"Abigail! What are you doing here?" Franklin stood at the top of the curved staircase leading to the second floor.

"Trying to find you. You *did* invite me, you know."

He hurried down the steps, greeting her with a light kiss on the cheek. "When did you arrive?"

"Maybe fifteen minutes ago."

"You walked here by yourself?"

"No, Joe's stable master drove me over in the cart."

"Genworth and Sorrell had a train to catch. Joe took them to the station. He should be back shortly. I was going to wait for him here. There are a few things he and I need to talk about. Privately."

She glanced toward the north wing and drew a tremulous breath. "So, you saw his museum?"

"Yes." He hesitated. "I'm afraid you may find it disturbing."

"I've seen it already. The doors were unlocked, so I went in. Appears as if Joe enjoys reveling in the misfortunes of others even more than I suspected. What he wants to call a museum is nothing more than a monument to voyeurism."

"Maybe, but Genworth and Sorrell seemed to find it interesting. They were eager to explain that such examples of human defects further illustrate the pressing need for their research."

"What proof do they have that birth deformities have anything to do with heredity? Maybe they're just random occurrences."

"Maybe, but Genworth and Sorrel certainly were eager to have Joe's ear. They'd like it fine if he were to give them rent-free space in his building."

"They want to use this place as a base for their eugenics research?"

Franklin sniffed. "I don't really think Joe wants them here."

How could a man as bright as Franklin deceive himself so completely? Joe was courting the eugenicists as much as they were courting him. Franklin ought to walk away from it all, right now. He didn't need Joe. He didn't need any of this.

"Are you worried Joe might change his mind about the Institute?" she asked innocently.

"Change his mind?" Franklin seemed surprised, even affronted. "No, he's not changing his mind. He's entirely committed to the Rome Institute and the potential of transformative surgery to alter human destiny. What I propose is to work *with* nature, not against it. Joe understands and appreciates the difference."

"Dr. Genworth may sense that Joe could be easily persuaded to a different point of view."

"Genworth doesn't understand that Joe has a habit of spreading himself too thin. Look how far he's come already with this museum of his. And yet, the south wing—the Rome Institute—is still just a pile of rubble. I need to get him back on track, and I'm the only one who can. Don't worry, I'll straighten him out.. He can't go off on a tangent anytime he feels like it. He needs to remember that we're partners, he and I."

His words fell like a slap across her face. *They* were partners. He and Joe.

Franklin consulted his watch. "I guess I have time to drive you back to the house. I just hope I don't miss Joe."

The thought of driving back together, having to listen to him go on and on about his partnership Joe, was more than she could stand. "Thanks, but I would rather walk."

.   .   .   .   .

Abigail easily navigated her way through the woods, but the entire way, her thoughts were on Franklin. Why couldn't he see the Institute was going to be more trouble than it was worth? He was much better off in Manhattan. He could be successful enough without Joe's money. And she could ...

This was always the point at which her mind spun into confusion. About Franklin and their affair. About her own behavior over the last few months. About what it means to be a doctor. Or even a doctor's assistant.

And, of course, the twins. She had vowed to be their advocate, but what had she done to help them? At least she must find out what happened to Ludwik. Did he really desert them, as Franklin thought? Lillian might know and be willing to tell her. If nothing else, Abigail wanted to hear her say she truly cared for the girls and would give them the stable home they deserved.

She quickened her pace, resolved to talk privately with Lillian, away from Joe's watchful eyes. But on her arrival at the Radcliffs' home, she found that Lillian and Ronnie had taken Joe's new Rolls Royce into the city and would not return until early evening. Her questions would have to wait.

Hot and sticky from her walk, she decided on a bath and rang for a servant to prepare the tub. Half an hour later, she was soaking in rose-scented water, the salts and heat working together to ease her tension. Still, she could not banish from her mind the disturbing displays she'd seen in Joe's museum. Granted, there were legitimate reasons to study human abnormalities, but Joe was neither a scientist nor a doctor. He was merely a collector of human misery.

She closed her eyes and sank deeper into the water. Resting her head against the rim of the tub, she tried to picture the lovely rose gardens surrounding the gazebo, hundreds of bright red blossoms bobbing in a gentle breeze. But that memory led naturally to another—sitting with Ludwik under the gazebo's sloping green roof, talking of nature and beauty and art. He said he once wanted to be a sculptor. She recalled his hands, the touch of them on her wrist, and how the tingling had lasted long after.

And then she fell into a dream.

She was wandering alone in Joe's museum when she heard a noise coming from one of the display cases and went over to investigate. The conjoined twins, the ones connected at the stomach, were moving inside their glass container. She watched as two pairs of eyes snapped open; four little fists started beating on the glass. Horrified, she tried to open the cabinet, but it was locked. She looked around for something she could use to smash the glass. In the dimness, she saw a baseball bat leaning in the far corner of the room, next to where the wax figures stood. She ran over, and as she leaned in to retrieve it, the wolfman's hairy hand grabbed her wrist. She screamed and pulled away. But when she turned around, she saw that the skeletons in the opposite corner had come to life and were trudging toward her. The giant and the dwarf, the two-headed child with an awkward hobbling gait. By now, all the babies were moving inside their glass bottles, their eyes rolling, their tongues dangling as they pounded and kicked the glass.

"I see you've grown accustomed to a life of leisure."

Abigail awoke with a splash to find Franklin standing in the bathroom doorway, hands on his hips, staring at her. Instinctively, she covered her breasts with her hands.

"No need to do that. It's nothing I haven't seen before." His tone was far from flirtatious. "I understand you were looking for Ludwik the other day. Joe said you called here and asked for him."

240 | THE BEAUTY DOCTOR

She swallowed hard, wiping the steamy sweat from her forehead. "I was just following up on some information Ludwik had promised me—about his camera."

"Oh, I see. And since when did you develop a passion for photography?"

Was he jealous? Or was it just that he disliked having found out about her call from Joe?

"Do you know when Ludwik left here?" she asked, ignoring his question.

"A few days ago. Why?"

"And he was going back overseas right away?"

He scowled. "I don't know—and I don't care. What is this obsession you have with Ludwik, anyway?"

"It's just that nothing makes sense. Starting with why Ludwik would abandon the twins after eight years as their guardian."

"I told you why. He needed money. And maybe he thought they'd be better off here." Franklin grabbed a towel from the rack and tossed it toward the tub. It landed in a heap on the floor. "Stay in there too long and you'll shrivel up like a raisin."

She reached down to retrieve the towel, wondering about Franklin. He seemed suddenly possessive of her, perhaps even a bit insecure about her affections. The change filled her with a peculiar sense of power.

"The telephone call that Joe mentioned—" she began, holding the towel but still not moving from the tub. "Yes, I was looking for Ludwik. But it's not what you think, nor is it what I told Joe. Ludwik had called me—"

"Spare me the details," he interrupted sharply. "That's not why I'm here. I came to tell you to get packed—right away."

She sat up, surprised. "I thought we weren't leaving until tomorrow."

"Something has come up."

"Do you mind telling me what?" Could he and Joe have had a falling out over the doctors from Indiana? Had he decided he was finished with Joe? He might be angry now, but soon he would realize it was for the best. They were going home.

"Prudence telephoned a little while ago. She said the police stopped by the apartment this morning."

"The police!" Abigail's heart stalled. Had something happened to the twins?

"Seems one of our patients has disappeared. And the last place she had been was our office."

Abigail looked at him, stunned. "Who?"

"Mrs. Moser."

The name she had feared he would say. Abigail thought hard, trying to reconstruct the exact chronology of events. Four days had passed since Mrs. Moser's last visit to the office. She had arrived at ten, undergone the corrective procedure to remove the paraffin from her face, and left in the early afternoon. Franklin had helped her out to the hansom at around one o'clock. "When you put her in the cab, did she say where she was going?"

"I told her to go straight home and rest. She said she would."

"I can't imagine she wouldn't have done as you said, especially after what she'd just been through."

"Let's not make too much of it, Abigail," Franklin said testily. "The procedure was a relatively minor one."

"But she was awfully upset. Do you think—" She stopped, recalling what Mrs. Moser had said: If Franklin couldn't restore her face to the way it used to be, she'd prefer to be dead.

"I think nothing. And I don't want you speculating about her either, especially in front of the police. We'll tell them what we know, and that's all. Just the facts: She was a patient, she came to the office for a minor procedure, left in a cab. That was all."

"But her state of mind ... it might be relevant."

Franklin gave her a stern look. "Did you not hear me? I said no speculation."

"The police will ask why she was at the office. You'll have to tell them there was a problem, and she was distraught."

"I will do no such thing, and neither will you."

"Franklin, you have to! She put her entire household staff on leave because she wanted no one to see her. I'm sure the police already are aware of it."

"Mrs. Moser is a highly emotional woman. Initially, she over-reacted to what was a minor problem. But by the time she left our office, she was feeling a good deal better. I had no concerns about her recovery or her state of mind. Otherwise, I never would have sent her home alone."

Franklin's assessment of Mrs. Moser's condition differed re-markably from Abigail's, but she kept quiet. He was upset, of course. Perhaps in denial of how serious a complication Mrs. Moser had experienced. Still, she knew that once they were back in Man-hattan, he would do whatever he could to help the police find Mrs. Moser.

And so would she.

CHAPTER 17

In the office the next morning, Abigail struggled for some sense of equilibrium but with little success. Nothing was going well. On the way back to Manhattan, she'd learned that Franklin had not severed his partnership with Joe, nor was he about to give up on the Rome Institute. Her concerns about Ludwik and the twins, and now the disappearance of Mrs. Moser, all remained unresolved. At that very moment, the police were upstairs interviewing Franklin.

She was sitting behind her desk, too distracted to work, when Isabelle Hadley walked through the front door, carrying a fresh bouquet of white roses. The young woman wore a lovely pastel frock trimmed in baby Irish lace, not unlike the dress Abigail had worn to Mrs. Chapman's tea party once upon a time. Her extraordinary hat was swathed in tulle and piled high with silk flowers in several shades of pink. But what captured Abigail's attention was Miss Hadley's radiant glow and the openness of her smile, both in sharp contrast to her own agitated state of mind.

"Good morning, Miss Platford."

"Miss Hadley, how wonderful to see you!" Abigail rose from her chair in greeting, but not without a touch of trepidation.

Though Miss Hadley appeared well, might there be some problem? A late complication of surgery? A complaint?

"I thought you would enjoy some decoration for your desk. The roses are so pretty right now. The maid picked these from Mother's garden just this morning."

"How very thoughtful of you." Abigail accepted the flowers, perplexed. Why would Miss Hadley bring such a gift?

"I just wanted to drop by and tell you the good news." Miss Hadley beamed as she removed her glove and held out her hand to display a magnificent round-cut diamond ring. "I'm engaged!"

Abigail broke into a smile. She was relieved, and genuinely happy for Miss Hadley. "Congratulations! And what a beautiful ring! But was this unexpected?"

"A bit. I've known Mr. Pilkington, my fiancé, for over a year. But truthfully, I was starting to think he'd never propose. Then last weekend, when we were out sailing on the Hudson, he asked me. The sun was just setting, and the sky was the most luscious shade of lavender with a touch of orange." She averted her eyes with a flutter of lashes. "You know what he said? *Look around you, Isabelle, and remember—all this beauty cannot compare to yours.*"

"How very romantic." Abigail couldn't help a twinge of jealousy, caught up as she was in an affair of a different tenor.

"Yes, he's very poetic for an accountant." Miss Hadley rotated her hand so the diamond would better catch the light from the desk lamp. "We're planning to honeymoon in France and Italy. I've always wanted to ride in a gondola."

"I'm sure Dr. Rome will be sorry that he missed you and thrilled to hear about your big announcement. You don't mind if I tell him, do you?"

"No, certainly not. But I really came to tell you."

"Me?"

"Yes, because—well, if it weren't for you, I wouldn't have had the courage to undergo surgery on my nose. When I first met you at Mrs. Chapman's house, I had the feeling that you wouldn't steer me wrong. If you said Dr. Rome could work miracles, then he could—and what better miracle than a marriage proposal?"

"Well, you do look beautiful." Abigail hesitated. "But Miss Hadley—"

"Please, you must call me Isabelle."

"Isabelle—I imagine Mr. Pilkington would have proposed even if you'd never done a thing to your nose."

She seemed surprised, and instantly Abigail regretted her remark. Perhaps too closely examining her fiancé's sincerity might temper Isabelle's elation.

But, responding with a light shrug, she seemed untroubled. "I guess I'll never know, but it doesn't matter. I'm happier this way. It's hard to explain, but changing my appearance changed me inside, too. Gave me confidence. Made me unafraid to be myself. I think that's what Mr. Pilkington finally fell in love with—the *real* me. The one I'd been hiding." She gave Abigail a playful smile. "Do I sound silly?"

Wasn't she saying just what Franklin had always insisted? Beauty surgery was not about saving lives, but it could change them for the better. It had done so for Isabelle Hadley.

"No, you don't sound the least bit silly. In fact, you've made me extremely happy. And I needed a bit of cheering up today."

The sound of footsteps on the back stairs set off an inner alarm. Franklin and the two gentlemen from the police department must be on their way down from his apartment. It would not do for Isabelle to see them.

"You'll have to excuse me," Abigail said, coming around from behind her desk, "but there is something urgent I must attend to in the operating room. I hate to rush off—"

"Of course. I understand you have work to do. I was about to leave."

She walked Isabelle to the door, trying not to seem as though she was rushing her. Thanking her again for the flowers, she hustled her out just as the three men entered from the hall.

"Miss Platford, this is Detective Baldwin and Officer Gerhardt. I've been talking to them about our patient, Mrs. Moser. You remember her, don't you?"

"Certainly."

"How do you do, Miss Platford?" The man dressed in a dark suit flashed his badge in front of her, while the officer next to him gave her a perfunctory nod. "I think we've gotten all the information we need from Dr. Rome, but I just wanted to see if there was anything Mrs. Moser might have said to you that could shed light on what happened to her after she left the office. I don't know if Dr. Rome mentioned to you that she's not been seen since last Saturday."

"Yes, he told me." She licked her lips and swallowed uncomfortably. What made her more nervous than talking to the police was the way Franklin's eyes were boring a hole through her. "I'm afraid she said nothing to me about where she was off to, though I assumed she planned to follow Dr. Rome's instructions and go home to bed."

"So, there was nothing in her behavior that caused you concern?"

"Well—"

Franklin broke in. "Actually, Miss Platford had minimal contact with the patient."

"Excuse me, Dr. Rome, but I'd like to hear what Miss Platford has to say, if you don't mind."

She swallowed again, feeling herself under scrutiny by all three of them. "The patient was quite agitated initially, but after Dr. Rome gave her the sedative—"

"Sedative?" Detective Baldwin turned to Franklin. "I don't recall you mentioning anything about a sedative."

"Possibly I didn't. It's more or less standard with a procedure such as I performed on Mrs. Moser. Just provides a bit of light relaxation, that's all."

"But are other effects possible? Could she have become confused, disoriented?"

"No, definitely not. I wouldn't have released her if there were a chance of that."

"So, Miss Platford," the detective said, turning his attention back to Abigail, "as far as you knew, Mrs. Moser was calm, rational, and had every intention of returning to her home at the time she left this office?"

She hesitated. The sedative had certainly calmed her down, but as for being rational ...

"I'm sorry, Detective," Franklin broke in again, "but it's unfair to ask Miss Platford to evaluate a patient's mental status. She's not been at this very long, I'm afraid. With surgery, patients exhibit a wide range of responses—any of which can be normal reactions to stress. In Mrs. Moser's case, I found her to be sensitive and emotional, but no more so than many other patients I've treated over the years. And by the time she was ready to leave our office, she was fine."

Abigail noticed that Officer Gerhardt had not taken his eyes off her face the entire time Franklin was speaking. Now it was he who questioned her. "Did Mrs. Moser have cause to be concerned about her surgery, Miss Platford?"

She couldn't look at Franklin. "I wouldn't blame her if she were, although Dr. Rome did an excellent job, and she was expected to make a full recovery."

"Recovery from what?"

"Well—her face, where she'd been injected, had become inflamed. Perhaps some sort of allergic reaction. But whatever the cause, Dr. Rome felt it necessary to remove the paraffin."

"I see." Detective Baldwin produced a small notebook from his jacket pocket, opened it, and scribbled something. When he was finished, he looked up at her. "Thank you, Miss Platford. You've been most helpful." He turned to Dr. Rome. "As have you, Dr. Rome. We appreciate your time. If there's anything else you think of that might assist the investigation, I hope you'll contact me." He handed Franklin a card, then gave a second one to Abigail. "All the information you need is right there. You can telephone the station day or night."

He signaled Officer Gerhardt, and the two of them headed for the door. Abigail was dreading the moment they would leave. She knew Franklin was furious and would waste no time in telling her so.

"By the way," Detective Baldwin said, turning to address Franklin directly, "you said that you walked Mrs. Moser to the cab? Personally?"

"That's correct."

"You noticed nothing unusual about the vehicle or the driver, did you? Anything that might distinguish them? That we could be on the lookout for?"

Franklin thought for a moment. "There wasn't anything unusual, not that I noticed."

"Just thought I'd ask," the detective said. He tipped his black fedora, again eyeing Abigail. "Like I said, call me."

· · · · ·

The lace curtains were drawn in the sitting room. Only a single lamp was lit, next to the overstuffed chair where Abigail often sat at night, reading or studying. But tonight, she wasn't doing either. She was waiting.

It was three in the morning. Franklin still had not shown up at her apartment. She knew she had disappointed him. He'd told her to say as little as possible to the two officers. But if there was any information that might help the police find Mrs. Moser, it was her duty to provide it. Even if Franklin might be forced to admit that his patient had suffered a serious complication.

Perhaps he felt she had betrayed him. But she had merely told the truth. Besides, if the police were to find out that either of them had withheld important facts, the consequences could be far worse. As it was, there were bound to be stories in the press. In a missing-persons case, newspapers seldom pass up an opportunity to assign motives where none exist, to destroy reputations merely based on rumor. And where do reporters get their titillating inside information? She surmised most of it must come directly from the police.

Weary of her sitting-room vigil, Abigail retired to the bedroom and changed into her nightclothes. In bed with the light out, she tried to fall asleep but couldn't. Her interview with the police kept running through her mind, though she could no longer remember everything she had said. Sitting up, she lit the bedside lamp. There it was on the night table—Detective Baldwin's card. Why had she placed it so conspicuously where Franklin was bound to see it? Where she would be forced to think again about the detective's parting invitation: "Call me."

But there was no reason she should call him; she had already told him everything she knew.

She opened the nightstand drawer and tossed the card inside before laying back down, the light still on. For a long time, she stared at the ceiling, thinking how eerily quiet it was without the sound of Franklin's breathing. She had grown accustomed to his presence, even the heat of his body next to hers. Yet, as much time as they had spent together, she often felt as though she didn't know him. Like his behavior this morning, with those two policemen: How could he have neglected to mention that Mrs. Moser was given a sedative?

In fact, hadn't he mishandled nearly every aspect of Mrs. Moser's care? He had not even followed up with her after the second procedure, to make sure she was all right. True, she had alienated him with her threats of a lawsuit; no wonder he dreaded another encounter. But Mrs. Moser had every right to be upset, and Franklin had a duty to endure whatever he must in order to take proper care of her.

Abigail sat up, clutching the comforter to her chest. She had heard the front door open. He was home. She wanted him here, yet a part of her didn't. She was afraid of what he might say. How she might feel if he expressed disappointment in her. But hadn't he disappointed her more times than she wished to remember?

The bedroom door flew open, slamming against the wall. Franklin stood there, holding his gray bowler in his hand, looking morose and rather wobbly. He tossed his hat on top of the dresser and ambled over to her. Without a word, he tore the comforter from her arms.

"Listen to me, Abigail, and remember this well." He bent down so his face was within an inch of hers. She could smell liquor on his breath: not the sweetness of brandy, but something stronger. He was clearly drunk. "A doctor who attempts to save a dying patient might fail, but he cannot allow that failure to consume him. If he did, he could no longer function as a doctor. And if other doctors were similarly affected by their failures, then who would be left? Confronted with failure, a doctor has no choice but to remain stoic. That is his duty."

"Franklin, please—"

"There are always going to be failures, Abigail. Every doctor, in every field of medicine, some time or another has let a patient down. But I know what you're thinking—that I should have been more indulgent with Mrs. Moser. I should have told her how upset and sorry I was. No! It doesn't work that way. A doctor can't allow himself that luxury. A doctor has to seem in control, even if he's not. He can't let his patient sense any weakness. That would be the worst thing possible, don't you see? A doctor must appear fearless. Never let down your guard—no matter what, no matter who might try to break you. Just keep going. Put your head down and never look back. That's the only way a doctor remains a doctor."

Abigail's heart was pounding. She had never seen him like this. So out of control. "You're tired. Come and lie down."

"I can't sleep. Not now," he said, raking his long fingers through his hair.

"Things will work out, Franklin. The police will find Mrs. Moser. She probably went away somewhere to recuperate alone. You heard what she said. She didn't want anyone to see her, not until she was better—but she'll come back, and everything will be all right."

He confronted her with bloodshot eyes. "You don't know that. You don't understand anything I'm saying."

"I *do* understand. Really, I do."

"You couldn't."

"But I do." She hesitated, wanting so badly to help him. Maybe she was the only one who could. "Those same feelings you're talking about—I've had them before."

He straightened up, took a step back. "You're not a doctor!" It sounded like an accusation.

Perhaps she should never have started. But something in his drunken rant had struck a chord in her. A regret so painfully deep, it was staggering. She had to tell him. To convince him that he was wrong about her. She knew exactly how he felt. "My father's death ... it was my fault. I killed him."

"You *what*?" Suddenly, Franklin seemed remarkably sober.

"I thought he was having a seizure, so I gave him potassium bromide. But it was his heart. I made a fatal mistake. He died, Franklin." Abigail could barely breathe, but she made herself continue. "Afterward, I couldn't stop looking back, blaming myself over and over. Finally, it was too much. I gave up everything. My hopes, my dream of becoming a doctor. My most basic belief in myself. All of it—gone."

For a moment, Franklin was silent. "Why did you say nothing about this before now?"

"I was ashamed. Maybe afraid you'd think I was incompetent, and you wouldn't want me around your patients."

"You ..." Staring at her with smoldering eyes, he ripped off his tie and tossed it onto the bed. "You're mine now." He seized her by the hair and pulled her head back, his lips on the hollow of her throat, his caresses so predatory she feared they might draw blood. When he finally let go of her, she fell onto the pillow, gasping.

"Can you accept what can't be changed?" he asked, his eyes probing like those of a relentless inquisitor.

Did he mean she should accept her father's death? Her own failure? She doubted that she ever could.

But if he was asking her to forgive *him*—to accept that Franklin Rome could make mistakes ... that he was not perfect ...

Perhaps she could find a way.

CHAPTER 18

Tis is my Auntie Riana."

The next morning, at half-past nine, Paddy and Shaena stood at the door to Abigail's apartment. Accompanying them was a woman wearing a garish, tattered cape over her shabby dress. Her age was hard to guess, but not only because she bore the wearied expression of hardship so common among the immigrant poor. For her, the reason was far worse.

"Please, come in. All of you." Abigail stepped aside for them to enter, grateful that Franklin had awakened early and left over an hour ago. But Paddy was supposed to bring Shaena to have her stitches removed at six this evening. Why had he come now? And brought his aunt?

"Thank you, ma'am." The woman bowed her head as the three crossed the threshold into the sitting room. Abigail quickly closed the door, worried that her neighbor, Mrs. Krueger, might happen into the hallway.

"I don't want to be bothering you, ma'am," Riana said, keeping her head down, "but I seen what you done for Shaena, my little niece. She's healing up nice. You done a good job."

Abigail kneeled down to examine the little girl's face. Everything looked as it should. No sign of infection, and the edges of the wound were perfectly aligned.

"It doesn't hurt like before," Shaena said sweetly, her eyes wandering to the open doorway of the bedroom. "You still have that bed with all the feathers?"

"Yes, I do."

"Can I sleep in it again sometime?"

Abigail smiled. "I don't see why not. In fact, you can lie in it while I remove these stitches. Would you like that?"

Shaena glanced up at her auntie, who answered with a slight nod. She turned back to Abigail. "Can I go there now?"

"We'll go in just a minute. But first, I have something for you."

Abigail stood up and went to the closet by the front door. Retrieving a small bag, she brought it to Shaena. "This is for being my very best patient."

The child reached into the bag and pulled out a stuffed animal. Squealing in delight, she hugged the furry gray kitten to her chest.

"What do you say, Shaena?" prompted Riana.

"Thank you."

"Thank you, *who*?"

"Thank you, Miss Platford."

"What about the soda shop?" Paddy piped up, a frown creasing his forehead.

"Not at nine in the morning, Paddy." Abigail was about to scold him for coming early, but then changed her mind. At least he had come, and there had been no harm done. "We'll save that for another time." She touched Shaena's shoulder. "Go on and take Kitty with you to bed. Don't forget to take off your shoes before you get in. I'll be there in a minute." The little girl scampered off to the bedroom, and Abigail turned her attention to the woman Paddy called Auntie Riana.

"Maybe you could fix her nose," Paddy said, though Abigail had already figured out the reason she'd come.

A tear escaped over the rim of the woman's lower eyelid and slid down her cheek.

"Is it syphilis?" Abigail asked, knowing Riana would accept the bluntness of her inquiry as being necessary. She already felt reasonably sure of her diagnosis. In its advanced stages, the disease could destroy the nose, leaving in its wake a gaping, irregular hole. Those afflicted often covered their deficit with a crude nasal prosthesis, but Riana wore no such apparatus this morning.

"Yes, ma'am. I'm ashamed to say it is. But whatever you may think of me, I'm not a whore. I never been. It's my husband what gave it to me. I swear."

"Believe me, I'm not here to judge. But I'm afraid I can't help you."

"Why not? You could fix it," Paddy said accusingly. "You make nice stitches."

Abigail felt awful about it, but they must be made to understand why she could do nothing. "I'm not a doctor, Paddy. I can't just decide to operate on somebody, anytime I want. It doesn't work like that." She addressed Riana, trying not to flinch when she looked at her. "You'll go to the hospital. Someone there should be able to help you."

Riana shook her head. "No, ma'am. I don't like hospitals."

"She won't go near Bellevue," Paddy said. "Not since they finished off Mum."

"But it's the only way," Abigail objected. "If you want me to, I'll go with you. I'll speak to them."

"I don't want nothin' to do with that death trap or any other of them so-called hospitals for the poor. They'd take one look at me and give me the black bottle for sure. If that's all I got left, I'd rather do myself in. Least there's some dignity in that."

Abigail remembered what her father had told her about the "black bottle." Rumors about it abounded in the tenements, especially among the Irish. It was said the hospitals gave you a drink from the black bottle when they wanted to get rid of you fast.

"What about Dr. Rome? He's a good doctor." Paddy gave Abigail a hard, steady stare.

"Dr. Rome is a *beauty* doctor."

"But Auntie wants to be beautiful."

"It's not that, ma'am." Riana hung her head. "I only wish I could walk down the street without people starin' at me. Without me seein' that look in their eyes and knowin' what they're thinkin'. That I'm some kind of monster, or worse." She looked up, a question in her eyes. "But are you sayin', ma'am, the doctor you work for don't know how to fix a problem like mine?"

Abigail recalled the two techniques she had read about in the book by Joseph Carpue. Both were complicated. One used a tissue flap brought down from the forehead; but taking the flap would badly disfigure the upper third of the face. That's why some doctors preferred the other approach, called the Italian method, first described in the late 1500s by an Italian surgeon with a long name she couldn't remember. It required a flap still attached to the forearm to be grafted onto the face. The technique was uncomfortable for the patient, since the arm must be kept bent in an awkward position for several weeks until the graft could be detached from its source and then molded into a nose. Judging from the illustrations she had seen, the result of either technique was only a crudely sculpted nose; still, compared to having nothing at all, it would be a decided improvement.

Of course, repairing the nose would not cure syphilis. Nothing could do that.

"Ma'am?" Riana raised her chin, forcing Abigail to confront her misery head-on. "I think maybe you're sayin' Dr. Rome don't want nothin' to do with somebody like me. Is that it? Because if it is, I understand. Really, I do."

Abigail couldn't bear having her think that, even if it might be true. "No, all I meant is that Dr. Rome is a very busy man."

Riana grabbed Abigail's hand and squeezed it. "I still think you're an angel of mercy, ma'am. What you done for my little niece—God hisself couldn't have fixed her any better."

Her gratitude made Abigail even more ashamed. If only she and Franklin could be of service to this poor woman who had nowhere else to turn! To restore her dignity, give her a chance to live again—for however long she had left.

What greater purpose could a doctor have?

·   ·   ·   ·   ·

Franklin looked up from the newspaper as Abigail entered his private office with their morning tea. After last night—with too much to drink and too little sleep—she had expected him to look frazzled. Yet he appeared well, even energetic. Might it be because of what had happened between them?

A change had occurred. The balance of power had shifted. Having confided in each other their deepest disappointments, they had forged a different sort of bond, based on compassion. Understanding. After so long, Abigail again had a reason to hope.

This morning, she would take it a step further and confess to him about Paddy and Shaena. There was no other way. Not if she wanted him to operate on Riana.

"Good that you're here. I've been waiting to tell you." Franklin paused dramatically. "We're operating on the twins tomorrow!"

Abigail stood frozen in place with the tea tray in her hands. "What? You can't be serious."

"You want to complain about working on a Saturday?" he quipped.

"No, I—I wasn't expecting it. That's all."

"I'll be happy to explain why we mustn't delay any longer—but after you pour me some tea, my dear."

She set the tray on the desktop and prepared a steaming cup of jasmine with a touch of cream, her mind in a turmoil. She was not prepared for this.

"I've thought about it all morning," he said. "The fact is, Joe has to be handled just right. From what I've observed, he needs to be kept in a constant state of excitement. Otherwise, he'll find something new to amuse him. Operating on the girls now—one of them, that is—should keep him engaged and encourage him to move faster on my project."

He smiled, oblivious to her disapproving silence. "It's no longer enough to be an accomplished beauty doctor; I must now be a psychiatrist as well."

A psychiatrist for Joe might certainly be in order. But at that moment, all she could think about was tomorrow, Valencia and Melilla laid out on the operating table. Feeling suddenly weak, she sat down in one of the side chairs.

"We'll operate on Melilla first. I want to start with the physically weaker of the two, get that over with. Performing the second surgery at the Institute, in front of an audience, it has to go smoothly. No slip-ups. We'll have been through it once, and if there are problems to be encountered, we will have dealt with them already. By the way, say nothing yet to the twins. No sense in getting them excited—or nervous. I don't even plan to tell Joe for a couple of days, not until it's all over and I know everything is fine.

"Which reminds me, I'll need your help to locate an ace photographer. I want some really dramatic shots, all the best angles—once the swelling goes down, that is. Imagine seeing them side by side, two heads on the same body, one nose beautiful, the other ..." He took a gulp of his tea. "Why, I'm willing to bet that after those first photographs are released to the press at the Institute's grand opening, they'll be plastered across the front page of every newspaper in the country. The calls for consultations will come flooding in."

"Flooding in," she repeated in a daze.

"Absolutely! First, you get their attention. The pictures of the twins will certainly do that. Then you go about closing the sale, as Joe would put it. Pose the question: *What is beauty worth?* The answer will be obvious. I can tell you exactly how a woman thinks! *If those Siamese twins can do it, with so little to gain, then why shouldn't I, with so much?*"

The more he talked, the more disillusioned Abigail became. Her earlier reflections now seemed nothing more than stupid sentimentality. Franklin had not been thinking of her this morning. He had only one thing on his mind—how to take maximum advantage of Valencia and Melilla's inevitable celebrity.

"You're sure about this, Franklin?"

His smile faded. "I suppose you're going to remind me that your friend Ludwik would not approve?"

"No."

"What then?"

She could think of only one thing that might dissuade Franklin. "If something goes wrong, anything at all, it will destroy your reputation forever."

"You sound as if you have no confidence in me."

"It's too risky."

He drummed his fingers on the desktop, his impatience rapidly escalating. "Are you done?"

But Abigail wasn't done. There was still the matter of Riana. This would be Franklin's last chance to salvage any vestige of the respect she had once held for him. If it wasn't already too late.

"I was wondering if you've ever done a nose reconstruction using a forearm flap. They call it the Italian method."

He gave her a puzzled look. "Why are you asking?"

"Because I met a woman who needs such an operation."

"Why? What happened to her?"

"She's suffering from syphilis. She hasn't a penny and—"

His teacup met the saucer with a clank. "This is not a charity hospital, Abigail."

"But the poor woman—"

"Have you lost your senses? I've been doing everything possible to build an exclusive beauty practice! You've seen the class of people we're attracting here. Do you think for one minute any respectable woman would want to lie on the same operating table as some lady of the night with a syphilitic nose? I am about to create the most ambitious beauty institute the world has ever seen, and I assure you the sick and indigent will not be among my patients. If that's the sort of medicine you prefer, then I suggest you join some holy order of sisters and become a missionary."

"I merely thought, as a doctor, you'd feel that some small part of your skills might be applied for the benefit of those less fortunate."

"If I might nudge your memory, you were the one to object when I fixed the ears of that young street urchin. Certainly, he qualifies as the *less fortunate* of whom you speak. Look what I did for him! And did I ask for anything in return?" He let out an exasperated sigh. "Listen, my goal is to be recognized as the world's foremost beauty doctor. Others have different goals that you may consider loftier, and that's fine. But I'm perfectly satisfied with mine."

His words only frustrated her more. "I see little difference between an operation to create beauty and one to restore it."

"You may be clever with words, but you're missing the essence of what beauty surgery is all about. Would anyone look at the result of a nose restoration such as you describe and say, *Oh, if only my nose could look like that*? No, they would never call a nose like that *beautiful*."

"The important thing is not what others say, but how the patient feels. And I believe that any nose, even an imperfect one, would make the woman in question feel a great deal better about herself." Impulsively, she seized on something else. "What about the twins? You're willing to operate on *them*. Are they the type of clientele you're hoping to attract to the Institute?"

"The twins are a unique situation. Obviously, there is much to be gained by operating on them in a public forum. Proving, in the most memorable fashion, the miracles a skilled beauty doctor can achieve. And by the way, for our publicity, the twins are allegedly the secret progeny of foreign royalty. All very hush-hush, of course." He chuckled, the cleverness of this little intrigue lightening his mood. "As you can see, I intend to compromise none of the Institute's reputation for exclusivity."

He turned back to his reading, signaling the end of their conversation—except for the casual question, "How many patients do we have this afternoon?"

"None."

His head popped up from the paper. "None?"

Abigail took vengeful pleasure in his dismay. "You sound surprised, but you know things have slowed down considerably."

"I suppose. So many of the ladies are away for the summer. And I have been preoccupied as well." He thought for a moment.

"All right, why don't you place another advertisement in the *New York Clipper*? A few more of those theater types wouldn't be such a bad thing in a slow season."

Abigail rose from her chair. "Yes, sir," she muttered, shutting the door behind her with a good deal more force than necessary. As she made her way down the narrow hall, thoughts of her father flooded her mind. She couldn't remember him ever refusing to treat a patient, regardless of their circumstances. Abigail had wanted so much to be like him. The urgency of her desire to help Riana proved that at least a part of her still felt the same. But she was not a doctor. She could do nothing on her own. There were people who needed her, yet she had no way of helping them. As for the twins, they would have surgery tomorrow—unless there was someone who could stop it.

· · · · ·

"Lillian?"

Abigail pulled the Strowger close, leaning forward in her chair until her lips were on top of the mouthpiece. Franklin was still reading his paper in the next room. "I hope this isn't a bad time to call, but I need to speak with you. About the twins—"

"I can't hear you." Lillian's voice sounded very far away. "Oh my, you'd think they could do better with these connections."

"How about now?" Abigail asked, cupping her hands around the mouthpiece, afraid to speak any louder for fear that Franklin might hear her. "Now?"

"Much better, yes. It's funny that you telephoned, Abigail. I was planning to call you within the hour. I'm throwing a little party tomorrow night in celebration of Joe's fiftieth birthday, and I'm hoping you and Frank can make it. I know it's awfully gauche to invite you on such short notice. But please say you'll come. Joe will be devastated if you don't join us."

The invitation was a godsend. If she and Franklin were off to Scarsdale tomorrow, it would be impossible for him to operate on the twins.

"I'm certain there's nothing else on Dr. Rome's schedule for Saturday. And even if there were, neither of us would dream of missing such a special occasion."

"Then it's settled! You'll stay with us overnight." Lillian paused. "But you were calling me about something?"

Considering the twins' temporary reprieve, it seemed better to approach the matter of their surgery with a bit more finesse. "I understand you and Joe are planning to assume guardianship of the twins. I wanted to offer my congratulations. If there's anything I can do to help—"

"I have no idea what you're talking about."

"Valencia and Melilla?"

"Yes, I assumed that's who you meant. But this business about guardianship—where did you ever get such a notion? Joe has bought them for the Radcliff Institute."

Bought them! And what was the Radcliff Institute?

"Are you referring to Joe's museum?" Nightmarish images paraded through Abigail's mind—twisted babies in bottles, the giant and the dwarf and the two-headed skeleton. All keeping their silent watch over the darkened room where Joe's growing collection of human oddities resided.

"Oh, you haven't heard?" Lillian said lightly. "Joe is combining the museum with a research laboratory. I'm sure you remember those gentlemen you met at our house—Dr.

Genworth and Dr. Sorrell? They're going to help him set every-thing up. Joe thought to call the entire enterprise the Radcliff Institute. So, it will be the Radcliff Institute and the Rome Insti-tute—each in its respective wing. After all, north is north and south is south, and never the twain shall meet!"

"But Lillian—" The word laboratory had sent shivers down her spine. "I thought you were very fond of the girls. And Dr. Rome said you'd always wanted children."

"My goodness! You really couldn't have thought I would want to take on a responsibility like that—not at my age. Or any age, for that matter. The Siamese twins are fascinating, but that's why they need to be studied. The doctors from Indiana seem in-trigued by the opportunity."

"Does Baron Rutkowski know about this?" Abigail blurted out.

"Ludwik? Obviously, he doesn't care. Joe must have offered him a lot of money for the twins. My husband wanted them badly. But I don't get involved in those things, Abigail. It's not my place."

"But do you know where he went?"

"You mean Ludwik? To London, so I heard. But dear, don't you worry about the twins. Joe still plans for Frank to have them for his grand opening. He's excited about their surgery. He says it will help make a name for both institutes—Radcliff *and* Rome."

Abigail closed her eyes, trying to grasp the enormity of all Lillian had just revealed. Ludwik would never have given up the twins if he understood why Joe wanted them. Either Joe had lied ... or Ludwik had not voluntarily relinquished the girls. They'd been stolen from him.

"Do you happen to have an address for Ludwik in London? There was something he asked me to look into for him—

something to do with his photography. I never had the chance to tell him what I'd found out."

"I don't know how you'd locate him. But I could ask Joe—"

"No, please don't! It's not that important."

"Very well, then. Maybe you can ask him yourself tomorrow night. We'll look forward to your company. The festivities begin at seven, but please get here early. Oh—and tell Frank not to say a word to Joe. The party is a surprise."

"Of course, not a word."

CHAPTER 19

A bigail sat at the dressing table in the Radcliffs' guest bedroom, a young maid deftly styling her hair in marcel waves.

Her eyes wandered to the tall window that overlooked the meadow and horse pastures. Low clouds hung like powder puffs in the gray-blue sky of early evening, the plaintive cooing of a mourning dove heralding the day's end. Such a peaceful setting, yet her thoughts were anything but tranquil.

Once again, Franklin had disappointed her. That he should find Riana undeserving of care because of her unfortunate circumstances went against everything Abigail had always believed about a doctor's moral duty. Yet Franklin's lack of charity should not have been a surprise. She knew what his ambitions were—and had gone along with them when it was to her benefit. What right did she have now to criticize them?

Except for what he planned to do with the twins. It was difficult to believe that he would be willing to imperil their lives for the sake of publicity. She had been wrong to trust him.

Had she been wrong about Ludwik, too? Could he have deceived her, convincing her he was a man of compassion and loyalty when actually he had always intended to profit from the twins? Perhaps he had only been trying to drive a harder bargain when he first threatened to leave Scarsdale with the girls.

"Would you like me to help you dress now, ma'am?"

Abigail came back to herself with a start. "Yes, thank you."

The maid assisted Abigail with her corset and its cover, then her petticoat and gown. The dress was fashioned from chiffon and lace in spring green, with an intricately beaded waistband and flowing train. It would have been impossible without help to fasten the tiny covered buttons that ran all the way down the back.

When they were finished, the young woman said shyly, "You look beautiful, ma'am."

Abigail hesitated, ashamed to ask but too curious to hold back. "Do you know what the countess is wearing tonight?"

"No, ma'am. I wasn't called to help." The young woman smiled. "But I'm sure you'll be the one everybody notices."

· · · · ·

Abigail hovered at the edge of the drawing room, waiting for Franklin to join her while taking stock of who Lillian had seen fit to include in such a special evening. She had assumed the Radcliffs to have many friends and acquaintances, but there were actually very few in attendance. A couple of minutes earlier, Lillian had told her their names, promising that once Franklin arrived, she would introduce them properly.

The notables included Sheriff Ray Hunter, a short, bullish-looking fellow with fat jowls and a thick neck, who oversaw the entire police department of the neighboring county seat, White Plains. The patrician-looking Mr. August Means, president of the Scarsdale Town Club, was accompanied by his wife, whose droopy face was cast in an expression of perpetual boredom. Mr. Frederick Eaton was Joe's attorney. Observed from afar, his loud, abrasive manner made it easy to imagine him intimidating some poor, confused witness on the stand. Dr. Genworth and Dr. Sorrell were also among the select few; they had brought with them another man, similarly grayed and bespectacled though vigorously lean. His name was Dr. Cornelius Whittaker.

"Sorry I'm late," Franklin said, coming up behind her.

Before she could ask what had taken him so long, she saw that Dr. Whittaker was making his way toward them. By the directness of his approach, she sensed he had a purpose other than small talk.

"Dr. Rome, a pleasure," he said, shaking Franklin's hand. "And this must be Miss Platford, your assistant. I have heard a lot about both of you."

Abigail nodded her acknowledgment. Something in the way he peered at her from behind his round eyeglasses made her wary. What could he possibly have heard about *her*, and from whom? "You're involved in the same sort of research as Drs. Genworth and Sorrell?"

"I am a psychiatrist, Miss Platford. I run the state asylum in Indiana."

She remembered well what Dr. Genworth had said. At the urging of eugenicists, the Indiana legislature had passed a law providing for the involuntary sterilization of inmates at state institutions. She could only assume that Dr. Whittaker must have approved the plan as well.

"It seems tremendous strides are being made in your field," Franklin remarked amiably.

"Yes, that's true. Of course, there are many facets to psychiatry. My particular interest is psychopathic personalities. Such defects, whether congenital or acquired, present an enormous problem to society."

"What kinds of *defects* are you talking about, specifically?" Abigail asked, wondering how wide a net he would cast.

"There are several classifications. Born criminals are one, but also pathological liars and those driven by what we call basic compulsions. One of the most interesting to me is *pedophilia erotica*—the unnatural sexual attraction of adults to young children. It has been well known throughout history, but we are only now beginning to recognize it as a true psychopathology. I'm working on a paper dealing with this very topic, which I expect will be published within the year—a series of highly unusual case studies."

Abigail was gratified to hear Dr. Whittaker speak of the abuse of children as pathological behavior. Society too often accepted such indecency without doing anything to combat it. Still, she mistrusted him. It was enough that he had come here with Dr. Genworth and Dr. Sorrell.

"But what about you, Dr. Rome? Have you published your work in the field of—"

"Transformative surgery," Franklin interjected. Though he had fallen out of the habit of using the more formal term, he clearly wished to make a favorable impression on Dr. Whittaker. "No, I've not published. There remains a very strong bias among the medical establishment against the sort of work I do; I imagine you are aware of it. While I've developed many exciting new techniques, they so far remain proprietary."

"A pity. I feel strongly that knowledge, especially in the medical field, should be shared openly. It's to the benefit of our patients that we do so."

"I agree. Right now, I'm designing an operating theater that will accommodate up to thirty spectators in the gallery. In time, the Rome Institute will be world famous, and transformative surgery will be recognized as the important advance that it is."

Dr. Whittaker raised one brow as he stroked his pointed beard. "And when do you think this institute of yours will be completed?"

"I'm hoping within the year. Mr. Radcliff and I haven't set a date yet for the grand opening, but he's as anxious as I am to get things rolling."

"And you're still planning to operate on the conjoined twins from Spain?"

"Yes, I am."

"Hmm, interesting ..." Dr. Whittaker took a sip of his champagne, which he'd not touched until now. "By the way, I'm going to be in Manhattan on Monday morning for a conference. I wondered if I might stop by your office around three to meet the twins."

Abigail's stomach dropped. "If I might ask, Dr. Whittaker, what is your interest in the girls? Not professional, I assume."

Dr. Whittaker turned to her with a subtle smile. "I hear you've developed a certain interest in them yourself, Miss Platford."

"I've become quite fond of them, yes."

"Miss Platford is a most compassionate young woman," Franklin said. "If it were up to her, she'd turn my office into a charity hospital."

The two men chuckled, regarding her with patronizing smiles. She smiled back, silently fuming.

"Society already has enough charity cases on its hands," said Dr. Whittaker. "Just imagine if all the resources devoted to caring for those with degenerative disorders could be used to further improve the health and education of the fittest and most productive among us. What a boon it would be for humanity."

"I suppose your services as a psychiatrist would no longer be needed," Abigail said smugly. Obviously, Dr. Whittaker shared the views of his colleagues from Indiana, which was enough to make her detest him.

"Very true, but there's no chance of that happening in my lifetime, I assure you." He turned back to Franklin. "Are we settled on three o'clock Monday at your office?"

"That should be fine. The best place for your interview would be my apartment, just above the office. I can assure no interruptions there."

She was about to again ask Dr. Whittaker why he wanted to meet the twins when Ronnie rushed into the room, signaling everyone to stay quiet. A minute later, Abigail heard heavy footsteps in the hall, and then Joe came into view, seemingly on his way somewhere else until a resounding "Surprise!" stopped him short.

He pivoted toward the drawing room. His mouth falling open, he threw his arms in the air. "What in the name of ..." He started to laugh, his stomach shaking beneath his too-tight shirt. "My dear Mrs. Radcliff, what have you been up to? Didn't I tell you I'd decided not to get any older?"

"But you rejected the alternative as well," Lillian replied, beaming lovingly at her husband. "Age has its rewards, and one of them is the companionship of like-minded people. I thought to console you on the eve of your fiftieth birthday with a little gathering of friends."

"And what a fine job you have done!" Joe exclaimed, glancing around the room. His gaze lingered a moment on Abigail.

"If you both will excuse me," Dr. Whittaker said, "I think I'll go over and wish Mr. Radcliff a happy birthday. Dr. Rome, I'll see you at your office on Monday afternoon."

Abigail was glad for him to leave—and terrified at the idea of his meeting with Valencia and Melilla. Turning to Franklin, she resolved to confide in him the worst of her fears. It seemed the only thing left to do. There was a chance he might be willing to help once he found out that Joe and Lillian were not to be be-nevolent guardians of the twins, as he thought. Hadn't he, too, been deceived?

"Franklin, we have to talk. I heard something yesterday from Lillian that—"

She was cut short by an announcement from the butler that dinner was ready to be served. Like an obedient herd, the guests began moving en masse into the hallway.

"Let's hold back a moment," Abigail said, touching Franklin's sleeve. "It's important."

"Not now. Come along."

"You go on," she said, turning a cold shoulder. Out of the corner of her eye, she watched him join Sheriff Hunter, who greeted him with a familiar slap on the back. In another minute, everyone had left for dinner except her.

"Excuse me, ma'am." The Radcliffs' elderly maid, Nessa, stood in the doorway carrying a silver tray. "Don't mean to disturb you, but I thought I'd gather up the empty glasses. Do you mind?"

"Certainly not. I was just about to go into the dining room," Abigail said, though she made no move to do so. Another night of being forced to listen to the pontifications of Joe and those self-anointed saviors of humanity from Indiana was almost more than she could bear.

"Thank you, ma'am." Nessa set the tray on a side table next to one of the love seats, remarking off-handedly, "Oh my, some-body forgot this." She picked up what appeared to be a notebook. "Dr. Whittaker, I guess."

Abigail snapped to attention. "Really? How do you know?"

"Says so right here." Nessa read from the cover: "*Clinical Notes: Case Studies. Dr. Cornelius Whittaker, Director, Eastern Indiana Hospital for the Insane, Richmond, Indiana.*" She looked up at

Abigail. "Sounds important. I'd best bring it to him right away before he misses it."

She had already taken a few steps toward the door before Abigail gathered her wits enough to stop her. "Oh, don't bother with that! I'm on my way to the dining room now. I'll take it to him."

"But I wouldn't trouble you, ma'am. Not for the world."

"It's no trouble," Abigail insisted, rushing over to take possession of the journal.

"Why, thank you, Miss Platford."

"Don't mention it."

The journal tucked discreetly under her arm, Abigail scurried out the door and down the hall, past the dining room to the ladies' powder room. Relieved to find it empty, she went inside and bolted the door. Leaning with her back against it, she hesitated. Sticking her nose into Dr. Whittaker's private clinical notebook was highly unethical. But wasn't it justified by her need to protect the twins? Perhaps there was something in these clinical notes that would shed light on why Dr. Whittaker wanted to interview them.

Taking a deep breath, she opened the cover. The first page was a table of contents, handwritten in a large, backward-slanting scrawl. A list of names, most likely the patients Dr. Whittaker was currently treating. She was about to flip to the next page when, with a gasp, she stopped.

Ludwik Rutkowski.

"Oh my God," she murmured. Never had she expected such a thing, but there it was: Ludwik's name, near the bottom of the page, written in the same bold cursive as all the others. Had Ludwik suffered some sort of mental breakdown? Frantically, she flipped to page ninety-seven. Her heart thumping, she read Dr. Whittaker's notes, the first dated just a few days ago.

Case #28

Diagnosis: Pathological Liar; Pedophilia Erotica, July 16, 1907

The patient is a male claiming to be 31 years of age. Identifies him-self as "Baron" Ludwik Rutkowski, of Polish birth, though his accent is distinctly British. Brought to EIHI from New York, where he was arrested for embezzlement and fraud. Further inquiry reveals a his-tory of sexual behavior consistent with pedophilia erotica. (Referred by F. G.) Of particular note is his peculiar preference for a pair of con-joined twins (female, approximate age 14) with which he has reportedly engaged in unnatural acts for the past eight years.

Patient arrived at the hospital with a broken ankle, which he in-sists resulted from an unprovoked attack by Mr. R., a highly respected philanthropist living near New York City. He further claims that the conjoined twins were removed from his custody as part of a kidnapping plot. These delusions may indicate additional psychopathologies.

Other than the ankle and a recent wound at the temple that is healing satisfactorily, the patient's condition appears unremarkable. He is of average height and weight; reacts normally to stimulus. Ex-hibits extreme anger and hostility toward his confinement; restraints are necessary. He holds to his identity as Baron Rutkowski; because of his apparent foreign-born status, no records are readily available. How-ever, law enforcement has confirmed patient's use of several assumed names recently.

In summary, the patient is afflicted with at least two forms of de-generation associated with the psychopathic personality. Studies on this patient will be conducted to determine which treatment methods, if any, yield results.

Abigail snapped shut the cover of Dr. Whittaker's journal, unable to read another word, too shaken by what she had learned already. Ludwik in a hospital for the insane? It was more awful than anything she had so far imagined.

At a loss for what to think or do, one thing was certain. She could not afford for Dr. Whittaker to realize his book was miss-ing and discover it in her possession.

She looked in the mirror. Her appearance was startling, her face completely drained of color. Giving her cheeks a hard pinch, she practiced a look of composure. A few deep breaths, a bright smile. Then a pat to her hair, and she exited the powder room.

Concealing the journal within the folds of her gown, she passed the dining room. Thankfully, the doors were closed and no one would see her heading across the hall to the drawing room. Nessa was still there. As Abigail entered, she looked up from her cleaning.

"Miss Platford! Is everything all right?"

"Actually, I feel a bit ill," Abigail said, touching her forehead. "I wondered if you would mind informing Mrs. Radcliff that I've gone up to my room? Please apologize for me, and tell her not to worry. It's only a headache. And here—" She handed Nessa the journal. "I guess you'll have to give this to Dr. Whittaker yourself." She glanced behind her, nerves on edge.

"And Dr. Rome? Should I say anything to him?"

"Yes, tell him I need him upstairs—right away."

· · · · · ·

Abigail paced the width of her bedroom, her mind reeling from the revelations in Dr. Whittaker's journal. Her first reaction had been not to believe any part of what she'd read about Ludwik. But the fact remained that Dr. Whittaker was a psychiatrist, an expert. Might he see in Ludwik what she could not? Perhaps so. If Franklin was correct about Arthur, her former fiancé had successfully hidden his predilection from her; though she would not have thought less of him, neither could she have accepted him as a marriage partner. But Ludwik ... he seemed so sincere in his feelings about the twins, like they were sisters.

She recalled what Melilla and Valencia had said about their guardian—how kind he was, how much they loved him. Could they possibly feel that way about a man who had abused them? Maybe it was a good thing for Dr. Whittaker to interview the twins on Monday. Perhaps their story would confirm beyond a doubt that Ludwik was not a pedophile, and the doctor would be forced to change his diagnosis.

As for the accusation of fraud, the assumed names—what evidence was there against him? The journal had offered no details except that Ludwik had been arrested in New York. She wondered if Sheriff Hunter had anything to do with it. He and Joe were obviously friendly. Would a word from Joe, and some money under the table, have been enough? Nothing would ever have to be proven in a court of law. Not with Ludwik safely shut away in the Eastern Indiana Hospital for the Insane.

But why would Joe do such a thing? Did he want the twins so badly that he would destroy another human being in order to get them?

Anxiously, she consulted the bedside clock. Fifteen minutes had passed since she gave Nessa instructions to tell Franklin she needed him upstairs. Why hadn't he come? She wondered if the maid had mentioned she was ill. If not, perhaps he had assumed she was merely insisting they discuss whatever matter had been on her mind in the drawing room. He might well have ignored her, figuring she would soon give up and join the others in the dining room.

The minutes ticked by. After an hour, there was no longer any excuse to be made for Franklin's failure to look in on her. Weary and discouraged, Abigail changed into her nightgown, performed a minimal toilette, and crawled into bed. She propped herself up with pillows and opened a book, but the pages might as well have been blank. Her thoughts kept turning back to Dr. Whittaker's journal.

If it was true that Ludwik had been unjustly accused, arrested, and imprisoned in a hospital for the insane, the corruption was staggering. Had it all started with Joe Radcliff and his desire to add the twins to his collection of so-called human oddities? Did the eugenicists cooperate in order to gain Joe's favor—and his money? Had the sheriff been duped, or did he know all along it was a sham?

There was a light knock at her door. Finally! She jumped up and hurried to open it, certain it was Franklin.

"I hope I didn't wake you." The countess was dressed in one of her embroidered kimonos, her head wrapped in a turban the same color as the yellow sash around her waist. "You rarely turn in so early."

"I have a headache," Abigail replied, crestfallen. Of all the people she didn't want to see ... "And why didn't *you* join the party downstairs?"

"Ronnie thought I'd better not. She said I might drink too much and perhaps that psychiatrist would have me committed." She shrugged nonchalantly. "But I wondered if you'd like to join me for a nightcap. It might even be good for your headache. I've always found alcohol to be the best cure for almost everything."

Abigail's first impulse was to say no; she had never enjoyed Alexandra's company. But with all the troubling thoughts on her mind, a nightcap might not be a bad idea. While it was not a habit in which she ordinarily indulged, a sip or two might help her to relax.

Besides, she still had a certain curiosity about the countess, perhaps even a strange sort of fascination with the woman she'd regarded as a rival for Franklin's attentions. What would she be like, face to face, just the two of them alone?

278 | THE BEAUTY DOCTOR

"All right, I'll be over in a minute."

She closed the door, already wishing she'd not been so rash. There was nothing to be gained but more aggravation. She would not stay long.

Slipping on her blue robe with the ivory lace trim and a pair of satin slippers, she ventured into the hall and through the open door to Alexandra's room. The countess seemed not to notice her arrival; she was gazing intently upon a large canvas atop a wooden easel in front of the windows, faced away from the door. An array of paints and a large palette were laid out on a nearby table.

"I didn't know you were an artist. Is this a new pastime?"

Alexandra looked up, hastening to drape a cloth over the canvas. "Oh no, I've been painting most of my life. Of course, that doesn't mean I do it well. Though Joe and Lillian seem to find my work to their liking. Maybe you've noticed some of my paintings in the drawing room?"

Those awful nudes! Abigail had wondered why the Radcliffs would display anything so crude and amateurish as those vile portraits. Perhaps they had done so only temporarily, to humor the countess.

"The paintings of ... women?"

"Yes, what do you think of them? Be honest."

She was tempted. Alexandra thought nothing of insulting everyone else; why shouldn't she have a taste of her own medicine? But no, Abigail couldn't do that—not quite.

"They're ... interesting."

"*Interesting?*" Alexandra gave a little snort. "That's what people say when they really don't like something but can't admit to it."

Abigail tried being a little more generous. "There are many painters who simply copy more famous artists. It's commendable that you have a style all your own."

"Well, thank you for *that*." Alexandra went over to her dressing table, poured two cognacs, and brought one to her guest. Raising her glass, she said, "A toast to my darling Ronnie!"

They both took a swallow of the amber liquid. Abigail nearly gagged.

"Did I tell you she *dis*invited me to her brother's birthday party tonight? Yes, I believe I mentioned it."

"I'm sure she didn't mean to hurt your feelings."

"Please don't make excuses for her. She can be every bit as boorish as any man. But tell me, Abigail, haven't you wondered about Ronnie and me? What we see in each other?" She smiled sardonically. "Maybe what we *do* together?"

The hot flush spreading over Abigail's face was not from the cognac. "Other people's relationships are not my business."

"Well, I don't mind telling you. What I love most about Ronnie is her lifestyle, much grander than anything I could afford these days. You see, my late husband, the Count, was not only a philanderer, he was a singularly unsuccessful gambler." She took a giant gulp of her drink. "As for what Ronnie sees in me, she used to find me entertaining but, sadly, not so much anymore. In fact, she's actually come to despise me. I have an interesting theory about it: I remind her of everything she hates about being a woman. I suppose that makes me ... what do you call it in English ... a *scapegoat*? I would have liked to talk with that psychiatrist downstairs. I'm sure he would be impressed with my insight."

Abigail was astonished by the entire outburst. Most of all that Alexandra, who loved to put on airs, would admit to sponging off Ronnie, for whom she seemed to have little regard.

"But who cares about Ronnie? I'd rather drink to you and Frank." Alexandra lifted her crystal tumbler high. "May the two of you live happily ever after, the prince and princess of beauty—in your beautiful castle, surrounded by beautiful children! Oh, it's just too lovely, isn't it?"

Biting her tongue, Abigail touched her glass to Alexandra's, thinking what a mistake it had been to come.

"Tell me, when is the wedding?" Alexandra turned and walked away, still without offering Abigail a seat. "After all, a *respectable* woman can't allow an affair to go on forever." She stood before the easel, running her finger along the edge of the covered canvas. "Would you like to see what I'm working on? It was going to be a surprise, but I'm rather excited to show it to you. It may be my greatest masterpiece. Actually, I was thinking of giving it to you."

"To me!"

"Yes, as a token of friendship. It's only fitting, since you were the inspiration. You and Frank." With a sudden flourish, Alexandra whisked off the shroud. "Voila!"

The portrait was huge, assaulting Abigail's senses in a bold flurry of form and color. For a few moments, she struggled to organize the images in her mind, to make sense of them. The two figures were entwined in a lovers' embrace. Lying in bed, the man was seen from the back, naked to just below his buttocks, his legs covered by the sheet. To his left, the woman lay sideways, her leg bent into the curve of his waist. His arms were wound around her, head turned to the side, his face mostly obscured by her long honey-blond hair. They might be almost any couple matching Abigail and Franklin's general description; Alexandra hadn't the skill of a true portrait painter. But how accurately she had captured Franklin's physique!

"Well?" the countess said, turning to Abigail with a faint smile. "I'm not finished. But it's coming together nicely."

"You have quite an imagination." Trembling with rage, Abigail took another swallow of cognac, feeling it burn all the way down.

"An inappropriate one, certainly. What would have *inspired* you to paint such a scene? Surely you didn't think I would want it as a gift."

"Really? I thought it might serve as a memento of that first night you and Frank spent together. The walls in this house are not as thick as one might wish. But don't worry about having disturbed me. I relished every minute."

"Perhaps you were only dreaming. Wishing you might indulge your own frustrated desires," Abigail said tersely.

"Dreaming or not, I have worked very hard on this painting. I'm sorry if it doesn't meet with your approval." She took a step back from the canvas. With a slight frown, she brought a finger to her chin. "You know, I just realized what's wrong. Details, Abigail, make all the difference."

She picked up her palette and a brush, which she dipped first into red, then blue, until the mixture was almost purplish, like a bruise. Abigail watched her lean toward the canvas, hesitate, and then place a tiny dab onto Franklin's left buttock, playing with it a moment until it had assumed more or less the shape of a strawberry.

Abigail stared at the spot, not sure at first what to make of it. Might it be a shadow or maybe a drip of paint that accidentally had fallen from the brush? But the dull ache in the pit of her stomach told her it was neither. Alexandra had placed the birthmark deliberately, knowingly.

"There!" she said, straightening up and stepping to the side so Abigail would be sure to have a wide-open view. "Now it's perfect."

Abigail stared for a moment at the countess's smiling face. She could not recall ever despising anyone so thoroughly. "Oh dear, I'm afraid you missed a spot," she said, hurling her glass straight at the canvas. It struck squarely in the middle before crashing to the floor, shattering into small diamond-like bits that scattered everywhere. Uncannily, the painting remained on its easel, unscathed.

"My, my! You surprise me, Abigail. I wouldn't have bet you had it in you. Neither would Frank, I dare say. He often remarks how docile you are, how pliable. Men enjoy that, I suppose. They like the feeling of power it gives them to control a woman. But then sometimes they prefer a bit more fire."

Alexandra turned toward the open window. The moon shone full and silvery bright. She took a few steps toward the glass, swaying slightly as though she were sleepwalking. Then she swung back around, her black eyes simmering. "Frank and me and that pretty little maid—the one who dresses you—we had a jolly time when he was here last. Have you ever tried a threesome, Abigail? You really must—that is, if you wish to call yourself a modern woman. But, whatever, you mustn't blame Frank. It was all Joe's idea. He's a bit of a voyeur, you know. It started out as a game, a wager, and Franklin lost. Maybe you didn't know that he likes to gamble. I suppose we'd all had a little too much vodka that night."

Abigail felt as if she were underwater, watching Alexandra's lips move, the sound of her voice fathoms away. She stood immobile, aware only of the pounding of her heart and the scene flashing through her mind: the countess, half-naked, swooning in Franklin's arms. She heard Franklin's voice, assuring her there had never been an affair, scolding her for having doubted him.

A flood of sickness swept over her. She saw Alexandra standing by the window, the matching yellow of her sash and her turban, the shocking red of her painted lips. It seemed a blur, a mirage. None of it real.

Clutching her robe, she turned and fled the room, only vaguely aware of the countess calling out to her, "Come now, you didn't really believe me about the maid, did you?"

In the hall, she glanced wildly about, half expecting to find Franklin there, with his deviously self-assured smile. She staggered into her bedroom and locked the door. Confronting the bed where she and Franklin had first made love, she had the bizarre idea of setting it aflame. In a fit of fury, she threw back the coverlet, ripped off the sheets. She would have torn them to shreds with her bare hands, except she hadn't the gall. Instead, she trampled them on her way to the armoire, where she pulled her spring-green gown from its hanger—the same gown Lillian's maid had helped her with that very night. In the drawer of the dressing table, she found a pair of scissors and began cutting, slashing the beaded waistband and the long swath of fabric that had trailed her every step only hours earlier. When there was nothing left but tatters, she tossed the dress aside, frantically searching for something else on which to vent her anger and humiliation.

But she was too exhausted. Her sobs came now in fits and waves that made it hard to breathe. Once, they would have been the tears of a broken-hearted lover; now, they were only the bitter salt of a woman done with being a fool.

She went to the window. The moon appeared just as it had through the countess's glass. Full tonight, but, of course, it could not remain so. The abiding law of the universe is that everything must change. Her time with Franklin was over. She would have to find her own way, without help from anyone.

The first step was taking care of those who needed her.

CHAPTER 20

They were back in the city by three the next afternoon. Franklin could not have failed to notice the coldness with which she regarded him throughout the entire drive. Few words were exchanged between them. At the conclusion, she had him drop her off at her apartment, saying the headache from last night still lingered and asking not to be disturbed. Sleeplessness lent her a pallor that made the story convincing. Franklin wished her a speedy recovery, saying he would see her at the office tomorrow. Seemed that he, too, had something on his mind.

By eight the next morning, she was on her way to the offices of the *New York World*, a newspaper in which Franklin often placed advertisements. As a result, Abigail had become friendly with a young woman who had access to the paper's "morgue," a vast biographical file on persons of importance.

"Samuel Storey?" she repeated after Abigail explained her quest, leaving out the more shocking details. "You say he's involved in the newspaper business—in London?"

"I think so, yes."

"Hold on."

She disappeared into the adjacent file room. Abigail heard the banging of drawers and several verbal exchanges of which she could make out only a few words—something about Carnegie and chains and profits. Perhaps nothing to do with Mr. Storey; she couldn't tell. As the minutes ticked by, she worried that Samuel Storey would be more difficult to find than she'd anticipated. Or maybe, though she didn't want to think it, he might not exist at all.

Finally, the young woman returned, clutching a single sheet of paper. "Samuel Storey owns a bunch of newspapers. Looks like the *Sunderland Echo* was the first of them, but there's an entire chain of them now. I jotted down the names. They're all over England."

Abigail breathed a sigh of relief. "So, he's a successful businessman? A person of note?"

"Seems to be. Here," she said, handing Abigail the list. "I also gave you the address for the *Sunderland Echo*. I'd say that would be the best place to contact him."

Abigail glanced at the paper and then the clock behind the desk. It was almost time for her to be at work.

"Where is the nearest telegraph office?"

Following her friend's directions, Abigail was there in less than ten minutes. After waiting in line, she gave the telegraph operator the delivery information and dictated her message. Considering the expense, it had to be brief:

Extremely urgent. Need information on background and character of Baron Ludwik Rutkowski. Contact Dr. Cornelius Whittaker, Eastern Indiana Hospital for the Insane, Richmond, Indiana.

Her mission accomplished, she headed for Franklin's office, arriving just before ten. He was already behind his desk, his head resting against the high back of his leather chair. She took a couple of steps into the room before seeing that his eyes were closed. She turned to go.

"Stay here, Abigail. I'm not asleep." There was an ominous tone to his voice.

He leaned forward to pick up something from his desktop, a piece of paper that he tossed in her direction. It landed on the floor a few feet in front of her.

"Go ahead, look," he said. "Read it."

She picked it up and quickly scanned the page; it was a legal summons. A complaint had been filed by Mrs. Ethel Stryder, who claimed she had suffered severe injury from paraffin injections performed by Dr. Franklin Rome on July 1, 1907. She demanded the enormous sum of $1,100 with interest and costs.

"Did you know Mrs. Stryder was having a problem?" she asked, glancing up at him.

"I was about to ask you the same question."

"If I knew one of your patients was in distress, don't you think I would have told you?"

His palm slammed the desktop. "Idiotic woman didn't even have the decency to telephone. She could have given me a chance to fix it before running to her damn lawyer."

Abigail wasn't in a sympathetic mood, at least not for Franklin's sake. She was worried, though, about Mrs. Stryder. Might her condition be as catastrophic as Mrs. Moser's? And there were at least two dozen other patients who had received injections during the time Abigail had been with Franklin. Would they all suffer the same fate?

"This is the worst possible thing that could have happened. And just when I thought everything was under control. I'll have to hire a lawyer. Maybe I can settle before anybody hears about it."

She knew *anybody* meant Joe Radcliff and that the Rome Institute was the only thing on Franklin's mind.

"I'll try to get an appointment with someone this afternoon," he said, thinking aloud, "You can handle that Whittaker fellow, can't you? Just take him upstairs to the apartment and let him talk to the twins. That's all he's interested in. Oh—by the way, we'll operate on them next Monday. I'd hoped to do it sooner, but I need to sort out these other matters first. I can't afford to be distracted."

Abigail nodded. At least now she had an entire week to work on reuniting Ludwik and the twins. But would that be enough? She had no way of knowing when Samuel Storey would read the telegram she'd sent, or if he would read it at all. She thought back to Saturday night and how close she'd come to telling Franklin everything—how desperate Ludwik had sounded on the telephone, her conversation with Lillian about the twins, and what she had later read in Dr. Whittaker's notebook. But now she considered it possible he might already know.

"How are you feeling? Your headache?"

She was surprised he remembered—or cared.

"Still there. I was sick to my stomach this morning. My temperature was over a hundred," she said, wanting to ensure he would keep his distance.

"You should be in bed."

"I'll stay until Dr. Whittaker arrives. Then I'll go home." She paused. "It's best if you sleep somewhere else tonight."

•   •   •   •

At half-past three, Dr. Whittaker—serious, self-possessed, and quite possibly ruthless—stepped through the front door of the office.

"Miss Platford, good afternoon."

"Hello, Doctor," Abigail said, rising from behind her desk. "I'm afraid Dr. Rome was called away unexpectedly. He said to offer his apologies for not being here to greet you personally."

"Very well. As you know, I'm here to see—what are their names again?"

"Valencia and Melilla Rosa."

"Did anyone tell them I was coming?"

"Not as far as I know."

"Good. I only want to ask them a few questions. Shouldn't take more than an hour."

"I was wondering, Doctor—might this interview have something to do with your research on psychopathic personalities?"

His eyes narrowed. "And how are you aware of my research?"

"You don't remember? You mentioned it when we were chatting before dinner at the Radcliffs' home. Dr. Rome was there as well. Sounds fascinating." She hoped the compliment would soften him, because surely what she had to say next would not.

"Ah yes." He smiled. "I recall it now."

"Of course, you didn't mention that one of your subjects is Baron Ludwik Rutkowski."

Dr. Whittaker's smile vanished. "I would never discuss a patient's case outside a professional environment, Miss Platford. That would be highly unethical."

"Dr. Whittaker," she began in her most earnest voice, "I am certain the goal of your research is to uncover the truth. But I fear there may have been a terrible mistake concerning Baron Rutkowski."

"What sort of mistake?"

She paused, suddenly questioning the decision she'd come to earlier. Might she be about to make a strategic error? There was that chance. But if she could get Dr. Whittaker himself to send a second telegram to Samuel Storey, it could only increase the chance of a reply. "I have located someone who might be helpful to you. He knows the baron and is a longtime friend of the family. His name is Mr. Samuel Storey. I remembered that Baron Rutkowski had mentioned him to me once, just in casual conversation. He owns a chain of newspapers in England." She opened her desk drawer, withdrawing the folded notepaper on which she had copied Mr. Storey's address. She handed it to Dr. Whittaker. "I thought you would want to get in touch with him right away."

He opened the note, glancing at it only a moment before stuffing it into his jacket pocket. "How enterprising of you."

Her heart sank. His reaction was not what she had hoped for. "You *will* telegraph him, won't you?"

Dr. Whittaker glowered at her. "Anyone who can shed additional light on a patient's condition may be useful. Now, if you don't mind, I'd like to get on with interviewing the twins."

"I assume you won't be telling them where Baron Rutkowski is?" Abigail had stopped caring what Dr. Whittaker thought of her. This was too important. "The girls believe he's gone to Poland to tend to his ailing father. They think he's coming back for them. That's what Mr. Radcliff told them, even though he intends to assume guardianship of the girls himself. Or he has *bought* them with something else in mind," she added caustically.

"I take it you don't approve."

"No, I don't. And I'm afraid I can't agree with your diagnosis of the baron either. He is not a pedophile. I'm certain of it."

Dr. Whittaker stroked his beard, studying her curiously. "Putting aside whether the baron of whom you speak is or isn't a patient of mine, how would you conclude that I have made such a diagnosis?"

Her throat tightened. "You said that pedophilia is an interest of yours—professionally, that is."

He pursed his lips. "Yes, well, you needn't trouble yourself about what I'll say to the twins. The purpose of my interview is to extract information, not to impart it."

"Please ask the girls about Mr. Storey. They may remember something, though I don't know for certain that they've ever met him."

Dr. Whittaker's nostrils flared. "Miss Platford, I don't believe I need your help in conducting my business with the conjoined twins—or with anyone else. Now, may we proceed upstairs?"

It was no use saying more. He would either follow up with Mr. Storey, or he wouldn't. "Very well then. Please come this way."

Reluctantly, she led him down the back hall and up the stairs to Franklin's apartment. Prudence promptly answered the door, stepping aside to admit them. The moment they crossed the threshold into the small foyer, Dr. Whittaker turned to Abigail.

"Thank you very much, but I won't need you further."

"I can let the doctor out when he's finished," Prudence offered.

A few seconds later, unable to think of an excuse to stay, Abigail was on her way downstairs. She already sensed failure. How foolish to imagine Dr. Whittaker would have an interest in contacting Samuel Storey. He didn't want the truth; all he cared about was publishing a paper promoting his theories of psychopathology. Ludwik was nothing more to him than a titillating case study. The only hope lay in the telegram she had already sent. Whether Mr. Storey ever received it or, if he did, whether he would feel compelled to respond was as yet unknown. But even if Mr. Storey were to vouch for Ludwik, Dr. Whittaker would be the one deciding whether to release him. Abigail had the feeling he would be in no hurry to do so.

She sat behind her desk to wait for Dr. Whittaker's return. Not that she thought he would tell her anything about his interview with the twins. But as soon as he was out the door, she intended to pay a visit to the girls herself, not only to find out what had happened, but to make certain they were all right. She did not put it past Dr. Whittaker to have filled their heads with nonsense about Ludwik, ideas that could only upset them.

It was half past four when she heard footsteps on the stairs. A moment later, Dr. Whittaker, accompanied by Prudence, entered the reception room. Both looked surprised to see her there.

"If you don't need me further ..." Prudence said, and quickly excused herself.

Dr. Whittaker turned to Abigail with a stern look. "There was no reason for you to wait."

"I thought perhaps—"

"You thought wrong, Miss Platford. You and I have nothing to discuss." He strode past her toward the door.

"But, Dr. Whittaker—"

"Good day," he said, clamping his bowler on his head and hurrying out. Abigail watched through the window as he hailed a passing hansom cab. Obviously, she had wasted her breath trying to reason with him.

She went to the door and locked it before making her way down the hall and up the back stairs. It took Prudence longer than usual to answer her knock. When she finally did, the look of distress on the elderly woman's kind, simple face told Abigail something was terribly wrong.

"Oh, Miss Platford! Thank goodness you haven't left. It's the twins—or at least one of them. Seems Melilla is sick."

"Since when?"

"Well, I noticed she looked a bit peaked yesterday. I didn't think much of it. But now, all of a sudden, she's taken a turn for the worse."

Abigail swept past her and ran down the hall to the girls' room. The door was open. The second she stepped inside, she could smell the acidic, cheesy odor of vomit. Valencia and Melilla were lying on top of the bed. She rushed over to them and placed her hand on the Melilla's forehead, then Valencia's. Only Melilla felt feverish, and not alarmingly so.

"Tell me what's wrong, Melilla. When did you start feeling poorly? And what are your symptoms—all of them?"

"Symptoms?"

"What other things feel bad besides your stomach?"

"My head. Her, too," Melilla said, giving a sideways nod a t her sister.

"You think it was something you two ate?"

"No, that man—" She stopped, her eyes filling with tears. "Why they take Ludwik? Why they lock him up?"

Abigail could barely contain her outrage. "What did Dr. Whittaker say to you?"

"He say Ludwik bad person," Valencia said. "Ludwik not come back."

Abigail sat on the edge of the bed, desperate to think of something she might say to cheer them. "Listen, I have good news. I've located someone who can straighten it all out. Ludwik is a good person. We know that. It's all been a terrible mistake. But Mr. Storey will tell them. Do you remember him? Mr. Storey—in London?"

If Samuel Storey was an old friend of the family, as Ludwik had said, it seemed likely the twins would know him. Yet her question drew only blank looks.

"He runs a newspaper—a bunch of them. Samuel Storey. Are you sure you don't know him?"

Suddenly Valencia's eyes grew wide. "Uncle Sammy?"

Abigail sighed in relief. "You see? We've nothing to worry about. Your Uncle Sammy will tell Dr. Whittaker all about Ludwik and how good he's been to you."

Melilla licked her cracked lips. "That doctor—he ask if Ludwik ever touch us—in bad places."

"We say no, but he ask and ask," Valencia said "He say awful things and then he want us say yes to them."

"But you didn't?"

"No, but he not shut up. Stupid man!" Valencia sounded like her old self, which made Abigail smile. She glanced at Melilla, hoping to see a hint of sparkle returning to her dark, troubled eyes.

"I want the two of you to rest now. Put Dr. Whittaker and everything he said out of your minds."

"But what we going to do with no Ludwik?" Melilla whined.

"You are not going to be without Ludwik. I promise." How Abigail wished she could be certain she was telling them the truth. What chance did she really have, pitted against men like Joe Radcliff and the doctors from Indiana, powerful men who could impose their will on others with no one questioning their right?

She stood up to leave.

"Where you go?" Valencia demanded, grabbing Abigail's arm.

Abigail had the idea that perhaps another lesson from *Gray's Anatomy* might take their minds off Ludwik. It was worth a try. "Just downstairs for a minute. I'll be right back."

She found Prudence standing just outside the room. The poor woman appeared nearly beside herself with worry. "They both were crying their eyes out," she whispered. "They didn't know what to think after what that horrible doctor said."

Abigail replied in a hushed tone, wanting to be sure the twins couldn't hear. "I'm curious—did Dr. Rome speak with them this morning? Did he tell them Dr. Whittaker was coming?"

"No, Dr. Rome don't pay the girls no mind. To be truthful, he's not been himself lately. He don't seem to notice too much around here."

She paused, wondering if Prudence had any idea of Franklin's current trouble. "Well, let's make sure they drink plenty of water. If you can, try to get some hot soup into them, too."

"Yes, ma'am. I'm sorry I didn't say nothing yesterday, but I thought they'd be all right." She shook her head. "That doctor—I know I shouldn't have been listening, but—"

"It's all right, Prudence. What did he say to the girls?"

"Sounded to me like he was practically threatening them. Said if they didn't tell him what that fellow—what's his name?"

"Baron Rutkowski. Ludwik."

"Right. Said he'd make things tougher on the man if the girls didn't cooperate. And then he started talking about all kinds of terrible things, obscene things, trying to get them to say this Ludwik fellow had forced them. Well, it was something to hear, Miss Platford! I just hope none of it was true."

"What did Melilla and Valencia say?"

"They said the man never laid a finger on them. They denied every accusation that doctor made, over and over."

"I thought it would be the case. I knew it."

"But what's going to happen to the girls now? Wasn't that fellow their guardian? If they've got him locked up ..."

"Baron Rutkowski is going to be released from the hospital. It's just a matter of time."

"Oh, that's good to hear, ma'am. I just hope those girls survive all this. I've never seen them look so bad."

"They'll be fine. You and I, we'll make sure of it."

CHAPTER 21

A bigail hurried over to her desk, intent on grabbing *Gray's Anatomy* and returning to the ailing twins. She considered it a blessing that Franklin was not around. Though she would have welcomed a doctor's opinion, the girls' condition did not seem overly serious to her, and his presence would only make her uncomfortable. Then, too, how would she explain her own sudden recovery?

"Miss Platford!"

Startled, she looked up to see Paddy standing inside the front door. He must have let himself in. She was surprised he would, after she had made him promise never to come to the office. But right away, she saw something was wrong. Disheveled and out of breath, Paddy had white trails running down his dirty cheeks. He'd been crying.

"What is it?" she asked, full of dread. Had something happened to Shaena?

"Auntie's dead."

Abigail caught her breath. "Riana?"

He nodded, his lip quivering. "Killed herself. With a rope."

"Dear Lord! When?"

"They said last night. Maybe early this morning. Nobody really knows. They found her in—in that place where she works."

"What place?"

"Mama Sally's. It's a—" He looked down, drawing a circle with his toe.

"A brothel?" She had always suspected that Riana's story about contracting syphilis from her husband might not be the truth—or not the whole truth.

He looked up at her, his eyes moist. "Auntie used to be the prettiest. But then—well, you seen her. Sally kept her around to clean up after the others, long as she didn't show her face. Said it would be bad for business."

Abigail thought back to the morning she'd met Riana and how the woman had begged for help. Riana had turned to her as a last resort. And she had let her down.

"Where is Shaena?"

"That's why I come. Without Auntie to watch after her, Sally's gonna take her."

"You mean the madam? *She's* going to look after her?"

"I guess. But—well, Mama Sally makes everybody work. There's girls in there not too much older than Shaena. She won't be no different—even with the scar." His eyes searched Abigail's face. "I know you like her. You took care of her once. I just thought maybe ..."

She was struggling to process everything she had just heard from Paddy, including this last not-so-subtle suggestion. But one thing she knew: She was proud of him for trying to protect his little sister. "You're a good boy, Paddy. A good brother."

"So, you'll come?"

"I don't—" She stalled for a moment. She was in no position to assume responsibility for a child. But at least she could talk to this *Mama Sally*. There had to be somewhere else for Shaena to go. Somewhere she would be safe.

"Yes, Paddy, I'll come."

·   ·   ·   ·   ·

Paddy rode with his nose pressed against the window of the hansom. "Mama Sally's don't need a sign. Everybody knows where it is."

Abigail paid no attention. She was back to worrying about the twins. The last thing she'd wanted was to leave them at a time like this. But every minute Shaena remained in that brothel was a minute in which harm could come to her—the sort of harm that a child might never recover from.

"There it is! Right over there, next to Fat Jack's Saloon," Paddy yelled up the hatch.

The driver reined in his horse, steering to the side of the road. Paddy opened the door and jumped out. In an unexpectedly gallant gesture, he turned and offered Abigail his hand—unfortunately, the same one he'd just used to wipe his nose.

"Are you scared?" Paddy asked after she had stepped down from the cab.

"Not really." She withdrew a couple of coins from her purse to pay the driver. "Will you please wait? I won't be long."

"I ain't no personal chauffeur."

"I'll be gone only about ten minutes, and I'll pay you double for the ride home."

He squinted at her, pulling his flat-brimmed cap down over his eyes. "I'll have a smoke, but if you ain't back by the time I'm done, you'll have to find yourself another ride."

Abigail knew she would do no better with him. She nodded, and then she and Paddy hurried off to Mama Sally's, a dilapidated two-story wooden structure crammed between Fat Jack's and another tavern called the King's Throne.

"I'll wait for you out here," Paddy said when they reached the door.

"You're not coming in?" Having never set foot in a house of ill repute, she had no idea what to expect. She had counted on Paddy being with her.

He shrugged. "Mama Sally don't like me much."

"You could have told me before," she scolded. "You might as well go back to the cab. Try to keep the driver from leaving."

Paddy nodded and took off, leaving Abigail to fend for herself. Resolutely, she opened the red door.

The air in Mama Sally's front room was dense with the smoke of incense and cigars. The drapes were drawn closed, and the only light came from an overhead gasolier. Several women wearing silk robes left open to afford a glimpse of creamy flesh lay about on red velvet sofas, talking and laughing with half a dozen men. Seemed that Mama Sally's attracted patrons from outside the neighborhood, as these gentlemen were somewhat fashionably dressed in jackets and ties. Everyone was having a fine time—except for one girl, thin and honey-toned, who appeared younger than the rest and sat off to the side, staring into space.

"Mama Sally!" One of the lounging women had spotted the new arrival. A moment later, Abigail heard the click of heels and a rustling of silk. The velvet curtain in a doorway to her immediate left opened with the harsh scraping of rings on the metal rod.

"Yeah?" The woman standing on the threshold was notable first for her size—not tall but extremely wide—and then her age, which was likely three times that of any other woman in the room. She wore an elaborately flounced gown, fancy but out-of-date, her reddish hair piled high in a mass of curls and adorned with several brightly colored feathers. Her powdery-white face looked as if it might crack if she were to smile; it did not appear she was likely to do so..

"Good evening. I'm looking for the proprietor of this—this establishment," Abigail said, her voice faltering.

"You're lookin' at her."

"You're Mama Sally?"

"I said so, didn't I?" She did not move from the threshold.

"I'm a friend of Riana, the young woman who—"

"Hung herself," Sally broke in. "Could have done it easier some other way, but in the end it don't matter. She's out of her misery now." She eyed Abigail suspiciously. "If you've come lookin' to collect her things, you can forget it. She didn't have a pot to piss in. I only let her stay here out of the goodness of my heart."

"I'm not here for her things. I've come about the little girl—Shaena."

Sally raised an eyebrow. "What about her?"

"I just wondered who will take care of her now."

"And what business is it of yours?"

Abigail suddenly noticed how quiet the room had become. She looked behind her. Everyone had left, except for the young girl sitting alone. She turned back to Sally, who was lighting up a cigar.

"I told you, I'm a friend of Riana's."

Sally extinguished the match with a flick of her wrist. "Riana didn't have no friends." She took a step toward Abigail, eyeing her up and down. "You're not one of them do-gooders, are you? Wantin' to stick your nose where it don't belong?"

"I just came by to make sure Shaena is all right." Abigail held her gaze steady. "I wondered what arrangements have been made for her."

"Arrangements?" Sally sniffed derisively. "As long as she does her work, I'll let her stay here. That's what her mother wanted."

"But Riana wasn't her mother."

"I'm well aware of that, missy. I guess you don't know—her mother was one of my girls, too. And that little one, she would have made a pretty whore one day. A shame her face got ruined. But I'm holdin' out hope for her yet. Men are funny that way; sometimes they don't mind a girl who's different, even like that."

Abigail felt woozy from the smoke and incense, or maybe it was because of what Mama Sally had just said. It seemed there was nothing she could do to help Shaena. But there had to be. She couldn't just walk away and leave her here.

"I'm taking Shaena with me."

Sally showed no emotion, leisurely blowing a couple of smoke rings before she finally spoke. "It'll cost you. Three hundred."

"Why, that's absurd! You don't own her."

Sally's eyes narrowed. "She may be young, but she's still worth something. I ain't just givin' her away."

Abigail drew herself up. "I can have her removed from here, you know. There are laws—"

Sally clenched the cigar between her teeth, regarding Abigail as she would a harmless insect. "I'll give her to you for two fifty, but that's my last offer."

Abigail couldn't believe it. H e r e she was, engaging in the same despicable game as Joe Radcliff when he'd sent Franklin to bargain with Ludwik for the twins. Except, of course, she meant to rescue Shaena.

"All right, two fifty," she agreed, realizing she would have to bluff her way out. "I'll take her now and bring you the money tomorrow."

"Afraid I don't do business like that, honey. Bring me the money, I give you the girl. Until then, we got no deal. And if I get a better offer in the meantime, you can bet I'll take it. So you best not dilly-dally." She smiled smugly. "Now, I suggest you be on your way.

A fine young lady such as you don't want to be caught in a place like this, I'm sure."

"But—"

Mama Sally's smile vanished abruptly. "Good day to you, miss." Turning her back with an air of finality, she passed through the doorway and drew the velvet curtain closed.

Abigail's emotions were in tatters. If she imagined herself some kind of savior, that naïve notion had been summarily quashed. She had failed miserably. Shaena would remain a prisoner here, no safer than before.

"Just turn quietly, and don't say a word."

Abigail froze. The voice coming from behind her was soft and breathy. When she swung around, she saw it was the girl who before had been sitting alone, lost in a dream, but now looked perfectly alert. Her finger was raised to her lips. "Shh."

She headed for the circular staircase at the far end of the room, motioning for Abigail to follow. Wearing a slim-fitting nightgown of black satin, she moved like a nymph, supple and quick, as she hurried up the stairs, looking back every few seconds. Abigail's feet followed unquestioningly, though she had no reason to trust this young stranger. Perhaps the girl was on drugs or luring her into a trap. Still, she appeared to want to help.

They reached the top and, together, stole silently down a long hallway. All manner of disturbing sounds—grunts and screams and shouted obscenities—could be heard from behind the line of closed doors. Finally, the girl stopped at one of them, opened it, and peeked inside. She motioned for Abigail to enter ahead of her.

The interior was dim, lit only by an oil lamp placed on a night table by the bed. The room's furnishings were decent enough, in a tawdry sort of way—red velvet curtains with black fringe, a four-poster bed with double-scalloped curtains and a satin coverlet, a mirrored dressing table, an elaborately carved chest of drawers.

On the wall was a huge gilt-framed painting of naked goddesses romping in the forest, and, on the floor, a leopard-skin rug—upon which Shaena lay asleep, curled up with her stuffed gray kitten.

Abigail rushed over, falling to her knees at the little girl's side. "Shaena!"

The child opened her eyes. At first, there was no sign of recognition. Then she broke into a smile, throwing her arms around Abigail's neck. "You came!"

Abigail pulled her close. "Yes, I'm here."

"You'd better hurry," said the girl who had been her guide. "Right now, it's quiet up here, but not for long. Some men are pretty quick, in and out. We encourage it that way, you know."

Abigail scrambled to her feet and lifted Shaena into her arms. The child had lost weight.

"Thank you so much. But—" She hesitated, considering what might happen to her young accomplice once Mama Sally found out Shaena was missing. "Are you going to be in trouble?"

The girl shrugged. "Doesn't matter. I can handle Mama Sally." She bent down, picked up the gray kitten, and handed it to Shaena with a wistful smile. "Don't forget your friend." The next second, she was at the door, checking outside in both directions before turning back to whisper, "I think we can make it. But hurry."

Abigail slipped into the hallway, hugging Shaena to her chest, and the three of them crept toward the staircase. They were almost halfway when a door behind them opened, and the sound of voices, a woman's and a man's, drifted into the hallway. In a panic, Abigail flattened her back against the wall, knowing it would do no good. Any moment they would be discovered.

"Here! The closet," the girl said, scurrying to open yet another door, this one narrower than the others. She urged Abigail forward, then pushed her inside. The door clicked shut. Huddling among the long gowns and furs, Abigail's senses were overwhelmed by the noxious fumes of mothballs, heightened by the suffocating heat. Shaena was crying. Abigail pressed the child's face against her bosom to muffle the sound, stroking her hair and whispering reassurances.

The man and woman were coming down the hall, closer. She could hear their conversation clearly.

"I'm not saying I don't like it, but you still owe me."

"You know how much this hat is worth? Look at that fancy label on the inside. Comes all the way from Paris, France." Abigail was struck by the man's voice; there was something familiar about it.

"Let me see it again."

She could tell they had stopped just outside the closet. But where was the girl? Had she fled?

"Look, right here. Paris, France. Just like I said."

"Hmm. Give it here. Let me try it on. Hey, Stella. Come over her and take a look. What do you think? Does it flatter me? Or is it too matronly?"

"Beautiful," Stella said. Thank goodness, the girl was still there! "I bet that came from one of those fancy stores—maybe even Bonwit Teller."

"You think so? Well—" There was a long pause. "All right, you win. But next time, bring me cash. Mama Sally's taking more than her share these days, and I need the extra. Can't eat a hat, now, can I?" She snickered. "Stella, honey—here, put this back in my room for me, would you? I don't want Sally getting a look at it. She decides it suits her, that'll be the last I ever see of it."

"Sure, I'll take it for you."

"Come on, let's go, Shark. I got other customers, you know."

Shark! She should have known. How could she ever forget that voice?

The two descended the stairs, their footsteps fading. After what seemed an eternity, the closet door opened.

"We'll have to go down the back stairs instead," Stella said. "It'll be safer."

Abigail followed her, thinking how narrowly she had missed running into Shark, and fearing at any moment someone else might venture into the hall and sound the alarm to Mama Sally. She watched her every step down the stairs, careful to avoid a slip or stumble. It was only when they had reached the bottom that she noticed the hat perched on Stella's head.

Blue felt draped with black chiffon, adorned with red silk rosettes and several colorful bird-of-paradise plumes.

Stella saw them out the door before giving Shaena a kiss on the cheek and disappearing without a word. Still clutching Shaena tight against her chest, Abigail arrived at the curb breathless. Paddy had done his job; the driver had waited. But after the boy helped Abigail and Shaena into the cab, instead of jumping in with them, he mumbled a hasty excuse and took off alone. Abigail wondered if he might be worried she would hand over his sister, and he'd be left to look after her.

The full weight of the responsibility she'd taken on now sank in. This little girl, for the moment, was hers. She would need to feed her, clothe her, shelter her. Certainly, there were places she could drop off the child, places where Shaena would be just one more among many poor, abused, and abandoned children. But Abigail knew already she could not bring herself to do such a thing.

Not today.

She settled into the seat, glancing nervously out the window. Apparently, no one had seen them leave Mama Sally's. Still, she was relieved when the driver flicked his whip on the horse's rear, and they were on their way.

Their escape a fait accompli, Abigail reluctantly turned her thoughts to the Parisian hat. It was not a hat that one forgets, and today was not the first time she'd seen it. The memory was quite distinct: Mrs. Moser handing her the hat, along with a pair of gloves and a parasol, to be placed in the closet of Dr. Rome's office. Abigail had made a point of complimenting her on it.

There was no way Shark could have gotten his hands on that hat unless he'd stolen it. And how would his path ever have crossed that of Mrs. Moser ... unless Franklin was involved?

That visit to the office had been Mrs. Moser's last. Abigail remembered how Franklin had gone up to his apartment while Mrs. Moser lay on the operating table, after she had become hysterical and he had administered the sedative. Abigail had wondered why he would leave her at such a critical moment, what he could be doing that was so urgent. Of course, he must have been telephoning someone. Shark or one of his accomplices. He must have been arranging for the horse-drawn hansom cab to come and pick her up, probably the same cab that had transported Paddy when he was chloroformed into unconsciousness, perhaps the same one that had brought them the fresh cadaver—from God knows where. They had taken Mrs. Moser away.

And now, nine days had passed. They must have killed her! What else could they have done? She buried her face in Shaena's soft hair, trembling all over.

"Why are you shaking?" Shaena said in her dear, squeaky little voice.

With an immense effort of will, Abigail pulled herself together. There was no sense in upsetting the child. Shaena had been through enough.

"I'm just glad to get away from that place. And excited that we're together again."

"Me, too! I had the best time ever with you. Even when my face was sore."

Then, sticking her thumb in her mouth, she leaned her head against Abigail's chest and promptly fell asleep.

• • • • •

She took Shaena home, bathed her, and settled her into the little girl's favorite spot, Abigail's luxurious feather bed. After asking Mrs. Krueger across the hall if she would mind peeking in on her little niece until she returned from a few errands, Abigail went straight to Franklin's apartment.

Prudence appeared tired and distraught. She reported there had been no further vomiting, but now Melilla was coughing.

"Let me take over, Prudence. I'll tend to the girls. Why don't you rest for a while?"

"Thank you, ma'am. I'm a bit weary."

"Make yourself a cup of tea and relax. Just be sure to leave the door from the stairs unlocked. I may need to go back and forth for supplies and such."

"What do you think is wrong with them? I'm praying it's nothing serious."

"I'll know better once I've taken their temperatures and listened to their lungs."

She patted Prudence on the shoulder and sent her off for a nap. Then she went into the twins' room and approached the bed where the girls lay sleeping. Placing the back of her hand on Valencia's forehead, she felt a slight warmth. But when she touched Melilla, her heart plummeted. The girl's forehead was on fire!

In a panic, she ran downstairs to retrieve the stethoscope and a thermometer. When she returned to the twins' room, wishing not to wake them yet, she started with the stethoscope. First,

Melilla's lungs. Abigail found her breathing somewhat labored, with congestion mainly in the right lung. Next, she listened to her heart; it was beating much faster than it should.

Checking Valencia, she discovered nothing out of the ordinary. The stronger twin was, so far, holding her own.

Armed with this new information, Abigail went downstairs again, this time to Franklin's private office. From his bookcase, she selected a volume on infectious diseases. Since she wasn't certain of a diagnosis, it seemed prudent to assume the worst. She looked up *pneumonia* and skimmed the entire chapter before sitting at Franklin's desk to jot down some essential notes.

"Milk punch to stimulate the heart ... quinine, two grains every four hours in a tablespoon of brandy ... opium for pain and to calm the cough ... linseed poultice covered with oiled silk over the affected lung ..."

When finished, she went into the operating room to search the medicine cabinet for the items she would need. Everything was there except milk for the punch and silk for the poultice, both easily obtainable from Prudence.

She put the items into a large bag and headed for the sickroom. The distressing sound of Melilla's coughing met her at the door. The girls were awake now and sitting up in bed.

"All right, the doctor is in!" she announced, sounding as cheerful as she could.

"Miss Abby!" Valencia squealed. Melilla tried to speak, but the effort only made her cough again. She held a napkin to her mouth, and when she lowered it, Abigail saw a glob of thick, green mucus.

While taking their temperatures, Abigail did her best to make light of their condition. She even joked about how lazy they'd become, lounging around in bed all day. But it was impossible to remain jovial when she saw Melilla's temperature—102°.

She immediately went to work, following the instructions she had written about the punch and the medicines and the poultice. Prudence brought milk and a piece of silk. After laboring for an hour in preparation of the various remedies, she administered them in the prescribed doses to Melilla, knowing that Valencia would benefit as well through their shared circulatory system.

As expected, the opium made them both very sleepy. As soon as they had drifted off, and knowing that nothing further needed to be done for several hours, Abigail tiptoed from the room and shut the door behind her.

"Can I get you some tea, Miss Platford? Or something to eat?" Prudence offered, appearing in the kitchen doorway.

"I'm fine, thank you. But could you manage here by yourself for a little while?"

"Oh yes, ma'am. I'm all rested up now."

"Please look in on them every fifteen minutes. I'll be back in about an hour. There are a couple of things I need to take care of right away."

Wearily, Abigail again descended the wooden staircase to the office. Her plan was to see if Mrs. Krueger would look after Shaena overnight. A lot to ask of a neighbor, but the elderly widow didn't seem to mind having company. Actually, Shaena was the one most likely to object. She loved that big, soft feather bed, and Mrs. Krueger had only a tiny cot in her spare room.

And there was something else Abigail must do at the apartment. Retrieve the card from the drawer of her night table.

The one with Detective Baldwin's number.

CHAPTER 22

That night, Melilla's temperature spiked to 103°. There was no sign of Franklin, either at his office or apartment. Abigail went about the business of caring for the twins with a calmness and competence that surprised her. She was engaged in a doctor's work. The sort of work she had always imagined herself doing.

She spent the night curled up on one of the tiny beds in the recovery room, getting up every four hours to give Melilla her dose of quinine. After the morning dose, at eight o'clock, she went downstairs to her desk, dropping into her chair like a dead weight. Exhausted as she was, there was no avoiding what had to come next. She dreaded picking up the telephone to call Detective Baldwin. But she needed to tell him what she'd discovered. Shark had Mrs. Moser's hat, or at least one just like it. He must have kidnapped her. And though it was possible he had acted on his own, most likely the trail would lead back to Franklin.

Thinking back, it all made sense. She had wondered what Franklin was doing upstairs while she waited with Mrs. Moser in the operating room. And when he didn't telephone his patient to see how she was feeling, she'd thought it both odd and irresponsible. Yet day after day went by until it seemed he had completely forgotten about her.

She remembered, too, the night he staggered into her apartment at three in the morning. Drunk and totally distraught, he had rambled on and on, trying to justify himself without ever telling her the reason. She could never have guessed it was murder, not in a million years. In fact, she found it difficult to believe, even now.

With a prickle of conscience, she realized that she would have to tell Detective Baldwin the whole truth, including her connection to Shark. She would have to admit that she knew about some of his questionable activities, that she had been present for two of his late-night deliveries to the operating room. Surely, the detective would think poorly of her, or worse.

She pulled the telephone closer, drew a tremulous breath, and lifted the earpiece.

• • • • •

At two o'clock that afternoon, Franklin burst through the door to the office. He whisked past Abigail, sitting at her desk, without a glance or a word. The next thing she heard was the slamming of his office door.

She waited a few minutes, anticipating he would come out again or call for her. He did neither. Not that she wanted to see him, but she needed to. Melilla's temperature was still dangerously febrile, and her cough hadn't improved. If anything, her breathing was worse. And now Valencia was almost as bad. As much as Abigail wished to avoid Franklin, it would be sheer arrogance not to ask him to examine the girls. He might be a criminal—good God, he might even be a murderer—but he was still a doctor.

Reluctantly, she went down the hall to his office, listening for a moment through the door. Everything was quiet. She took a deep breath and knocked.

"What is it?"

"May I come in?"

"I suppose."

As soon as she entered, she could feel the tension stretched between them, like a taut wire.

"Well, well. Look who's here! Have you come to gloat? To revel in your victory?"

"Victory?" What could he possibly be talking about?

"Don't play innocent with me!"

With a sudden stab of fear, it occurred to her that, somehow, he might have found out about her call to Detective Baldwin. Surely the police wouldn't have told him. But what if they did?

"You knew I needed the twins." Franklin spoke with a needling edge to his voice. "Joe needed them, the Rome Institute needed them. And still you interfered."

So that was it! Samuel Storey must have responded to her telegram. She felt a flood of relief—and a touch of revenge.

"Yes, I interfered! And I'm not sorry."

Franklin jumped up from his chair, nearly knocking it over in his anger. Slamming his palms on the desktop, he leaned toward Abigail, a threatening snarl on his face.

"You filthy little betrayer!"

"There's no way to justify what happened to Ludwik, and you know it."

"I don't have to *justify* anything to *you*!"

"What about to yourself? They've accused Ludwik of horrible things, just so they can lock him up and Joe can do as he pleases with the twins. It's all a lie. I don't believe a word of what they say."

"It doesn't matter what you believe. No one asked for your opinion. Ludwik was arrested. He was deemed to be dangerous. Not my decision or yours. Normally, one leaves such matters to the authorities. But no, you had to stick your perfect little nose into it! You had to stir things up. Your meddling has cost us the twins."

For a moment, she thought that by *us* he meant the two of them. But, of course, he was talking about himself and Joe. "You had no right to them, neither one of you."

Franklin's eyes narrowed. "How did you know about this Storey fellow—that he used to be in partnership with Andrew Carnegie?"

Her mind raced back to that morning in the newspaper office—banging file drawers, snippets of conversation floating through the open door. Chains and profits ... and *Carnegie*. She had thought nothing of it then.

"I'm afraid that's none of your business."

"Damn you!" With a wild sweep of his arm, he pushed a slew of papers off the desktop, scattering them willy-nilly. "I suppose you remembered Genworth saying that Carnegie is his biggest donor, too. Well, your precious Ludwik is on his way to being released. The twins are going back to him. They won't be having surgery at the Institute. All thanks to your treachery."

If only Franklin knew how happy he'd just made her! Mr. Storey must have enlisted the help of his friend, Andrew Carnegie. Carnegie's connection to Genworth was nothing more than a fortunate coincidence, but she was not about to admit that to Franklin. She lifted her chin, emboldened to the point of recklessness. "Someone had to show Joe that he can't have everything he wants. You were too much of a coward to do it. I imagine you even helped him to sabotage Ludwik. But you weren't content to stop at that. You had to go after poor Mrs. Moser, too. To make sure she couldn't tell anyone what you'd done to her, so Joe wouldn't change his mind about the Institute. You'd sooner have your patient dead than see your precious hospital go up in smoke."

Franklin leaped from behind his desk, his face dark with rage. "You ungrateful little whore! When I think of all I've done for you—"

A hard slap landed on her cheek, followed by another.

"You sold me out!" he shouted. "You and that miserable so-called *baron*. He deserved everything he got." He raised his hand to strike her again, but then, suddenly, he stopped. "My God, what is happening to me?" He backed away from her with a look of bewilderment. Stumbling like a drunk, he returned to his chair and collapsed into it.

Abigail stood frozen in place, stunned by his attack. She'd been a fool to tell him of her suspicions. She should have realized how dangerous he was. What might he do next?

Coming to her senses, she took flight through the open door, terrified he might pursue her. But only his seething rants trailed her down the hall.

"And I'm not your damn *father*, either. I'm not anything to you. And you're nothing to me. Do you hear me? Nothing!"

Her heart felt like it would burst as she ran to her desk, yanked open the drawer, and swept up her *Gray's Anatomy*. After that, the pen her father had given her and the clinical journal in which she'd written every step of every procedure she and Franklin had performed together over the past three months. Clutching them tightly, she hurried to the closet for her hat and parasol. She had nothing else.

Except—what about the twins?

"Good afternoon, Miss Platford." Startled, she spun around. Dr. Genworth rose from the sofa. "There was no one here, so I let myself in. I hope that's all right."

He approached her, his bowler in hand. She did not offer to take it from him. There was no call for it now.

"I assume you are here to see Dr. Rome. He's in his office, down the hall," she said.

"You don't intend to announce me?"

"I'm afraid not. I no longer work here. In fact, I was just leaving."

"I see."

"Good afternoon, Doctor!" Franklin entered the room, all smiles. "I wasn't expecting you until later."

"I know, but I just got out of my meeting with Mr. Carnegie, and it seemed best to come right over."

"Yes, certainly. Well, please come this way to my office. We'll be more comfortable there."

"Actually, I won't be staying long," Dr. Genworth said. "What I have to say requires only a minute."

"I see." Franklin shifted uneasily. "Well, at least you'll have a seat here. I can have my maid bring us some tea."

"No, thank you. Let me get straight to the point. Mr. Carnegie is entirely in agreement with my assessment that the Radcliff Institute would be an exceptional facility for our eugenics research. He does not, however, believe it is in our best interests to appear to be affiliated with your little enterprise—your *beauty surgery* institute."

Franklin blanched. "Believe me, Doctor, we've only scratched the surface of what transformative surgery can achieve. I can prove to you how perfectly it complements your efforts, if only—"

"The only true perfection," Dr. Genworth interrupted, his tone openly contemptuous, "comes from *eliminating* inferior elements, not *disguising* them. That's what is wrong with your ideas, Dr. Rome. They, and many other things about you, don't hold up to scrutiny."

"Mr. Radcliff obviously feels differently."

"Not anymore, he doesn't. Not after all that's happened. This whole matter with Baron Rutkowski left a sour taste in Mr. Carnegie's mouth. I assured him it was only an unfortunate misunderstanding. Still, he instructed his investigative people to poke around a bit, and they came up with some interesting findings." He turned to Abigail. "Miss Platford, do you know anything at all about the man you've been working for?"

"Please leave Miss Platford out of this," Franklin broke in. "In fact, I would prefer that she be on her way. This is a private conversation."

"I don't see why it should be private." Dr. Genworth seemed to enjoy Franklin's growing agitation. "You told Joe Radcliff that you studied medicine at Hopkins, isn't that so?"

"Yes, but—"

"There are no *buts* about it, Dr. Rome. There is no record of you ever attending Johns Hopkins or any other institution of medical training. Which perhaps explains why you've never applied for a license to practice medicine in the state of New York."

Abigail stared at Franklin, incredulous. What Dr. Genworth was saying couldn't be true. The diplomas were on his wall. If he were not legitimately credentialed, he would never have had the audacity to proceed with so bold a plan as the Rome Institute.

Dr. Genworth turned his gaze toward her. "You didn't know about this, Miss Platford? You, who worked with this man day in and day out?"

From his disparaging attitude, Abigail wasn't sure if he was remarking on her startling ineptitude or accusing her of being an accomplice.

"No, I wasn't aware of any of it."

Apparently satisfied with her response, he resumed with Franklin. "I've already informed Mr. Radcliff, and he asked me to convey his bitter disappointment at such a flagrant abuse of trust. The Rome Institute is off the table."

Franklin's hands were clenched into tight fists. "I'll believe that when I hear it from Mr. Radcliff himself. I was just about to telephone him with the news that we have an additional investor in our project. Someone who might be interested in your work as well. Someone with very deep pockets."

Abigail looked from Franklin to Dr. Genworth and back. He had to be bluffing about having another investor. Was there no end to the lies?

"I suggest you keep that investor of yours on a tight leash, Dr. Rome. Because if he were to find out that you are no more qualified to perform surgery than the local barber, I doubt he would be interested in opening up those deep pockets."

"And what about you, Dr. Genworth?"

He looked at Abigail, his brows raised. "I beg your pardon, Miss Platford?"

She had not intended to speak nor had she considered what she might say. Or why she felt the need to say anything. It was certainly not in defense of Franklin. But suddenly her pent-up rage toward Joe and the eugenicists had come bubbling to the surface. "You believe yourself and your colleagues to be so far above everyone else. You act as though you are the only ones who know the truth, the only ones worthy of being saved. What you propose to inflict upon the weak and the sick and the helpless is despicable, sir. And yet you call yourself a *doctor*! You disgrace the title."

Dr. Genworth drew himself up, regarding her with a look of pure enmity.

"Miss Platford, yours is the sort of ignorance that the eugenics movement must contend with far too frequently. All I can say is that someday you will thank me for what I'm doing. Someday your children will thank me."

"Don't count on it," she said, picking up the bag with her few possessions. "If you gentlemen will excuse me, I have two sick girls to attend to."

She approached Franklin, needing to pass him in order to make her way down the hall. Her decision was made; she was taking the twins to the hospital as fast as she could.

"When I'm finished, I want to speak with you," Franklin said in a low voice. "Please."

* * * * *

Once upstairs, Abigail called for an ambulance to transport the girls to Bellevue Hospital. But there would be a delay. The crash of an electric train in the Bronx, with seventeen dead and sixty injured, meant that all the ambulances were in use. There was no choice but to wait. She could only hope that she and the girls would be gone before Franklin came looking for her.

Entering their room, she found them both asleep. Grateful for a few moments of quiet, she sank into the bedside chair and closed her eyes.

It was over. Today was her last day as Franklin Rome's assistant. She would never again sit at her mahogany desk with its embossed leather top and elegantly turned legs. Never again would she pass Franklin the blade or the chisel, or hear him explain each skilled maneuver of an operation. Never would they share their morning tea in his private office, surrounded by his official-looking diplomas, none of them worth any more than the paper they were printed on.

The revelation that he was not a doctor had been a bombshell; she'd not seen it coming. Certainly, there was no justification for deceiving his patients. Deceiving *her*. But however he had learned his craft, he was good at it. Was it shameful to mourn, even for a second, the waste of such talent?

Because he was finished now. Forever.

And what about his beloved beauty surgery? Doubtful it would ever be counted among the more significant achievements of modern medicine. How could it hold a candle to the work of doctors like her father, called on to render service to gravely ill patients, often contagious with some incurable disease? She had always thought of medicine that way: as a matter of life and death. Yet, to transform a human face, to sculpt from flesh and bone, requires skill and judgment; such surgery is both science and art. Franklin taught her that. He had taught her many things, some good and some bad.

Now he was gone from her life.

Forgiveness was out of the question. The list of his transgressions was too long, the nature of them too serious. Dear God, what if he was a murderer? It was hard thinking of him that way—but not impossible. His ambition had become toxic, an insidious evil, a poison deadly to the soul. It was too late for the antidote.

"I want to apologize."

Her eyes flew open. Franklin stood in the doorway, his tie loose, his jacket askew.

"I was angry, but I shouldn't have slapped you. That was out of line."

"It doesn't matter now." She glanced nervously at the twins. She had wanted to be gone before Franklin could even think about trying to stop them.

"Does that mean you forgive me? We can forget it? Because, Abigail—" He looked at her imploringly. "I want you to stay."

She stood, afraid of what might come next. "I don't want these girls disturbed. They're ill." She took a step toward him.

Would he grab her? Threaten her? In his unstable frame of mind, realizing she was onto the worst of what he'd done, he might be capable of anything.

But he seemed calm enough as he stepped aside, letting her pass into the hall and shut the door behind her. Leaving the two of them face to face, alone.

"Please understand, Abigail. This is all some sort of conspiracy. Genworth and Sorrell—they want me out of their way. They want Joe Radcliff's money all for themselves. So let them have it. But they won't stop us! We'll go someplace else and start a new practice. Maybe Chicago. Or how about California? You'd like that, wouldn't you? San Francisco?"

She could hear the desperation in his voice, but she felt no pity. He cared nothing for anyone but himself. He'd not even asked what was wrong with the twins.

"You're not a doctor, Franklin."

"You despise those eugenicists and everything they stand for. Yet you're willing to take Genworth's word over mine?"

His delusions unnerved her, but right now she was more anxious about the time. Twenty minutes had passed since her phone call. When would the ambulance come?

"It's my fault," Franklin went on. "I should have realized who I was dealing with and never gotten us involved. But it's not too late. We don't need Joe Radcliff. We can pack our bags, be on our way, and this unfortunate chapter will be behind us. And Abigail—" He paused, licked his lips. A light sweat glistened on his forehead. "You know I care for you. If it would make a difference ... I'll marry you."

"You're proposing marriage?" His sudden ardor was too insulting to ignore. Was everything just a game to him, an opportunity to prove how well he could play? From the beginning, he had taken advantage of her innocence, her trust. Never again. "Don't you think you should ask Alexandra? I'm sure she'll have an opinion."

"Alexandra?"

"I know that you've slept with her. Probably more than once. Not that I care."

"Is that what's been bothering you?" He snapped his fingers. "Damn, I should have known! That's why you went behind my back about Ludwik. You were jealous."

Abigail might have laughed in his face if it wasn't all so tragic. He was pathetic. So different from the dashing Dr. Rome who had drawn the eye of every woman at the Hennessys' banquet. The one who had escorted her through the aisles of Bergdorf Goodman, confident he could transform her into the perfect foil. How expertly he had slipped the Parisian gown from her shoulders. Explored every inch of her body. Guided her through her first dissection. Taught her how to stitch a wound with finesse. But no, this man before her now was an entirely different person. Someone Abigail didn't know.

"Believe what you like," she said, straining to hear the wail of a siren.

Suddenly, there was an urgent banging at the front door. Could it be the ambulance had arrived?

Prudence came from the kitchen, scurrying past them. A few moments later, a steely-eyed Detective Baldwin stood behind Franklin, hands on his hips.

Franklin turned to confront him. "I don't recall that we had an appointment, Detective."

"We didn't." Detective Baldwin acknowledged Abigail with a nod. "But it seems the trail of Mrs. Moser's disappearance has led us back to you. A surprising bunch of fellows you associate with, Doctor. Too bad one of them has a weakness for Parisian hats and

Lower East Side whores. The combination of the two proved to be your undoing."

Franklin's face had assumed a grayish pallor. "I have no idea what you're talking about."

"I'll be happy to explain everything once we get to the station. You're coming with me now."

Franklin looked imploringly at Abigail. "You'll come along. You can straighten this out."

"I'm taking the twins to the hospital." She turned to Prudence, who was standing in the foyer, bug-eyed. "Why don't you go with us, Prudence?"

Only when Officer Gerhardt came through the front door wielding a pair of handcuffs did it hit Abigail in full force. Franklin was going to jail. And she was the one who had turned him in to the police.

She felt light-headed, her legs unsteady.

"If you'll excuse me—" she said, asking Detective Baldwin's permission with her eyes. He nodded.

Slipping into the twins' bedroom, she closed the door and leaned her back against it. She was shaking uncontrollably. "It's all right," she said, talking to herself. It wasn't her fault. She had to go to the authorities. If he was guilty of engineering Mrs. Moser's disappearance, then he deserved to go to jail. What he had done was a crime, heinous beyond anything she had ever imagined possible. "It's all right," she said again.

"Miss Abby? You okay?"

Her head snapped up. How could she have forgotten about the twins?

"Yes, of course. I'm fine, Valencia. Please, go back to sleep. Please ... everything will be all right."

CHAPTER 23

I t was morning in the open ward at Bellevue Hospital. Sitting on the edge of the bed where Valencia and Melilla lay sleeping, Abigail had a perfect spot from which to observe the constant stream of activity. Sick and injured being wheeled in and out on carts, doctors making rounds, nurses delivering medications and retrieving bedpans. This was her fourth day at their bedside. By now, she was used to the commotion, the unruly patients, the piercing shrieks and muted sobs. It was an atmosphere far removed from the pristine operating room where she had assisted Franklin—and into which she would never set foot again.

Her diagnosis had been correct: pneumonia. She'd been told that the measures she took in caring for the twins were exactly right. The several doctors who had been called in for consultation were optimistic about a full recovery.

She looked over at Ludwik, slumped in a straight-back chair, snoring loudly with his mouth open. He had arrived late last night. After all that he'd been through, no wonder he was out cold. He'd lost weight, and his color wasn't good. His crutches leaned against the wall next to him. It would be some time yet before he could walk without them.

Perhaps feeling her gaze, he awakened, quickly shifting into an upright position.

"Sorry I fell asleep. How are they doing?"

"Resting for now."

"Good," he said, patting down his disheveled hair. "I can't remember much of what we talked about earlier. Who knows, maybe they did something to my brain while I was in that godforsaken place."

"You're just tired. You need a few days to get back to normal." She had not asked what tests, or so-called treatments, he had been subjected to—and wasn't sure she wanted to know. Probably it was best for Ludwik to put the entire ordeal out of his mind, at least for now. No doubt he needed healing as much as the twins, though of a different sort.

"I'm not sure I thanked you sufficiently for what you did," he said, his eyes meeting hers. She had almost forgotten how very blue they were. "I doubt any amount of thanks could be enough. You saved me, and my girls as well."

"It was Mr. Storey and his friend Andrew Carnegie who saved you. I'm disappointed in Mr. Carnegie's support of the eugenics movement, which is an abomination. But at least he made sure the twins would be returned to you."

"Dr. Rome must be awfully upset that he won't have my girls to publicize the grand opening of his institute."

"Dr. Rome?" She hardly knew where to begin. "I didn't have a chance to tell you, but Dr. Rome is under investigation. He's been detained by the police for the last four days, suspected of being involved in the disappearance of one of his patients. And there's something else." She hesitated. "He's not really a doctor after all."

She had never felt so ashamed. What must Ludwik think of her for having associated with a man like Franklin Rome? She wondered, too, if he remembered that *work* was not all she had done with Franklin. And what would he think if he knew how close she had come to masquerading as a doctor herself—a dermatologist—simply because Franklin had suggested it?

He leaned forward, his expression full of concern. "I'm glad you told me. I understand now just how difficult the last few days must have been for you. Is there anything I can do to help?"

"Thank you, but no."

She didn't want his sympathy, though there might be ample cause for it. With no immediate prospects for another position, she would be forced to move out of her apartment in a couple of weeks. And there was Shaena. Prudence had been watching her so that Abigail could spend time at the hospital. But she couldn't afford to keep a maid, and Prudence already was interviewing for other jobs.

"Good morning, Miss Platford." Detective Baldwin strode up to the bed with a smile, breaking the solemn mood that had settled over them. "I knew you'd be here, and I wanted personally to deliver the news. Mrs. Moser has been found."

Her heart leaped. "She's all right?"

He shook his head. "No, I'm sorry. What I meant to say was that her body has been found."

Abigail had expected as much, but that didn't prevent her from feeling anew the absolute horror of it. "Where?" she asked.

"Buried in a shallow grave on Hart Island. That fellow Shark and his accomplice led us straight to her."

"And Dr. Rome?" she said hesitantly. "Has he been charged with anything?"

"We have substantial proof he was an accessory to the crime, though he's still not admitted to anything. I believe he will, though. Once he understands it's in his best interests." He craned his neck toward the bed where the twins lay sleeping.

"And how are the Siamese twins doing? I've always wanted to get a close look at them."

"They're making progress. By the way—please excuse my manners—this gentleman is their guardian, Baron Ludwik Rutkowski." She turned to Ludwik. "Detective Baldwin has been in charge of the investigation into Mrs. Moser's disappearance."

With difficulty, Ludwik rose from his chair. "Pleasure to meet you, Detective," he said as they shook hands.

"Thank you, sir. Miss Platford has told me about your situation. I'm wondering if you intend to press charges in the matter. Against Mr. Radcliff and the others."

"No, I don't relish a long, drawn-out battle. Mr. Radcliff is very well connected. I'm not even sure I could bring him down. What I intend is to take my girls back to England with me, just as soon as they're well enough."

A lump came to Abigail's throat. It was unlikely she would ever see any of them again.

"But we'll be returning to New York," Ludwik added, as if he'd read her mind. "The twins never got to see the sights. Obviously, none of us is in any shape to do so now. But I doubt they will let me off the hook for too long." He smiled warmly at Abigail. "I'll keep my fingers crossed that Miss Platford might be free to show us around next time."

"If you're sure you don't want to bring charges," Detective Baldwin said, "I'll go ahead and close the book on that part of the case."

"Yes, I'm sure."

"Oh, Miss Platford," he said, appearing to have just remembered something important, "I was wondering when you'd like to come down to the station?"

Before Abigail could ask why she was needed there, she noticed Prudence across the crowded ward, weaving her way toward them with Shaena in tow.

"Sorry to interrupt," Prudence said, arriving breathless, "but I just heard from Mrs. Cameron, the lady who interviewed me yesterday afternoon. She offered me the position. Said she needs me right away. Today." Prudence was clearly torn between relief and regret. "The pay is awful good, and I can't afford to pass it up, Miss Platford. Afraid I'll have to leave Shaena with you now. Wish I didn't."

"Come here, sweetheart," Abigail said, bending down and opening her arms to the little girl, who ran into them willingly, snuggling as close as she could. Abigail looked up at Prudence. "Please, don't worry about us. And thank you for everything. I hope the new position is exactly as you hope."

"I wish you the best as well, ma'am. Lord knows you deserve it. But tell me, how are the twins doing?"

"They're going to be fine."

Prudence clasped her hands in front of her. "Thanks to God!" She smiled down at Shaena, her eyes misting. "As for you, sweet pea ... I know you'll be a good girl."

Shaena buried her face in Abigail's skirt.

"Well, then. I guess I'll be on my way." Biting her lip, Prudence nodded once and left in a rush, disappearing among the ward's bustling tide of humanity. Watching her go, Abigail felt a touch of envy. Prudence had settled on a new life within days. She wondered how long it would take her.

"And who's this?" Detective Baldwin asked, eyeing Shaena.

"Oh—my little niece." Shaena came out of hiding, and Abigail gave her a kiss on the cheek before straightening up. "You were saying something about coming to the station, Detective?"

But Detective Baldwin was already down on one knee in front of the little girl, looking at her face. "Dog bite?"

"Yes," Abigail answered reluctantly. She hated for Shaena to feel like an object of curiosity. "She has a lot of healing yet to do."

"Same thing happened to my younger sister when we were kids. Whoever stitched up this little one did an excellent job."

"Actually, I repaired the wound." Abigail knew she shouldn't boast, but she couldn't help herself.

Detective Baldwin stood up. "Looks like she's going to do just fine," he said, brushing off his trousers.

"But you were saying?"

"Ah yes, the reward money."

Abigail's eyes widened. "Reward?"

"Maybe I never mentioned it, but soon after Mrs. Moser's disappearance, her husband offered a substantial reward for information leading to the discovery of her whereabouts. Three thousand dollars."

Three thousand dollars! Her gaze traveled back to Shaena. The child's arms were wrapped around her hips, as though holding on for dear life. Abigail stroked her soft hair.

"Congratulations, Miss Platford." The good news seemed to have brought a bit of color back to Ludwik's face. "That's quite a sum. Do you know what you're going to do with it?"

Suddenly, she recalled Franklin's bitter admonishment: *Surely by now you realize that medical school would be a complete waste of your time ...*

She smiled. "Yes, Ludwik. I know precisely what I'm going to do."

ACKNOWLEDGMENTS

It would take many pages to list all the resources that were vital to my research for *The Beauty Doctor*—resources without which my story and characters could never have come to life. A few of the most extraordinary were: *The Correction of Featural Imperfections*, by Charles C. Miller, MD, first published in 1907, which details the methods by which Miller performed many of the early cosmetic operations mentioned in my novel; Elizabeth Haiken's fabulous book *Venus Envy, A History of Cosmetic Surgery* (The Johns Hopkins University Press; 1997), which provided colorful historical context; the research of Keith A. Denkler, MD, and Rosalind F. Hudson, MD, presented in "The 19th Century Origins of Facial Cosmetic Surgery and John H. Woodbury" (*Aesthetic Surgery Journal*; www.aestheticsurgeryjournal.com), which disclosed new findings concerning how beauty surgery was practiced at the turn of the century; and Museum Vrolik (University of Amsterdam) and the Countway Library of Medicine (Harvard University), whose displays and other resources on the eighteenth- and nineteenth-century study of teratology were helpful in developing the concept of Joe Radcliff's museum. I am grateful to public historian Lauren Markewicz for her expertise in the Edwardian era and her painstaking review of my first draft for historical accuracy.

The Beauty Doctor was originally published in 2017. Many thanks to my publisher, Black Rose Writing, for encouraging a Second Edition with a spectacular new cover.

I am appreciative of my many writing friends for their advice and encouragement, and for always giving me their honest opinions. Eternal love for my late mother, Helen Hutchison, and my late father, Stanley Hutchison to whom this book is dedicated. Finally, I am so fortunate to share life with my wonderful husband, Bob, whose love and friendship will always mean the world to me.

READING GROUP GUIDE

1.   In what ways does Abigail's relationship with her father influence her self-image? Does it strengthen or weaken her?

2.   What does the way Abigail handles her decision not to marry Arthur say about her as a person?

3.   Abigail's attitude toward beauty surgery changes rather quickly. Is this change motivated by self-interest, by a genuine appreciation of its value, or by something else?

4.   As players in Joe Radcliff's Socratic game to define beauty, what does each character's definition reveal about him or her?

5.   Baron Ludwik Rutkowski exhibits unusual kindness toward Abigail. How does his offer of help affect her?

6.   Why does Abigail still want Franklin as her lover, even after he treats her in a manner that so deeply disappoints her? Is she primarily motivated by desire? Ambition? Pride?

7.   Should Valencia and Melilla, the conjoined twins, be able to decide for themselves whether to undergo surgery on their noses?

8. What is it about Franklin Rome that attracts Abigail? In the beginning? Later on?

9. What attracts Franklin to Abigail?

10. How does Abigail's notion of what it means to be a doctor change over the course of the story?

11. How does it affect Abigail when she first recognizes Franklin's weakness? When she sees him finally crumble?

12. How do Abigail's relationships with children change her? With Paddy and Shaena? With Valencia and Melilla?

13. How does the juxtaposition of beauty surgery, Joe's museum of human oddities, and the eugenics movement illuminate the book's major themes?

14. What about Franklin's infidelity bothers Abigail the most? His lies? Alexandra revealing their affair? That Abigail truly loves him, or that she should have known better than to trust him?

15. What is the turning point at which Abigail takes control of her own future?

ABOUT THE AUTHOR

Elizabeth Hutchison Bernard is a bestselling author of historical and women's fiction. Her 2023 novel *Sisters of Castle Leod* is the Winner of the 2023 Maxy Award for Historical Fiction and Adventure; a Finalist in the 2022 American Writing Awards; and an Editors' Choice of the Historical Novel Society. It is a #1 Bestseller on Amazon Kindle for Historical Biographical Fiction and Biographical Literary Fiction. *The Beauty Doctor*, first released in 2017, was a Finalist for the prestigious Eric Hoffer Book Award. *Temptation Rag: A Novel* (2018) has been hailed as "a deeply human portrait of racial and gender inequality in the ragtime era." (Pulitzer Prize Winner Fredric Tulsky).

A summa cum laude graduate of Northwestern University (Evanston, Illinois), Bernard is a former touring musician, public relations professional, and executive editor of *Aesthetic Surgery Journal*. She now is a full-time author living with her family near Phoenix, Arizona.

www.ehbernard.com
https://www.facebook.com/EHBernardAuthor
https://www.instagram.com/EHBernardAuthor
http://www.X.com/EHBernardAuthor

HISTORICAL FICTION BY ELIZABETH HUTCHISON BERNARD

Sisters of Castle Leod: A Novel

Temptation Rag: A Novel

The Beauty Doctor (Second Edition)

YOUR OPINION COUNTS

Word-of-mouth is crucial for any author to succeed. If you enjoyed *The Beauty Doctor*, please leave a review online—anywhere you are able. Even if it's just a sentence or two. It would make all the difference and would be very much appreciated.

Thanks!
Elizabeth Hutchison Bernard

We hope you enjoyed reading this title from:

www.blackrosewriting.com

Subscribe to our mailing list – *The Rosevine* – and receive **FREE** books, daily deals, and stay current with news about upcoming releases and our hottest authors.
Scan the QR code below to sign up.

Already a subscriber? Please accept a sincere thank you for being a fan of Black Rose Writing authors.

View other Black Rose Writing titles at www.blackrosewriting.com/books and use promo code **PRINT** to receive a **20% discount** when purchasing.